The Lone Star

—

Independence

by

Don Emmitte & Alex Pazdan

AUSTIN
BROTHERS PUBLISHING

The Lone Star: Independence
© 2020 by Dom Emmitte and Alex Pazdan
Published by Austin Brothers Publishing

ISBN: 978-1-7359739-1-3

Printed in the United States

Acknowledgements

From Don Emmitte:

It seems that writing the Acknowledgements is more difficult than writing the book. There have been so many people who have encouraged, affirmed, and helped with the writing it is difficult to know where to begin. With that in mind, I will begin at the foundation of all my inspiration and encouragement—Jesus Christ, my Redeemer and constant source of strength and wisdom. I am motivated and driven by my deep faith in Christ. Thus, He is the foundation of my life and work.

Further I must acknowledge the incredible contribution of my family in the process of this work. My wife, Mary, has been a constant source of encouragement for over fifty years, and continues to amaze me with her affirmation and assistance. My sons, Kyle, David, and Aaron were indispensible in the writing of this book; and my oldest grandchildren, Faith and Logan, provided the initial backdrop and setting of much of the book.

My close friend and co-author, Alex Pazdan, continues to amaze me at the depth of his knowledge, and capacity to recall history, which was invaluable in our many collaborative conversations. The Lone Star would not have been if it were not for him. I am also in debt to the wonderful work in professional editing of Laurie Chittendon in the final weeks of writing as well as the incredible contribution of Terry Austin and Austin Brothers Publishing.

From Alex Pazdan:

There are many people I would like to thank in the production of The Lone Star. First, I must acknowledge my children, Jonathon and Ashley, who gave me the idea to write a book in the first place.

Their faith in me to accomplish such a goal continues to inspire and encourage me. I also want to thank my parents and sister, who encouraged me on this journey. Of course, my friend and co-author, Don Emmitte, who turned the story into a great book. I must also acknowledge the Founding Fathers. This book is really the retelling of what they did and accomplished. And, last, but not least, I thank my faithful Savior Jesus Christ, who died for me, loves me, forgives me, and intercedes for me in spite of all my sin and failure. To Him be all the praise, glory, and honor.

Contents

Chapter 1

The Beginning

October 25, 1992 – October 23, 2018

Texas will again lift its head and stand among the nations. It ought to do so, for no country upon the globe can compare with it in natural advantages.

— Sam Houston, War Hero, General and President of the Republic of Texas

COME AND TAKE IT

Lieutenant Commander Dylan Walker sat with his team in the secure conference room at the Navy Special Warfare Center in San Diego, California, waiting for a briefing from the Commander of the base. Typically these meetings were casual brainstorming sessions about a prospective assignment. However, when Commander Richards entered the room with Deputy Director and the Special Agent-in-Charge of the FBI's station in Waco, Texas, Walker knew this would be anything but a typical planning session. It looked like it was going to be a full-moon kind of day. Walker and the other men from Seal Team 7 stood when the commander entered.

"At ease, soldiers," Richards formally ordered. As an aide distributed the mission guides, he continued, "A situation has been developing in Texas. SAC Diane Hernandez from the Waco Station is here today to provide additional details not specified in your mission guides."

Walker was a fourth-generation navy man, a graduate of the Naval Academy, and decorated Seal, with over fifty successful missions all over the world, chafed at the presence of the FBI. However, he understood the chain of command and hadn't risen so quickly from his academy rank of Ensign to Commander in just eight years by making his personal feelings known. It didn't help that the location of this operation was in his home state.

Hernandez stepped forward and began the briefing. "We have been working in conjunction with the Bureau of Alcohol,

Tobacco, Firearms and Explosives in Texas since 1984 when Mr. David Koresh and some of his followers split away from a religious sect known as the Shepherd's Rod and formed a splinter group called the Branch Davidians. They have developed a compound outside of Waco, which is heavily guarded and fortified by the male members of the sect. There have also been numerous allegations filed with the local authorities that Koresh is physically abusing the children in the compound and committing statutory rape by taking multiple underage brides. You can see from the article in a local Waco newspaper included in your mission briefing that Koresh has gone on record saying he is entitled to at least 140 wives and that he is entitled to claim any of the women in the group. He has claimed, according to the interview in the paper that he has fathered at least a dozen children, and that some of these mothers became brides as young as 12 or 13 years old."

Walker interrupted, "Ma'am, what does this have to do with us? Isn't this a matter for the local authorities?'"

Hernandez stared him down and curtly responded, "They've done all they can down there. They just don't have the manpower to get the job done."

Walker pressed a little, "Have they called in the Texas Rangers?"

Hernandez smirked, "I've been stationed there for nearly a decade, and I've never known the Rangers to be able to do anything more than lead a July 4th parade on horseback."

Commander Richards cleared his throat and said, "Please go on Agent Hernandez." It was a clear signal for Walker to be silent.

Hernandez continued, "In addition to allegations of sexual abuse and misconduct, Koresh and his followers have been stockpiling illegal weapons. In May 1992, Chief Deputy Daniel Weyenberg of the McClennan County Sheriff's Department called the ATF to notify them that his office had been contacted by a local UPS representative concerned about a report by a local driver. The driver said a package had broken open on delivery to the Branch Davidian compound, revealing firearms, inert grenade casings, and a large shipment of black powder."

Walker was scanning the mission guide when Hernandez said, "Am I boring you, Lieutenant Commander?"

"No ma'am," Walker quickly responded with his best blank stare. Then added, "We are trained to multi-task, ma'am."

Their relationship had gotten off to a rocky start, and it was deteriorating rapidly. Hernandez could see this was not a man accustomed to being second in command to anyone, much less a woman. She made a mental note to talk to Commander Richards about the wisdom of going forward with Seal Team 7.

Hernandez pressed on, "On June 9th, the ATF opened a formal investigation, and a week later, it was classified as sensitive, 'thereby calling for a high degree of oversight' from both Houston and headquarters. They had already received reports of automatic gunfire coming from the Mt. Carmel compound. ATF agents David Aguilera and Tom Skinner made contact with the Branch Davidians' gun dealer Henry McMahon, and as a result, were able to speak with Koresh by phone. However, the ATF agents declined to make the inspection and began surveillance under the cover of college students. The investigation included sending in an undercover agent, Robert Rodriguez, whose identity we now know has been compromised and is being held hostage at the compound."

Commander Richards continued the briefing, "This is where your team comes in, Dylan." He used Walker's first name in an effort to de-escalate the tension.

The men of Seal Team 7 had been together for a long time. They were fiercely loyal to Walker. In fact, there were two other Texans, Carson Bradley and Jack Reece, who had been with him from the beginning, forging an unbreakable bond.

"Any questions?" Richards asked.

"What's the timetable, Commander?" Walker inquired.

"We will deploy tomorrow morning at 0600. I want a preliminary plan by arrival in Waco." Richards said.

Walker simply said, "Yes Sir." The team remained in the briefing room, gathering all the materials before reconvening later.

It was a long afternoon of planning and packing their gear before they broke for supper together and the last meeting to fine-tune their plan. They still needed to do several run-throughs of the actual scenarios before wheels-up. After finishing, they gathered their gear and bedded down for a short night of rest. As dawn broke, they loaded the Globemaster III transport plane they had boarded so many times before. Joining them on the plane were several support personnel, Commander Richardson, and SAC Hernandez. The accompaniment of the latter two was unusual. Walker knew this operation must have been rooted much higher up the command ladder.

The trip from San Diego to Fort Hood, which was located in Killeen, Texas, just 60 miles from the Davidian compound, was uneventful. It always was. Walker and his team had been deployed enough now that they knew the trip was downtime. They relaxed in their hammocks, listening to Walkmans to drown out any thoughts of the coming mission.

Once they reached Ft. Hood, they supervised the offloading of equipment into ground vehicles. Once that was finished, they met in one of the nearby hangars. It was still warm in Texas, even though October was nearly spent. Hernandez and Richards were the last to arrive at the makeshift command center. Walker began the briefing pointing out the ingress points for his team to enter the compound covertly, assess the situation, grab the hostage, and egress as a team through the tunnels located at the west end of the compound. There was agreement that they would overwhelmingly have both the element of surprise and superior weaponry to handle the civilians without bloodshed.

There was a long pause as Commander Richards reexamined the details of the plan and SAC Hernandez was the first to speak. "What if you meet resistance?"

Walker answered without emotion, "Our rules of engagement clearly state that we will not fire unless fired upon."

She insisted, "There will be armed guards in the room with the hostage."

Walker simply answered, "Yes ma'am. As the plan outlines, we will use flash-bangs and tear gas to quickly immobilize all the people in the room."

"What about Rodriguez?" she almost screamed.

Walker began, "Ma'am..."

"Stop calling me 'ma'am'!" she shot back.

Walker was already in deployment mode. He wasn't fazed in the least by her apparent panic. Before he could answer, Richards said, "Agent Hernandez, Lieutenant Commander Walker, is merely being polite. They are trained and prepared to deal with the temporary effects of the flashbang and tear gas on the target."

She said, "I would remind you, Commander, 'the target' is the son of the Secretary of Defense. He is no ordinary hostage."

Carson Bradley leaned over to his friend, Dylan Walker, and whispered, "Man, this is fubar."

Walker simply nodded and whispered back, "Full moon."

Arriving at the on-site command center, introductions were made, and Walker went over the plan with the ATF commander, the captain representing the Texas Rangers, the local Agent-in-Charge from the FBI, Texas Guard representatives, the Sheriff of McClendon County, a DOD representative, and a representative from the Texas Governor's office. Walker thought to himself, "Man, what a friggin' circus!" In the middle of the outline for the extraction plan, the DOD representative, who actually was there to relay information back to Secretary of Defense Rodriquez, the father of the hostage, said, "It won't work."

Walker said, "Excuse me?"

The Agent-in-Charge answered quietly, "It won't work. You've been misinformed, Lieutenant Commander. We've been at this for 51 days now. We tried to breach the compound with force. We lost four good agents. We got six of them, but there are still too many people armed with fully automatic weapons, grenades, and at least one 50 caliber machine gun. We negotiated a cease-fire, hoping we could bring this to a peaceful solution. All we've gotten so far is the release of a few women and children in exchange for food and medical supplies. They aren't going to surrender easily."

Walker and Richards exchange glances. Dylan knew the commander was surprised by this as much as he was. The DOD representative continued with another surprise, "We've already secured the go-ahead from the Attorney General to use tear gas and armored vehicles to push down the walls going in with full force."

Walker had noticed a lot of temporary structures, tents, and bivouacs coming in. He asked, "How many men do you have?"

A man, who had stood off from the group almost in the shadows, said, "More than enough to take care of these crazies."

The DOD, quickly interjected, "We have 900 regular army with supporting armored personnel. We also have all the heavy equipment in place to advance and push down the walls."

Walker saw the disaster unfolding and simply said, "I may have an alternative with less risk to the hostage."

Richards said, "Go ahead, commander."

Walker offered, "Myself and two others from the team can enter through the tunnels, secure the hostage in a safe zone before the breach begins. We can defend a position at the rear of the compound easily while you come in from the front." They agreed on the new approach, but would not back off from an overwhelming assault. They would have thirty minutes to enter and retrieve the hostage. It would be a tight window of opportunity, but it should be enough for them to accomplish the mission a minimum of risk to the team or the hostage.

Walker chose his fellow Texans, Carson Bradley and Jack Reece. They made their way around to the entrance to the tunnel, which was in an old school bus at the rear of the compound. It was not locked or guarded. They quickly reached the end of the tunnel and quietly disabled the guard placed there. He couldn't have been more than sixteen years old. Bradley easily rendered him unconscious with a non-lethal chokehold, easing him to the floor. They were making their way to the room where the hostage was being held with twenty-two minutes left in their window of opportunity when all hell broke loose. They heard small arms fire, the 50 caliber began to sound, and then there were huge explosions in the front rooms. The assault had begun early. Racing through makeshift hallways, they nearly reached the room where their target was being held when the propane tanks exploded. Reece caught the brunt of the explosion and was killed instantly. Bradley's uniform exploded in flames. Walker rushed to Bradley, taking him and rolling with him to extinguish the flames. Some of the debris from the collapsing wall must have hit Walker as everything went to black.

Walker awoke the next day in a hospital room, still under the influence of the concussion and the drugs, he stammered, "Where's my team?"

Richards had been waiting outside the room and went in immediately, "Take it easy, Dylan. You're OK."

"Where's Bradley?" he asked.

"He's gonna make it, but we had to transfer him to the burn unit at Baylor Medical," Richards quietly said.

"What happened? We had twenty-two minutes left?" Walker asked.

Richards just said, "Fubar."

The next weeks and months were a circus of media with politicians and agency representative finger-pointing. Carson Bradley, badly burned, barely surviving, received a medal of honor. However, he was left with rage and bitterness toward the US government, and Dylan offered his resignation, which was firmly refused. He agreed to finish out his twenty years, but he never forgot. That moment he vowed to himself, he would make it right for Bradley. He couldn't let this go. The government had let them down and cost his childhood friend everything. No medal could ever ease that pain. The time passed quickly, and finally free of the Navy, Walker returned to his home in Texas.

Carson Bradley was discharged from the Navy. Returning home to Texas, where he began a group of equally passionate men and women from Texas who rallied around the idea that Texas had to secede from the Union. He was surprised that it was so strongly supported. Texans for Independence became the largest group in the state over the intervening years until Dylan comes home. Dylan Walker, hero and patriot, was immediately approached by the Governor to join the Texas Guard with the rank of Brigadier General, the highest-ranking officer and commander of nearly 21,000 troops, including its army and air components. He also commanded two companies of the 19th Special Forces Group and Air Guard fighter and attack wings that provided strike and drone capabilities. It was an army rivaling the foreign armies of the world.

Dylan Walker often met with his old friend, Carson Bradley; however, as the Brigadier General of the Texas Guard, he could not be a part of Texans for Independence even though he was very sympathetic to their cause. He often attended their meetings in disguise, but every time he saw his old friend, his face and body burned almost beyond recognition, it reminded him of that fateful day in Waco.

One of Dylan's good friends was John Lucas III. He was a powerful and extremely successful cattle rancher and Texas state legislator. He had died while Dylan was away serving in the Seals. He knew his son, John Lucas IV, from his earliest years as a boy. He had followed in his father's footsteps and was now a member of the Texas State Legislature. Dylan and John IV had semi-regular lunches at various locales throughout the state. This time it was Dylan doing the inviting, and he asked him to meet for lunch at Buzzard Billy's Swamp Shack, perched on the Brazos River in Waco.

John readily accepts as he always liked Dylan and enjoyed reliving old memories of his Dad. After they had eaten some of the best gumbo outside of the swamps of Louisiana, enjoying a cold Shiner beer, with the Brazos quietly flowing under them, Dylan asks John if he has been paying attention to the legislative battles in Alabama, Georgia, and Missouri over abortion. It's a hot button for John. "Of course I have!"

Dylan finishes his beer and asks John if he'd take a short ride with him. He said, "I'd like to take you to where it all began for me." Of course, he meant the site of the Waco Siege as it had come to be known.

They drove silently for the next twenty minutes. Dylan pulls his truck up to the site where a simple granite marker was set with the engraved names of the 82 men, women, and children who were killed there. Dylan said, "You know John, we still had twenty minutes left in our planned window of opportunity to extract the DOD's son. We were almost there, just a few feet from entering the room. We'd have gotten him out alive. Instead, somebody decided they couldn't wait. Did you know that eighteen of those children killed were under ten years old? None of that needed to happen."

Quietly John said, "I didn't know that, Dylan."

Walker pressed on, "Well, it's true. But that's not why I brought you out here. The truth is those innocent kids are nothing compared to the 60,000 abortions that are performed in Texas every year through legal clinics. John, we can't do anything about the lives that have already been lost, but maybe we can stop more from being added to their number. I lost someone very important to me at Waco, and your family lost someone very important from abortion."

John can only say, "I know."

Dylan continues to press, "John, we have the strategic advantages of being the only state strong enough legally to put a stop to this senseless practice. Texas can avoid the legal strangleholds that have plagued the other states."

John nods approvingly and says he will definitely pray and think about this. John is good to his word. John is a cautious man. He wouldn't even buy a truck without talking it over with four or five people. Before committing to any course of action this important though, he would need to talk to those closest to him. The first meeting he decides to have is with his friend and pastor, David Edwards.

Chapter 2

The Struggle

October 24, 2018

"Government big enough to supply everything you need is big enough to take everything you have ... The course of history shows that as a government grows, liberty decreases."

— *Thomas Jefferson*

COME AND TAKE IT

Fall in South Texas always provided a time of rest and rejuvenation for both people and land. Texas, especially on the far southern border of the Rio Grande, has never been known for the passing of the seasons. In fact, it was the local joke in Webb County. You could stroll into the downtown café in Laredo and find the old ranchers sitting around the big table in the back, drinking their coffee and solving all the world's problems, from high taxes to global warming.

David Edwards and John Lucas IV usually found themselves at one of the booths enjoying the comfortable atmosphere of their regular haunt. David was the local pastor of the First Baptist Church and somewhat well known in both the county and the state. He'd been there nearly twenty years and often served as counsel for local and state leaders during those two decades. He was especially close to John, who owned and operated the largest cattle ranch in Texas. David had known John and his Dad for years. He had been instrumental in the most challenging times of his life. After John's dad died, David became more than a close friend. Today they met just to "chew the fat," as the locals would say.

John arrived first and secured the booth with the chalkboard hanging over the bench seats. He knew David liked to draw as he wove stories of life and the Bible into some point that somehow always gave him clarity for his current problem, even if John didn't understand right away. And that was one thing he needed today – some clarity. In just a few months, the new Texas legislative session would begin. There was a lot on John's mind, and for the first time in his legislative career, he was considering taking the lead on a new bill.

David greeted John as he walked through the door with his usual, "Howdy!"

David got up, and they shook hands and hugged one another. "What's up?" David began.

"I'm done, preacher," answered John.

"It's good to see we're starting with something light-hearted," David replied with a grin.

That wasn't the first time he'd heard that lament from John. John's personality was somewhat like Eeyore from *Winnie the Pooh*. His glass was half empty on his best days, though this time seemed different. There was a serious look in his eyes that communicated a crisis point had been reached far beyond any of the challenges his friend had ever faced before. It looked as if he had the weight of the world on his shoulders. That was a great concern for the old pastor and friend.

John began without preamble, "Have you been following any of the news concerning Alabama's new abortion law?"

"Yep. It looks like they decided to do whatever is necessary to protect life. It is going to be a dog fight."

"I think Texas needs to make a decision about that soon," John stated flatly.

Not one to mince words, David answered plainly, "Been coming for a long time."

David allowed his answer to hang there, waiting to see if John would continue to talk about what was really bothering him. The silence was palpable. The only noises in the café were the other locals engaged in conversations about their day ahead. A television in the corner had a news channel on, though the volume was muted. The local weather reporter was pointing to the daily forecast for the coming week. John hardly glanced up from his coffee when David asked, "So, John, what are you prepared to do?"

That question opened the valve on the fire hydrant style David was so used to from John. John was animated as he began to talk faster than David could listen. He was never able to listen as fast as John could talk. Making matters worse, David had become deafer than ever as he aged. His wife would often prod him to get a doctor's opinion, but as was true with most things, the Reverend David Edwards was not a compliant man.

John began in one of his common races to finish his verbal thought, "Alabama has got it right. But, we can get it done. Even Georgia and Missouri have passed bills to protect the unborn child. The problem is none of them have the legal right or resources to make a difference. Texas does. Those myopic lawmakers have lost sight of our own Declaration of Independence. They ought to know what it says. John Adams, Benjamin Franklin, Thomas Jefferson, Roger Sherman, and Robert Livingston wrote it with the plainest of language: 'But when a long train of abuses and usurpations, pursuing invariably the same Object evinces a design to reduce them under absolute Despotism, it is their right, it is their duty, to throw off such Government, and to provide new Guards for their future security.' I don't know how anyone could mistake that!"

David simply said, "Indeed. I can see you've done your homework. But, again, what are you prepared to do?"

John was exasperated, "I'll write our own bill. I know enough folks to get it passed, and then we can have what we need in Texas to really protect every child, in or out of the mother's womb."

"Are you sure you want to go down this road, John?" David asked.

John quickly answered, "What do you mean? You know the history. You know the pain my family has been through. You know what it was like standing beside my sister's bed when we had to decide to have her committed just to save her life. You were there. You know."

"I do know," David quietly answered. Then he went on, "I also know what it means for you. It won't end with a bill in

Texas. It will go much farther than that. This path is much longer than that. How much are you willing to sacrifice?"

John looked at him with deep sadness and said, "But it's the right thing to do."

David said, "Yes, it is. But are you doing this now because it is the right thing to do, or to try to make things right for your sister?"

John quickly said, "Both, I guess."

They finished their coffee in silence. Finally, John pays the bill and gets up to leave when David gives him one of those looks he was known for and says, "You are more than enough to do what God gives you to do. I'm always going to be standing with you, John. You're good stuff!"

With that, John hugs his old friend and confidant, walking out of the café, hardly noticing all the others staring at him.

He got into his old truck and began the ride home. John had a lot to think about after that morning with David at the Downtown Café in Laredo. He made the drive back to the ranch in the quiet. Normally that would be peaceful for him. Today was different. As he turned on to the old Farm-to-Market 20 going south from the city, the mesquite covered land did nothing to quiet his spirit. David's words weighed on his mind. "What am I willing to do?" ran over and over like an echo across the Palo Duro Canyon.

After all, he had never done anything of note. He had grown up under the tutelage of his Dad, who was certainly not a man of indecision. All his life, growing up on Lucas Farms, he knew he'd never be the man his Dad was. Feelings of insufficiency and self-doubt plagued him. No matter what he had accomplished, he always felt out of place in such a powerful and connected family as his was. His wife was the only bright spot in his life; she and his two children.

John met Rebecca at Texas A&M in an agricultural law class. She was almost out of place in the class. She certainly didn't look like a *country girl*. She was stunningly beautiful, with long raven hair and dark eyes that seemed always to be focused beyond the ordinary. John would have never thought to risk getting to know her had it not been for the professor's serendipitous appointment of her to his study group. John was the leader of the group because of his achievement, though he always thought it was because of his lineage and land.

Rebecca was a quick study. They soon excelled in every assignment with her contribution. After three months, he finally awkwardly suggested they go to the Dixie Chicken and get a burger after class. She accepted, and over the next two years, they seemed inseparable. She just understood him. Even when his insecurity seemed smothering like the dark clouds of distant thunderstorms coming from the north, she always found a way to shelter him from his introspection.

After college, they were married and moved to the ranch, where he would continue to take more responsibility for the family's ranch. Their two children, John V and Abby, were proud of their father, especially Abby, who seemed to dote on his every word. Rebecca enjoyed the benefits of being a part of a powerful and connected family, much more so than John. She often spurred him on with her dream for him to embrace his position and use it for good. Over the years, this became a significant point of tension in their marriage. He was always more than content with the family's position, power, and money, while Rebecca wished he would be more like his father and take things to the next level. John was content to ride the *senderos* to the top of the rise, sit on his horse, and watch the cattle meander through the grassy pastures so carefully planted and kept in the South Texas heat. He would think, "They are always the same—just happy to be grazing, not a care in the world."

He couldn't help remembering the first time this issue arose in Alabama. He recalled how that ended. When the Alabama law dealing with abortion had run its course through all the lower courts, dealt with every civil suit, and finally ended with the state nearly bankrupt from the sheer expense of the extended legal battle, they were no closer to resolution than when they began. He wondered if his course of action was worth it. The US Supreme Court had finally heard the last of the appeals and ruled in a split decision that Roe vs. Wade could not be overturned in favor of the state's law. The case, 410 U.S. 113 (1973), was a landmark decision of the U.S. Supreme Court in which the Court ruled that the Due Process Clause of the Fourteenth Amendment to the U.S. Constitution provides a fundamental "right to privacy" that protects a pregnant woman's liberty to choose whether or not to have an abortion.

Of course, John had studied all of the opinions regarding that case extensively. He was a young lawyer when it was heard. In June 1969, when then 21-year-old Norma McCorvey discovered she was pregnant with her third child. She returned to Dallas, Texas, where friends advised her to falsely assert that she had been raped in order to obtain a legal abortion, with the incorrect assumption that Texas Law allowed abortion in cases of rape and incest. This scheme would fail because there was no police report documenting the alleged rape. In any case, the Texas statute allowed abortion only "for the purpose of saving the life of the mother." She attempted to obtain an illegal abortion but found that the unauthorized facility had been closed down by the police. Eventually, she was referred to attorneys Linda Coffee and Sarah Weddington. Ironically, Ms. McCorvey would end up giving birth before the case was decided, and the child was put up for adoption. In 1970, Coffee and Weddington filed suit in the United States District Court for the Northern District of Texas on behalf of McCorvey under the alias Jane Roe. The defendant in the case was Dallas County District Attorney Henry Wade, who represented the State of Texas.

John had known Wade, meeting him for the first time with his father in 1996. They continued a cordial and personal relationship after he joined the bar remaining close until Wade died in 2001. In fact, he still remembered those evenings playing dominos and smoking custom rolled Cuban cigars discussing all the cases he had tried. Wade was flamboyant and unforgettable to Texans. After all, as Dallas County prosecutor from 1950 to 1986, he never lost a case he personally tried. He prosecuted Jack Ruby after he shot and killed Kennedy assassin Lee Harvey Oswald in the Dallas police headquarters in 1963.

Those evenings spent with Wade had forged resolute respect for the law. While many may have never known that Wade was a Democrat, they certainly had no idea why he had McCorvey arrested at all. Wade was never out crusading against abortions. But, because abortion was illegal in the county and he was the top law enforcement official in the county, he was compelled to move against her. Roe wanted to challenge the law and his authority. The question became, "Should he prosecute her if she underwent an abortion?" For him, the answer was yes.

Meandering down the old road, he finally reached the main gate to the ranch and turned in. As he stopped in front of the ranch house, he made his decision. He would begin to test the waters with some of his close friends in the legislature. There were many risks involved. Abortion in Texas was as prickly as the cactus so common to his beloved South Texas. And, it was not an issue that people were neutral about. Even his friends in Austin, some who were facing reelection, would hesitate to be a part of changing any of the laws that were presently on the books. After all, Texas did have some of the strictest pro-life regulations of any state in the union. In addition to regulations concerning when a woman might have an abortion, and the addition of mandatory approved counseling, last year the Senate passed legislation that banned abortions based on the sex, race, or disability of a fetus, and criminalized doctors who perform discriminatory abortions. There were a large number of legislators who simply didn't want to fight this fight any longer. And he thought about the repercussions he might face in his home. Rebecca and the kids would be on board. Prudence Lambert, a childhood friend of John's and, more importantly, the CEO of Lucas Ranch, might not be as easily swayed. He certainly did not want to lose Prudence's leadership on the ranch. She had been invaluable since joining the staff.

Perhaps if he met with these groups and built a coalition big enough to sway the Governor and the other lawmakers, it would be worth it. Maybe this was his path. In fact, that's exactly what he would tell David tomorrow morning when they met again over coffee. After all, he was a Texan. Those roots ran as deep as the mesquite of his beloved state.

Chapter 3

The Decision Is Made

October 25, 2018

"Those who would give up essential liberty to purchase a little temporary safety deserve neither liberty nor safety."

—Benjamin Franklin

COME AND TAKE IT

It was early when John arrived at the Downtown Café in Laredo. The temperature was cool for that time of the year in South Texas. As was typically the case, it would get hotter as the day wore on; but, now, he enjoyed the crisp air and cool breeze blowing in from the north. He lingered in his truck, trying to formulate his thoughts, steeling his resolve for what he anticipated as a crossroads moment in his life.

He had tossed and turned through the night after meeting with David the day before. His words still rang in his mind. What was he willing to sacrifice? He wasn't sure how much it would cost him; however, he was sure that liberty, real liberty, has always been costly. Anyone who knew any part of the history of the Lone Star knew the sacrifice made by the 257 Texans. They made the ultimate sacrifice at the Battle of the Alamo. Abortion was an extremely personal issue for John and his family. It's what made this battle worth fighting, and, if it was also the start of Texas asserting a little more independence, then all the better.

He got out of his truck and strode to the front door of the café. When he opened it, he saw David in their usual booth. John tipped his hat to Rosita, who had been at the café as long as he could remember. She was a local fixture in Laredo's downtown. She was an immigrant's daughter who had grown up there. She had been to the University of Texas with an academic scholarship majoring in business. After graduation, she returned home and bought the old downtown building off the courthouse square, opening the café. Hardly seemed possible that was forty years ago. John and his dad made the trip into town often enough that she got to know them. In those early days, Rosita did anything that needed to be done to make her business a success. Now, she had become such an important part of the city that everyone knew her. She was elected to serve on the city council and had represented her district well.

"*Bueños Dias, Señor* John," she greeted him. She liked to use the familiar Mexican greeting when she saw him. After all, she was the one responsible for John being fluent in Spanish.

"*Bueños Dias*, Rosita!" John replied. He continued to walk to the back booth, where David waited, talking with all the other old ranchers and businessmen who had gathered that morning.

He slid into the booth opposite David and was greeted warmly. David said, "Sleep well last night?"

"You know I didn't. How could I? Way too much to chew on," John began.

"Wanna chat about it?" David grinned.

"I've got so many things bouncing around my mind, I'm not sure where to start," he began.

David used that as an excuse to do what he so often did. He liked to lead with questions designed to see the choices. He grabbed a napkin, and John knew what that meant. He was about to get the drawing with an explanation of his three choices—again. This was David's fallback position. He some-how could distill every circumstance into three choices: stay the same, quit, or change. And, it was getting ready to happen again. John knew before David ever got to the *change* that was going to be the decision he had to make.

He knew staying the same wasn't possible. If he didn't do something, he could never face Sarah again. Sarah Lucas was his younger sister. She had grown up as a difficult and rebel-lious child. She followed a course of rebellion and experimen-tation with drugs, alcohol, and wild living in high school and college. This led her to attach herself to any boy who shared her attitude about life and fun. She somehow managed to graduate from the private academy run by the Catholic Sisters of Mercy. St. Augustine's was run tightly. Sarah chafed under the philosophy developed as a result of the vows of poverty, chastity, obedience and service that the Sisters observed. The last thing she wanted was poverty; her dad was one of the wealthiest men in Texas. And, chastity, obedience, and service were things for other girls, not her.

She made it out of St. Augustine's relatively unscathed. Her Dad used his influence to secure her acceptance into the University of Texas in Austin. That was like pouring gasoline on a fire, though. John remembered that one day, the day that changed everything. She had been dating a boy who was the worst in a long succession of abusive boyfriends. The drug and alcohol abuse only worsened when she became pregnant. Of course, she didn't tell anyone other than her boyfriend. His pressure and abuse continued unknown to anyone in the family until she agreed to an abortion. It was the bottom for her.

Just after that decision and the finality of the procedure, Sarah realized what she had done. She called John and asked him to meet her for lunch at Cooper's Barbeque near the capital on Congress Avenue.

They got their food, though Sarah couldn't really eat. John knew something was going on. He thought it might be her grades. He had no idea of the news he was about to receive.

Sarah began to softly cry as she said, "John, I've messed up. I know I don't have the right to ask for your help, but I know how much you've helped all the hands at the ranch whenever they needed you, and I can't think of anyone else I can turn to."

John was startled, thinking how much this sounded like the Prodigal Son returning home. In fact, he had just heard his friend David Edwards preach that sermon Sunday. He said, "You're my sister. That's never going to change. What's going on?"

She told him everything. She confessed the drugs, the alcohol, the sex, the abuse, and the pregnancy ending with an abortion. It was worse than he had feared. As he listened to her, he remained silent, helpless, paralyzed. How could he have let this happen to her? How did he not protect his little sister? How could he have failed her so badly? He never wanted to fail his family again. Over the next few months, he helped Sarah turn it around. And she worked hard with her recovery, ultimately graduating from the university.

It was a good story with a happy ending for Sarah. She moved home and began to organize a pro-life advocacy group, Texans for Life, which had gained enormous support in the intervening years. Soon after she came home, David introduced her to a young minister he knew, Jeremiah Lyons. They were soon married, and both committed to the work of the advocacy group. It had become the largest, most powerful pro-life group in the state due to Sarah's story and work.

John knew he could never face Sarah again if he shrunk from this challenge to change the law in Texas. He believed this could be the final redemption in his sister's journey. Now was the time, and he had decided he was the man to do it. He just didn't know if he was enough.

"I can't let Sarah down," he told David.

The preacher said, "So, I'm guessing you will not stay the same?" then he marked an "x" through that choice on the napkin drawing. "How about just quitting?" he asked.

John became intensely animated and grabbed the pen from David's hand and scratched through the "quit," and said, "I not only can't stay the same; I can't quit either! I just don't know if I can succeed!"

David never strayed very far from the Bible. It was his ultimate truth. He often remarked that it was "the truth that sets us free." This moment was no exception. He looked at John and said, "I reckon Joshua felt the same way when Moses handed him the reins to take all those folks into the Promised Land." After recounting the story of Joshua, David simply said, "Change is never easy, even when you know what it should look like. This change is going to evolve as you go. However, we can work our way through it by following a logical plan. The key is in knowing what the beginning should look like?"

John knew where to start. He had gained a strong following in the state legislature. He would talk individually with each of those people. He also knew he had to win the support of Perry Thompson, the Governor of Texas. The timing was right. He had about six months before the next session would begin. Sarah would help. She had enormous support throughout the state. His conversation continued to pour out ideas and strategies until he absolutely had to take a breath. David was accustomed to drinking from the fire hydrant with John, and he merely let him exhaust the line of thought.

Then David said, "Maybe you should start with Rebecca. What does she think?"

He was right. He had to start at the beginning. He would talk to his wife as soon as he got back to the ranch. He was certain she'd be supportive. She always had. It was her support that got him into politics in the first place. There were plenty of days when he'd just prefer to sit and watch the cows graze though she'd prod him to "saddle up." That was her way of urging him to move forward. He fondly remembered her sitting in the front row when he announced his campaign for State Senator. He knew if he was going to do this, he needed her in his corner.

"I'll talk to her when I get back to the ranch," he told David.

David's response was typically understated, "I guess you better get moving. You're burning daylight."

John paid the bill and walked from the café to his truck, resolutely determined. He had made his decision.

Chapter 4

The Coalition's Beginning

October 25, 2018

"But when a long train of abuses and usurpations, pursuing invariably the same Object evinces a design to reduce them under absolute Despotism, it is their right, it is their duty, to throw off such Government, and to provide new Guards for their future security."

—Declaration of Independence 1776

COME AND TAKE IT

It was still early in the day, though John felt as if he'd already put in a full day. Any meeting with David Edwards was always challenging; however, it was always worth it. John didn't have many friends, but he was very close to the few he had. He considered David, his best friend. Very little was filtered or restrained between them.

John arrived at the ranch house and walked in only to be caught by Prudence. Prudence Lambert was never *off the clock*. She had grown up with John attending high school with him as well as Texas A&M. She received her business degree from the nationally ranked Mays Business School, graduating Magna Cum Laude. She had multiple offers for a position as auditor and consultant with Deloitte, Ernst and Young, and Price Waterhouse Coopers. She ultimately decided on a position with Price Waterhouse Coopers at their corporate headquarters in London, England. She'd stayed there for several years until John approached her about coming home to run his ranch. After all, he wasn't very good at it, and when his Dad turned the business side of it over to him, he had barely managed to keep it moving in the right direction. In the ten years since Prudence had taken over, she had overseen the most profitable and highest growth period in the ranch's long and storied history.

Prudence assailed him as he came in, "Slow down. I need a few minutes."

Her few minutes were always longer than that, and they always involved him making decisions he really didn't care to make. Today was no exception. She began to relate the condition of some of the pumpjacks on the ranch. Not only did they have a large cattle operation, but a large part of the revenues also came from the production of oil and gas wells on the property. Lignite had also become a part of the ranch's business in the last decade, though that was relatively new. She needed his permission to go forward with replacing some of the equipment, making it necessary to shift some of the contracts and file the necessary papers with the federal government.

Prudence had all the documentation and paperwork requiring his signature. She began to go over each of the documents when John said, "Prudence, you know I trust your judgment. Just point where I need to sign."

That merely gained him a lecture of how important all of these things were, "I might not be here forever, you know."

An hour later, John walked out of her office and found Rebecca. She was just about to sit down with a few friends from church for brunch when he walked on to the large covered porch at the back of the house. Of course, everyone was cordial. They knew one another well from church and other social events. John felt obliged to exchange pleasantries. He was always out of his comfort zone when forced to be around women. He always felt they didn't understand him at all. Most women simply tolerated him as a gesture of kindness to Rebecca.

"May I speak with you a bit later?" he asked his wife.

"Of course, dear. Is it something that can wait, or do you need me now?" Rebecca cooed. She certainly was in her element.

"No, hurry. It can wait," John answered.

He retreated to the wooden swing hanging on the porch that overlooked the pasture nearest the ranch house. This was the pasture where they kept the herd of registered longhorns. As he sat, he thought how majestic they looked. Some of them were old enough to have grown horns that spanned over seven feet, tip to tip. He was always amused when he saw Bevo, the current mascot for the University of Texas since he was an Aggie. Football season was over, and the steer had been returned to the ranch to be wintered on its home pasture. The season had not ended nearly as well for the "T-sips" as it did for his beloved Aggies.

He saw that the newest acquisition couldn't be missed. The six-year-old longhorn, aptly named Pancho Villa, was rowdy in his new surroundings. Though that was not the reason he was easily the stand-out in the herd. John had recently negotiated his purchase from the Pope family, who owned a small farm outside of Goodwater, Alabama. The Pope family had come to Texas years earlier and become interested in getting a longhorn as a family pet. They were connected with a veterinarian who procured the steer as a six-month-old. They had raised him to become the Guinness World Record Holder for possessing the longest set of horns measuring tip-to-tip at 10 feet, 7.4 inches. The Popes could no longer care for the animal, but couldn't bear to see him sold at auction. He was a steer, after all. His usefulness genetically was nil. John heard about their plight from a friend and was happy to bring him home to Lucas Farms. He seemed to empathize with the way they must have felt.

As he watched the huge longhorn graze, he thought how ironic it was that he was named after the famous Mexican revolutionary Pancho Villa. He recalled his history. It was Francisco "Pancho" Villa, who was the Mexican revolutionary leader advocating for the poor and land reform. He helped lead the Mexican Revolution, which ended the reign of Diaz and led to the creation of a new government in Mexico. John recalled, Villa is remembered as a folk hero and a champion of the lower classes and wondered if his *revolution* would be remembered as fondly.

Thinking about his decision, it was easy to go back to his memories of his father. Their relationship was good. He admired him and deSired to be like him in the earlier years of his childhood. As he grew into his teens, he always felt he could never fill those boots. John Lucas III was legendary in Texas. He cast a long shadow across the state in business and politics.

John's father was a Texan through and through. Most of the family's wealth came from the land they had settled, defended, and developed since it was first granted to his great-great-great-grandfather in a land grant from Stephen F. Austin. From defending their land in the height of the Comanche raids to the ultimate fight for freedom from the Mexican government, the Lucas name was at the forefront. It symbolized the pioneer spirit of Texans past and present.

When his father was elected to the Texas Senate, he quickly gained a reputation for doing the right thing for the people of Texas regardless of how the political party power brokers might perceive it. This was at the root of the long-standing differences that developed between John Lucas III and Governor Thompson. Thompson, then the Speaker of the House, started the feud with his penchant for backroom deals and promises to powerful lobbies. His dad could not sit idly by and see the people of Texas sold out for Thompson's political benefit. While it couldn't be proven in a court of law, it was common knowledge that Thompson had played a pivotal role in advancing the social agenda of some of the liberal factions of the state legislature. If a vote could be bought, he knew exactly how to buy it.

On more than one occasion, John Lucas III blocked the then Senator Thompson's self-serving political deals. Surely, this time would be different. Surely, this time he could reason with the Governor.

Lost in those thoughts, he didn't hear Abigail, his daughter, approach. She came up from behind him and put her arms around his neck and gave him a gentle kiss on the cheek. There was nothing unusual about that. Abigail Lucas was quiet and introverted, much the same as her Daddy. She never liked the attention and power of their family. She was fiercely loyal to John. She, more than anyone, liked to sit with her Dad on the porch and while away the time watching the cattle.

She came around the swing and sat next to John, sing-songing in her best Texas drawl, "Penny for your thoughts."

He needed no further provocation. He began to outline in fire-hydrant fashion his struggle and the subsequent decision to throw his full energy into the drafting, introduction, and passing of a bill protecting the life of the unborn children of Texas. "I think it's high time we did something for all these innocent children and their mothers, so no one ever needs to endure what your Aunt Sarah had to endure!" John exclaimed.

He must have been a bit too animated with that last remark as his wife rounded the corner and said, "John, are you okay?"

Startled, he stammered, "Fine… I'm fine. Did I interrupt your group?"

Rebecca answered, "Of course not. We just broke up, and the ladies have left. I came looking for you and thought I'd find you out here."

Rebecca took a seat on the swing with Abigail and John. She put her arm around Abigail with a warm embrace. They chatted about school, her art, and a few other inane things for a few minutes when John said, "Abigail, would you mind if I talked to your Mom alone for a little while?"

That question piqued Rebecca's curiosity. This was certainly not going to be a typical conversation with her husband. The practice session with Abigail helped John, though talking to Rebecca was certainly not going to be as simple. He still felt unworthy of having her, even after all these years together. So he just jumped into the whole story. He talked about how he'd never really felt he had done anything of importance since taking his father's seat in the state legislature. He shared how he had watched other states pass laws defending and protecting the unborn child.

He said, "Did you know that there are nine states that now have stricter abortion laws than we do? Even Louisiana passed a bill. Alabama passed theirs before that! How could we be so backward in our state? None of their laws will be able to stand up to the federal government. We're the only ones with the resources and legal right to govern ourselves without federal intrusion. When Texas was a nation unto itself, we joined the union by treaty. Even with the confusion after the Civil War, I think Texas can lead the way on this. I've got to do something about it!"

Rebecca waited for him to take a breath. She was used to his way. She quietly said, "I know John. What do you have in mind?"

Calmer now, he outlined his plan. "I'll begin to build a co-alition with the others who are like-minded. We'll draft a strong bill for introduction into this year's legislative session. We can convince the Governor to support it and sign it into law. Then we can protect every child in our state, especially those who are yet to be born."

Rebecca smiled, took his face in her hands, and said, "I am so proud of you. We can do this together. I'm always going to be sitting on the front row, John."

Life had never been any better than this. He felt as if he had finally arrived at the center of his purpose and calling. They sat there, his arm around her, holding her close, watching the sunset across the *sendero*. It seemed as if the colors were especially brilliant. It was as if God was giving him His support too.

Chapter 5

The Movement Is Born

October 26, 2018

"You will never know how much it has cost my generation to preserve YOUR freedom. I hope you will make a good use of it."

—John Adams

COME AND TAKE IT

The 2019 Texas Legislative Session was set to convene on Tuesday, January 8th. With just six months to build a coalition, draft a bill, and get it to the floor of the House and the Senate, John Lucas knew there was not a moment to waste. The time for sitting on the swing watching his beloved longhorns graze was a luxury he could not afford. That would have to wait until he saw the bill signed into law by the Governor.

John knew the procedure. Any representative or senator could write a bill for introduction on the floor of their chamber. John, being a senator, would only need a simple majority of the 31 members in the Senate to send it on to the House of Representatives. That might be a little more of a challenge since there were 150 members of that chamber. He would have more time to lobby some of the members in the house as the bill progressed. Even though the Democrats did not control either of the chambers, there were still some very influential people that he would need to get the bill passed through both Houses of the Legislature. Of course, most importantly, the Governor would need to be on board for the bill to become law.

Governor Perry Thompson was an interesting study in the world of Texas politics. He received his political science degree from Baylor University. Baylor, as it is commonly known, is a private Christian university in Waco, Texas. Located on the banks of the Brazos River next to I-35, between the Dallas-Fort Worth Metroplex and Austin, the university's 1,000-acre campus is the largest Baptist university campus in the world.

A degree from Baylor went a long way toward gaining entrance into one of the top five law schools in the country, the University of Texas. None of this was hurt by the fact that he was also part of a powerful Texas oil family with its corporate offices in Dallas. Some of his close friends would even chide him by asking if his real surname wasn't actually "Ewing," referencing the very popular 80's television drama, *Dallas*.

Perry Thompson rose up quickly through the ranks of the Texas Democratic party to become Speaker of the House, the Lieutenant Governor, and then Governor. Even in the red state of Texas, he had won his first term in a landslide and didn't see any decrease in popularity in his second and final term either. However, Thompson's aspirations were not limited to the historic Governor's Mansion; his political ambitions stretched to the White House.

John's father was a contemporary of Governor Thompson. As a result of their working relationship, John IV enjoyed a congenial relationship. Of course, it did not hurt that Thompson's family owed some of their business success directly to John Lucas, III. Even more importantly, however, was the fact that John Lucas, IV, delivered the Latino vote of South Texas to the Governor in both his elections. That fact was not lost on the Governor or the Democratic Party.

When Perry Thompson's cell phone rang with the caller I.D. showing "John Lucas," he took the call immediately.

After some brief pleasantries, John said, "Perry, I need an hour or so of your time as soon as possible."

Knowing it would never be an hour with John, the Governor asked, "How soon can you get away for lunch here in Austin?"

"I'll be there tomorrow. Can I meet you at the Austin Land and Cattle Steakhouse at noon?" John asked. It was on Lamar and offered hand-cut aged beef and chops served in a dark, old-fashioned setting. John knew the Governor well. He couldn't resist a show at one of the best steakhouses in Austin.

They were one of the few restaurants that served Garrison Brothers Bourbon, which he was very fond of drinking.

Perry said, "Sure. See you at noon."

John thought of one more request and asked, "One more thing, Perry, can you arrange clearance for me to land the helicopter at the capitol helipad?"

"No problem at all, my friend." And, with that, the conversation ended. The Governor was certainly curious now. This request was well out of the norm for John Lucas.

John worked on a brief outline of his thoughts for his conversation with the Governor. He used some bullet points to remind him of the current laws on the books concerning abortion in Texas. This was not one of the typical political issues in the state. Most of the legislative sessions recently had dealt with the border and public education. Abortion had found its way to the bottom of the list when it came to reform. After all, Texas still had one of the strictest laws on the books regarding abortion. It did not allow for partial-birth abortions. Nor was it legal to perform abortions during the third trimester except to prevent death or substantial risk of serious impairment to the mother's physical or mental health or if the fetus had a severe and irreversible abnormality.

As John's thoughts recalled the conversation in Waco with Dylan Walker, he also recalled that even with these laws, 60,000 abortions took place in Texas every year. And, for John, that was 60,000 too many.

It was a surprise to everyone at the ranch house when John arrived at the breakfast table dressed in a suit and tie. That was not his usual pattern at all. Even when he was in Austin, he would have been seen on the floor of the Senate dressed in starched Levis, with his well-worn custom Mercer and Son's boots. J.L. Mercer and son had been in business since 1923. In those 90 plus years Lyndon Johnson, John Wayne, and Charlie Daniels were all in the company of those who took their boots seriously, settling for nothing but Mercer's handcrafted Texas footwear.

Abby looked at her dad and playfully asked, "Where are you preaching today?" That was the family joke. John wouldn't allow himself to dress in anything but a suit and tie if he were going to church, much less speaking at church.

"I've got a meeting in Austin today with Perry Thompson. I've got the chopper ready to leave in an hour." John informed them.

Abby couldn't resist the opportunity to ask if she could go with him, nearly begging, "Can I go? You know all the new clothes are out now, and I really need some things, please, Daddy?"

Rebecca recognized both how comforting that would be for John and how she could rearrange her schedule to go with Abby to spend some time with her shopping in downtown Austin. "I can rearrange my schedule and go with y'all if you like? Abby and I are overdue for some shopping in Austin any-way," Rebecca remarked.

John jumped at the suggestion, "That would be great!"

Abby chimed in with a sly grin and said, "JV would love to spend the day without us underfoot anyway."

John Lucas V, shortened to JV to his family and friends, was a senior in high school. He reminded John of his father in so many ways. He relished the prominence of being born into such a powerful family. He was naturally an extrovert, very handsome, and excelled at everything he tried. He was pop-ular in school, captain of the football team, president of his class, a leader on his debate team, and voted "Most Likely to Be President." There was no doubt about who he was and where he was going with his life. With all of this innate talent, he was not arrogant or conceited; he was simply sure of himself in ways John never was.

As JV joined them for breakfast, John said, "Hey! Your mother and I are going to Austin for the day. Abby is going with us so that she and Mom can do some shopping while I meet with the Governor. Would you like to go, or would you rather stay at the ranch for the day?"

JV was quick with an answer, "If I can have some of my friends over, I'd rather stay."

"Sure, no problem," John answered.

They finished breakfast, excited for the adventure. It was a short walk from the main house to the helipad where the Bell 230 LM was already warming up, ready for the short hop to Austin. The cabin of this luxury model was especially quiet, allowing for John, his wife, and daughter to enjoy some casual conversation. John usually listened a lot more than he spoke. However, the experience provided him with a wonderful break from the anxiety that was building in this first real step into a world that was relatively unknown to him. He was always a great support to others, but never the leader of the cause.

They landed about an hour after take-off. John had called ahead and arranged for a car and driver for Rebecca and Abby so they could easily navigate their way to their favorite stores. As they disembarked, Rebecca took John's hand and said, "You're going to do great. I'm on the front row."

He smiled as she kissed him lightly on the cheek and walked to the waiting car. John thought to himself that it had been a long time since she looked at him that way. It reminded him of when they had first met and begun to date.

The Governor sent an aide to meet John at the helipad. After introducing himself, they walked in silence to the car. It was a short ride to the steakhouse, and John was a little early but was seated immediately at the table reserved for their lunch.

The Governor arrived shortly after and asked, "How was your trip in the Swag-copter?" Thompson was not above a little jibe from time to time. It was a reference to the football rivalry between the University of Texas and Texas A&M.

John's personal preference was not to travel in the helicopter. It was often on loan to the head football coach at A&M to make his visits to recruits all across the state. Its maroon and white themed paint was dubbed "the Swag-copter" by Sports Illustrated when it was first used. He smiled broadly at the familiar rivalry reference. John, in relatively rare form, said, "I guess I could have come in the truck with Bevo in the trailer." Bevo was the longhorn mascot for the University of Texas. John owned the steer and pastured him on his ranch during the year. They both laughed as they sat down. Food was ordered and delivered quickly.

"What's on your mind, John?" the Governor began.

"I am going to introduce a bill to the senate when we convene," John said without preamble. That was both a surprise and a concern for Thompson. John had not been involved directly in the legislative process in the past. However, the Governor was enough of a politician that he knew to let things play out with measured patience. It probably was going to deal with the border. John's ranch ran for over a hundred miles along the Rio Grande, and it was no secret that it was becoming increasingly more difficult to police it. With the federal government tightening border security at the entry points, the vast distances between them through private land like Lucas Ranch were ideal crossing points for the hundreds of people who crossed monthly into the United States.

The Governor listened, still practicing patience. John opened his notebook for reference, which caused the Governor to raise an eyebrow.

John began, "Perry, you know Sarah's story."

"I do. She has done a marvelous job in developing Texans for Life. I know you are proud of her."

John pressed on, "Her story is merely a beginning for me. I have often wished I could have done something different back then. Perhaps I would have another niece or nephew to celebrate with on holidays and birthdays. However, Perry, there are none of those, because that child's life was ended unnecessarily. Sarah was too young to make such a decision, and it was too easy to walk into the clinic for the procedure."

The Governor interrupted, "John, you know we have the toughest laws of any state regarding abortion without infringing on the rights of women to govern their own bodies."

"But those laws are not tough enough," argued John. He went on, undaunted, "Let me take you back to an experience I had not long ago in Waco with Dylan Walker."

The mention of General Walker's name in this conversation both alarmed and puzzled the Governor. However, he merely replied, "Go on, John. I'm listening."

"We had lunch on the Brazos and then took a little trip out to the site of the Waco Siege. I saw the memorial placed there to the 82 people who were killed that day. Did you know 18 of those were children under ten years old?"

"It was a tragic sequence of events, though entirely legal," the Governor remarked.

John dropped his voice to an even more serious tone, "Sometimes, what is legal is not what is right." He continued the conversation, outlining the bill he was going to introduce. "I will get with the Legislative Council and dot the 'i's' and cross the 't's,' but I want to know if you will support me moving forward. I need to know I can count on you going forward."

There was a long pause before the Governor answered, "John, you know I'm a Baptist. I support life. And even though it has always been a tough sell to the DNC, it has always been one of the planks of my platform. While we aren't known as a pro-life party, I can rest on my history as more of a centrist, especially with this issue. That has not changed. However, you know the trouble other states, like Alabama, have had in recent years trying to do much less than you are attempting. I'm not even sure the Supreme Court would allow it as constitutional."

John was prepared for that response. He had done his homework well. "I think the Texas Nationalist Movement might argue that last point, but that's beside the issue. I don't want to secede. I want to stop killing our children."

Then the Governor knew he was caught between being labeled a 'baby-killer' or going along with John for the moment. That label would kill any hope he had of the White House. He said, "Let's get the bill passed, John. If it passes, I'll sign it." He never thought it would get that far.

The rest of the lunch was relatively benign in the context of the conversation. The Governor was politically savvy enough to recognize when a strategic retreat was necessary. They talked about their families and football. Even though they no longer played in the same conferences, Texas A&M having moved to the Southeastern Conference and Texas remaining in the Big 12, they were fierce rivals. They traded polite jabs at one another, hoping to renew the rivalry on the field in the postseason.

Governor Thompson looked at his Rolex President Day-Date with an obvious move both to indicate his busy schedule and the extravagance of the $12,000 watch and said, "My, the time has gotten away. I need to run."

John began to thank him for the time, and Thompson was out of his seat and moving away before he could finish the first sentence. John was not a man who could be impressed by such shows of power. He smiled and simply paid the bill while leisurely finishing his Garrison Brothers Small Batch Whiskey.

John had some time to kill. He knew Rebecca and Abby wouldn't have finished their shopping yet. He directed the driver to take him back to the capital. As he walked through the corridor toward the exit where he could walk the short distance to his office complex, John saw some of the paintings hanging in the alcoves along the way. He wondered why he hadn't really noticed them before now. As he entered the south foyer, he stopped at one of the two large paintings near the foyer entrance. Both were the work of William H. Huddle.

One was titled *Davy Crockett*, and the second was *Surrender of Santa Anna*. It was the first that caught his attention. It presented the popular frontiersman in his fabled garb, coonskin cap included. It was an unusual interpretation compared to the many other paintings depicting Crockett at the Alamo. This one showed him standing with a long rifle in one hand and his coonskin cap in the other with a backdrop of serene forest. John thought that was certainly a long way from the scene Crockett must have faced at the end of the battle for the Alamo. And it was a stark contrast to the other Huddle work across the Gonzalez alcove. *The Surrender of Santa Anna*, which had been hanging in the alcove since 1891, showed the morning after the April 21, 1836, battle as Texian fighters presented Mexican General Antonio López de Santa Anna, dressed in the white pants of a private, to Texas General Sam Houston, who is reclined with a battle wound to his leg. It was the moment in history when the decisive victory securing the rebels' independence from Mexico was final. John recognized some of the figures from his study of Texas history. He saw the scout Erastus "Deaf" Smith, seated on a log, Secretary of War Thomas Jefferson Rusk, standing to the rear left of Houston, and Colonel Mirabeau B. Lamar, to the left of Rusk. The more he thought about these men, the more he felt his inadequacy for the task ahead. He was encouraged that his task was so much less than theirs. After all, he just wanted to change the abortion laws, not start a rebellion!

He walked out of the building and was greeted with a fresh breeze under the live oak-shaded walk. He arrived at the offices and was greeted by his Chief of Staff, who knew nothing of his reason for being in Austin. John took him aside after greeting those who were in for the day and began to tell him in brief terms what he was about to do. They discussed some of the preliminary details necessary to introduce the bill and the possible reaction of the media and potential opposition. John wasn't ready to do any specific planning at this point. For him, he was still laying the groundwork. The afternoon flew by, and he saw he needed to leave to meet Rebecca and Abby for the flight back to the ranch.

He arrived at the helipad about the same time as Rebecca and Abby drove up. Of course, they were all smiles as they walked with both arms full of bags from Wildflower's, Adelante's, and Spring Frost Boutique. They were some of their favorite shops in Austin, though he didn't understand why. Fashion was certainly lost on him. They loaded their bags and were belted in their seats as the helicopter warmed up for take-off and the return trip to the ranch.

Rebecca could always tell when John was withdrawing into the solitude of thought and typically left him alone to work through those thoughts in his own time. However, this time she began to engage him in conversation. At first, she described the fun she and Abby had in their little junket. She told him about a little denim dress that Abby had picked out, "It has straps made from overalls!"

John realized she had been talking and tried to engage her. "What color is it?" he asked.

She smiled. That was her signal to really talk to him. They began to banter a bit back and forth when Abby said, "Tell Daddy who we met for lunch at the bistro."

John was in a much better mood now and playfully asked, "Was it an old boyfriend?"

Rebecca smiled and said, "Of course not. We saw Lydia Smithson. She joined us for lunch."

"Really?" John said with a bit of surprise in his voice. They hadn't seen Lydia in a long time. She and Rebecca had known one another in school but had gone separate ways early in their relationship. Lydia had become one of the toughest litigators in the state and started a very influential pro-choice lobby group. She would not have taken the news of John's interest in banning abortion in Texas well at all.

"I bet that went well," John said.

Rebecca continued, "Oh, you know Lydia. She is always ready with a quick retort. She likes the debate. Abby and I just changed the subject."

Abby joined the conversation with a simple statement, "She's not very nice."

John, more reasonable, answered her, "She's just passionate about her beliefs."

Abby said, "Like I said, she's not very nice."

They continued the flight bantering back and forth about everything from the upcoming football game against Alabama to the unusually cool weather they were having. John was less and less interested in the conversation and more concerned with the coming fight getting the bill drafted, adopted, and signed into law.

Chapter 6

The Coalition Grows

October 27, 2018

"The first duty of government is the protection of life, not its destruction. The chief purpose of government is to protect life. Abandon that and you have abandoned all."

—Thomas Jefferson

COME AND TAKE IT

Saturday in the fall was usually a time of relaxation for John. Of course there were always things that needed to be done on the ranch, but it had been a while since John was responsible for any of those duties. When the legislature was not in session, his typical Saturday started by enjoying a late breakfast with Rebecca on the back porch overlooking the *sendero*. This side of the ranch house facing the southwest always had a slight breeze coming in. It was cool enough this time of the year, so overhead fans circulating the air were not needed.

The rest of the day was taken with various recreational activities. Even though they had a Luxury Suite in the newly renovated Kyle Field and it was an easy enough flight to College Station in the helicopter, he had given the suite to the director of Special Olympics of Texas so that they could use it for some of the children who were going to compete later at the field. He and JV were a little nervous about the game. Last Saturday, they had played South Carolina and won in a squeaker with just a field goal separating the teams as the buzzer sounded. Today they would face off against Mississippi State. This year's schedule was tough. That was football in the SEC West. However, even with a first-year coach at the helm, they seemed to be better than most of the pundits predicted. He hoped he could be that kind of surprise to the folks who knew him. The task he was facing was so much more than a game.

That thought kept him going as the day before was exhausting with the trip to Austin. There wouldn't be any rest today either. In fact, he rose earlier than usual and began to put together a list of people he needed to enlist in preparing the bill.

Rebecca walked by his office and saw him sitting at his desk. She curiously asked, "You know its Saturday, don't you?"

He looked up and said, "I've got so much to do. I'm not sure where to start. I'll need all the help I can get if yesterday is any indication of how difficult this is going to be."

She read between the lines very well. She thought the meeting with the Governor hadn't gone nearly as well as Thompson had let on. On top of that, her conversation with her friend, Lydia Smithson, was met with much more opposition than she had revealed. He would need some heavy-hitters in the political arena—well respected religious leaders, powerful lobbyists, and key legislators to get this bill passed and signed into law.

Almost nonchalantly, Rebecca said, "You know Jeremiah and Sarah are coming over today."

He remembered that several months earlier, he had invited them to stay over for the weekend before they returned to DC. They were headed back next week for a final push on some pro-life work with several other heads of pro-life organizations from across the nation. While Texas for Life was primarily concerned with legislation within the state, being the largest pro-life organization in the nation, they were a very important influence at the federal level as well.

"Oh, yeah, I remember," he said.

Rebecca suggested, "Might be perfect timing to bring her into the loop."

John smiled and thought to himself, "She really is in the front row on this." He felt invincible when Rebecca was like this. "Do you think she'd mind talking a little business?" John asked.

Rebecca flashed that infectious smile she was so well known for and said, "I might have mentioned it to her last night when she called."

John just laughed.

"Come on, let's get some breakfast and see if Pancho Villa is up near the fence," Rebecca said.

He joined her, and they walked to the back porch.

Abby and JV joined them shortly after they were seated at the table with their morning meal. Abby went to John and Rebecca and hugged them both as was her custom; JV greeted his mom with a hug and slapped his dad with a more *manly* greeting. After all, he was 17 now, and hugs stopped for him when he became a teenager. John and JV talked about the coming game. Rebecca and Abby were politely bored by the topic. Finally, there was a pause in the sports talk, and Rebecca reminded them that Jeremiah and Sarah were coming for the weekend. She anticipated they would have a family cookout that evening, and their presence was unstated, though understood.

JV said, "Mom, I've got a date tonight. Can I invite her to come over?" JV was not one to usually bring his dates to the ranch for a family meal. Rebecca thought there must be something special about this young lady. "Do I know her?" she asked.

"I think so. Her dad is the new doctor in town. They just moved here last summer," JV offered.

Laredo was a big city, and while Rebecca knew most of the news, she wasn't sure who JV was talking about. The hospital had expanded, and several new specialists had moved to Laredo that summer to begin their practice. John thought he knew who JV was talking about. The only doctor who seemed to be old enough to have a senior in high school was Dr. Fitzgerald. Before moving to Laredo, he and his wife lived in California with a thriving practice in pediatrics. He and John had been introduced at the Downtown Café by David one morning as "Fitz" had come in for his morning coffee before rounds.

In casual conversation, John learned they left California because the political climate had grown increasingly more liberal through the years. They chose Texas because of its history of conservatism; and, more specifically, they moved to South Texas because of the climate and the people. San Diego had a southern climate much like Laredo. They were accustomed to a large Hispanic population. John knew of Dr. Fitzgerald's active involvement in starting and maintaining the Diamond Neighborhood Family Health Care Center. It was well known in the west as a place where people of all walks of life could receive quality care.

Rebecca was glad to have JV's date coming to the cookout. "Why don't you invite her mom and dad to come as well? I'm sure we'd like to get to know them and welcome them to our area."

"Uh, I don't know about that," JV stammered.

John said, "JV, I promise we won't gang up on them."

And Rebecca added, "You know there's always room for a few more folks at our table. Would you rather I called and invited them?"

JV knew when the trap had been sprung. He said, "No, Mom. I'll invite them."

"Good. Do they have any dietary restrictions?"

"No, Mom. They are just normal people like us," JV said with a tone of surrender. John knew that Rebecca had an agenda. He just didn't know what it was.

He was still oblivious to the plan that Rebecca saw developing when she said, "John, I wonder if the pastor and his wife would also like to come over for dinner tonight. I'm sure they would like to see Jeremiah and Sarah; and, they could get to know Dr. Fitzgerald and his wife better as well. In a church our size, it's always hard for the pastor to get to know all of his members."

Then John knew he was caught just as surely as JV was. John complied and simply acknowledged her suggestion with a promise to call them as soon as he finished eating.

They finished up their breakfast and John retreated to his office to make a few calls. He was a bit hesitant to call David, though a promise was a promise. He sat down, and his eyes began to wander across the room. Nothing in the room was purely functional. Every piece of furniture held some memory or meaning for him. Even the pictures and mementos on the wall held a special place in his heart. His gaze finally came to rest on an old black and white picture of him standing on the steps of the Administration Building at Texas A&M with his squadron. It was his freshman year. It was a tough year.

David had often told him how powerful these things could be in your life. They elicited a series of almost tangible reactions. The process usually began with just the one seemingly isolated memory, though it quickly raced through a series of things almost unrelated. They always ended in a compilation that brought peace and resolve. This time was no different. He thought about all of the experiences he had that year. That brought him to football season, the building of the bonfire, winning the Southwest Conference, and beating Alabama in the Cotton Bowl. The memories coalesced into greater thoughts.

He began to think of Muster, the annual gathering of Aggies all over the world, to commemorate the sacrifices made by Aggies for freedom. Coincidentally, Muster was always held on April 21st each year, which is also San Jacinto Day. That day is the celebration of the Battle of San Jacinto, which took place on April 21, 1836. It was the final battle of the Texas Revolution, where Texas won its independence from Mexico.

Musing, he admitted to himself that almost every school has a football team, albeit not as great as his. After all, no one else has the Twelfth Man. Many other colleges and universities have great schools of agriculture and engineering. Some even have alumni gatherings that celebrate days of old. And a few have military cadets. But none combine all these elements of excellence and remembrance, tradition and affiliation, and bring them together in a single, solemn ceremony that signifies what Aggies are at the core of their being. When culture tells people to look out for themselves, they still honor the core attribute of "ole army fight!" Texas A&M still calls us to look out for one another.

He remembered that very first day of Freshman Orientation, "Fish Week." He and all the other freshmen were taught the sum of the whole is greater than the individual parts. They were taught this when they were all given the same first name. It was the ubiquitous designation of "fish." No one was elevated above another; you are all just Fish. You are *fish*. And then those fish from various communities, backgrounds, and ethnic roots over that first year, reach final review, and suddenly, they know they are not alone. They have become one. They had learned to look out for each other, to march together, to eat together, to study together, and sometimes even to share a date. It was this process, the many becoming one that the Scripture describes as "the body of Christ – the Church" that they were forged into something far greater, far more powerful than simply students at the same institution.

They did countless push-ups together. They spent late nights cleaning their *fish hole* together. They were screamed at *on the wall together*. These things and many more caused their individual personhood to be broken down, and their collective sense of one was formed. The cause of one another became greater than self. And it was this crucible that sent Aggies out into the world; and, this was true not just for those who had been a part of the Corps, but all who had been a part of the many great Aggie traditions that taught service ahead of self.

And the proof was in the pudding. It was the Class of 1917 that graduated en masse to get overseas and fight and die to liberate Europe in World War I. It was those classes of the 1930s and 1940s who fought on the high seas; who flew missions from the air; who bled and died in foxholes and lonely islands to free millions from the forces of oppression in World War II. It was the Aggie heroes in Korea, Vietnam, and the Cold War who brought down the Iron Curtain and a murderous Soviet regime, freeing millions of Russians, millions of neighboring Republics, and people throughout Eastern Europe. And it was Aggies who fought, died, and today bear the scars of the first Persian Gulf War, the War in Iraq, and the war that continues in Afghanistan today, who continue to do themselves proud. But it was not just Aggies on the field of battle who had advanced the cause of service. It was all the Aggies in classrooms and board rooms; Aggies in factories and mills; Aggies on oil rigs, in soup kitchens, involved in charities and private giving who had put a love of country and neighbor first.

That old black and white photo steeled him even further for the cause. He wasn't going to save thousands of lives with military might or intellectual acumen in the world of science. He had the opportunity to save thousands in the world of government. With that thought, he picked up the phone and called David Edwards.

John was a little surprised that David answered. He was not an idle man. He expected the call to go to voice mail. However, David answered the call with his characteristic cheerful greeting, "Good morning John. What's up?"

John went straight to the request, "Rebecca and I are having a cookout tonight. We were wondering if you and Meg would like to come. Sarah and Jeremiah are in for the weekend, and we thought it would be a great chance to catch up."

David was a bit surprised at what seemed like a spontaneous invitation from John. However, he politely accepted, "Sure. We don't have anything on the calendar tonight that I'm aware of. Let me check with Meg. What time?"

John said, "Around six?"

"Sounds great," David said.

Then John belatedly added, "Oh, we've also invited Dr. Fitzgerald and his wife, Barbara. JV is dating their daughter, Katy, and Rebecca has also invited them."

"Sounds like an interesting group for the evening. Can we bring anything?" David asked. John laughed and said, "Not unless you've got a side of beef ready for the grill!"

With a chuckle, David said, "That's your job."

Rebecca had already begun preparations. She had some of the ranchhands get the fire pit ready, chairs set at the table, and the meat prepared for cooking. It wasn't long after those preparations were given that she thought she'd check on JV. He was a responsible young man but sometimes tended to procrastinate like his dad. She found JV in the family room watching a football game and asked, "Any word from Katy's parents yet?"

With a lot less enthusiasm than she had hoped for, he said, "Yes ma'am. Katy said they were very glad to come." And, after a short pause, he added, "Mom, you're not going to embarrass me, are you?"

With that great smile and a wink, she said, "Of course not!"

Chapter 7

A New Friend and Partner

October 27, 2018

"You may all go to hell and I will go to Texas" *(Angrily said after losing his bid for reelection to the US congress from Tennessee.)*

—*Davy Crockett*

COME AND TAKE IT

John sat in his study and contemplated the day. It would be good to see Jeremiah and Sarah. He was excited about the prospect of discussing the introduction of a strong pro-life bill in the legislature. His mind drifted to the years between that dreadful day when she confided in him about her pregnancy, the abortion that followed, and all of the physical issues that were the result of that one decision. So much good had come of that experience, though she and Jeremiah were denied what they had sought so tenaciously. After their marriage, they busied themselves with the task of developing the ministry embodied in Texans for Life. Their success in that endeavor was nothing short of astounding. However, their personal lives were not as rewarding.

As Sarah began to approach her thirties, she and Jeremiah felt it was time to begin a family of their own. A year passed quickly, and while they had not done anything out of the ordinary, she had not conceived. There wasn't any great concern in the early days, though Jeremiah was right in asking her if they should see a specialist in reproductive endocrinology. There were all sorts of initial tests performed with both Jeremiah and Sarah. The results were both conclusive and cruel. Sarah's abortion years earlier had resulted in Asherman syndrome. The scarring on the uterine walls made it impossible to conceive. They elected to remove the scarring, though it was not successful. They continued to move through the various treatment steps, trying to conceive, though none were successful. That was a long five years. Finally, they were told their best option was adoption. They were certainly not opposed to adoption, though heartbroken that they could not have a child of their own.

John had been very supportive throughout those years. He had done all he knew to do, supporting them with his presence and resources. He never regretted any of that. His only regret was that he felt he had failed Sarah in those early years before the abortion. This feeling of failure was not a result of any bitterness or anger from Sarah. John always seemed to take responsibility for others' pain personally. He and David had talked about that so many times he had lost count; and, it seemed to do little to absolve his feelings of guilt.

His mind continued to drift across the years. Jeremiah and Sarah had done everything possible in their quest to adopt. They sought every legal option. John used all of his influence and networking. However, it still resulted in the same tragic truth. They were ultimately denied for one reason or another. They were childless and would remain so. Their strong faith and love for one another brought them to a place of acceptance and understanding that John admired, though he had difficulty sharing it.

The morning was getting away from John as a knock on the office doorjamb gently separated him from his thoughts. John never shut the door to the office, though Rebecca was always respectful of his thoughts as he worked. She questioned, "Am I interrupting?"

"No, of course not," John answered.

"Your thoughts seem awfully heavy today. Can I help lighten the load?" Rebecca chimed as she sat on one of the two leather wingback chairs near the desk.

John got up from the desk and joined her in the other chair. He said, "I was a million miles away. So much has happened over the years. I am amazed at Sarah with all she and Jeremiah have been through. Their faith and commitment have never wavered."

Rebecca smiled warmly and said, "She's had a great example in her older brother."

He was always amazed at how she knew what exactly to say to ground him in the present.

"Thanks, you do know how much I love you," he replied.

Rebecca teased, "We don't have time for that right now, but maybe later..."

John smiled and asked, "What's on the menu?"

Rebecca said, "I thought I'd have the hands prepare some bone-in ribeyes to throw on the pit."

John knew that she would have them get the best cut of meat. He was never concerned about her choices for the menu. The original question was just a way of starting a new conversation with her. He loved being able to talk to her. It was good medicine for his cluttered mind.

A thought came to him, and he said, "I wonder if it would be too Texian of us to cook some cabrito too?" For most people, *cabrito*, or goat meat, might not elicit great food memories, but nothing compares to the *cabrito* served in South Texas. And, his ranch hands were the best in South Texas.

Rebecca was pleased he had thought of that. She said, "I think it would be a great way to welcome the Fitzgerald's to the ranch." She bounced up and walked out of the office, looking back as she exited, John saw the mischievous look on her face as she gave him a wink and a smile.

John sat in the chair and returned to his reflection. Texas is an interesting state. It is the second largest of the fifty United States based on both area and population (Alaska and California are first, respectively). The largest city in Texas is Houston, while its capital is Austin. Texas is bordered by the U.S. states of New Mexico, Oklahoma, Arkansas, and Louisiana and the Gulf of Mexico and Mexico. Texas is also one of the fastest-growing states in the U.S. Throughout its history, Texas was ruled by six different nations. The first of these was Spain, followed by France and then Mexico until 1836 when the territory became an independent republic. In 1845, it became the 28th U.S.

state to enter the Union, and in 1861, it joined the Confederate States and seceded from the Union during the Civil War. Texas is known as the "Lone Star State" because it was once an independent republic. The state's flag features a lone star to signify this as well as its fight for independence from Mexico.

The state constitution of Texas was adopted in 1876. The economy of Texas is known for being based on oil. It was discovered in the state in the early 1900s, and the population of the area exploded. Cattle is also a large industry associated with the state, and it developed after the Civil War. His family was deeply rooted in both of those enterprises. In addition to its past oil-based economy, Texas had invested strongly in its universities. As a result, it has a diverse economy with various high tech industries, including energy, computers, aerospace, and biomedical sciences. Agriculture and petrochemicals were areas of growth in Texas. Texas is unique. It should take the lead in the fight for life.

Not only was Texas a leader economically, but just the shear vastness of its geography also made it special. After all, Texas has ten climatic regions and 11 different ecological regions. The topography types varied from mountainous to the forested hill country to coastal plains and prairies in the interior. Texas also has 3,700 streams and 15 major rivers, even though there are no large natural lakes. So many people knew so little about this second-largest state in the union. Most folks thought of it as a desert wasteland. Actually, less than 10% of Texas is considered desert. The desert and mountains of Big Bend are the only areas in the state with this landscape. The rest of the state is coastal swamps, woods, plains, and low rolling hills.

Texas also has a varied climate due to its size. The panhandle portion of the state has bigger temperature extremes than the Gulf Coast, which is milder. The Gulf Coast region of Texas is indeed prone to hurricanes. Even there, Texas has shown a strength and resilience unique to any other state. In 1900, a hurricane hit Galveston and destroyed the entire city and killed 12,000 people. It is recorded as the deadliest natural disaster in

U.S. history. Yet, Galveston has become a strong city with its tourism rivaling that of New Orleans. He remembered Mary Lasswell, who grew up in Brownsville and wrote the famous book, *I'll Take Texas.*

One of his favorite quotes from the book was: "I am forced to conclude that God made Texas on his day off, for pure entertainment, just to prove that all that diversity could be crammed into one section of earth by a really top hand."

John heard the mantel clock chime noon and realized he needed to get going with some of the evening preparations. He knew that this day would be key to everything he wanted to accomplish. He got up and walked with a firm conviction that this course was not just good but the time was right as well.

Abby caught him as he walked down the hall leading to the great room. "Dad, everybody else is going to have someone with them for the barbeque. Can I ask someone too?"

John smiled and asked, "Someone or someones?"

She laughed and said, "Just one, Dad. I thought it would be fun to call Josh Fitzgerald."

Josh was Katy's younger brother. She thought if JV was going to have Katy as his date, maybe she should have Josh as her designated *other* for the night.

"Do you know him?" John asked.

She said, "Sure. He's in my AP Math and History class. We're studying the Battle of Gonzales right now. I thought he'd like to see your *Come and Take It* flag."

The Battle of Gonzales was the first military engagement of the Texas Revolution. It was fought near Gonzales, Texas, on October 2, 1835, between rebellious Texian settlers and a detachment of Mexican army soldiers. It began the War for Independence. John had a flag from that battle passed down from generation to generation since the Battle of the Alamo. The flag was a treasured heirloom first passed on through his great aunt, several times removed, Gertrudis Alsbury, who survived the Alamo along with her sister, Juana Navarro Alsbury, and a part of the family of James Bowie.

John smiled and said, "I'm sure y'all will be just interested in history."

She pleaded, "Come on, Dad. I don't want to be the only one without someone."

John stopped, put his arm around her, and said, "You will never be alone as long as I have breath."

"It's not the same," she lamented.

John smiled and said, "I know. And, of course, it's OK."

Abby skipped off, delighted as John walked into the great room. He saw Jeremiah and Sarah pulling into the front-drive and walked out to greet them. Shaking hands with Jeremiah and receiving a giant hug from Sarah, he said, "I hope you guys are hungry. We've got the pit fired up for steaks and cabrito tonight."

Sarah said, "I heard. Rebecca called us earlier. I also understand we've got a crowd gathering."

John should have known Rebecca would take care of the details.

He still tried to apologize, "I hope that's OK?"

Sarah said, "Of course. I always enjoy seeing the preacher." She had always known David Edwards simply as "the Preacher."

John added, "We have some other folks coming as well."

Sarah said, "I know. We are looking forward to meeting Fitz and his family."

John was a bit confused. He said, "Fitz? How do you know Dr. Fitzgerald?"

Sarah explained, "I met him through Michael Brody, the head of the Texas Christians United."

Texas Christians United was the largest evangelical organization in the state. It was a non-denominational group dedicated to advancing Christian principals through collective political action. It was also one of the most powerful lobbying groups in Texas. Sarah added, "They are family friends. Did you know they were roommates at Vanderbilt? I'm told they have worked very closely together on some ground-breaking legislation dealing with family issues and public education. They are both strongly pro-life. We are helping them with some collaboration in that area."

John was astonished, though he knew he shouldn't be. Rebecca was typically one step ahead of him on most things. It looked like this was a part of her plan all along. It made him smile broadly. He said, "I didn't know that. Though I'm sure, Rebecca did."

They all laughed at that reference. John said, "Let's get your stuff unloaded, and you can relax a bit."

It didn't take long for them to gather their things and take them to the guest quarters. By the time they had unloaded them from the back of their SUV, Rebecca had joined them with welcoming hugs all around. She and Rebecca had grown very close over the years and couldn't wait to have some time together. John and Jeremiah had grown close due to their relationship, so it was a natural separation when the girls went into the kitchen, and they walked out to the back porch. They both grabbed a cold drink from the rustic cooler John had received as a gift from David several years ago. It was more of a piece of furniture than an ice chest. David enjoyed woodworking and had built it as a surprise for John's birthday several years ago. It was made from cedar and emblazoned with Aggie logos. It fit the décor of the porch where there were plenty of things to remind John and Rebecca of the days at A&M as well as their state heritage. Two of the more prized pieces in the collection of historical artifacts John had collected were relatively new to Jeremiah as he had added them since Jeremiah and Sarah had come to the ranch last. When the Texas Museum was being refurbished, and renovation had begun in earnest at the Alamo, Phil Collins had donated his entire collection of historical papers and artifacts to the Texas Museum, and John had one of the pieces on permanent loan. He had collected other pieces as well, but this was his favorite. It was a rifle owned by Davy Crockett, along with his leather shot pouch and a pair of powder horns that were widely believed to have been given to a Mexican officer before his death.

As they sat down overlooking the pasture full of John's registered longhorns, Jeremiah nodded to the long rifle and said, "I heard you had gotten Crockett's rifle." He chuckled a bit and then quickly added, "You're not going to use that to start another war for independence, are you?"

They both had a good laugh as John said, "Of course not!"

They both sat in silence for a moment, looking at the cattle peacefully grazing when Rebecca and Sarah joined them.

Sarah sat next to Jeremiah, and Rebecca said, "Have you heard the news?"

John knew he'd need to bring up the topic though he wasn't exactly sure how to do so. He should have known Rebecca would break that ice for him. Sarah playfully said, "I've heard some rumblings in the ranks of the conservatives that things are going to be a little hotter than usual on the floor this session."

That really surprised John. "What have you heard?" he asked.

Jeremiah jumped in to try to ease John's fears a bit and said, "Nothing really, John. We got a phone call from Governor Thompson's chief of staff about some legislation you were planning on introducing this session. He said the Governor was worried about it. He also said it would be one of the most important pieces of legislation Texas has ever attempted and long overdue. He also said that if anyone could get it passed, it would be John Lucas."

John didn't know whether to be relieved or embarrassed. In actuality, he was a bit of both. It was his opening to the news, and he plowed ahead. "News sure travels fast. I just met with the Governor yesterday. How did it get to you that fast?"

Sarah said, "John, you poked a sleeping bear. Folks have been used to you being quietly supportive. They've always been afraid you'd rise up to the full strength of your power like Daddy did."

John Lucas III, John and Sarah's father, was the patriarch of the Lucas clan. He had served in the Texas legislature for over thirty years. He inherited the family ranch from his father, though the land had been in the family since it was first settled under the Adams-Onis Treaty. His family worked closely with Stephen F. Austin in gaining the land when Texas was still under the control of Mexico. He was a powerful cattleman, though his wealth was gained more from oil and gas. If John Lucas III wanted something done, it got done. He was not a silent participant; he was a vocal leader. The Governor was one of those among Texas's political power brokers that was relieved when he had died.

John defensively said, "I am not trying to be like Dad. I just want to do something to finally protect the unborn and the women who carry them to birth."

Sarah said, "John, I didn't mean to offend you. You are a different man than Daddy. You have patience, compassion, and grace toward all people. Because of that, you have more power and influence than he ever did or could."

Rebecca stepped into the conversation, "John, tell them the whole story. Start with your meeting in Waco with Dylan."

John took a deep breath, and said, "It goes back much further than that. He started with his lunch with Sarah all those years ago and went through his meeting with the Governor. It was like he had dammed up all of those thoughts and feelings, and now finally, the waters were being released. He felt the freedom and strength he had never felt before.

Jeremiah and Sarah were amazed that they were able to see him in this chrysalis moment. He was truly being transformed. Jeremiah said, "John, we have always been with you; and, we are with you in this fight."

John was overwhelmed and didn't know what to say, though he finally replied with a simple, "Thanks!"

Sarah told him that they could mobilize their legal and financial resources within days. And Jeremiah half-joked, "Maybe we will need that rifle after all!"

Rebecca and Sarah didn't catch that reference, though John laughed heartily with Jeremiah.

Sarah broke the reverie when she asked, "Are you going to tell the Edwards and Fitzgeralds?"

Now John really laughed as he looked at Rebecca and said, "Do I have any choice?"

She smiled and said, "Always, though, I like to think I make it easier for you to choose what I would choose too."

They spent the next few hours waiting for the others to arrive while visiting and catching up. John and Jeremiah got up to stretch their legs and walked across the back to the longhorn pasture. As they approached, Pancho Villa was the first to meet them at the fence. He was spoiled and always looking for some handout of fresh apple slices, which John regularly supplied to the enormous longhorn. Though he was first to arrive, the other longhorns soon joined them, waiting for their treat as well.

"Where's Bevo?" Jeremiah asked.

"Oh, its football season, and they've got him in Austin for the game," John replied.

Jeremiah shook his head and smiled as he said, "I've always thought it was ironic that an Aggie would take care of the University of Texas' mascot."

John replied in his best drawl, "Heck, you know them teasips cain't ranch." And they both had a good laugh.

Walking back to the porch, they saw that David and Meg were there. They walked up and greeted them warmly. David already had a Shiner beer in his hand and laughingly teased John, "I see I had to bring my own beer since you were too bashful to ask if it would be all right to ice some down with Fitz and his family coming over."

David was not your typical "Baptist" preacher. In fact, he really wasn't Baptist at all any longer. Some years before, during a personal health crisis, David had been treated rather badly by some of the church's leadership, which resulted in a forced resignation. Their ultimate reason was that they felt they "needed a change," whatever that meant. John always

suspected they didn't like David's style of direct and unwaver-
ing truth when it came to the Gospel. They used his illness as
an excuse to force him out. It wasn't long before David began
another church, though it was independent and non-denominational. Grace Restoration Church became the largest church
in South Texas very quickly, and David's respect in the state
and national evangelical community grew even more.

John nodded and said, "Thanks, preacher. I always love
being called out with the truth!"

While they were getting comfortable and enjoying talking
about everything and nothing at the same time, they saw some
of the ranch hands getting ready to put the meat on the pit, and
David saw the whole goat on the spit and said, "*Cabrito*, huh?
You must have something very special planned tonight." He
looked over at Rebecca and smiled. She had already prepared
the way with a bit of information.

John noticed the look and said, "I see Rebecca has been
talking to you, too."

David chuckled a bit and said, "Nothing I didn't expect,
John. This has been coming for a long time."

About that time, JV came out to the porch with the
Fitzgerald's in tow. John walked to Fitz and began to introduce
everyone. While he didn't see it before, he realized this could be
the beginning of a core group of friends for the coming years.

JV and Katy quickly retreated to the bonus room, where
they planned to spend some time watching the football game
and enjoying their *date*. JV was especially excited to try to convince Katy to participate in the Aggie tradition of kissing your
date after every football game score. Abby and Josh wanted to
hop into the four-wheel-drive *Mule* and ride around the ranch a
little before dinner. She hoped that this would give her a chance
to impress him, and maybe he would be inclined to ask her to
the annual homecoming dance.

The ladies retreated into the kitchen and began some
last-minute preparation. Barbara, Fitz's wife, had a bottle of wine
that she has brought as a gift to the host. She was apologetic as

she gave it to Rebecca, "I hope this isn't inappropriate, but Fitz and I thought you might like to have some of this vintage from the Diamond Collection of the Coppola Winery in Sonoma."

Rebecca said, "Oh, that's wonderful. Thank you for your thoughtfulness. We'll open it after we eat. John is more of a beer kind of guy, but I'm sure he will be very glad you brought it."

Barbara smiled and said, "Sounds like Fitz's kind of friend."

Meg added, "They're all just regular guys when you take away all the titles."

And they all laughed.

Dinner began with little formality. They all sat down after serving themselves at the buffet. Fitz was particularly interested in the cabrito. While the Southern California version of *cabrito* was slightly different from South Texas, he confessed it was one of his favorite foods. In fact, they all enjoyed the cabrito as much as the ribeyes.

The conversation around the table ranged from sports to the weather, though nothing was mentioned about the pro-life legislation. Fitz and John seemed to enjoy poking at one another over the baseball and basketball program's value at Vanderbilt while avoiding any discussion about football. The Commodores were notoriously in the bottom of the SEC in that sport, while A&M was typically in the top.

As the sun began to set, and the air turned cooler, they finished dinner and went into the great room to relax and enjoy the rest of the evening. The teens retreated to their space and left the adults to their conversation. They'd had enough adulting for one night.

David was the first to speak, "John, do you want to tell us more about the coming session, or should I?" He was always just that direct. And, he would be the first to acknowledge that he was an *acquired taste*.

John said, "It's a long story; and, some of it is not mine to tell. However, because of these experiences and the recent legislation from other states, I am committed to bringing a strong bill to the floor for passage into law in our state guaranteeing protection for all pre-born children and their mothers."

That seemed to be more than enough to get the ball rolling in the conversation. Fitz was the first to speak up when he said, "What do you want to do, John?"

He answered, "I want to make it impossible for even one child to be taken in abortion."

It seemed as if time had stopped. Every eye seemed to be focused on John. He was uncomfortable until Fitz turned to Barbara and said, "I knew we made the right decision to move here." Barbara just smiled. Fitz continued, "We moved from San Diego because we could no longer be in a place that valued life so little. When I took the Hippocratic Oath, it was much more than a mere formality. It was a vow to the Lord for me. What can I do to help?"

John was overwhelmed. David merely smiled at John and said, "I'm not much for religious formality, but if ever there were a time for a prayer of thanksgiving, this surely is such a time." With that, they all held hands, and David prayed over the people there and the work that was beginning.

They spent the rest of the evening talking with one another and sharing some of their personal stories. Preliminary plans were laid for further work. And, new friends and partners in the future were cemented. When the last goodbye was said, and John and Rebecca were alone, John put his arms around her and whispered into her ear, "Thank you."

She answered, "Always and forever, John."

Chapter 8

The Opposition Gathers

October 29, 2018 – November 2, 2018

"The dons, the bashaws, the grandees, the patricians, the sachems, the nabobs, call them by what names you please, sigh and groan and fret, and sometimes stamp and foam and curse, but all in vain. The decree is gone forth, and it cannot be recalled, that a more equal liberty than has prevailed in other parts of the earth must be established in America."

— John Adams, in letter to Patrick Henry, June 3, 1776

COME AND TAKE IT

It was entirely fitting that the week of Halloween would see John Lucas IV and his core of support, so soon founded, face the demons of doubt. The opposition led by Governor Thompson and fueled by Lydia Smithson and other pro-choice groups had already been mobilized. Soon after John's luncheon with the Governor, they had received a call indicating the need for a face-to-face as quickly as possible. The Governor was not a novice in the political arena. He also recognized that should John take up the mantle of leadership his father had worn so well, it would be a long and politically bloody battle to oppose him. Of course, he had no way of knowing that John had already garnered the support of some very powerful groups. With the cookout meeting, John had secured the backing of Texans for Life and Texas Christians United.

Texans for Life was very powerful on both the state and national stage. Thompson had tried to face off against Jeremiah and Sarah Mann once before. It had not gone well. It was regarding a provision in a public education bill containing some new language suggesting that abortion was an acceptable birth control method. What he thought would have been an easy presentation turned into a nightmare of negotiation and ultimately ended in his acquiescence on every point.

Texas Christians United was led by Michael Brody. With 56% of the state's population claiming *strong ties* to Christianity, Brody represented a huge majority that ran across denominational, cultural, and racial lines. They could not be ignored.

While individual churches might fight among themselves, they could be counted on to unite over the issue of life rather than choice. Brody, the lead pastor of the largest church in Houston, had personally debated the issue publicly with no less than the Acting President and CEO of Planned Parenthood, Ms. Ashton Linley-Harris. It was a spirited exchange. The fiery style of Ms. Linley-Harris was powerful; however, the years of experience and soothing baritone voice of Brody seemed to carry the day with most of the pundits from the media. Texas Christians United alone would be a difficult force to turn away.

Governor Thompson had scheduled an informal meeting for Wednesday, October 31st. He had spent most of Monday working with his chief of staff, Peter Bridges, planning both the meeting's agenda and guest list. Peter had been with Perry Thompson through all of his campaigns, advising him on many issues. However, when Thompson was elected Governor, Bridges experienced a betrayal from him that soured his relationship and evaporated his loyalty. Bridges' wife had an affair with an Austin attorney and became pregnant. She elected to have an abortion, which Thompson quietly arranged to save the embarrassment of the scandal. Peter and his wife ultimately divorced in Thompson's first term. As a result, he had come to know Jeremiah and Sarah, who helped him through those days. He had become a vital source of information for them.

Thompson wanted the list of people to be small enough to manage, but large enough to exert pressure from several directions should it be necessary to stall or even defeat John. They finally decided on a mix of people from the government as well as the private sector. All of them were powerful in their own areas, and all of them were committed to the legal status quo concerning abortion in Texas. This was especially true of Lydia Smithson and Ashton Linley-Harris. Also on the list were the leaders of the minority groups from both the Texas Senate and House. The Democrats had made significant gains in both the House and Senate, though they were still in the minority. Texas had always been a red state and remained so, even with the influence of eight years of a very liberal president of the United States. Bridges also suggested that they include the Lieutenant Governor, who was very conservative; and, in Texas, held absolute power over the Senate.

The meeting was arranged to be held at the Governor's Mansion. Thompson hoped it would be relatively unnoticed by the press. Even if it was, he could spin the agenda by directing them to think that it was primarily a meeting to get to know Ms. Linley-Harris, who had only recently taken the position as acting president and CEO of Planned Parenthood. If John questioned him, he could convince him that he was already making some progress before introducing his bill, ensuring smooth passage.

The meeting began informally with brief introductions, and Lydia Smithson was the first to speak, "Governor, I'm sure you've not called us to the mansion to discuss how we plan to dress for the trick or treaters tonight. What's the agenda?"

A fiery reproach from Ashton Linley-Harris quickly followed. "I hope this isn't an ambush for some new legislation that continues to erode women's rights, which are already woefully deficient in this state."

The Governor cleared his throat as if he had just swallowed something wrong. Linley-Harris smiled, knowing she had touched a nerve. She pressed harder, "Governor, we are already aware that new legislation is being drafted to be presented this session that will eliminate the legal status of a woman's health choices concerning her pregnancy. Planned Parenthood will not be silent nor sit on the sidelines if this is true. We are prepared to fight it with all of our considerable influence and resource." She was never one for a subtle approach. And, this meeting was beginning very badly for the Governor.

"Well, Ms. Harris..."

And, she interrupted quickly, "My name is Linley-Harris."

The Governor began again with a conciliatory tone and in his best Texas drawl, "My apologies, Ma'am. Perhaps we can dispense with the formalities for our meeting today. Please call me Perry."

With that, Lydia caught Aston's eye as a gentle reminder that silence was a better approach now. Lydia then said, "Let's give the Governor a moment to set the agenda, shall we?"

Thompson was relieved she had come to his rescue, though he knew she had set it all in motion to indebt him to her all the more as she prepared her run for the Supreme Court.

The Governor opened his pad and said, "I wanted to informally meet with each of you today because Ms. Linley-Harris is partially correct. John Lucas has informed me of his intent to introduce a bill that deals with abortion."

Linley-Harris drew a breath to begin again with her remarks of protest, and Lydia once again, though more forcefully, gave her a withering look. The stares of the others were riveted on the Governor.

The Lieutenant Governor said, "John is going to introduce a bill? He's never been at the forefront of any legislation. He certainly isn't his father. And, I might add, thank the heavens for that little blessing. His father was a thorn in our side for years. What John Lucas III said was as good as law in this state."

The Governor added, "I have met with him, and he is very serious and committed to this legislation. I suspect this has been brewing for a long time. John has some very personal connection to this legislation. I think it would be a mistake to underestimate his ability or influence."

The Lieutenant Governor responded, "Perry, we might be able to slow it down, though I suspect he will have substantial support. I don't think we can fight this one head-on." He looked at the majority leaders and said, "Perhaps y'all can keep it in committee for as long as possible." They both nodded their approval.

Lydia Smithson did not want to reveal her conversation or relationship with Rebecca Lucas. However, she knew this bill was not going to be able to be slowed down. In fact, she knew it would take on a life of its own. Like an avalanche, it would gather momentum and power as it moved downhill. She inserted, "I think that's a good first step; however, we should be ready to litigate this bill and tie it up in the courts. It may be that the US Supreme Court will be our only hope to defeat it. That's what happened to the other states that have tried this."

They all agreed, and she was unofficially appointed to lead that part of the counteroffensive. All in all, she was very pleased with how this was looking for her. She might even get to argue the case before the SCOTUS. That would look good on her resume. The Governor assured them he would keep them informed, and the meeting broke into other less inflammatory conversations with Lydia and Ashton excusing themselves rather quickly.

Once they were outside, Ashton confronted Lydia, "What were you doing in there? We had a chance to exert our power, and you rolled over!" She was nearly yelling.

Lydia said, "Calm down. Your passion will be your undoing. These men are not accustomed to being told anything by a woman. We'll catch these flies with honey, not vinegar."

Ashton answered, "Fine, but I don't intend to wait on them to *slow things down*."

"I should hope not," Lydia matter-of-factly answered. "If I were you, I'd immediately alert my legal department, as well as mobilizing the media department for a preemptive campaign. You're going to need to budget for a state-wide campaign."

Ashton scoffed, "What can a cowboy from South Texas do to stop the most powerful lobby in the nation?"

Lydia simply said, "He's no ordinary cowboy." And for the second time that afternoon Ashton heard the caution not to underestimate John Lucas IV.

Meanwhile, the others present in the meeting adjourned for a drink and a cigar in the sitting room. Peter was no longer necessary and excused himself, hoping to get in touch with Sarah as quickly as possible. Governor Thompson reached for a bottle of Garrison Brothers Small Batch Bourbon. He had first received it as a gift when he spoke to honor the Texas Distillery located in Hye, Texas, as they won the American Craft Spirits Award for the fourth year in a row. He had grown very fond of this particular bourbon. Feeling superior, he liked to taunt his friends in Kentucky and Tennessee with a bottle for Christmas.

They were all concerned at this development, feeling conspiratorial and just a bit superior. After a while, Thompson said, "We're going to need to watch that Harris woman. Her Yankee ways are going to be a problem." They all grunted their agreement.

Peter Bridges was able to reach Sarah on the phone before her flight left. "I hope this is not a bad time?" Peter began.

"Sarah said, "Not at all. How did the meeting go?" She had already been alerted that the Governor had instructed him to call the meeting.

Peter went on, "It went better than I thought it might. There's not going to be any trouble from Thompson. He wants to slow the bill down, but he has no stomach to fight John. He has much higher hopes for his future in politics. He can see it as a win either way."

Sarah said, "That's as we expected."

Peter continued, "However, we may have a problem from Lydia Smithson or Ashton Linley-Harris."

Sarah replied, "I understand and thanks for the update, Peter. I'll convey this to John and Rebecca when we get together later. I hope your Halloween costume isn't too spooky tonight." They both laughed and said goodbye.

Jeremiah asked Sarah, "How was the meeting?"

She said, "Not as bad as it could have been. We'll talk more about it with John later."

Chapter 9

The News Spreads

October 28, 2018 – November 2, 2018

"We view ourselves on the eve of battle. We are nerved for the contest, and must conquer or perish. It is vain to look for present aid: none is at hand. We must now act or abandon all hope! Rally to the standard, and be no longer the scoff of mercenary tongues! Be men, be free men, that your children may bless their father's name."

—Sam Houston (Before the Battle of San Jacinto)

COME AND TAKE IT

John woke on Sunday morning refreshed and renewed. The cookout the day before had gone better than he could have imagined. It seemed that everything was falling into place to make a stand for life once and for all. Jeremiah and Sarah had pledged their support as expected; however, with the full support of Fitz and his contacts with Texas Christians United, the end result was all but guaranteed to be successful.

Sunday morning was always busy. They rose early enough to have breakfast and get ready for church. This Sunday was a bit more harried than normal as Jeremiah and Sarah were guests for the weekend. Everyone fell into a natural rhythm, and they all loaded into the Suburban to drive to worship together. David Edwards was a special part of all their lives, so Jeremiah and Sarah were looking forward to hearing him preach. He was a very accomplished orator, though his sermons were never without the simplicity of the Gospel. They appreciated his candor and directness in communicating the grace of God and forgiveness through Christ.

While the church was a huge structure with modern architecture, it was also very simple. David was a practical man. Extravagance was not a part of his life in anything. John always chuckled a bit at that but felt very comfortable because of it. They arrived a bit earlier than anticipated, so they could park close enough that they would not need the shuttle from the parking lot to the entrance. Since the church had exponentially grown, the original structure had long since given way to parking as the new building now seated five thousand and still required two morning services and a live feed broadcast to five other remote locations in Austin, Dallas/Ft. Worth, Houston, El Paso, and San Antonio. David Edwards preached to 20,000 people every Sunday, yet it always seemed he was just talking to you.

John and his family were well known at the church; and, though not as well known, Jeremiah and Sarah were welcomed warmly by the stationed greeters. Fitz and his family were in the foyer near the Coffee Corner as they entered. Rebecca smiled, knowing that was not a coincidence. Either JV or Abby had undoubtedly engineered the rendezvous so they could sit together. They greeted one another, and the teens separated quickly to find seats with others of their age group. It took the adults a bit longer as friends or acquaintances often stopped them.

A young woman came to Sarah, threw her arms around her, and gave her a warm embrace. John did not recognize her, though Rebecca also greeted her with a hug. Fitz also knew her and said, "It's good to see you. How's your little boy doing?"

She nearly gushed, "He's so wonderful! I can't believe that I nearly missed this great gift of God. I will never be able to thank y'all for helping me so much when I first came to you."

Rebecca saw the confusion on John's face and formally introduced him with an explanation, "John, this is Cindy. One of the high school counselors called me last year and asked if I would be able to help her."

Cindy interrupted, "And, that was the best day of my life. Being pregnant is hard enough. However, when you are just sixteen, it's a lot harder. Rebecca and Sarah helped me decide to keep my son. I met Dr. Fitzgerald in the hospital when Danny was born. That was the day I became a mom and a Christian!"

John's crusade was beginning to take on a new dimension. What he was attempting was not just about the past but the future. He wondered how many other girls were out there who didn't get to meet a Rebecca or Sarah and ended their pregnancy. He remembered Dylan Walker's words at Waco. Every year there were at least 60,000 women in Texas whose story didn't end like Cindy's.

They finally reached a place where they could be seated. As usual, the worship began with contemporary music led by the worship team. Though the music was not John's favorite style, the first song caught his attention. It was one that the team often used, *You Never Give Up on Me*. It was perfect for him at that moment. The lead female vocalist sang, and the chorus rang true in his mind and spirit:

> You never give up on me
> No, You never give up on me
> Though I'm weak, you are strong
> You told me I still belong
> No, You never, never give up on me.

David's message was just as impactful as always. It echoed the same theme of God's grace. However, it seemed to John that he was listening with a different perspective today. At the end of the service, just before the crowd was dismissed, David returned to the stage. That was a bit unusual as he normally used the time to make his way to the exit to greet people personally as they left.

David said, "I have a little something unusual to ask the community today. As I explain it, I want to ask my dear friend, John Lucas, to make his way to the platform."

John was a bit uncomfortable, as this was well outside of his normal behavior. He had never sought the spotlight, and it would be brightly shining on him now. Never-the-less he made his way to the front and stood beside David.

David went on, "For those of you who have never met John Lucas, one of our State Senators, let me introduce you to him. Don't worry; he's not running for reelection this year." The crowd chuckled, though the attention nearly paralyzed John. David then said, "He's doing something much more important this year. He will be introducing a new bill supporting life and effectively banning abortion in this year's legislative session. I want us to pray for him today."

With that, the congregation began to stand and applaud. Those near him gathered around him and laid their hands on him as David prayed. It was brief but powerful.

After all the hugs and handshakes, John finally made his way to Rebecca and the others. He looked at Rebecca and said, "I don't know if you had anything to do with this, but thank you."

She smiled and said, "I wished I did, but that was all David following what he believes is what God wants him to do."

Fitz added his support again and asked if he could call him tomorrow for a further chat about some strategy going forward. John agreed that anytime would be fine.

Unlike church, lunch was relatively uneventful. They determined to spend the day relaxing and enjoying the quiet before the storm. Unfortunately, the *storm* hit about mid-afternoon.

John received a call from Mateo Garcia, his Chief of Staff, who maintained the Austin office when John was not there. He was informed that his official state email had been flooded with emails over the last few hours. They had received over two thousand emails all related to the events at church that morning. His staff had been called into the office to respond, but they didn't know what to say. They had also received inquiries from all the major news outlets asking for a statement or interview. It looked like David's prayer was prophetic, as well as practical. John was curious as to the first survey of the emails. He was told that the ratio was running overwhelmingly in support of his "new bill." Mateo Garcia, who had been with John from the beginning, was confused and asked, "What new bill, Senator?"

John laughed and said, "I will be in Austin tomorrow. Call for a general staff meeting, and I'll give everyone an update."

Always polite and respectful, he said, "Thank you, Sir, but what shall we do with these emails."

John sighed and said, "Go ahead and send out a general answer expressing my gratitude for the support of those who are supportive; and ignore the others until I have our meeting tomorrow. And, answer the news media with a very general response indicating that we are still in the process of developing a final draft for the new legislation, and a press conference will be forthcoming when it is done."

"Yes Sir, but they won't be satisfied with that."

John simply answered, "I know; but, it's the truth."

Jeremiah, Sarah, and Rebecca were all sitting on the porch with him when he got the call. Rebecca questioned him, "Everything all right?"

John said, "I guess we don't need a press release. David took care of that this morning. I've already received over two thousand emails in support of the bill."

Sarah laughed, "I guess you better get it written pretty soon."

With that, they all laughed.

Rebecca said, "You've got this."

And John knew that things had just gotten very real.

Later that same day, Dylan Walker had also heard the news. He decided it was time to meet with both Carson Bradley and John Lucas. He thought his first visit ought to be with John, though. He made the call. When it went to voicemail, the General simply said, "I saw David's call to prayer today while I was at church in Austin. I hope we can get together this week. Call me when you can."

John really didn't want to meet with Walker until he had some concrete news, but the General could be very persuasive. He would call later and set up something for early in the week. He needed to see Jeremiah and Sarah off tomorrow and meet with Fitz; then, he could take the helicopter into Austin for a meeting with the staff in the afternoon.

Chapter 10

The Plot for Freedom Is Initiated

October 29, 2018

"War is when the government tells you who the bad guy is. Revolution is when you decide that for yourself."

—Benjamin Franklin

COME AND TAKE IT

John woke to a brisk day for South Texas. It was not unusual for him to rise early in the morning; however, he was up even earlier today than usual. He had a lot to do and knew he needed an early start to be able to finish his list for the day. He made his way to the kitchen and saw that Rebecca, Sarah, and Jeremiah were already sitting at the island in the large kitchen center. Rebecca asked, "Are you going to the café for breakfast this morning, or do you want me to fix you a plate?"

John answered, "I thought I'd see Sarah and Jeremiah off and then drive into town. I'd like to see David this morning."

She knew he had to go to Austin soon, though she didn't want to ask him about that part of his schedule. He would have that in his plan, and it would happen soon enough.

Jeremiah said, "You've got plenty to do this week. We're leaving in a few minutes for the airport. You don't need to hang out with us this morning."

Sarah echoed Jeremiah's comments and said, "We'll call when we get to Washington. Perhaps we can get a reaction from some of the other pro-life leaders at the meeting. There are many resources at your disposal, John. We are behind you completely."

"Thanks," John said. He did need to get ahead of the brewing story in Austin. He needed to call his staff and schedule a meeting for tomorrow. He also had to return Dylan's call and arrange to meet with him mid-week.

As he drove into town, his phone began to ring. It was Dylan Walker. John answered the phone, and the General said, "Good morning, John. I hope I haven't called too early. I need to meet with you as soon as possible."

John said, "I'm glad you called. I got your voice mail yesterday and intended to call you later today. I plan to be in Austin tomorrow. Would Wednesday work for you?"

The General quickly agreed, "Sure. Just tell me where you'd like to meet?"

"How about lunch at Cooper's?" John suggested. "That works for me. See you around noon?" Walker suggested. "Perfect," John said.

Well, that was one thing he could check off his list. While on the way to the cafè, he called his Austin office and informed his chief of staff that he would be in the office later that day. He wanted to meet with all the staff today after his arrival.

When he arrived at the café, it seemed busier than usual. He walked in and saw David at their normal table, drinking a cup of coffee. He wasn't able to walk through the café without everyone in the room, speaking to him and shaking his hand. It was a bit uncomfortable for John to be the center of such attention, though he was kind and responded to each one. He finally got to the table and sat down as David said, "Celebrity status seems to suit you."

John just laughed and said, "Thanks to you!" They both laughed heartily, and Rosita came by with coffee, "*Buenos dias, Señor* John."

"Thanks, Rosita. Big crowd today?" John responded with the familiarity of their long relationship. She smiled broadly and said with a twinkle in her eye, "Si. They all came in looking for you this morning. I think they are wondering when the revolution is going to begin."

Rosita left him with that short statement, and John looked at David with confusion on his face. David simply said, "Why are you surprised, John?"

He said, "What revolution?"

David just laughed and said, "Remember this day, John. It is just a beginning, and there will be many more steps taken in this journey." David always was cryptic, but this was more so than usual.

John merely shrugged and began to tell him about the call from his staff. He also recounted the response he had already received. "I'm flying to Austin later today to begin writing a formal statement for release. I've got to get ahead of this before it gets too big."

David, knowing how big it was going to eventually get, merely said, "That's a good plan, John. You do know that this is already beyond you and me, don't you?"

John knew better than to ask him to elaborate. Thankfully his regular breakfast came, and they talked about football and deer season for the rest of the time together.

John returned to the ranch and told his pilot that he'd like to leave for Austin as soon after lunch as possible. He informed John that Rebecca had already told him to get the helicopter ready for the flight, and he was ready to leave as soon as John wanted. That brought a smile to John, and he thought, "Of course she has. She's always a step or two ahead of me."

He told the pilot, "Let me get my bags together, and I'll be out in a bit."

The pilot said, "Oh, I've already loaded your bags, Sir. Rebecca told me you'd need to get your briefcase together, but I've got all the rest stowed away."

John just grinned and walked into the house. He found Rebecca and laughed as he said, "Thanks for packing my stuff."

She smiled and said, "No problem. I packed enough for the week, though I didn't know how long you planned to stay."

John said, "Are you trying to get rid of me?"

Rebecca quickly answered, "Of course not, but I knew there were lots of things that would need to be done."

With that, he went to the office, packed his briefcase, said his goodbyes to Rebecca, and boarded for the flight to Austin.

While John was in the air, enjoying the ride and watching the change in topography from the *sendero*s of South Texas to the Hill Country leading into Austin, things were abuzz in Austin. His staff was readying for his arrival and their meeting.

The Governor was already preparing his staff for what was sure to be a very busy week as well. However, unknown to John or the Governor, Dylan Walker had arranged to meet with Carson Bradley later in the day at the gun range on the Texans for Independence headquarters. Texans for Independence was a group dedicated to Texas's secession from the Union and the state becoming an independent nation. Since Bradley founded the group, he had been the driving force in its phenomenal growth. He had connected hundreds of thousands of Texans, conducted scores of media interviews, participated in international conferences on self-determination, and grown the Texas independence movement into one of the largest groups of its kind in the United States. In fulfilling his mission, he had given a home to all Texans who believe that Texas would be better off as an independent nation.

The stated mission of Texans for Independence was: "... to secure and protect the political, cultural and economic independence of the nation of Texas and to restore and protect a constitutional Republic and the inherent rights of the people of Texas." They were very well connected both statewide and nationally. In 2009, the TFI had engaged the Texas Legislature advocating for a referendum on Texas independence. They had drafted the Texas Independence Referendum Act and gathered strong support to put the question on a ballot for statewide decision. Bradley had high hopes that it would make the 2020 ballot bringing an end Texas' affiliation with the United States.

Dylan met Bradley at the TFI headquarters and after a warm welcome they transferred to an off-road vehicle to ride to the range. Walker said to his old friend, "You're even more careful than usual. What's going on?"

Bradley said, "I have some news I want to give you that cannot be overheard. The range is the safest place we have free from the prying eyes and ears of Homeland Security."

Walker indulged his old friend. They arrived at the 500-meter outdoor range, which was typically deserted this time of the week, and Bradley said, "I saw David Edwards' announcement yesterday. Does Lucas even know what's about to happen?"

Walker replied, "Does it matter?"

Bradley retorted, "Of course not; however, things are about to begin moving quickly now." With that, Walker began to walk him through all the developments he knew about, and a preliminary plan was made for the ultimate move toward secession.

Walker had no idea of the plans Bradley had already put into place. He also did not know the seriousness of his old friend's health. He had battled lung disease as a result of the injuries he received in the Waco debacle. In fact, it appeared he would lose that battle soon, and he had vowed that he would not lose his battle for Texas' independence regardless of his health issues. Independence would be achieved whether he was alive to see it or not.

Neither of them could ever resist a little competition, and the temptation to shoot at long-distance targets was too great to let slip away. They spent the remainder of their time talking and shooting a few hundred rounds punching holes in the paper targets downrange. When they finished, they retrieved their targets and returned to the office. Walker said, "I guess I owe you dinner. You outshot me again."

Bradley laughed at his old commander and said, "I'll put it on your tab."

They shook hands and the General got in his truck to return to Austin. Bradley told him before he left, "Tell Lucas we're watching him."

They both laughed, and the General left. As soon as Walker had driven away, Bradley made a call to his lieutenant,

"Looks like things are going faster than we thought. Get the Houston Plan finalized and ready to implement."

John arrived in Austin and was greeted at the helipad by his Chief of Staff, Mateo Garcia. They loaded the car and drove to the office immediately. Along the way, Mateo briefed him on any further developments. Emails had slowed a bit, but they had been replaced with calls and texts from fellow Republican legislators and media representatives. His colleagues were generally supportive and offered their assistance. They were also inundated with requests for media interviews or comments.

John listened and waited for him to take a breath. As soon as there was a break in the deluge of words, John said, "It's going to be OK. Let's respond as we are ready. We'll have a staff meeting later today and begin to formulate a strategy to deal with every request."

Mateo answered, "I've put the staff on alert. They are waiting for us at the office. I've also requested additional interns to be assigned from the legislative pool. They'll be in attendance as well."

It was a short ride to the office. John didn't expect the welcome he received when the car arrived. The door opened, and a dozen reporters met him with recorders and cameras pointed toward him. As soon as he got out of the car, they began talking at once, questioning him about the new legislation. They were all were talking at once as was typical of a group of reporters hot on a breaking story. John held his hands up, "I am both pleased and surprised by y'all being here today. However, we are in the early stages of drafting the bill. We will release a statement shortly to be followed by a press conference later in the week. Again, thank you for your interest in this new bill." Sensing a hot story, they followed him to the door of the building still shouting their questions. John couldn't remember a time when he was happier to get inside that door.

His chief of staff apologized, "I'm sorry, Sir. I don't know how they knew you were coming."

John laughed a bit and said, "No problem. It seems we no longer have a low profile here in Austin!"

His chief of staff answered with a shake of his head, "No Sir, Pastor Edwards saw to that last Sunday."

John made his way to his office and, upon entering, noticed a lot of new faces. He asked, "How many interns did you request?"

His chief sheepishly answered, "A few... maybe a few more than a few." They both smiled, and John went to his personal office to collect himself before the meeting.

He saw the stack of messages that were left on his desk. John was "old-school" and still required a paper note from his scheduler with missed calls. In the past, there were never more than a handful; however, this time, there were dozens. It was actually a little terrifying that so many people wanted to talk to him. He was accustomed to operating in the background. That was simply not going to be the case any longer. He took a deep breath and steeled himself for the next step.

All of the staff gathered in a large room that had been set up quickly with tables and chairs for everyone. John was not a formal man, and he merely walked to the head of the room where he could see everyone. He said, "Thank you for your presence here today. I am not quite sure where to begin, but we will start with a quick recap. Then we will address the steps we need to take between now and the opening of our legislative session in January."

He proceeded to give them a little background of how he had arrived at this point. Then he informed them that it was his commitment to both introduce and get passed into law a bill that would ensure the end of abortions in Texas. That first fifteen minutes of narrative resulted in three hours of non-stop questions and led to a comprehensive plan for going forward. The staff was divided into specific groups according to areas of need and corresponding to their expertise in each area. Their work would begin immediately.

After the meeting adjourned, he returned to his personal office and flopped into his chair, exhausted by the afternoon's pace. His first thought was to call Rebecca. When she answered, her voice was just the medicine he needed, "I'm so glad you called. How was your afternoon?"

He sighed, "Awful."

"Really, what happened?" she inquired.

He began with the reporters and the missed calls, the staff meeting, and, like falling rain, he spoke in the rapid-fire way that he often drifted into when he was either overly excited or agitated.

She interrupted, "John, take a breath. We've got this. We'll do it one step at a time."

He was exhausted and quietly said, "Maybe I've bitten off more than I can chew this time."

She said, "I don't believe that for an instant. Neither does David, Sarah, Jeremiah, or anyone that knows you."

They talked a little while longer, and as John said good-bye, Rebecca said, "Remember, I love you, and I'm on the front row."

By that time it was early evening and too late to make any return calls. His chief of staff slipped his head in the door and asked, "What time do you want to begin in the morning, Sir?"

John said, "Let's get started early. I'll be in the office by 8 AM."

"Yes Sir. See you then."

John left the office and went to his Austin residence. The penthouse apartment at AMLI Downtown was more than big enough, though it seemed claustrophobic and lonely tonight. His phone rang, and he saw it was Sarah. Answering, he said, "I am so glad you called."

He explained the day to her, and she quietly laughed. Then, she said, "I have some good news to relay to you. We couldn't do anything today due to all the talk about the bill. Somehow it must have hit the national wire. Everyone at the conference is pledging support and resources."

He was amazed, though he wasn't as surprised anymore at the life it seemed to take of its own accord. He went on to tell her the schedule and plan for the week. She agreed that it was a good plan going forward.

Chapter 11

The Gathering Storm Clouds of Conflict

October 30, 2018

"Texas has yet to learn submission to any oppression, come from what source it may."

—Sam Houston

COME AND TAKE IT

John Lucas easily drifted into a reflective mood as he made the short ride from his Austin residence to his capitol office. He did his best to push aside all the distractions of the day's schedule. As he did so, he began to think of the opening celebration of the new Museum of Texas History. It seemed like that had been an eternity ago, though he remembered it had only been seven years. He recalled meeting the newly hired PR Director at the opening, whom he came to know quite well because of his key involvement with the museum.

Sean O'Sullivan was one of the most unlikely hires for the museum he could have imagined. He was a recent graduate of Georgetown University. Originally, he hailed from Breezy Point, located in the borough of Queens in New York City. He was highly recommended to the museum as they began to expand their Texas Collection. He came from Irish immigrants and had the personality to match. He was a fiery, no-nonsense young man.

During his tenure at Georgetown, he met a young professor who originally came from Texas. While his major did not demand a language, he had developed a deSire to learn one of the Romance languages. Even though Spanish was the most popular of those languages, he had heard much better things about the French Department than the others. He began taking some of the introductory courses in his first year. He also enrolled in the summer study abroad program. During those eight weeks in France, not only did he develop a working fluency in French, he was able to learn a great deal about Texas history. The young professor was the director of the study abroad program, and they spent some time together in France talking about their immigrant backgrounds as well as the culture of the state. This summer study pushed him into a deep appreciation for Texas history, ultimately leading to the focus of his work at Georgetown being done in the Texas War for Independence.

Before John was given the giant scissors to cut the ribbon for the museum's addition, he remembered O'Sullivan standing by the refurbished Goliad Cannon. O'Sullivan started his brief remarks with the shouts of "'Come and Take It!', 'Remember the Alamo!', 'Remember Goliad!' What Texan is not familiar with these phrases? Phrases to stir the soul, inspire courage, and incite rebellion. Each phrase is associated with a pivotal point on Texas' road from revolution to independence."

Going a bit further with his combination of history and marketing, he said, "On October 2, 1835, the Mexican commander at San Antonio ordered the people of Gonzales to surrender their small brass cannon. Local officials refused and sent runners into the surrounding areas to gather armed men. The Mexican colonel ordered about 100 soldiers to take the cannon by force. Buried until reinforcements arrived, the cannon was then mounted on a wagon and decorated with a white flag proclaiming, 'Come and Take It.' The Mexican soldiers arrived to confront 160 armed Texans, and a brief battle ensued. One Mexican soldier was killed, but no Texans. The Mexicans withdrew to San Antonio. News of the "battle" spread and ignited fervor among Texans."

John knew the rest of the story well, though this young red-headed man continued. "By early 1836, the Texans in San Antonio occupied the abandoned mission, San Antonio de Valero. The old mission had once housed a Spanish company from Alamo de Parras in Mexico. So, most people referred to it as the Alamo. Colonel James Bowie and his men joined Colonel James C. Neill, commander, in January 1836. In February, William B. Travis and his men joined them. Bowie was chosen commander of the volunteers, Travis of the regular army. However, Bowie became ill and passed the entire command to Travis. Although the Alamo was a fairly good defensive position, Travis knew they had too few men, less than 200.

"There were also gaps in the Alamo walls, closed only with sticks and dirt. Regardless, Travis was determined to hold the Alamo, which had come to symbolize so much for its defenders. This would also tie up Santa Anna's army and give Sam Houston more time to raise a Texas army. Despite written appeals for help, help did not arrive in time. As Mexican troops encircled the Alamo, Travis explained that remaining there would mean certain death. According to legend, he drew a line in the sand with his saber, asking those who wished to stay to cross over the line. All but one stepped across.

"At about 5:00 AM on March 6, 1836, the battle began. Mexican buglers played the notes of *El Deguello*, an ancient chant indicating that no mercy would be shown. The Texans put up a stubborn fight, but the third assault by the Mexican troops successfully breached the walls. By 8:00 AM, the battle for the Alamo was over. Bowie, Travis, and volunteer Davy Crockett were all killed. 'Remember the Alamo!' became a battle cry for Sam Houston's army.

"Also by 1836, the Spanish presidio, La Bahia, near the town of Goliad was under Texas control, commanded by Colonel James W. Fannin. General Sam Houston had ordered Fannin to retreat to Victoria, but Fannin delayed and found himself surrounded by Mexican forces at the Battle of Coleto. He and his men surrendered and were imprisoned inside the presidio at Goliad.

"Many Texans believed they were prisoners of war and would be treated fairly by their Mexican captors. Though the surrender document, in Mexican archives, shows no such promise, eyewitnesses testified that Mexican General Urrea assured Fannin that he and his men would be treated fairly. General Urrea even wrote to Santa Anna, requesting that the lives of the prisoners be spared. Santa Anna responded with immediate execution orders.

"On March 27, 1836, Palm Sunday, Fannin, his men, and other Texan captives were divided into columns and marched out onto the prairie. They believed they were going on work detail; some even assumed they were going home. Upon a signal, Mexican soldiers opened fire on them, killing them all. Colonel Fannin was the last to be shot, forced to watch the execution of his men. 'Remember Goliad' joined 'Remember the Alamo' as the battle cry of Sam Houston's army, soon to be victorious at San Jacinto."

John had become so absorbed in his thoughts; he was startled as the driver stopped the car and said, "We're here, Senator. May I get your briefcase?"

John was always a bit embarrassed by the attention he was given. He replied, "No thanks. I got it."

He exited the car and walked into the office, where he was immediately met by his chief of staff, Mateo Garcia, "Good morning, Sir. I have a tentative schedule for your approval on your desk."

Mateo followed John through the outer offices, where he greeted each of the staff. When they arrived at Lucas' office, he said to Mateo, "Will you see if you can get me Sean O'Sullivan on the phone? He's at the Bullock Museum."

Mateo went over the schedule, though John was more absorbed with his thoughts about the key meetings that day. He had to meet with General Walker, which was always a bit intimidating. He nodded his approval of the schedule, and Mateo left the office to arrange for a meeting with O'Sullivan.

He passed John's scheduler's desk and said, "Would you get Sean O'Sullivan on the phone for the senator, please?"

She responded, "Of course. May I tell him what this is concerning?"

Mateo said, "I have no clue. This is a new day!"

It was early in the day and O'Sullivan happened to be in the museum when John's scheduler called. "Mr. O'Sullivan,

Senator Lucas would like to have a word with you. Is now convenient?"

Sean did not live under a rock. He was well aware of the political buzz surrounding the Senator's new abortion bill, though he saw absolutely no reason why he would be involved. He made the time for the call. "Actually, now is a perfect time. I'm in between meetings at the moment."

He was placed on hold for a moment while John took the call, "Thank you for taking my call, Mr. O'Sullivan."

Sean replied, "Please, Senator, call me Sean."

John continued, "Very well. I would like to visit with you at your earliest convenience. I am preparing to introduce a new bill to the legislature in the coming session and would like to talk to you about some strategies concerning the media."

O'Sullivan was taken completely by surprise with both the direct nature of John's opening remark and the possibility of being involved at all with this ground-breaking legislation. "Of course, Senator…"

John interrupted, "It's only fair, Sean, that you call me John if I have that privilege with you."

O'Sullivan said with a note of surprise and respect, "Yes, Sir… uh, John." He continued, "I can come by your office around three this afternoon if that is soon enough?"

John said, "Perfect. See you then."

John walked from his office to the coffee machine and said to Mateo and his scheduler, "Clear the calendar at three this afternoon. I need some time for a meeting I've just added with Sean O'Sullivan. And, Mateo, I want you in that meeting as well."

Mateo was not insecure, but he asked, "May I ask what the meeting concerns, Sir."

John answered, "I'm sorry, things are moving a bit fast for me. I remembered him from a ribbon-cutting at the museum several years ago. He seems to have a good hold on both Texas history and marketing. I want him on our staff."

Both Mateo and the scheduler raised their eyebrows, to which John said, "I know it is a different day. But if I've got to handle the Governor, General Walker, the media, and God only knows who else, I think he will be a great asset to our team."

They both were agape with surprise.

John had enough time before his lunch with General Walker to meet with the legal team. They concluded that the bill needed to go further than the present law already provided. John instructed them to work closely with Jeremiah and Sarah's team from Texans for Life to get the wording correct and prepared for presentation to the Texas Legislative Council as soon as possible.

Cooper's Barbeque wasn't far from his office. John left with time to spare for his lunch with General Walker. Arriving near noon, John walked into Cooper's and was seated in the back at a table for four. Cooper's opened in 1962 and has been a staple of Texas Barbeque ever since. Students of the university often had lunch there, though it was also a regular stop for tourists and natives. The old barn wood style of decorating was not a part of the current fad; it was original to the restaurant from the beginning. It reminded John of a much simpler time. The sights and sounds, even the smell of the mesquite grill, were somehow comforting.

John was seated, and General Walker joined him within minutes. As Walker walked toward the table, John stood to greet him, and the General said, "Good to see you, John. Thanks for meeting with me so soon."

"No problem, at all, General," he said.

"Please, John, call me Dylan," the General insisted.

John felt every eye staring at them. After all, Walker was dressed in his military uniform with five stars across his epaulets, six rows of ribbons across his left lapel, and his Navy Seal Trident above the ribbons. He commanded attention, and this time, John couldn't help but feel it was intentional. John was dressed more casually than normal. He had not felt like standing out today. His starched Levis and shirt were his standard casual look. He did indulge himself when it came to the hat he chose for the day. He wore a charcoal gray Stetson El Presidente with a Cattleman crease in the top. His children had given it to him several years ago, and it had more sentimental value than the thousand dollar price tag.

The server came to their table to take their order, and John deferred to Dylan. Part of the deference was to see if he was going to eat or not. If he ordered a meal, the conversation might be lighter than John expected. To his surprise, the General ordered a two meat plate. Maybe this was going to go easily after all. John played it safe and ordered brisket with potato salad on the side. They both ordered a Shiner on tap to drink.

As soon as their beer arrived, Dylan began, "How's the political weather, John?"

John laughed and knew it wasn't going to be a light conversation after all. He said, "Hotter than South Texas in August." And they both laughed.

Dylan went on, "I saw where David announced your new legislation Sunday."

John said, "That was a bit of a surprise to me."

"Have you got the bill written yet?"

"We're working on it," John said.

Walker wasn't one to be subtle. He said, "Well, there's blood in the water, and the sharks are already circling."

Being a seal early in his career, Walker knew the dangers of swimming in shark-infested waters with an open wound. It usually didn't end well.

John said, "We're definitely playing catch-up, but I've increased my staff and begun to build a coalition from outside the legislature.

"How did your meeting with the Governor go?" Walker continued with his inquisition.

John wanted to ask him how he knew he'd had a meeting with the Governor but thought better of it. There probably wasn't much that happened in Texas that Walker didn't know about. John offered a brief answer hoping that he would pursue other lines of questions, "I thought it went well."

Even though Walker knew he was taking a chance, his deep relationship of trust in the Lucas family, he was quick with a response, "John, he's not a man who can be trusted with the truth. He has his eye on Washington. I'd be careful if I were you."

John was not going to be drawn into a conversation like that. He knew how much his father trusted Walker, but he was not quite ready to do the same yet. He simply nodded and asked Walker, "What's the real agenda here, General?"

Walker was surprised. Something had happened to John Lucas. This is not what he had come to expect from him based on his dealing with John over the years. He was beginning to sound a lot like his father. John Lucas III was not a man to be trifled with in any conversation. If his son followed in those footsteps, he knew he could trust him with anything, especially the real agenda.

Walker smiled and said, "I remember our conversation well from Waco. My purpose today is to ask the same question. How far are you willing to go?"

John answered quickly, perhaps too quickly, "It will get done. On that, you have my word. By this time next year, every abortion clinic in Texas will be closed."

Walker said, "Even Houston?"

"Even Houston," John said matter-of-factly.

With a deeper, very serious tone, Walker said, "Then you have my pledge to be by your side with all of the resources I can muster." They finished eating with small talk. General Walker paid the tab, and they left Cooper's, even if it was with very different ideas of what the future would hold.

Walker would wait a while before he began to enlist others, though he needed to call Carson Bradley as soon as possible. He placed that call on the road back to his office. Bradley was expecting it and answered immediately. "How was lunch?" he asked.

Walker related most of the information to him and asked, "How many men do you have at your disposal, Bradley?"

He answered, "About a thousand who are immediately available, though I can get about a thousand more with two week's notice."

The General was thinking ahead and said, "I think we need them to enlist in the Texas State Guard."

Bradley asked, "Are you expecting trouble?"

Walker answered, "Not if we have a big enough show of force. Washington doesn't have the stomach for another Civil War." Bradley smiled at the other end of the phone and thought that might be true, except he had other plans.

By the time John reached his office, Sean O'Sullivan was waiting for him with Mateo. John looked at his watch and realized it was early. He walked into the office and said, "I'm sorry if I've kept you waiting. I thought our appointment was for three."

Sean said, "It was, but I wanted to get here a bit early and meet your Chief of Staff."

John said, "Great. I've asked him to join our conversation."

They continued into John's office and sat in the rawhide sofa and wingback chairs custom covered in maroon material with Texas A&M logos printed on it in white in front of the desk. John was not pretentious; however, no one came into his office and walked away unimpressed with the luxury and uniqueness of the man who occupied the seat behind the desk. In this case, however, John wanted Sean to feel at home, so rather than sit behind his desk, he sat on a guest chair and joined them.

The beginning of the conversation was a little awkward. John didn't want it to feel like an interview. However, he did want some answers before offering Sean such an important position on his staff. "Tell me about how you got to Texas, Sean," John began.

Sean had anticipated that question as it was often a question posed to the New York native. He answered quickly. "I remember reading Elizabeth Abrahamsen's blog during my freshman year at Georgetown. She calls it *Wide Open Spaces.* She said something that caught my attention: 'People from all over the United States can pick Texas out on the map. Even if they're not American, people know about Texas. All over the world, traveling Texans tend to identify as Texan rather than American, because, well, we get treated like celebrities when we do.' And, I knew I wanted to be a part of that. So, when the museum called, I jumped at the chance."

John allowed his drawl to surface distinctly and said, "Well, we are different. I'll give you that."

Sean went further, "Sir, if I may be bold enough to ask you a question."

John was comfortable with this Yankee from Queens and said, "Sure, shoot."

Sean paused for a moment and then asked, "Why am I here, Sir?"

John explained what he wanted to accomplish with the new legislation he was working on and looked Sean in the eye as he said, "I want you to join our staff for this fight."

Sean was silent. And John went further. "In Texas, we can see a long ways. We know when a storm is brewing long before it hits. Some folks take shelter; others get ready to fight the storm. I know a storm is brewing. I've never been one to take shelter. But I also know that I need good people around me to win this fight. I think you're one of those people. Are you?"

Sean quietly said, "Yes Sir. I believe I am."

John said, "Good. Mateo will be your direct supervisor, as he is with all my staff. He'll get the transition started immediately."

Then he turned to Mateo and said, "Let's get him up to speed as quickly as possible. I want him to concentrate on the public relations aspect. He'll work with the media team exclusively."

Mateo, smiling because he now knew that they could win this fight, said, "Yes, Sir. When do you want him to start?"

John said, "Yesterday would have been great!"

This was a very different John Lucas. Storm clouds or not, like his father before him, he was becoming his own storm!

Chapter 12

The Line Is Drawn in the Sand

October 31, 2018

"It is much easier to pull down a government, in such a conjuncture of affairs as we have seen, than to build up, at such a season as the present."

— John Adams letter to James Warren, 1787

COME AND TAKE IT

The date was not lost on John as he arose early in the morning of October 31, 2018, and began the drive to his office. While most people readied themselves for the onslaught of children who would make their way to their doors with the query "Trick or Treat?" John knew the more important significance of the day. On this day in 1517, Martin Luther, a German Augustinian monk, posted 95 theses challenging doctrine of the Roman Catholic Church on the church door in the university town of Wittenberg.

That simple act began what we have come to see as one of the most transformative events of world history: the Protestant Reformation. John and David had many conversations about that seemingly innocent call for debate from Luther. Initially, it was aimed at reforming the beliefs and practices of the Roman Catholic Church. Still, ultimately it ended the unity imposed by medieval Christianity and, in the eyes of many historians, signaled the beginning of the modern era.

John mused about the lines drawn in the sand throughout history. In reaction to Luther's actions, Leo X issued the papal bull *Exurge Domine*, condemning 41 errors from Luther's writings and sermons. If Luther didn't recant within 60 days, he would be arrested and brought to the fires of "holy recompense." Luther would recognize the pope's authority or face the consequences, but Luther did what was natural to him. He went forward with what he regarded to be right. His response was well known: "Farewell, thou unhappy, lost, sacrilegious city! Let us hand this Babel over to the servants of Mammon, the unbelievers, apostates, pederasts, devotees of Priapus, robbers, simonists, and all the other wild prodigies with which this pantheon of godlessness is filled to the brim. Let it become a dwelling place of dragons, lemures, vampires, and ghosts, and, in keeping with its name, become an everlasting chaos."

Despite his bravado, this farewell was painful for Luther, as he admitted. But the die was cast. Luther and Rome would proceed along divergent paths.

John certainly didn't want his bill to cause division. However, his mind jumped from one historical event to the next, and in each case, the result had been similar. The Founding Fathers of the United States did not want a war. However, he could only imagine what the people of Lexington and Concord in Massachusetts must have felt when faced with 700 British soldiers as they marched out of Boston after the massacre on King Street and the Battle at Bunker Hill. Crossing the line to open rebellion, citizens known as *Minute Men* attacked the British soldiers as they marched out of Boston, which signaled the beginning of the Revolutionary War.

He couldn't forget the most famous of all the lines drawn in the sand, the one traced on the ground by Travis during the last days of the Alamo. John didn't want to draw any lines in the sand; however, he did want change. With that last thought, he arrived at the office, and to his relief, the horde of reporters had left.

Mateo Garcia met him at the door with the daily briefings and a summary of the previous day's work. He couldn't help but notice that Sean O'Sullivan was in the office. He asked his chief of staff, "What's Sean doing in the office?"

Mateo answered, "When he offered his notice at the museum, the director was unusually direct in telling him to leave effective immediately. It seems he is on the opposing side of our bill."

John shouldn't have been surprised by that news, though he was. "Ask Sean to step into the office for a few minutes," John instructed Mateo.

"Yes, Sir," Mateo answered.

When Mateo walked over to Sean's desk, Sean said, "Am I in a lot of trouble?"

Mateo smiled and quickly said, "Nope. I think you just scored some major points with the boss! He does want to see you as soon as possible, though."

Sean gathered some papers and his iPad and went immediately to John's office. After knocking, John said, "Come on in, the door is always open, Sean."

Sean took a seat in one of the wingback chairs in front of the desk and said, "Would you like a report on our progress thus far, Sir?"

John was a bit surprised that there was anything to report. He said, "In a moment, yes; however, first, I'd like to know what happened at the museum. Are you OK?"

Sean learned a very valuable lesson at that moment. John Lucas IV was not a man who cared more about reaching goals than the people who were a part of his team.

Sean said, "I'm really not sure what happened. I went back to the museum after our meeting, and before I could say anything, the director called me into her office, where she confronted me about meeting with you."

"News certainly traveled fast around the capitol; however, this was even faster than he thought possible."

Sean went on, "After I explained our meeting and my decision to offer a customary two week's notice, she began to lecture me on the negative effect this would have on my career. She ended the lecture with her telling me she would accept my immediate resignation. She said, 'You've chosen the wrong side in this one.' So, I typed a simple letter of resignation, packed my box, and left."

John smiled and said, "Good choice, Sean. You're on the right side of history on this one.

Sean shared his own thoughts, as well as with the team. Then he asked John if he wanted him to draft a formal speech for the press conference?

John was surprised. He asked, "What press conference?" He'd told reporters that there would be a press conference later in the week, but he had not expected it to be already arranged. "What press conference?"

Sean said, "I'm sorry Sir, I thought you said you want to meet with the press this week?"

John couldn't help but chuckle. "Yes, I did. When have you scheduled it?"

Sean said, "Friday morning, Sir."

John said, "We do have some work to do, don't we?"

"Nothing we can't handle, Sir. I believe the Texan phrase is: 'Keep your saddle oiled and your gun greased.' We'll have both done by the end of today, Sir."

John believed him.

John's scheduler buzzed in and asked if she could bring him his messages. As she walked in, she had a stack of notes indicating it would be quite a day again. She handed them to John and explained, "I've separated the notes removing those that staff could handle. I've also taken the liberty of giving all the media calls to Mr. O'Sullivan if that meets with your approval?"

John heartily agreed. He was very fortunate to have such a strong staff. When this was over, he would have to do something very special for them.

As John leafed through the notes, he saw one was from the Governor's scheduler requesting that he call back at his earliest convenience. Based on the warning he'd received from General Walker, he wasn't anxious to make that call just yet. He needed to call Rebecca first. He hadn't had a chance to talk to her today. They had never gone a day since they were married that he didn't talk to her every day when they were apart. Sitting at his desk, he placed that call.

When Rebecca answered, he said, "Hey. Sorry I'm later than usual. How's your day going so far?"

She laughed in her magical way and replied, "My day? I'm not in the middle of the fiery furnace." She knew he would recognize that reference from the Old Testament and the story of Daniel's three friends who disobeyed the king and were thrown into a furnace for their execution.

John laughed and said, "Well, it's not that hot yet!"

She got a bit more serious, "How are you doing, John?"

"Really well," he answered. "I've hired a new staff member to handle the PR and media. I think he's going to be a great addition."

They chatted for a bit more, and Rebecca said, "Call me if you need anything. I can be there in an hour." John knew she meant that; however, he wouldn't impose his need for her assurance to that length, at least not yet.

John knew it was time to get to the more difficult calls. He asked his secretary to begin at the top with a call to the Governor. He wanted her to use a landline, hoping that they may be able to play telephone tag for a bit so he could avoid the conversation for as long as possible. Unfortunately, the call was connected quickly.

Governor Thompson greeted John warmly.

John always felt a little like he was talking to a master salesman when he spoke with that tone of voice. He answered the Governor's greeting with brevity, "Doing well, Governor. How are you?"

Thompson answered, "That's actually part of the reason why I wanted to talk to you. I received a call from some of the national news representatives asking me about your proposal to submit a bill changing our abortion laws."

John was a little taken aback at his use of the word "proposal" as if that somehow meant the Governor had misunderstood John's intent. He had not asked for permission to submit a bill; he had informed the Governor he was going to submit it. John answered, "I'm not surprised."

Thompson countered, "Well, John, I thought we had an agreement that you'd run that by me before you went this far."

John had never personally heard this side of the Governor. He bristled and replied, "I'm sorry if you misunderstood, Sir. I thought I told you I was going to write it for submission to the Legislative Council in time for to both the House and the Senate consideration in this year's session."

The Governor tried to get the upper hand but realized this was not the John Lucas who could be intimidated any longer. He said to John, "Perhaps I did misunderstand. But, John, isn't it premature to leak it to the press? The last thing we need right now is a media circus here. Washington and a large part of the country isn't going to be happy with that. Actually, I wouldn't be surprised if you alienated your own party with such a quick move. I'm sure they'd want the credit."

John could care less about what would make Washington or the Republican Party happy. In fact, that may be a large part of the problem in dealing with the abortion issue in the first place. He'd already seen how the federal government's dealing with immigration along their southern border had gone. And, while that was another issue for another day, he certainly didn't agree with how that had gone down.

He merely replied, "I can imagine they may not be very happy with my bill."

The Governor shot back, "John, the last thing we need is more Marines in our state. The immigration mess is more than enough for us to deal with right now."

John said, "Governor, there wouldn't be any reason for Washington to send anyone here when we pass this law. It is the right of our state to regulate this issue within our border."

Thompson merely replied, "I hope you're right." With that, he said goodbye. He knew he couldn't sway John off the mark.

Governor Thompson realized that he had less time to mount a counter to John's direction than he at first thought. It would be more difficult to stay out of the center of this storm. He immediately placed calls from his personal phone to Lydia Smithson and Ashton Linden-Harris. He also called Peter

Bridges in and asked him to get an appointment with General Walker as soon as possible.

Lydia Smithson answered on his first try.

He said, "We need to accelerate our efforts. Somehow the media got wind of Lucas' bill, and we know where that's going to end."

She was not surprised at his lack of knowledge as to the events of the week. He was not familiar with the enormous following of David Edwards and had no reason to have seen or heard about his call for prayer for Lucas on the previous Sunday. She said, "Governor, did you not see David Edwards' church service Sunday?"

"Of course not. Why would I listen to that washed up, old preacher?"

She was very measured in her next words, using his first name to remind him that he has not ascended yet, "Perry, that washed up, old preacher has a weekly live audience of over 20,000 adults. They all love him and listen to him very closely on every issue he deems as important. His call to prayer for John Lucas, his friend and member of his church, was as good as an endorsement. The media was listening. That is a certainty."

The Governor was not a prudent man. He almost shouted back at her, "I don't care how many voters he has in his back pocket. I'm not running for reelection."

She quietly answered, "You may not be running for re-election to the Governorship, but you are running for a chance to be nominated for the white house. If you get into a fight publicly with John over this, you will lose it all."

He was frustrated, "Why now? Why has Lucas decided to take the reins of his father's legacy now?"

Lydia was thoughtful in her reply, "I'm not absolutely sure. But, whatever the reason, he's got a firm hold on them. Governor, you need to be careful not to cross the line on this one."

He then said, "Perhaps you should give Ms. Linley-Harris a call." He didn't know that they would be having a conversation this week about the next steps to take.

She said, "I will."

They hung up just as Peter Bridges walked into the office. He informed the Governor that General Walker happened to be in the building and could drop by in about an hour if that would be acceptable. Feeling more in control now, Thompson said, "Make it happen, Peter."

When the general arrived, he was shown immediately into the Governor's office. Peter accompanied him and sat with them, taking notes for follow-up and other tasks that might come from the meeting. This was not a meeting Bridges could afford to miss. While it wouldn't be recorded, he could pass the information on to Jeremiah and Sarah, where it could be very useful going forward.

The Governor greeted the general with a salute. That always grated on Walker. To think that the leader of this great state had so little knowledge of the correct protocol when greeting him made him inwardly seethe. He reminded himself that he shouldn't expect anything more from a man who had used every favor and excuse he could muster to avoid any military service.

Walker merely nodded and seated himself across from Thompson. The Governor said, "We have a situation brewing general."

Walker was surprised it had happened this quickly. He knew things were gathering momentum, but this was better than he could have hoped for. The Governor went on, "You may have heard about a potential bill that Senator Lucas is developing for submission in this year's session. It will be very unpopular and inflammatory. Even so, I think he has enough power to push it through. We need a contingency plan if he does."

Walker acted as if he didn't know anything about the bill. "May I ask what this has to do with the Guard's mission, Sir?"

The Governor was about to lose his temper. The hour between his conversation with Lydia Thompson and this meeting had not been enough time for him to calm down. He rose from his desk and went to the bar to pour a glass of Garrison Brother's, "Would you like a drink, General?"

Walker gently rebuffed him, "No Sir, it's a bit early for me."

That only made Thompson angrier, though the bourbon allowed him to calm himself before replying, "General, if this bill takes effect, we could end up with the Marines on our doorstep."

Walker said, "Sir, I find that hard to believe. Perhaps if I knew more I could begin to formulate a plan that would ensure peaceful reaction to any contingency. What exactly do you expect to be the precipitating event or events?"

The Governor then replied, "I don't know the answer to that yet. However, I want you to be included, and at the table of every meeting we have in the future concerning this issue."

The general asked, "Yes Sir. What group is this again, Sir?"

The Governor realized he had revealed more than he should have, but it was too late to recall that information. He tried to walk it back, "Well, I'm going to get a few people from within the government, and the public and private sectors to discuss countermeasures. I want you present. However, I also want you to treat this information as of the highest priority and hold it in the strictest confidence."

Walker replied, "Certainly, Sir. I understand. Will that be all?"

The Governor tried to act dignified and said, "That's all, General. You may be dismissed." As he was saying this, he stood and left the room, smiling.

Thompson then turned to Peter and asked how soon he could get the group together for a strategy session? Peter suggested Friday at lunch. The Governor wasn't happy about the delay, but it was reasonable to expect it would take that long to coordinate all of the principles involved.

The line had been drawn in the sand, and the Governor had just refused to cross it. He had made a choice placing him on the wrong side of Texas.

Chapter 13

The Bill Is Drafted

November 1 - 2, 2018

The time is now near at hand which must probably determine whether Americans are to be freemen or slaves; whether they are to have any property they can call their own; whether their houses and farms are to be pillaged and destroyed, and themselves consigned to a state of wretchedness from which no human effort will deliver them. The fate of unborn millions will now depend, under God, on the courage and conduct of this army. Our cruel and unrelenting enemy leaves us only the choice of brave resistance, or the most abject submission. We have therefore to resolve to conquer or die.

— George Washington (spoken in his August 27, 1776 Address to the Continental Army before the battle of Long Island)

COME AND TAKE IT

It was only Thursday, a mere three days since he came back to Austin, and John was exhausted. He desperately needed some time in the swing overlooking the *sendero*. Pancho Villa would be a welcome sight grazing peacefully in the pasture with the other longhorns. However, there was much to be done with very little time in which to get it done.

The first order of business was to begin the work of writing the first draft of the bill. He was well aware that the 1973 Roe v. Wade Supreme Court ruling legalized abortion at the federal level. He also knew that many states had enacted state-specific laws restricting the procedure. Texas did have some of the most restrictive abortion laws in the country, including mandatory ultrasound imaging and parental consent for minors. Additionally, women seeking abortion-inducing medications must make four visits to a doctor and obtain an ultrasound.

He also knew the danger of passing a law that would result in the SCOTUS striking it down as unconstitutional. Just two years ago, in June 2016, in a 5-3 decision by the United States Supreme Court in Whole Women's Health v. Hellerstedt, a Texas law was struck down which placed specific requirements on abortion clinics, including requiring doctors to have admitting privileges at a hospital within 30 miles of the clinic and setting clinic standards similar to those of surgical centers. The court ruled that these laws are unconstitutional and unduly restrictive of a woman's right to abortion services. However, he was also convinced that the Constitution's language in no way supported what was often referred to as the *fundamental right to abortion*.

He had come to believe it was the height of intellectual dishonesty to argue that the authors of the Constitution and its amendments intended to protect abortion under some vague and unwritten *right to privacy*. That so many courts and judges had for so long upheld a legal doctrine antagonistic to the Constitution revealed the modern judiciary's rogue nature. Too many had become enslaved by the few privileged and empowered people within the ranks of the professional politicians of the day. This bill had to be different than any other attempted in the past.

As he had each day previously, John arrived at his office to be greeted by Mateo Garcia. The schedule for the day was packed. He would meet first with the legal team to begin the draft; then, he was scheduled to meet with Sean and the media team. Hopefully, they could work through lunch, which Mateo had already anticipated and ordered in from the Austin Daily Press. The sandwich shop began as a quiet addition to the campus regulars who visited the food trucks for a quick lunch between classes, but it quickly transitioned to a brick and mortar establishment known for their unique Texas sandwiches.

John saw that Fitz was on the schedule for a phone conference later in the afternoon, being joined in the call by Michael Brody. He also wanted to make time to talk with Jeremiah and Sarah. He would need their legal team to be involved from the beginning. He asked Mateo to see if some time could be squeezed in for a call to them. Mateo smiled and said, "I have them on video conference when we meet this morning."

Once again, John had underestimated the mutual commitment and competency of his chief of staff. He graciously said, "Mateo, you're a marvel. Thanks!"

"Just doing my job, Sir," Mateo quickly answered.

And John said, "And, so much more. Again, thank you!"

John gathered himself before going into the conference room, where the monitors were already on standby, waiting for the group from Texans for Life to join the meeting. While it was 9 am in Texas, Washington was in the Eastern Time Zone and thus an hour ahead. John walked into the room and greeted all the staff members; both Jeremiah and Sarah were the first to appear on the monitors.

Sarah was the first to speak, "Good morning, John. How's the heat in Texas?"

John chuckled at the double meaning of her question, which he knew was intentional. He said, "It's hotter than a two-dollar pistol!"

Everyone in the room stifled a laugh at the distinctively Texas reference, and Sarah retorted, "I'll bet it is. We've heard the thunder all the way here."

John invited Sarah to begin with some history and pertinent information from the perspective of both their state and national work. She began to bring them up to speed with an introduction concerning the most recent actions taken in other states: "In early May, the Georgia Governor had signed into law what is commonly called 'a heartbeat bill.' This law bans abortion as early as six weeks into pregnancy. Georgia is the fourth state to pass such a law this year alone. The bill prohibits abortion once a fetal heartbeat can be detected. But reproductive rights advocates and doctors say the laws, which prohibit abortion before many women know they are pregnant, amount to a near-total ban on the procedure."

John interjected, "Is this bill going to be challenged seriously?"

Jeremiah answered that question, "Yes. It's already receiving significant protest from all of the pro-choice groups. The ACLU has even jumped on the bandwagon against this law. And, of course, Planned Parenthood has thrown their full weight and resource against it. They have already filed a brief with the Supreme Court challenging the Georgia law. That case will be heard early in 2019. There is hope for the law with the new appointees to SCOTUS. We have some degree of confidence that it will be upheld since the heartbeat, while not the beginning of life, is the universally recognized indicator of life."

One of John's staff asked, "Do any of the heartbeat bills include rape or incest as exceptions?"

"Good question," Sarah said. She went on, "In fact, the Georgia law also includes medical emergencies involving the life of the mother. Ohio is the only state that does not include these exceptions; however, they require a sonogram to determine the heartbeat. That functionally will ban all abortions since very few women are able to recognize their pregnancy until a lapse in the menstrual cycle, which usually does not occur until later than the development of a heartbeat detectable by a sonogram."

John stepped into the conversation again and asked, "Does this really ban abortions?"

Jeremiah answered, "Well, John, the short answer is 'no.' However, it does come close, especially with the provision of the potential of prosecution of the medical personnel performing the procedure, with up to ten years of jail time; and, the potential for charging the mother with murder."

"Again," Sarah began, "it does provide a significant challenge to Roe v. Wade. However, not all pro-life groups are willing to get behind the idea. That's been one of the discussions we've had this week in virtually every session. With the news from Texas, a lot of people are waiting to see what you do."

The discussion went on for another hour. There were numerous questions raised. John could tell his staff was very supportive, though he had some doubts about their willingness to go as far as he wanted. He wanted to stop all abortions. They closed their discussion and planned to have a preliminary document finished by Monday morning.

As the meeting wrapped up, Mateo began to rearrange the room to accommodate the smaller media team. Sean joined him while John excused himself to make a call to Rebecca. He didn't like calling her from the car on the way to the office. It always seemed less personal, especially with the driver within earshot.

"How was the first meeting?" Sean asked Mateo.

Mateo answered, "I thought it went well, though I'm not sure we're all on board. It's a lot to process for some of the interns."

Sean's response was unusual as he said, "Everyone has an agenda, Mateo. We just need to discover what it is and do our best to give everyone something of value." Mateo was growing to admire Sean more each time they interacted.

Just as the media team gathered, the delivery from Austin Daily Press arrived. There was an assortment of sandwiches, called *tortas* in Texan, though John always chose the Cuban. It was filled with pork belly carnitas, Black Forest Ham, pickles, Aioli, Swiss, and White Cheddar cheese, with spicy mustard. Everyone settled in with something to eat, and their iPads open. John thanked them for their quick response to the challenge. He then turned to Sean for the opening remarks and updates.

Time was indeed short. A press conference had been called for Friday at 10 am. After welcoming the press and making a few remarks, Mateo would turn the podium over to Sean, who would field any questions. John would be present though silent through the briefing. If anything needed to be walked back later, this strategy would be easier to handle. It was also decided that they would avoid any publication of the bill being distributed at that time. It would need to be presented through all the early channels before that.

John then began to summarize these steps so everyone could be on the same page. Texas was a bit different than other states. The first step in a bill becoming law was the introduction to the respective chamber of the originating author. For example, only a Texas Senator can introduce a bill in the Senate. The bill will also be assigned a number according to the order it was introduced. John hoped that this would be one of the first introduced and therefore receive a number of SB-1. It must be introduced separately in both chambers and if increasing taxes or raising funds are required from the bill, it must begin in the House. Bills must be introduced in the first 60 days of the regular session. After that, the bill's introduction requires a four-fifths from either chamber, unless the Governor has declared an emergency and the bill pertains to that emergency. Once the bill is introduced, a caption (short description of the bill) is read aloud, this is also considered the first reading, and the presiding officer assigns the bill to a committee.

John continued to summarize by explaining that the next group to consider the bill would be *The Committee*, which was often known as the Little Legislators. They would hear testimony for or against the bill and decide to take no action or issue a report on the bill. If no action is ever taken, the bill dies; the Committee's Report would include a record of how everyone voted, the recommendations regarding the bill. After this, a copy of the Committee's Report is sent to all Texas Legislature members; the bill is read again by the caption and then debated by Legislators. The chamber members then cast their votes, either through voice or a record voted, on the bill. The bill needs to obtain a majority vote for it to pass; once it passes, it is sent to the other side of the chamber.

After all of that, it would be sent to the Governor. Then the Texas Governor has four options when a bill reaches his desk. He could sign it into law; not sign it, in which case, if Congress is in session, the bill becomes law within ten days without his signature, or within 20 days if Congress is not in session; veto the bill, which means it is denied, the veto can be overridden by a two-thirds vote from the Legislature; or the Governor could use a line-item veto, which means the Governor could eliminate certain parts of the bill without killing the entire document. Since this bill was not a state budget proposal, the line-item veto could not be used.

One of the new interns asked, "Which one do we want, Senator?"

They all chuckled under their breath. John, always patient with the younger, less experienced staffers, said, "We'd like it to sail through the legislature and the Governor sign it immediately with all the appropriate fanfare. Maybe we could get the Aggie Band to back him up and play *Texas, Our Texas.*"

Someone mumbled a little too loudly not to be heard, "Fat chance."

John turned to the offending staffer and chided, "Which part, the Governor signing the bill into law, or the Aggie Band playing on the steps of the capitol?"

They all laughed. When the laughter died down, the same staff member said, "Both, Sir."

Now, no one was laughing. John simply said, "That's where we come in. We can carry this one over the goal line. Let's play 'em one down at a time. If we make enough first downs, we'll get across the goal eventually. Heck, if A&M can beat LSU in seven overtimes, we can do this. We sure ain't all hat and no cattle!"

Sean divided the team into smaller groups to work independently on various parts of the conference. They would meet together again at the end of the day to coordinate their responses and make certain every eventuality was anticipated and provided for a positive answer.

Sean closed the meeting and said, "OK folks, let's saddle up."

Sean using particularly Texas language, always seemed to be a bit strange to John. His Queens accent and a Texas idiom somehow just didn't go together. John did recognize his effort to fit in and let it go without any comment.

John retreated to his office and readied himself to talk with Fitz and Michael Brody. Right on time, the phone buzzed, and his scheduler announced, "Dr. Fitzgerald and Reverend Brody are on line two, Senator. Shall I ask them to hold, or are you ready for their call?"

John was surprisingly ready. The day's meetings so far had steeled his resolve. "I'm ready. Send the call back."

Fitz began, "Thanks for taking our call, Senator. I know you must be busy."

John wanted to make this as casual as possible, and he answered quickly, "Never too busy for your call, Fitz; and, please call me John."

John recognized Brody's deep baritone voice instantly, "I appreciate you taking our call, John. Fitz tells me you are about to introduce some groundbreaking legislation."

John answered, "We are. I have come to a firm commitment that we need to speak on behalf of those who are unable to speak for themselves."

John explained some of the bill's preliminary parts, as they had outlined earlier in their discussions that day. He also explained that he was getting a lot of help with the bill's draft from Texans for Life. Fitz came into the discussion with the understanding that Jeremiah and Sarah Mann were John's sister and brother-in-law. He had already given him some of the background of the cook-out discussion at John's ranch the weekend before.

Brody said with a chuckle, "Things are moving pretty fast, Senator. What can I do to help?"

John replied, "I'm not really sure, except for your wisdom and influence within the evangelical community."

Brody answered a little too quickly with a quip, "I've never shied away from a good fight."

John was a bit surprised by his humor and immediately realized Michael Brody was a lot different than his public persona.

John said, "I'm not really looking to provoke a conflict, though I am very aware that it may be that we will face some stiff opposition from some of the more pro-choice legislators."

Brody got serious and said, "I'm sure you will. I want to be very clear about one thing as we go forward. Our organization is founded on the principles we believe to be central to the Scripture. While we have often found ourselves embroiled in a political battle, our focus is much broader than politics. You can be assured of our support and help in the effort. One of our guiding principles revolves around our unshakeable belief of the sanctity of life from the moment of conception."

John responded with his gratitude. They chatted a bit more and just before the call came to a close.

Brody said, "John, we want to help; however, we would not support violence or insurrection."

John laughed and said, "Let's hope it never comes to that."

John was very pleased with Brody's response. It looked as if the road was being paved as he made his way. He had little time to relax, though. Just about the time his mind began to relax, he was jarred out of his reverie when Mateo stuck his head in the office, "We're ready for you, Sir."

"Ready for me for what?" he asked.

Mateo answered, "The final briefing and mock press conference. We have the brief ready and wanted to go over the potential questions to rehearse your answers. The press conference is scheduled for 10 am tomorrow, Sir."

John almost groaned, "Oh, I almost forgot." He knew both Mateo and Sean were not going to let him forget anything.

And, then, as if on cue, Sean breezed into the room and said, "Ready to go, Sir?"

John gathered himself and walked with them to the conference room, wondering why there wasn't a porch swing for him to retreat to. He missed those days of quiet reflection that seem to have become so distant now.

Chapter 14

The First Shot Is Fired

November 2, 2018

"We view ourselves on the eve of battle. We are nerved for the contest, and must conquer or perish. It is vain to look for present aid: none is at hand. We must now act or abandon all hope! Rally to the standard, and be no longer the scoff of mercenary tongues! Be men, be free men, that your children may bless their father's name."

— Sam Houston

COME AND TAKE IT

The week had been a blur of activities for John Lucas IV. He could not remember a time when so much had been accomplished, and yet, so much remained. His drive from the Austin residence to the capital office complex was relatively uneventful. He had already talked with Rebecca that morning before leaving. Their conversation was warm and familiar. It was always a source of strength for John to talk to her. That had been their pattern for all the years since meeting at Texas A&M. He asked how the kids were doing, and she informed him that JV seemed to be taken with Katy Fitzgerald. He had never been a "player," and this developing relationship was something extraordinary. John simply smiled at the thought of how his relationship with Rebecca had begun in a similar way. He truly couldn't imagine a day when she was not a vital part of his thoughts.

The driver noticed the senator seemed to be lost in his thoughts. He knew something about the schedule that day. Mateo had texted him earlier in the morning that he should be aware that there might be a large gathering of the media waiting for the car to arrive. The press conference was scheduled for mid-morning, though most reporters wanted a jump on the news cycle with some quote from the senator.

As was predicted, he turned the corner to approach the parking area in front of the complex, and there were dozens of reporters with their crews and equipment standing near the door. The driver broke into John's thoughts, asking, "Sir, the media is waiting at the front, would you like to park at the rear entrance?"

John focused a bit and saw the crowd of media and said, "That's OK. They can't eat me! Anyway, I suppose I have to start getting used to this sometime. It might as well be today!"

The car pulled into his space and John got out of the car, briefcase in hand, and the shouts cascaded into a roar of voices. Mateo exited the front door to handle the press, and John waved him off. John stopped for a moment, as reporters shoved microphones, phones, and recorders toward his face to get the clearest recording of the senator's remarks as he said, "Good morning, y'all. Isn't this a wonderful November morning? I bet the deer are moving today. Looks like a great start to the season this year."

The last thing anyone in the media wanted was a quote about hunting season. John always had a knack of ignoring the obvious and turning to the obscure. However, it had the de-Sired effect. They were so stunned at that remark it gave him just the opening to quickly enter the office while Mateo stopped the horde and invited them to the conference room to prepare for the briefing at ten o'clock. They grumbled but complied.

Sean met him as he came into the main office and asked if he wanted to go over the notes, handing him a fairly thick folder. John chuckled and said, "Sure, but I need a cup of coffee first."

Mateo quipped, "Already on your desk, Sir."

John knew he was being handled by the staf, but it was reassuring that they had so quickly proven their loyalty and competence.

The team briefed John over the central points of the bill that the legal team had outlined. Sean also reviewed the draft of the opening remarks. John made a few changes, and they reviewed possible questions that the media might have. He was a very quick study, and the preparation went smoothly.

John spent the remaining time reviewing the one-pager, making sure he was ready for the briefing. Ten o'clock came quickly. As he entered the conference room, he was both pleased and surprised at the crowd of reporters. Mateo had already informed him that all the major outlets were present: ABC, NBC, CBS, MSNBC, CNN, Fox, and both the AP and UPI. There were also several newspapers and magazines represented. He was very surprised that the Washington Post and the New York Times were there. However, he also knew things were always a bit larger than life in Texas.

The bigger surprise came from some of the other representatives he saw. The Governor's office was represented by no less than Peter Bridges, the Chief of Staff. Also in attendance were Ashley Linley-Harris and Planned Parenthood; Michael Brody and Texas Christians United; and Texans for Life had representation present. Small groups of reporters had gathered around some of these representatives, though everyone took their places as John walked to the lectern. As John began, Sean distributed the official press release and one-pager.

John began with little ceremony. After all, he was not a man who stood on pretense. Even his dress was casual, though he did take Rebecca's advice and wear slacks instead of his typical starched and creased Levi's. He welcomed all of the media and others present, "It is good to have all of you here today, though I must say I'm a bit surprised. I guess it's a good thing my dad built the conference room as large as he did, though I never imagined why, at least until today!"

Everyone in the room laughed except for the representative of Planned Parenthood. She knew why the former senator had built it so large; his reputation was one of being as big as the state itself. No one in her office wanted John to step into his father's shoes. That might be a force too great to be reckoned with successfully.

John began to speak:

"In the Declaration of Independence, Thomas Jefferson articulated fundamental truths upon which the United States of America was founded. These truths included that each of us possess a set of inalienable rights granted by God. Included among these God-given prioritized rights are the rights to life, liberty, and the pursuit of happiness.

Recognition of these inherent rights once helped propel our people into revolt against a tyrant. Respect for our God-given rights is an essential component of our American Civilization. Congress has a responsibility to ensure the Jeffersonian Truths of the Declaration of Independence are protected for current and future generations of Americans.

"As Texans, we understand these truths better than any other members of the Union. We have also fought our own War for Independence. Even our flag speaks to our State's deep understanding of the commitment and sacrifice necessary to ensure that every citizen of our land enjoys these fundamental rights. We only have two bars of color beside the bright white Lone Star centered on royal blue. The red bar is always flown on the bottom because we recognize it was the blood of our citizens in the ground of this great state that gave these rights.

"We should all recognize that of these rights, the right to life received primacy in Jefferson's list for a reason: without the right to life, how would an individual's rights become vested? How could any other rights be realized if one's very life could be taken away by another? Jefferson articulated a prioritized set of rights; first, the right to life, then the right to liberty, then the pursuit of happiness. Each right was carefully prioritized in sequential order because the right to life trumps all other rights. No one can take a human life in exercising their liberties, and no one can take a life or take away the liberty of another in their pursuit of happiness. If the right to life can be taken, then no rights are ultimately protected.

"Nearly sixty years after the Declaration of Independence was written, upon the assembly of the Convention of 1836, on March 1st, a committee of five of its delegates were appointed to draft a document declaring Texas a free and independent nation. The committee, consisting of George C. Childress, Edward Conrad, James Gaines, Bailey Hardeman, and Collin McKinney, prepared the declaration in record time. It was briefly reviewed, then adopted by the delegates of the convention the following day.

"While we are not drafting a Declaration of Independence, we must acknowledge regrettably that our nation has seemingly forgotten the importance of adhering to Jefferson's vision; and, further forgotten our own adopted beliefs in these same truths. Instead, we have allowed a new tyranny composed of nine unelected Justices on the Supreme Court of the United States to erase our foundational truths. We have traded off the brilliance of Thomas Jefferson's specificity insuring life for a vague and inherently meaningless set of legalistic "emanations" and "penumbras" seemingly conjured out of thin air whenever activists on the Court want to replace Jefferson's self-evident truths with black-robed judicial activism.

"It's time that we reclaim our hard-earned rights, beginning with the right to life. To this end, I will introduce a bill at the beginning of the 86th Legislative Session named the Heartbeat Protection Act. It will cut through the obscuring haze of illogical judicial rhetoric and return the right to life to the primacy our Founding Fathers intended. Under this legislation, abortionists who end the life of an unborn child whose heart is beating will be subject to imprisonment and the loss of their medical license. As a matter of law, the bill will ensure that if a heartbeat can be detected, that baby is protected by the same power and authority of the great Lone Star of Texas won by the heroes of the Alamo, Gonzales, Goliad, and San Jacinto.

"By listening for a child's detectable heartbeat, we can save the lives of over 95% of aborted babies in this great state, and we will extend protection to the unborn to as early as 6-8 weeks from conception. What better way to recognize the inalienable right to life than to ensure that all babies with a beating heart are protected in the womb where all our lives began?"

For more than a few moments, reporters and representatives were stunned into silence. Not even a whisper or murmur could be heard from the gathering. Even John's staff was stunned at the power and presence he commanded in the delivery of his opening remarks. No one had expected this from John Lucas IV. This was much more like his father. Few had opposed that Lucas and politically survived.

Eventually, the media stirred, and the barrage of questions began. Sean O'Sullivan fielded the questions attempting to maintain some semblance of order, though the crowd soon deteriorated into a cacophony of voices determined to be answered first.

Sean was savvy enough to single out the most positive of those voices first. He knew the Fox News representative from his time at Georgetown University. While the reporter was conservative, he was also fair. Sean recognized him first. The question was brief but potentially inflammatory: "Will the Governor sign the bill if it is passed by the legislature?"

Sean, serving as the moderator, turned to John who had been briefed on this question. He simply answered, "Based on my preliminary meeting with Governor Thompson, I have every confidence in his support and affirmation of our efforts to protect the unborn of our state."

With that statement, Peter Bridges smiled and recognized the deliberate move to box the Governor into making a definitive stand on the issue. Bridges stayed for the remainder of the briefing but knew his report to the Governor was going to cause enormous consternation within his office. Thompson would not be happy that he was being drawn into this fight so quickly.

There were many other questions, most of which were referred to the one-pager. Some of them were deferred until the final draft of the bill had been made public. John's legal team felt it was premature to release the draft before it was presented to the Legislative Team.

The representative from MSNBC was finally recognized and asked, "What would the penalty be if an abortion were performed after the detection of a heartbeat?"

John answered, "Under the new law, performing an abortion in Texas would be a felony. The legislation, when signed into law by Governor Thompson, would define a fetus as a legal person 'for homicide purposes.' However, the woman who receives the abortion would not be held criminally culpable or civilly liable."

CNN jumped in without recognition and shouted, "Are there any exceptions?"

Sean was about to protest the question as out of order, but John turned to him and looked him off as he said, "When the law goes into effect, there would be only two reasons a person in Texas could have an abortion: First, if the fetus has a 'lethal anomaly' which would cause death soon after birth or a stillbirth, or if it would 'present serious health risk' to the mother. The legislation also specified that it isn't enough for the mother to have an 'emotional condition' or mental illness; and, a second doctor would need to agree that the mother has such a 'serious illness' that could cause her or the baby to die.

Sean regained control of the questioning and recognized the representative from the Associated Press. He asked, "Where and who may perform the abortion if it is deemed necessary?"

John answered, "These medical procedures could only be performed by state-licensed medical physicians in recognized, fully equipped and staffed hospitals."

The reporter from the Washington Post blurted out, "You are functionally prohibiting every abortion!"

John firmly and quietly said, "Yes. It is my conviction that every unborn child has the right to life."

Sean finished the briefing by fielding a few more questions, though the news-bite had already been captured with John's last remark. The meeting was adjourned quickly. The reporters all rushed to deliver their reports as quickly as possible. John stayed a bit to talk to the representatives from Texas

Christians United and Texans for Life. They were both supportive and affirmative in their response.

Finally, the building was empty of everyone but John's
staff, and he retreated to his office. No one at the briefing realized it, especially not John, but the first shot had been fired in
this new war of independence for Texas.

Chapter 15

The Opposition Is Plunged Into Chaos

November 2-3, 2018

"These are the times that try men's souls: The summer soldier and the sunshine patriot will, in this crisis, shrink from the service of his country; but he that stands it now, deserves the love and thanks of man and woman."

—Thomas Paine, on December 23, 1776, in The Crisis Number 1

COME AND TAKE IT

The reports from the press conference were virtually immediate. With every television outlet flashing "Breaking News" in a red banner scrolling across their broadcasts, the Governor knew the outcome before his Chief of Staff, Peter Bridges, could even make his report. Bridges was not in a particular hurry to write the report and made a cursory call to Governor. By the time Bridges arrived at the Governor's office, Thompson was already in a near panic mode because of the initial news reports. He immediately called his chief of staff into the office.

"What is going on over there, Peter? Has Lucas gone completely off the rails? Is it true that he wants to ban abortions altogether in Texas? Doesn't he realize the Supreme Court has already settled this issue?" Peter knew it was best just to remain silent and let the Governor vent at times like this.

Peter waited for the Governor to take a breath and said, "Let me clear your calendar for an hour so we can go over the press briefing in its entirety." The Governor walked to the bar and poured himself two fingers of Garrison Brother's Select, hoping to settle his anger. Thompson said, "I don't need a briefing. I need to stop Lucas."

He took a drink and said, "Peter, we've got to do something to head this off at the pass. The last thing I need to deal with at the start of this legislative session is abortion. It's bad enough that we are trying to get some property tax reform done in response to the crisis in our public education system. You know the fight we face in that area. We should never have borrowed from the State Teachers' Retirement

Fund. We've got to replace that money before my term ends, or I'll have no shot at the White House."

Thompson was regretting the backroom deals he had struck attempting to broaden his base of support for his run at the presidency. The agreement he made with the Senate's vocal minority to provide greater health and educational benefits for the immigrants was a problem. He agreed with them to fund it from various surpluses in operating expenses. However, his only ready access to the necessary funds was to redirect it from the Teacher's Retirement fund. He thought it could be replaced easily from greater receipts from the state lottery, though that had been grossly miscalculated. He managed to defer most of the spotlight from budget watchdogs, but it was coming into sharp focus now that he had been reelected. He struck a deal with Planned Parenthood to fund the deficit in exchange for property tax relief and facility expansion incentives. What he had done was unethical and illegal. If he got caught, it would do much more than ruin his chances of a presidential run. That did not make him happy.

Peter responded, "Would you like to see if we can get the group together for a Monday meeting?"

The Governor nearly shouted back his answer, "Monday! Are you crazy! We need to meet today! Call them and set it up immediately!"

With that, Peter replied, "Yes, Sir." He walked out of the office and retreated to his own office to place the calls.

He called Lydia Smithson first. She answered on the first ring and said, "I was wondering how quickly you'd call. I'm guessing the Governor has already begun hitting his Garrison Brothers!"

Peter was an accomplished navigator of the political scene and merely said, "The Governor would like to call a meeting this evening. Is 6 pm all right with you?"

Lydia laughed as she said, "I'm surprised he wants to wait until then. Yes, Peter, I can rearrange my plans. I assume we're meeting in his conference room?"

Peter simply answered, "Yes, ma'am."

Peter also contacted the others, and they agreed to meet that evening. He had saved his last call for Ms. Linley-Harris. Peter had spoken briefly to her at the end of the press conference. He knew she was fully aware of the challenge this was going to be to the present laws. In fact, she had already called her staff in Houston and had them schedule a strategy meeting for Saturday morning. She needed to mount an aggressive counter-campaign quickly before the Sunday morning news shows.

While Peter finished the calls, the Governor's scheduler buzzed into Thompson's office with a very unusual call. She announced to the Governor that the Democratic National Committee's chairperson was on hold, waiting to talk to him. Thompson said, "Can you send her to Peter?" She answered, "I'm sorry, Sir, she was very clear that she wanted to talk to you. Shall I tell her you will call her back?"

The Governor finished the rest of his bourbon and steeled himself for the call. He nearly spit out the words, "Fine. Just put her through."

The DNC had been relatively uninvolved in state politics over the years. However, with the new chairperson, there was a much more active role. They had developed an in-house technology incubator called Para Bellum Labs. This new DNC unit was first headed by an engineer with a Ph.D. in computer science from MIT. The effort was designed to help the party, and its candidates bridge the technology gap. It was no accident that Para Bellum, translated from Latin, meant "prepare for war." She was more of a war-time general than an administrator.

The chairperson said, "Governor, what's going on in Texas? I thought you had a better handle on politics down there than the reports seem to indicate."

Thompson replied in the calmest voice he could muster, "Everything is fine. I've got it under control. The media has blown this story way out of proportion. We can handle Lucas."

She replied, "Good. I'd hate for something like this to come between you and your goals for the future."

Governor Thompson *knew exactly what she meant; and, he also knew that without the endorsement of the DNC, he would have no chance of any further political career after his present term was over.*

In this "war," she wouldn't take any prisoners. The enemies of the DNC were politically executed without hearing or appeal.

The time flew by, and the group began to arrive at the capital. The same group, who had met earlier, was invited. Lydia Smithson and Ashton Linley-Harris arrived at the same time, though they did not travel together. Ms. Linley-Harris was still in town after having attended the press conference at Senator Lucas' office. She had also brought two others from her office. One was the PR/Media Director, while the other was the Chief Legal Representative of Planned Parenthood. The leaders of the majority and minority groups from both the Texas Senate and House also arrived, along with the Lieutenant Governor. The only person who had not been in the first meeting was General Walker. The Governor had insisted that Peter include him in this meeting.

The Governor welcomed them and thanked them for extending their workweek by coming in on Friday evening. As might be expected, Ashton interrupted his remarks, as she said, "Cut to the chase, Governor! We were told at our last meeting you had things under control. You said there was no hurry to move to any action. I think those in attendance at today's press conference know how badly you misinterpreted the timeline. What I want to know is how you plan to stop this insanity from going any further?"

After venting with Peter, the Governor was better prepared for this meeting. He quietly replied, "We all may have underestimated the urgency of our situation. However, we are still in control of the schedule going forward."

She fired back, "Spare us the platitudes as you try to cover your ass."

Perry Thompson could not remember dealing with such an inflammatory person in his life. However, he ignored the remarks and addressed the group as a whole. "I think everyone here knows one another from our previous meeting. We are also happy to welcome General Walker, from the Texas State Guard to our informational session tonight.

There was an awkward silence until Walker said, "Thank you, Governor, although I'm a bit unclear as to the reason I am here."

Dylan Walker was not new to politics. He could not resist the subtle provocation to inflame the meeting further. Sometimes the real motivations for people's actions were best revealed when they were the angriest. It was always more difficult to think before you spoke when you were in the heat of what was perceived as a battle. The Governor knew he was losing control of the meeting and turned to Peter for help, "Peter, would you mind briefing us all concerning the announcement by Senator Lucas?"

Peter swiped his iPad to open the documents he had earlier scanned and summarized the meeting. He ended his presentation with the now-familiar sound bite from Lucas: "It is my conviction that every unborn child has the right to life."

He went on and said, "The senator has outlined a bill that appears to ban all abortions in Texas effectively."

Linley-Harris said, "Finally, someone who is willing to call it for what it is. These heartbeat bills prohibit abortion once a fetal heartbeat can be detected. All of the reproductive rights advocates and doctors I know agree that these laws prohibit abortion before many women know they are pregnant, and amount to a near-total ban on the procedure. It's a forced pregnancy bill. It's a health care ban bill!"

The Lieutenant Governor asked, "Do we actually possess a copy of the proposed legislation?"

The Governor answered, "No. It has not been presented to the Little Committee as of yet."

Linley-Harris continued, "Similar bills have been presented in other states like Alabama, Ohio, and Georgia. Some of them include a penalty for performing abortions of up to 10 years in prison as well as loss of their license to practice medicine. They also do not explicitly exempt women who perform their own abortions with medication, leading to speculation about whether they would also be subject to criminal charges.

Some have suggested that it could even lead to murder charges for women who have abortions. If this bill is passed in Texas, it would lead to the closing of every woman's health clinic and thus deny them many basic health needs which they would not be able to receive from anywhere else."

The minority leaders from both the senate and house were enraptured with this young woman's fiery nature. As they nodded their assent, they were both tempted to say, "Amen!"

The Governor, however, tried to soften the remarks by saying, "Ms. Harris, we don't know that to be true. In fact, none of these laws have finished their course through the courts. I am confident they will be struck down once they reach the Supreme Court."

Linley-Harris looked directly at the Governor and said, "You are correct, Governor. I have not consulted with every health clinic providing services for women; however, I do know what Planned Parenthood would do. We would be forced to close our doors in Texas. That would result in a direct loss of $500 million dollars of federal aid coming into the economy of this state."

That last comment had the deSired effect on the politicians in the room. It was nearly thirty minutes later before the Governor could restore some semblance of order to the chaotic bantering. All the while, Dylan Walker was smiling inwardly at how his simple plan with a visit to the Waco Siege site with John Lucas had resulted in what he knew was a giant step toward a break with the federal government. Abortion wasn't the main issue here. He was much more pragmatic than that. He cared about being free once and for all from an oppressive federal government. They would all be on board soon enough. They would have no choice. The Houston location of Planned Parenthood would be the final stage in this drama.

The meeting adjourned with a renewed sense of urgency to counter the momentum Lucas had already gained; however, it felt like a hollow victory since none of them could agree on what needed to be done. It seemed as if each of them had their own agenda.

Once everyone was gone, Thompson asked Peter to stay for a few minutes. "Peter, this looks very bad. I received a call from the DNC before the meeting. She informed me that my career would be over if we allowed any attention to be diverted to an abortion bill. You know what that means for your career too. If I'm retired, I really won't need any staff, much less a Chief of Staff."

Peter merely nodded his head in understanding. The Governor still had no idea of Bridges' commitment to this legislation. Peter Bridges knew if it required him to lose his career, that would be a small price to pay.

Bridges walked toward his car across the capital grounds, determined to call Sarah as soon as he got into his car. It was only an hour later in DC, and she needed to know about this latest development. In his mind, the Governor's group's chaos would indicate the sooner they pressed forward, the better.

Chapter 16

The Plot Thickens

November 3-10, 2018

"All new states are invested, more or less, by a class of noisy, second-rate men who are always in favor of rash and extreme measures, but Texas was absolutely overrun by such men."

—Sam Houston, President of the Republic of Texas and hero of the revolution.

COME AND TAKE IT

The first week of November was almost sacred for Carson Bradley and his trusted inner circle within the Texans for Independence. They had been together in their quest for an independent Texas for nearly three decades. This week was significant because it signaled the start of deer season. Bradley and his lieutenants met together at his ranch to hunt together during the day and sit around the campfire, telling their tall tales at night. They hadn't missed an opening day together in over twenty years.

While Bradley's ranch was small compared to some of the other privately owned high fence preserves in the area, it still covered 500 acres of some of the best deer country in South Texas. He ran a few cattle, though they were more a hobby than a business enterprise.

His cattle were crossbred with Longhorn cattle. Hardy, aggressive, and adaptable, the Texas Longhorns were well suited to the rigors of life on the ranges of the southwestern United States. They survived as a primitive animal in the most primitive ranges and became the foundation stock of that region's great cattle industry. These crossbred cattle seemed to be a fit symbol for him. He felt that Texas' roots bred with a renewed surge in patriotism for his state made the perfect mix to bring freedom back to Texas.

His ranch was located just a few miles from Presidio la Bahia, also known as Fort Defiance. This location from the Texas War for Independence was not as widely remembered as its sister fort, the Alamo, but its stone walls housed 270 years of Texas history, tragedy, and according to some, the ghosts of those who died in that war. It stands near the south bank of the San Antonio River, which also ran through his ranch's edge. It is a fortress that stands out against the local backdrop of Anaqua trees and warm blue skies. Through two revolutions, countless skirmishes, and untold hours of everyday life in times gone by, Presidio la Bahia had stood on that spot since 1749. Although the cannons on its parapets have long been silent, many believe that the history of this place is every bit the inspiration that other more well known spots were to Texans.

As Bradley and his inner circle gathered around the fire, he decided to tell the story of the Presidio as an introduction to the looming implementation of the Houston Plan. As he began his recitation of the history, they all listened with rapt attention. He said: "The Presidio la Bahia was originally established as a Spanish stronghold to defend Spain's mining interests in the area, but after French colonists withdrew from the Texas territory, the fort became a vital waypoint along major trade routes and a gateway to the river. At first a show of military might, it soon became a vital landmark of the region.

"As the fort transformed into an economic hub, the town of Goliad sprouted and blossomed around it, and the fort chapel, Our Lady of Loreto, was constructed to serve the soldiers, their families, and the townsfolk. Being the only consecrated ground for miles in any direction, the chapel courtyard soon became home to countless graves, both marked and unmarked, unrelated to the wartime bloodshed on the grounds.

"Civilian life persisted around the fort even as it changed hands between the Spanish and the rebels multiple times throughout the Mexican War of Independence, but the worst was yet to come.

"During the Texas Revolution, Presidio la Bahia was commanded by the Texan Colonel James Fannin, who renamed it 'Fort Defiance.' Running critically low on supplies, fighting frigid storms, and unable to offer support to the falling Alamo,

Fannin was ordered to abandon the fort and fall back to neighboring Victoria. The troops of La Bahia had barely left the gates when they were captured by the forces of Mexican General José de Urrea and corralled back into their own fort, now as prisoners. When Urrea refused a presidential order to execute the prisoners as pirates, his lieutenant took up the order and had Fannin and his men divided up into groups to be killed.

"Francita Alavez, the common-law wife of another of Urrea's officers, argued passionately for mercy for the prisoners and was fortunate enough to have some luck in this venture. She succeeded in having 20 men spared for their medical, linguistic, or other useful knowledge, and managed to hide an unknown number of others, saving their lives. For this and her other humanitarian efforts throughout the war, Alavez became known as the 'Angel of Goliad,' in time earning a statue that now stands in her honor in the Presidio's plaza.

"In spite of Urrea's refusal, and the best efforts of Alavez and other objectors, the majority of Fannin's men, over 400 in total, were led outside in groups and shot. Those too injured to walk were dragged to the fort's quadrangle, and those who survived the initial firing were beaten and stabbed to death. Only 28 escaped by hiding among the corpses. Fannin himself was saved for last and forced to sit in a chair in the chapel courtyard due to his wounded leg. He requested that he be shot in the heart, given a Christian burial, and that his watch be sent to his family. The soldiers performing the execution shot him in the face, stole his watch, and burned his body along with the rest.

"Over the last few years, our organization has grown in number and strength. However, the time for planning and waiting is at an end. We are taking our place in our day's Fort Defiance. Some of us will be called on to make the ultimate sacrifice. After all, what is life without liberty? We cannot forget we are Texans, not Americans. The United States government has taxed us, regulated us, invaded our privacy, and attempted to silence our dissent. My fellow Texans, this is what we have labored and strived for. The tyranny of the federalistas stops now. We are bringing this fight to everyone who lives in the great state of Texas. All will need to answer the question: Are you a Texian, or are you an American?"

Every man gathered in the flickering light of the campfire, raised his Lone Star longneck, and agreed with a whoop and a holler!

Chapter 17

The Evaporation of Peaceful Days

November 3, 2018 – January 8, 2019

"When once a republic is corrupted, there is no possibility of remedying any of the growing evils but by removing the corruption and restoring its lost principles; every other correction is either useless or a new evil."

— Thomas Jefferson

COME AND TAKE IT

Friday's press conference had gone well. John's staff had prepared everything necessary to communicate the basic outline of the bill that would redefine abortion in Texas. Functionally it would end the possibility of all abortions except in extreme instances. Even then, it would require much more than a nod of the head from those in the medical community performing the procedure.

As he ended the day, he wanted to take the helicopter back to the ranch, though he knew he still had too much to do in Austin. Riding back to the apartment, he thought how he needed to have Rebecca with him, at least for the weekend. It was an easy decision to call her immediately.

Rebecca answered her phone as soon as she saw the caller ID, "Hey! How did the press conference go? I bet you were perfect."

He was always amazed at how she could say just the right thing at just the right time. He answered, "It went well. I sure missed having you there, though."

She could read between the lines with John very well. She playfully said, "I was thinking that I could come up for the weekend if you're not too busy to show a girl a good time?"

John almost shouted, "Are you kidding? That would be great!"

"I'll call you when we have an ETA. Perhaps you could pick me up, and we could go out to eat at The Carillon?" Rebecca answered.

John said, "I can handle that!"

It didn't take long to ready the helicopter for takeoff. While Rebecca packed a few things, the pilot made the final checks and warmed the engine.

When she boarded the helicopter, the pilot told her she could expect to arrive at 6:30 pm. She called John and told him when she would arrive. He was thrilled that she was coming. This was just what the doctor ordered. He would call the Carillon immediately and make the arrangements.

The Carillon was located in the heart of Austin, near the University of Texas campus. John didn't pay attention to their football schedule, and as luck would have it, they were scheduled to play a home game against West Virginia on Saturday. While John usually relied on his staff to handle reservations, he decided it would be quicker and more personal if he dialed the restaurant himself. When the reservation's attendant answered the call, he was gently rebuffed.

She said, "Sir, you do know the Longhorns have a home game tomorrow? I'm afraid we have nothing left at this late date. Perhaps I could put you on a waiting list? Could I have your name?"

John was never one to use his position or name to curry favors. He simply answered, "This is John Lucas. The reservation would be for my wife, Rebecca, and I."

Quickly the attendant said, "Just one moment Senator Lucas."

Before John could say anything, the Maître d'Hôtel answered and said, "Senator Lucas, I am sorry for any confusion. Of course, we can accommodate you and Mrs. Lucas this evening. What time should we expect you?"

John was grateful and finished making the reservations for the evening.

John had his driver pick him up, and they rode to the helipad near the Capitol to meet Rebecca. They arrived a bit earlier than expected, which merely added to his excitement of seeing Rebecca.

They hadn't waited long until John heard the familiar sound of the helicopter's blades as it made its approach and landing. After the pilot powered down, John opened the door for Rebecca and tightly embraced her. "Sure missed you this week," he said.

She smiled, gave him a gentle kiss, and said, "I missed you, too."

The overnight bags were loaded into the car, along with a box that John did not recognize.

As they settled into the back seat, John asked, "What's in the box?"

It wasn't very large. It looked like the boxes of plain paper for the printers at the ranch office from Amazon.

Rebecca said, "It's a little surprise for you."

John didn't do well with surprises. He continued to ask her what was inside it. This was a little game they played with one another, pretending as if Rebecca was not going to tell him. She liked to wait until he nearly begged her to reveal the surprise. Finally, she relented and said, "David had it sent over yesterday. He said you would enjoy it."

Now John was more curious than ever. However, it would have to wait; they had arrived at the Carillon.

They were greeted at the curb by the valet and shown to the front where they were taken to their table. While walking through the restaurant, they noticed it was very full. John said, "I see you're very busy tonight."

The server said, "Yes, Sir. Texas is playing West Virginia tomorrow. It's a big game, and there are lots of alumni in town."

"I'm glad we could get a table, then," John offered.

She went on, "We always have a table for you and your wife, Senator Lucas."

Rebecca looked casually around the room and recognized four people sitting in a corner, almost hidden from the rest of the room. She saw they would pass close enough to divert the route to their table and pass by. She said, "Oh, John, look there's the Governor and Lydia with their spouses."

John was typically oblivious to his surroundings and wouldn't have noticed had she not mentioned it. Rebecca steered their way by the Governor's table purposefully. He had his back to the room, though Lydia saw John and Rebecca coming their way and waved. As the Governor turned, he had the look of the cat that swallowed the canary!

The Governor stood and gathered himself quickly, saying, "Good evening John. It is a pleasure to see you and Rebecca here. Are you in town to see the game tomorrow?"

Lydia and Rebecca both laughed at the thought. Lydia tried to save the Governor, and said, "I doubt that Governor. They're both Aggies!"

They exchanged polite greetings to the stares of many who were eating in the area. Rebecca inwardly smiled, having achieved her goal. She knew what that dinner meeting would be about and wanted to fire a warning shot across the bow, so-to-speak. This subtlety was not lost on Lydia Smithson. She was an astute student of such communication.

John and Rebecca were seated and served Kir Royal, a popular French cocktail made with a measure of crème de cassis and topped with champagne, along with the menu for the evening. They both decided on the Texas Cheese Board to start, followed by Spring Lamb Chops with the cauliflower-chalaza chili casserole, topped with a pumpkin seed pesto.

When the appetizer arrived, Rebecca said, "Wasn't that a surprise seeing the Governor and Lydia with their spouses?"

John knew better than to bite on that bait and simply said, "Probably plotting their next move to get to Washington."

Rebecca laughed and said, "More likely plotting how they're going to deal with you."

He knew she was right, but he just wanted a quiet evening without any political interruptions.

Rebecca didn't push that topic anymore. She could tell he was tired. The best medicine for John was an uneventful dinner talking about the kids and the ranch, both of which he loved greatly. She had always admired the simplicity of his loyalties.

His love was predicated on family, and nothing would ever change that. She just hoped he hadn't gone too far because of that loyalty. They finished their gourmet meal with her doing most of the talking and John listening attentively.

When they arrived at the AMLI Downtown, the valet helped get Rebecca's luggage and the mysterious box she had brought with her. They hardly entered the penthouse door as John said, "Can I open the surprise now?"

Rebecca laughed and said, "Why don't you open a bottle of wine first. I'll change into something more comfortable, and we'll open it together in front of the fireplace."

While it was November, Austin was certainly not a cold-weather location this early in the fall. Rebecca wanted to create a relaxed atmosphere for John. She knew Saturday would be anything but restful as she had talked with Sarah on the flight up from the ranch. Peter Bridges called Sarah after the Governor's meeting. As a result, she and Jeremiah were ending their conference early to come to Austin.

John did as was requested and settled into the comfortable sofa near the fireplace. Rebecca joined him wearing jeans and an old oversized Aggie sweatshirt she often wore when relaxing. He was always amazed at how she could look beautiful in whatever she wore.

She joined him on the sofa, and John opened the box. It was stuffed with hundreds of handmade cards and letters from the children of the church. He began to take them out one by one and read them becoming more and more emotional with each one. Some of the children had drawn Aggie logos on them with a child's scribble of "Gig 'em!" in big letters; others had big hearts drawn in the center of the page with Scripture references of encouragement and affirmation; and, even more, obviously written by older teens and young women were stories of how they had been affected by the pain of abortion.

One particular note grabbed at his heart. It was from a young woman who had graduated from college last May. Her mom had raised her because her father had abandoned them at the news of her mother's pregnancy. They were juniors in high school when her mom became pregnant. Everyone wanted her to get an abortion. She nearly did. Somehow, as she was getting ready to go to the clinic for the procedure, her mother stopped at a red light two blocks away from the clinic, and an old man approached the car. It looked like he was going to be begging for a hand-out like many who stationed themselves on the downtown corners of Laredo, though he didn't. He walked up to the window and handed her a piece of paper, as he said, "God is enough. He loves you." There was a copy of the picture included with the note. It was a pencil drawing of Jesus gathering the little children to Him and smiling broadly. She wrote, "My mom told me that was the moment she knew she could never do anything to hurt me because I was God's gift to her."

As John finished reading, tears began to fall down his cheeks gently. The tears were not as shocking to Rebecca as his look. It seemed as if the weight of the world were on his shoulders as she heard him whisper through his tears, "It will all be worth it, won't it?"

Without another word spoken, she rested her head on his shoulder, and they watched the fire flicker on the hearth until John quietly said, "Thank you."

She kissed him deeply, and they went to bed.

Rebecca woke up earlier than John. She always did. He got up to the smell of bacon and fresh coffee drifting in from the kitchen. He threw on his jeans and walked into the large open living area. "Good morning! I hope you slept well."

Rebecca said, "I did! I always sleep well next to you." They ate breakfast on the balcony looking down Lavaca Street to the Colorado River, which ran through the center of Austin's downtown. It was a lovely morning. The weather was certainly cooperating for the games later that day.

Rebecca knew she would need to tell John of Sarah and Jeremiah's arrival later, but she hated to disturb the simple pleasure of the moment. She tried to be subtle, "Have you heard from Sarah lately?"

John answered, "No. I hope all is going well in DC."

Rebecca smiled.

He said, "What? Did I say something wrong?"

"Of course not," she answered. "But, she called me yesterday when I was in the air coming up here. She and Jeremiah are flying into Austin today."

John enthusiastically replied, "Great! Maybe we can see them while you're here."

Rebecca said, "I'm glad you feel that way. I told them we'd pick them up at the airport."

Once again, John finally got it. Rebecca was always a step or two ahead of him. John mused, "I wonder why they're coming back early?"

The morning flew by. John and Rebecca took the Suburban out to the airport themselves, giving their driver the weekend off. If John was going to drive, he preferred the SUV to the car. It felt more familiar to him, almost as if he were driving his old Chevy pickup along the ranch roads. Arriving at the airport, they met Jeremiah and Sarah as they exited the secured area to walk with them to the baggage claim. After gathering the luggage and getting into the SUV, they decided to get some lunch at the Cosmic Café. It was out of the way enough that they wouldn't need to worry about the football crowds and the outdoor setting was perfect for a day like today.

They arrived and seated themselves at a shaded table outside near the water feature. A myriad of colorful Koi swam lazily in the pool at the end of the constantly flowing waterfall. John and Jeremiah ordered one of their fall craft beers on tap, while Rebecca and Sarah opted for sweet teas. They all ordered from the Leroy and Lewis Food Truck. John's favorite was the Akaushi brisket from the Beeman Family Ranch in Gonzales County. Akaushi brisket is beef derived from a breed of cattle imported to Texas from Japan in the early 70s. It's even more expensive than "standard" Wagyu but well worth it. The girls opted for the Barbacado, a half avocado stuffed with barbacoa, and dressed with a light cilantro sauce.

After they had eaten and enjoyed some light conversation, Sarah said, "I heard the Governor switched sides, John. Do you need our help?"

John wasn't terribly surprised, though he was curious about how she had heard that news. He said, "Who is your source?"

Jeremiah laughed and said, "She has eyes and ears all over this town, John."

Sarah continued, "That's not important now. We think that it is going to be a bigger fight to get the bill signed than it is to get it passed." Sarah continued and named the legislators she knew would be supportive and some initial thoughts on a strategy of getting enough votes. And, just like that, John saw his peaceful weekend with Rebecca evaporate.

John remembered the letter from the young woman and realized that losing his peaceful days would be a small price to pay.

John said, "I have felt the Governor's support was disingenuous from the start. I guess I was just hoping it wouldn't come to a fight when he realizes he can't win."

Sarah smiling, said, "You're changing John. You've got the best of Daddy combined with your courage and compassion. I have never quite seen you like this before."

He said, "Thanks... I think!"

They all laughed, and he added, "Why don't we get Mateo and Sean together for lunch tomorrow and see if we can develop a more specific strategy for the staff on Monday?"

Chapter 18

The Team is Completed

November 3-4, 2018

"The sacred rights of mankind are not to be rummaged for among old parchments or musty records. They are written, as with a sunbeam, in the whole volume of human nature, by the hand of the divinity itself, and can never be erased or obscured by mortal power."

—Alexander Hamilton, "The Farmer Refuted,"
February 5, 1775

COME AND TAKE IT

Jeremiah and Sarah's arrival forced him to put the introduction of the new bill at the forefront of his schedule. He did take comfort in the fact that Rebecca was there. In fact, they had both agreed it would be better for her to remain in town for at least a week. She'd need to get some clothes sent up from the ranch, though that was a problem with an easy solution. She made a call to David Edwards and asked if he wouldn't mind Prudence Lambert to have them packed and loaded in the helicopter. Pastor David was already planning to be in the church's Austin location to preach Sunday, and it was his custom to take the helicopter in from Laredo.

Rebecca also phoned Prudence and requested she has them pack enough for a week. She was very familiar with Rebecca's preferences. She had grown up with John, going to high school and college with him. Their families were close. When John invited her to come home ten years ago, joining the business as the Executive Manager and CEO of the ranch with all its subsidiaries, she and Rebecca became fast friends. Prudence had become like a beloved sister during the years. The request would not be interpreted as an imposition.

Having the luggage delivered to the penthouse at AMLI wouldn't be difficult. Rebecca could check that detail off her list of things to do. She also wouldn't need to arrange the luncheon meeting for Sunday; Mateo would take care of that, though John would certainly forget to invite their spouses. She'd offer to take that off his plate. Of course, he was relieved at the suggestion.

It was early evening when Rebecca was able to talk to Mateo. After she told Mateo about Sarah's information concerning the Governor, she invited him and his spouse to lunch following church Sunday at the penthouse. She also asked him to contact Sean and invite him and his spouse. While she didn't know Sean well, she was acquainted with him through Jeremiah and Sarah. Besides, she was absolutely confident in John's choice.

Mateo was happy to do as she requested, however, he thought he'd better not surprise John and Rebecca with Sean's husband. He said, "No problem at all, Mrs. Lucas. However, I'm not sure if you are aware that Sean is gay. He and his husband, Patrick Beeman, have been married for three years. Is that OK?"

Rebecca quickly answered, "Of course it is."

Mateo apologized, "Yes ma'am. I just didn't want to cause any problems."

Rebecca laughed. She knew Mateo was worried about what John might think. She said, "John's a much bigger man than that, Mateo."

He stammered back, "Yes ma'am."

And, she reassured him again, "It's going to be all right, Mateo. Jeremiah and Sarah have collaborated with Patrick in DC. While they don't always agree, they are agreeable."

Rebecca wasn't quite sure how she was going to make sure John knew about Sean and Patrick. She'd have time to deal with that before lunch on Sunday. She would need to call a caterer to bring in a meal. She didn't have time to prepare anything at such short notice. Thinking it would be better kept simple, she decided on Pascal's. They specialized in Tex-Mex food and were excellent. She had used them in the past for many of John's political events. She made the call and had no trouble scheduling them, even though they typically required twenty-five people to cater an event.

Sunday morning, they all woke early enough to have a bite of breakfast on the balcony. John was the first to get up. He was sitting outside, drinking his coffee, and looking toward the Colorado River as the early morning mist rose. Rebecca joined him first, followed by Jeremiah and Sarah soon after. Their conversation was more about Saturday's football games than what might lay ahead politically.

John said, "Well, if nothing else goes right, "tu" lost to West Virginia, and the Aggies beat Mississippi State yesterday."

They all had a good laugh at that. Even though the University of Texas hadn't played A&M since the Aggies joined the SEC, the rivalry was still as fierce as ever. John was not one of those Austin politicos who wanted to revive the series. He remembered well how bitter the split was when A&M finally decided to leave the Big 12. He had no regrets in the regents' decision to change conferences. It had been an incredible move for Texas A&M.

Rebecca asked, "Are you going to brave the traffic and drive us to church?"

He laughed and said, "I think I'd rather let Jeremiah drive. The roads aren't nearly as empty here as they are in Webb County!"

That suited Rebecca fine. She was hoping she could steer the conversation toward Sean and Patrick while casually talking with Sarah. When they got into the SUV, Jeremiah took the driver's seat and John the front passenger seat, leaving Rebecca and Sarah in the second-row seating.

Rebecca began the conversation, "I've got Pascal's bringing in lunch today. I hope that's OK?"

John was first to voice his approval, "That's great! How did you pull that off? I thought they only catered big events."

She answered, "The Lucas name has some pull in this town."

Sarah laughed and said, "How many did you invite?" Rebecca said, "Only eight. There are Mateo and Sean with their spouses and us."

Sarah took the hint and said, "I'm glad you invited Patrick. He's an exceptionally bright young man. He's one of the best

lobbyists in Washington. We've worked with him quite a lot
over the past year."

John was lost. He said, "Patrick? Who's that?"

Sarah rescued Rebecca and said, "Oh, haven't you met
Sean's husband yet?"

John answered, "Obviously not." He smiled and knew he
had been set up perfectly again.

Sarah continued, "You'll like him. I'm sure you know his
father. They own the Beeman Ranch."

"Really?" John answered. "I can't wait to hear how he and
Sean met. An Irish Yankee and a cowboy from South Texas is an
interesting match."

Jeremiah turned into the parking lot and parked as close
as they could to the front door. As they were walking to the entrance, he said, "I wonder what kind of surprise Pastor David
has in mind today."

John immediately said, "Do you know something I don't?
I really don't want any more attention than I've already gotten."

Sarah said, "It's way too late for that, John."

As they walked into the large gathering place before entering the worship area, John noticed a crowd had gathered near
the bookstore in the far corner of the large room. The church
was very contemporary. They had developed the Austin ministry to reach young families and had been successful. It was the
biggest of the satellite locations with an average attendance of
two thousand people each Sunday. They had a coffee shop that
rivaled Starbucks in the gathering room. It had tables scattered
about for people to engage in conversation while watching the
broadcast from the worship service on strategically placed flat
screens. The bookstore was added to allow people to purchase
various media as further study and reference material accompanying David's current sermon series.

John was not particularly curious about the crowd gathered near the bookstore until he noticed the broadcast camera
and microphone set up. Sarah said, "I guess the media found
out Pastor David was in town today."

Before they could get through the entrance to the worship area, one of the greeters approached the group and said, "Good morning, Senator Lucas. Pastor David told us you would be here this morning and asked if you could meet him near the bookstore?"

He looked at them and asked, "Did y'all know about this?"

With angelic faces, they all assured him they had no knowledge of the ambush.

Rebecca said, "Go ahead, John. Remember, I'm on the front row."

He smiled broadly and followed the greeter.

David Edwards was already there, though obscured by the crowd of people. He noticed John approaching and interrupted the questions, "Excuse me. I see my dear friend coming in."

The reporters turned and saw he was talking about Senator Lucas. All of a sudden, their interview had gotten much more important. They separated for the pastor to walk through and greet John warmly. Of course, all of that was recorded for later broadcast. They gathered quickly around David and John and began to pepper them with questions.

David simply said, "The Lucas' are here with their family to worship. Let's allow them to find their places. After all, you're here to interview us about our new series for the Advent Season."

With that, he led them away from John, and they dutifully followed.

With just twenty minutes to conduct the interview, the media wanted to know more about the abortion bill than the Advent series. It was a cacophony of questions. One reporter raised her voice loudest as she asked, "Is the Senator here today to promote his anti-abortion bill?"

David Edwards was old and wise enough to deal with the inflammatory question easily. He turned to the camera and said, "I'm glad you've asked about the new legislation, though I think you may be surprised by my answer. I've known John

Lucas since he was born. If he is here today, he is here to worship the Lord. This is not a political venue for him or his family.
This is his community of faith."

A reporter interrupted, "But what about the timing of his
presence here today and the announcement last week of his
proposed abortion bill?"

David refocused their attention, "You will recall that I
called this interview to draw your attention to our new book,
'A Woman of Faith.' The first sermon in the Advent series that
I'll be preaching today is what the book is built around. We're
going to focus on the angel Gabriel's announcement to Mary,
the young virgin of this little town of Nazareth, that she would
give birth to God's Son, who would be the Savior of the world.
While it must have terrified her to hear those words, she accepted them with a faith rooted in her trust of God's will and
purpose for her."

Reporters are nothing if not persistent. Another said,
"What does that have to do with abortion?"

David said, "Who said it had anything to do with abortion? It has to do with life. Let me leave you with one question today: What did this young Jewish woman choose? Did
she choose life or not? Now, I must go to worship. You might
find it interesting to stay and hear the sermon. I'm going to be
answering those questions this morning."

With that he left them standing speechless. It would be
interesting to see how they spun his words.

John was very glad to get into the worship area without
any other interruptions, though he wondered what David was
up to. David Edwards rarely did anything without purpose.
Why did he want him to be ushered to him if not to speak to the
reporters? What plan was he executing? Fortunately for John,
all of these questions dissolved as the worship team began to
sing. The service went without any further incident until the
message.

David was in rare form today. His sermons were always
Biblically based with an absolute focus on the grace of God;

however, today was even better than usual. He began with a brief reading of the Annunciation to Mary in the first chapter of the Gospel According to Luke. In great detail, he described the tremendous sacrifice her pregnancy would mean for both she and her betrothed, Joseph. He also made it clear that Joseph at first was hesitant to accept the news. He wanted "to quietly put her away" as Luke recounted the experience.

David drew the parallel to Jochebed, the mother of Moses, from the Old Testament. He said both of these women, even in the face of severe challenges, found a way to choose life for their children. While he never used the word abortion, it was a masterful way of emphasizing God's great gift in life. He clearly showed the good in choosing life while not shaming any women who may have made other choices. He was, first and foremost, a man of grace. He was more concerned with correcting the future than condemning the past.

John and the others were leaving the church and purposefully walked out the door where David conversed with people as they left. They all greeted one another. John told his mentor, "Great message, pastor. Thank you!"

And, Sarah hugged David, and whispered into his ear, "Thank you pastor. You always help me see the wonder of God's grace."

David had tears well up in his eyes and smiled at her. He then looked back at John and said, "I'm in town all week if you'd like to buy me breakfast?"

John answered, "Count on it, Pastor. How about Wednesday?"

David said, "Perfect."

As they left the parking lot, Jeremiah said, "I wonder why Pastor David had the press here today?"

John said, "You must have been reading my mind. I was thinking the same thing."

Sarah merely laughed while Rebecca took up the challenge of stating the obvious for them. "Do you both really not understand?"

John and Jeremiah both said in unison, "No."

Rebecca went on, "Stereo ignorance, I see." Sarah laughed even more.

Jeremiah was a bit indignant, "Really, you don't need to mock us." They all laughed at the jovial repartee.

Then Sarah got serious and said, "He is making it impossible to sit this one out. His audience is too large to ignore, and, with so many legislators facing re-election, he just made pro-life the focal point of the debate. He has functionally shifted the political landscape."

They arrived at the AMLI and took the private elevator to the penthouse. They had a little time to change clothes before the others arrived. Their timing was near perfect. The doorbell chimed the "Aggie War Hymn about the time they finished dressing," announcing someone at the door. It was Pascal's with the food. As soon as the servers set everything up on the kitchen island for a buffet style meal, the door chimed again. Mateo and his wife, Sean and Patrick, had met in the lobby and rode the elevator up together.

Sean asked Mateo, "Is this typical when you work for the Senator?"

Mateo laughed and said, "Nope. You're getting to see a transformation of the apprentice to the master. I've been told that John's father was like this. He was driven and focused, a man who wielded his influence precisely as a surgeon would use a scalpel. He was a man to be reckoned with."

Sean said, "I hope I haven't made a mistake coming on board."

"You haven't." Mateo went on, "John has the best of both in him; and, he has Rebecca to balance him."

Standing at the door, they heard the chime play the "War Hymn," and Patrick said, "He takes his alma mater seriously, I see."

They were still laughing when John answered the door. Looking a little confused at their laughter, Mateo shifted to

Chief of Staff and said, "Sorry, Sir. The 'War Hymn' caught us a little off guard."

John laughed and said, "It's a bit pretentious, but Dad was like that. He had it installed years ago when he used this place for his Austin residence."

Introductions were made all around. Sean and Patrick were immediately put at ease by John's warmth and welcoming demeanor. Rebecca said, "I hope you like Tex-Mex. I had Pascal's cater today's lunch."

Then John said, "I have two rules for this afternoon. First, we are not in public; please relax. Call me John. I believe you're already on a first-name basis with everyone else. Second, I am interested to hear from everyone. Please feel free to speak your mind freely. We've set the table outside on the balcony. There's a nice breeze today. We'll eat out there and come inside for more discussion later. Please, help yourself."

Chapter 19

The Political Landscape Is Sharply Focused

November 5, 2018

"Now my venerated friend, you will perceive that Texas is presented to the union as a bride adorned for her espousal. But if, now so confident of the union, she should be rejected, her mortification would be indescribable. She has sought the United States, and this is the third time she has consented. Were she now to be spurned it would forever terminate expectation on her part, and it would then not only be left for the United States to expect that she would seek some other friend, but all Christendom would justify her course dictated by necessity and sanctioned by wisdom."

— Sam Houston to Andrew Jackson, February 16, 1844

COME AND TAKE IT

Sunday's lunch and informal planning session were incredibly productive in more ways than mere political planning. John was energized by the group's diversity and positive debate. However, he had no idea of the importance that it would become in the months ahead. The addition of Patrick Beeman to the core group was a great coup in light of his knowledge of the political landscapes of both Texas and Washington.

John was a little later than usual arriving at the office and was surprised by Sean and Mateo at the front entrance. After all these years, he was still surprised that Mateo seemed to know the precise time of his arrival to meet him before he walked into the building.

Mateo cheerfully chimed, "Good morning, Senator. I hope you slept well."

John was both flattered and glad to see him first that morning. "It was a great evening. Thank you again for coming over." He looked toward Sean and added, "I was so glad to meet Patrick."

An apprehensive look appeared on Sean's face, and John added, "All is good, Sean. However, I do have a question."

They continued their walk up the stairs to the entrance as Sean simply said, "Yes Sir, what can I do for you?"

John stopped for a moment and looked directly at him, asking, "Why is it that I haven't met Patrick before now?"

Sean had been preparing for this moment since he accepted the position on the Senator's staff. He had a little speech prepared and rehearsed, though it seemed completely inappro-priate in light of the acceptance he had been extended over the last few weeks. He almost stumbled with his words, "Well, Sir, I guess I wasn't sure that I could keep my job if you knew."

John said, "Keep your job... I cannot imagine going for-ward without you. Just because we disagree in some areas doesn't mean we cannot work together. I've found disagree-ment and congenial debate brings us to a stronger position. And that brings me to my next question. Do you think Patrick would be willing to join our staff?"

They continued walking into the main office as Sean gath-ered his thoughts for an answer. John said, "I see I've surprised you. That was not my intention. I really think he and I ought to talk about coming on board. I like his honesty."

"But, Sir," Sean said, "he isn't an advocate of strengthen-ing the laws against abortion."

John countered, "Exactly. I think it would be very prof-itable to have his voice on our staff. He strikes me as someone who could balance my emotional investment in this legislation with a clearer understanding of those on the opposing side."

Sean went on a bit further, "Well, Sir, there's also the fact that he makes a lot of money in his position."

John chuckled, "I think I can manage it, Sean."

"Yes, Sir," he said in return.

John said more seriously this time, "I mean no disrespect, but I am willing to make personal sacrifices to finish this job. If that means I need to supplement his salary personally, I am committed to this course."

Sean was nearly speechless. Taking the pressure off Sean, John said, "Mateo, could you contact Patrick and see if he'd be willing to visit with us before he returns to Washington?"

Mateo said, "I will be happy to do so, Sir."

John said, "And, Mateo, please stop with the 'Sir.' Call me John."

Mateo would not do that, especially in the workplace. He smiled at the Senator and said, "Yes, Sir." They all laughed.

As all three of them entered the office, they were greeted by the other staff. John's scheduler handed him his messages. John saw an addition in the smaller conference room. Whiteboards had been hung with the names of all the legislators divided by their Senate or House positions with columns beside each name labeled "for," "against," or "undecided." Several interns were already engaged on the phone that morning. Mateo explained they were already polling the members of the House and Senate concerning their positions. They would be more decisive as the bill came out of the Little Committee and was printed and delivered to their offices. John saw there were already some legislators identified as "for." That was encouraging. He continued into his office while Mateo went to his desk.

Leafing through the phone messages, John was surprised at the number of calls from the media. He also noticed there were a few calls that would require his immediate attention. Those included messages from Peter Bridges, the Governor's Chief of Staff; Lydia Smithson; Dylan Walker; and David Edwards. He decided to return them in order of easy to difficult. He buzzed his scheduler and asked her to phone David Edwards, Dylan Walker, Peter Bridges, and then Lydia Smithson. He also told her that if Patrick Beeman called, he wanted to take that call immediately. He had the feeling that his day was going to be challenging and harried.

When his scheduler called David Edwards' office, she spoke to his office administrator and realized it was merely a confirmation of a breakfast meeting with John on Wednesday. She was familiar with their relationship and confirmed it without bothering John with that detail.

Before she could get General Walker on the phone, she received a call from Sarah's administrative assistant at Texan's for Life. It seemed that things were as hectic in their office as they were in the Senator's office. She asked if the Senator could be available for a conference call that day with Jeremiah, Sarah, and the State Attorney General. She thought that call would need an immediate answer and put them on hold while she

went directly to the Senator. John knew that neither Jeremiah
nor Sarah would ask for that call if it was not urgent. He told
her to set it up at their earliest convenience, clearing his schedule if necessary.

The Attorney General was one of the most influential
members of the Tea Party in Texas. The Tea Party was born out
of a conference of conservative legislators whose goal was to
examine how government works and how they could force
changes to make officials more accountable. It was a seed that
quickly blossomed on the national stage with calls from grass-
roots activists to cut federal spending, taxes, and the size of
government, and reduce the federal deficit. It burgeoned in size
when the Democratic Party was installed in the White House,
as well as both the Senate and House in 2009. This forced an expansion of focus in state government, especially in Austin. The
Tea Party transitioned to a coalition approach in government
having great influence in Texas. Tea Party caucuses had grown
their ranks in both the Texas House and Senate and were now
recognized as the "Freedom and Liberty Caucuses."

The conference call was scheduled for mid-afternoon.
Jeremiah and Sarah, along with a few other key staffer members from their office, would meet John and his principle staff at
his office. John had a larger conference room where they would
use the more advanced video conferencing technology. Even
though John did not like technology, he had equipped his staff
with the latest equipment allowing much more efficient flow of
information.

Before any other calls could be made, Mateo informed
John that Patrick was planning to return to DC later in the week,
and his schedule was flexible until then. John seized the serendipitous opportunity, "Can he meet us for lunch?"

Mateo answered, "I'll set it up. How many shall I make
reservations for?"

John said, "Make them for four."

John wanted Sean to be a part of the conversation. It would
expedite the decision process after he offered Patrick a position.

While the office continued to buzz with activity, John was connected to General Walker. The General told John he had developed several engagement plans and was going to present them to the Governor later in the day. He wanted to know if he'd like to be present at that meeting. John's day was already developing into a scheduling nightmare; and, it didn't seem appropriate for him to be in that briefing.

As he declined, Walker asked, "May I email you copies for your records?" That seemed very odd to John, but he agreed.

Dylan Walker was always cautious. He had practiced careful planning for every possible contingency before any engagement. However, just as it happened in Waco years ago, he did not know others had made plans he could not have anticipated. Carson Bradley's *Houston Plan* would take everyone by surprise.

Mateo secured reservations at Perry's Steakhouse and Grille downtown. He, Sean, and John met Patrick at the restaurant at noon, giving them plenty of time before the three o'clock conference call that afternoon. Patrick had arrived before them and was seated at the table. John was glad to see he was dressed casually. He must have taken his cue from Sean as he left for the office that morning. After greeting one another, they seated themselves and were immediately approached by their server for lunch.

He addressed John first, "May I get you something to drink, Senator Lucas?"

John thought, "Does everyone in Austin watch the news?" He was accustomed to being able to sneak into a restaurant before the media had made him the focus of their nightly news. That was another thing that had evaporated since the press conference. At least they didn't see any other legislators in the restaurant. John ordered an Old Fashioned, which was one of the signature non-alcoholic drinks at Perry's. The others added their orders.

The server then asked if they wanted to start with any appetizers, and John replied, "Can we get a double order of Bacon

Wrapped Scallops and a large order of Tempura Fried Lobster Tails?"

The server continued and asked if they were ready to place their *entrée* order or would they need additional time.

John said, "I think we're ready." They all ordered the Lunch-cut Filet, and the server retreated to place their orders.

As soon as the server had left, John said, "Thanks for meeting us here, Patrick. I know your schedule is hectic enough without things being added at the last moment."

Patrick answered quickly, "No problem, Senator. It is my privilege."

Once again, John felt the formality of titles pinching his deSire to conduct business with more cordiality. He smiled and said, "As I said yesterday, please call me John."

"Yes Sir," he replied immediately. John knew these young men were too professional to let go of his title and seniority. John continued, "What are you working on now?"

Patrick remarked that things were relatively slow in Congress right now, and said, "With most of the emphasis being placed on immigration, I've been primarily involved with the Catholic Legal Immigration Network, the ACLU, and the National Immigration Law Center. We are lobbying the House and Senate concerning the lack of medical care currently being provided in the detention centers. They are being forced to operate well over capacity as a result of the new Executive Orders signed in recent months."

Patrick went on, "The children being detained, often separated from their family members, don't deserve this lack of treatment. They have little control over their situation and how they got there in the first place."

John couldn't help making the connection between the work Patrick was doing and the issue of abortion, but he reserved his comments for another time. He wanted to hear more from Patrick about his motivation for this kind of work. John asked, "What brought you to this kind of work?"

Patrick laughed and said, "Well, Sir, that's a long story. I'm not sure you have the time for that."

John became serious and said, "I have as much time as it takes. I am very interested in getting to know you better."

The appetizers came at just the right time. It gave Patrick a moment to think through why John Lucas would want to know his story. He concluded it was an expression of a genuine deSire to get to know him. He began his story with being raised on his family ranch and studying at Texas A&M University.

John interrupted, "I noticed your ring yesterday."

Patrick said, "Yes, Sir, though I don't have the Aggie War Hymn as my doorbell!" He went on to say that he had developed a great love for politics and especially Texas history. "That's actually how Sean and I met in Georgetown." John made the connection now. They were both Texans.

Their food came and Patrick continued his story through the meal. "I have always felt that there are so many people who are disenfranchised from the basic rights guaranteed to them in our constitution. I believe that the words of President Lincoln in his Gettysburg Address are true. His exhortation was that we should resolve ourselves 'that all those who have died shall not have died in vain—that this nation, under God, shall have a new birth of freedom—and that government of the people, by the people, for the people, shall not perish from the earth.' I am convinced that will not happen without committed advocates. I am one of those advocates. And I feel the best way for me to be an advocate for those without a voice is as a lobbyist."

John realized there was a depth to this young man far beyond his years. He had made his decision. Both Mateo and Sean had been silent during the entire meal. They almost interrupted the moment, but John said, "I agree. That's why I want you to join our staff."

Patrick was completely surprised by the offer. He said, "Sir, I'm not sure I can support your efforts. I believe a woman ought to be the sole decision-maker when it comes to her health."

John was quick to respond, "I do too. However, I also believe that every child, born or unborn, also has certain rights, but somewhat like the children along the border being separated from their parents, they have no one to advocate for them. Help us get this right for both the mother and the child."

Patrick was amazed at the depth of John Lucas. He had misread him. That was not something he often did. However, he recognized something very different about him than the other politicians he had met. "How long do I have for a decision, Sir?" he asked.

John said, "How long do you need?"

Patrick looked at Sean, and said, "Can Sean and I talk about this and I will get back to you tomorrow?"

"John said, "Absolutely."

As John and Mateo returned to the office, Sean stayed behind with Patrick to talk about the offer. Sean was the first to speak, "I hope you don't think I ambushed you. I had no real idea that the Senator was going to offer you a job immediately. He asked me earlier whether you might consider it, and I told him you differed with him on his abortion position."

Patrick replied quickly, "You know I'm not mad at you, right? Besides, I'm not so sure we're that far apart. I might be able to make a much bigger difference here than in Washington. And working with you would be a lot better for us than traveling so much." Sean was grateful he had found such a great partner in life.

Patrick did voice one question, "I do wonder if he knows how much I make. I don't think it's a good idea for me to take a pay cut right now."

Sean said, "I told the Senator you made a lot more money in the private rather than the public sector. He practically laughed that away while he said money was not going to be a problem."

Patrick said, "There's really something vastly different about him than some of the folks inside the beltway."

They talked a bit more and agreed it was the right move to make. They would go back to the office and tell John immediately.

John and Mateo returned to the office just as busy as when they had left. Phone conversations were being held by the interns and staff as they tried to move the legislators from "undecided" to "for" on the board. It didn't seem they were having much success. John thought, "This is why we need Patrick."

Jeremiah and Sarah were in the conference room, making sure everything was set up for the video conference call when John walked in and asked, "Got everything you need?"

Sarah said, "Sure, it's our new home away from home."

John had a little time and thought he'd better return Peter Bridges' call before the video conference. He asked his scheduler to make that call and put it through to the conference room. Before calling Peter, she told him that he had called three additional times while he was at lunch. When John picked up the phone, he was a little surprised to be told that the Governor was waiting on the line instead of his Chief of Staff.

John said, "Good afternoon, Governor. I'm sorry I didn't call earlier. I have been otherwise engaged."

The Governor responded, "I'm sure you have, although I'm not accustomed to being placed at the end of the line, Senator."

John knew better than to take that bait. "What can I help you with, Perry?"

It irked the Governor to be called by his first name from someone he considered a subordinate. John knew that but couldn't resist a gentle reminder that he did not consider himself to be his subordinate.

The Governor plowed ahead, "I was disappointed to see you conferring with the Mann's Saturday night. I hope you are not going to bring your family ties with Texans for Life into the fight."

John returned with a deflection, "Fight? What fight are you referring to, Perry?"

Then John heard Peter Bridges voice in the background. Peter said with more clarity, "John, I've put us on speaker. I hope you don't mind?"

John replied, "Of course not, Peter. It is always good to hear your voice of reason in the conversation."

Peter thought this was not typical for John Lucas at all. He was relentless, though subtly demanding positional equality, if not superiority, from the Governor. Peter smiled at that thought. He had long ago grown weary of the backroom deals and bullying from the Governor.

Peter said, "I think what the Governor was referring to is the need for patience while your bill makes its way through the normal legislative process before being introduced to the House and Senate. We don't want to complicate its approval with any unnecessary politicizing of such a hot issue."

John replied with restraint but still firm, "As you both know, I am completely committed to doing whatever is necessary to have this law take effect before the close of the coming Legislative Session. I will pour the full weight of my resources and influence into accomplishing that goal."

With that, the Governor disconnected the call leaving his Chief of Staff to apologize for the breach of etiquette. John thanked him and said, "No problem, Peter. I'm beginning to get a clearer picture of the political landscape now."

Sarah said, "That seemed to go well." Jeremiah and John both burst out laughing.

John said, "Well, he boils my blood!"

Sarah simply replied, "Good."

John looked toward the office's main door and saw Sean coming in. He walked out just about the time Patrick entered the doorway. John smiled and said, "You're back earlier than I expected."

Sean was first to speak, "I wouldn't miss this call for anything, Sir."

Sean made his way to the conference room, and Patrick said, "Never thought I'd be working for a Republican, Sir, but here I am. What can I do?"

John said, "Who said I was a Republican? I'm not sure I like that label anymore. If you need a few days to wind things up in DC, you don't need to be here. We can wait."

Patrick said, "I don't think you can, Sir. No disrespect to you or your staff."

Jeremiah and Sarah walked out to greet Patrick, and Sarah said, "No disrespect taken. And, you're absolutely correct. John just had a wonderful conversation with the Governor as he told him to go to hell."

"I didn't say that, Sarah," John quickly protested.

She said in her deadpan voice, "Might as well have."

Patrick looked at Sean, and he shrugged his shoulders as if to say, "Don't ask me. I have no clue."

John gathered everyone's attention and said, "This is Patrick Beeman. He will be our Legislative Director and in charge of our lobbying initiatives in both the House and Senate. He will also be working with any outside groups who have an interest in helping us get the bill passed."

Jeremiah and Sarah exchanged a look, and Sarah said, "Guess I'll need to set another plate at the table. Welcome aboard, Patrick."

She was very pleased with her brother. Daddy would be proud. She would tell him so later.

As the call began to connect and each participant was added to the conference screen, Sarah wrote a note on the personal iPads each of them had been given for private communication within their group during the call. It was a simple means of testing their connectivity. John's group consisted of himself, Jeremiah, Sarah, the Director of Litigation for Texans for Life, Mateo, Sean, and Patrick.

She made sure everyone knew the participants joining the Attorney General by noting each on their iPads. Perhaps the biggest surprise was Lydia Smithson. How she got an invitation to this call was a mystery to Sarah; however, she identified her to the group with her name and a witch riding a broom drawn beside it. John scowled at her from across the table, and she smiled innocently. Jeremiah just shook his head, knowing the playful way Sarah had of provoking her brother at times. It did have the deSired effect of lightening his mood, especially in light of the governor's earlier conversation.

Once everyone was in place, the Attorney General introduced the people from his office; Lydia inserted herself as the Governor's representative; Jeremiah introduced himself and Sarah along with their Director of Litigation from TFL, and John introduced his group.

The meeting was congenial and informational. It seemed like it was more of a fishing expedition on the Attorney General's part than anything else. John was glad that Sean was there. He was able to recap the bill's basics that were being printed for submission to the Little Committee this Wednesday. The AG remarked that they had expedited the process incredibly well. He also expressed his concerns about the constitutionality of a few points to which the Director of Litigation of TFL cited several opinions and decisions already made by SCOTUS due to the challenges of similar laws passed in other states.

The only real flare-up came when Lydia Smithson asked John if the bill passed his plan for handling all the protests when the clinics began to be shut down was? John couldn't help but notice the use of "if" instead of "when" in her question. He knew Lydia well enough to know it was purposeful.

While Lydia was asking the question, Sarah drew a big smiley face on the iPad, which popped up in front of John. It immediately drew a smile on his face, and he calmly answered, "I can understand the Governor's concern in this regard; and, I'm glad you asked this question. In an earlier conversation with General Dylan Walker today, I was informed the Governor has already contacted him with a request for rules of engagement and specific plans for each of the sites in question. He offered to email them to me once the Governor has been updated this afternoon. I'm sure the Governor will update you as well, Lydia."

Sarah wrote, "Home Run!" on the iPad.

The others added their own exclamation points to the message and pressed "send."

There were a few more questions, though they were all benign. The conference call ended, and John physically slumped in his chair at the relief of that being behind him.

By this time, it was nearly five o'clock. John asked if they would like to get a burger at Wink's.

Sarah said, "Rebecca's already got food ready for us at the penthouse. I think she'd be disappointed if we went to Wink's."

John looked at her and said, "How do you know that?"

Sarah smiled and said, "I FaceTimed her on my phone so she could be on the front row, John."

He was speechless. He said, "I don't know what to say."

Sarah said, "Let's eat would be sufficient. By the way, you did great today, John. I'm proud of you."

Tears were beginning to form in his eyes, and he could only reply, "OK, let's eat!"

John arrived first at the penthouse. When he walked in, Rebecca was finishing a floral arrangement for the center of the buffet the staff had set for everyone. She rushed to him and threw her arms around him, kissing him deeply.

He said, "What was that for?" She said, "Just because I love you. Now, get comfortable. Our team will be arriving soon."

As the others began to arrive, Rebecca greeted them warmly. When she got to Patrick, the team's newest member, she said, "Glad you joined us."

He still couldn't quite put his finger on it, but there was something much bigger happening here than a new piece of legislation.

Chapter 20

The Conflict Escalates

December 15-25, 2018

"If ever the time should come, when vain and aspiring men shall possess the highest seats in government, our country will stand in need of its experienced patriots to prevent its ruin."

— Samuel Adams

COME AND TAKE IT

John finally found himself resting in his swing, home for the holidays. South Texas winters were mild enough to allow for a pleasant afternoon outdoors. It was still too cool for Rebecca to join him for more than a few minutes, but she had been with him throughout the months spent in Austin. Even when she had to go home to help JV and Abby with school activities, she came back to Austin to support him.

The two months since his visit with David Edwards in Austin were revealing. The political landscape had become crystal clear. Some he thought would be staunch supporters who had turned against the bill as a result of the heavy-handed coercion of the Governor. Lydia Smithson had become an outspoken critic of the bill succumbing to the pressure of the funding for her political aspirations of a seat on the Texas State Supreme Court. Their promised support by the pro-choice groups was essential to her success.

He understood how that could happen, but he still struggled with the idea that anyone could put personal gain above others' needs. It was easy to see the opposition born out of true conviction; however, most of his opposition was not rooted in belief. The Governor had told him in one of his more candid moments: "It's just how politics work." If that was true, he hoped he never became a politician.

David had warned him about the motives of people as they pressed forward. He hadn't missed it by much. One of his drawings about choices still burned in his mind. David often drew three circles in a line and one centered beneath them, each connected by a line. The bottom circle was always labeled with whatever choice might be in question. The circles above were labeled, left to right, "stay the same," "quit," and "change." He would always firmly assert that "you get what you get because you go where you go." It was a personal interpretation of a passage from Paul's writing that a man "reaps what he sows." John believed that truth, which led him to conclude that he had chosen not to remain the same and therefore taken away the status quo. However, many had chosen to "quit." That looked like a full assault on John, his family, and his team. It had nothing to do with the issue before them.

The bill, now dubbed "Sarah's Law," had made its way through the Little Committee and was ready for reading into the session, which was to begin in two weeks. Along with Jeremiah and Sarah, his team had worked tirelessly in the intervening months to get to this point. It appeared the coalition that had been built was holding together, and the vote would be anticlimactic.

As Christmas drew nearer, John concentrated more on spending time with JV and Abby than the 2019 Legislative Session opening. He felt that he had been away far too long while getting Sarah's Law ready for the vote. He knew they understood, but he was very sensitive to his absence. He was looking forward to a hog hunt with JV on Monday. That would be JV's first day of Winter Break. Abby would tag along, though her preferred *weapon* was the Sony Cyber-shot DSC-RX10 IV Digital Camera John gave her last Christmas. She also enjoyed being the designated driver on the expedition across the *sendero* while John and JV looked for a sign to begin their stalk.

Jeremiah and Sarah were due in town later that week. They always spent Christmas with John and Rebecca at the ranch. Perhaps he and Jeremiah would take the old Crockett rifle down and fire it a time or two to be able to say they did. It was still in working condition, and firing it a few times during the year actually helped maintain the long rifle's condition.

Perhaps that would quiet Jeremiah's continued jibes that he would need that weapon for the coming revolution. The absolute last thing on John's mind was any sort of revolution, much less one needing weapons.

However, unknown to John, such an event was indeed brewing. Carson Bradley had been hospitalized earlier in December with continued complications resulting from the debacle at the Waco Siege.

It was ten days ago when Bradley had been admitted to the Houston Methodist Lung Center. That was not unusual. However, this time some complications extended his stay. It was not lost on him when the director of his respiratory team informed him that they had found a mass in his upper right lobe that might involve a lung resection. The timing couldn't be any worse. He felt he was so close to seeing the Houston Plan executed. One of the first calls he made was to his old friend Dylan Walker.

General Walker immediately left for Houston to visit with his old friend when he received notification of his condition's seriousness. It wasn't a long drive from Austin to Houston, though it felt like he couldn't get there fast enough. Dylan's mind wandered back to that day. He had always felt responsible for his friend's injuries. If he would have protested more to the FBI's plan, if he would have insisted on more time, if he would have picked someone else, if he would have delayed entrance to the hostage's room, if he would have retreated to regroup, all of these *if's* had never gone away since that day. The woulda-coulda-shoulda haunted him as much now as ever before.

General Walker arrived unannounced at Carson's private suite finding him talking to his chief lieutenant from the Texans for Independence. Just before he entered the room, he heard him them talking in hushed tones. There was something about concrete encasements and the radio transmitters' distance, but they immediately stopped talking when he entered the room. It struck him as odd, but his concern was the health of his friend, not some crazy fireworks display they were planning to ring in the New Year. He walked in, and warmly greeted his friend.

Bradley said, "Today's a good day for war, isn't it, General?"

Dylan was stunned by that greeting. Bradley quickly disarmed any alarm his friend might have when he said, "It is December 7th, Dylan. Lighten up, soldier."

They both had a good laugh, and the General remained in the dark concerning any plans Bradley had. He then turned serious and said, "The only war I'm worried about right now is the one going on in your lungs."

Bradley smiled broadly and replied, "Awe hell, General, I fought worse than this off with a lot less help. The doctors around here have everything under control."

And, with that, Bradley began to reminisce about some of their old missions while serving together. They visited together for most of the day until Bradley lit up a hand-rolled Cuban cigar smuggled in by his lieutenant. Alarms sounding and nurses rushing in to see the patient smoking were more than enough to get the General politely dismissed. Dylan left with a promise to return soon. Bradley assured him he'd call if there were any change in his condition.

On the way out, General Walker found the charge nurse and asked if he could be contacted should any change in Bradley's condition occur. He was informed that he was not on the list for release of information and that it would have to come from the family or patient. Bradley had no family. And the General was unsure whether he would receive that call from him. He pressed the charge nurse harder with his position, and she held firm. Finally, she relented a little and gave him a form to fill out and promised to have Bradley sign it. Dylan filled it out with her waiting and all but marched her into Bradley's room, where he said, "Sign the release, you old dog. It's the only way I can find out how you're doing."

Bradley laughed and scribbled his signature across the bottom.

Monday, December 10th, saw Bradley's health continue to deteriorate and the doctors determined that both radiation and chemotherapy were no longer options. Their recommendation was for resection of the upper lobe of his right lung. While the recuperation time was lengthy, they felt his condition would only worsen should they attempt chemotherapy or radiation, perhaps making the surgical procedure less viable. Bradley agreed to the surgery, and it was scheduled for the following day.

General Walker was informed of the scheduled operation and immediately called one of his old friends in the Navy. Rear Admiral Samuel Schultz was the chief medical officer of the Marine Corps and familiar with the injuries Bradley had received at the Waco Siege.

Dylan called him and asked without preamble, "Have you heard about Bradley?"

The Admiral answered, "I have Dylan. The doctors have been in touch with us, and we have sent everything we have on the scarring in his lungs."

Dylan started, "If anything happens..."

The Admiral continued, "He's in the best hands in the country. Houston Lung is the best in the world."

Dylan calmed down a bit and said, "I don't care what it costs; I want him to have the best."

Again the Admiral assured him, "The Navy has got that covered. He has the best right now; but, remember, this was always an eventuality."

On the day of surgery, Dylan was there before his friend went in. He assured him he would be waiting there when it was over. It was a lengthy procedure. It went without any complications, though the scar tissue slowed the procedure. Bradley was in surgery for four hours during which the General became more and more anxious about his old friend's condition.

Finally, the head surgeon came out to talk to those waiting. Being directed to Dylan, who was the only designated *family*, he said, "The surgery went well. However, we won't know the full extent of the results from the lymph nodes we removed until tomorrow."

"Lymph nodes?" Dylan asked.

The surgeon explained that the process included both the removal of the lobe where the mass was located and the removal of as many lymph nodes as possible to attempt to eradicate the cancer cells before it spread further completely. Dylan's anxiety was further escalated, and his determination to make things right for his friend only grew.

During the intervening hours, as Bradley recovered from the anesthesia, Dylan called the Governor to inform him of Bradley's status. While the Governor was not a fan of Texans for Independence, regarding the movement as frivolous and a mere distraction, he was genuinely concerned for the well-being of one of Waco's heroes. He knew the history of the federal overreach and the lives lost because of it. He had often remarked how things would have been different had he been President.

When the Governor answered his call, Dylan said, "Good afternoon, Governor. I hope your day is going well."

The Governor answered quickly, "It is. How did the surgery go for Bradley?"

The General replied gravely, "I'm afraid there is good news and no news, Sir. Bradley did well through the procedure, but we won't know all the results until tomorrow concerning the spread of the malignancy."

Genuinely, the Governor said, "I'm sorry, Dylan. I hope there is good news there as well. I know how much your friendship has meant through the years."

Of course, as was usually true for Governor Perry Thompson, he was never thinking only about others. In this case, he recognized that being concerned about Bradley would help his opposition to the bill sponsored by John. He didn't want to risk pushing TFI toward supporting John's bill.

The next day Dylan was still at the bedside of his friend when the surgeon made his rounds. Walking into the room, the doctor greeted everyone, but spoke directly to Bradley, "Good morning, Mr. Bradley, I hope you slept well?"

Bradley answered with as much bravado as possible, given his condition, "I did as well as can be expected with all those nurses hovering over me all night." Dylan smiled, knowing that was a good sign from his friend.

The doctor continued, "We have your results back from the tissue and lymph nodes. It appears we were able to resect the entire lobe containing the mass successfully. It was confirmed to be a non-small cell cancer, more specifically squamous cell carcinoma. We also removed a number of lymph nodes that contained the same cells."

Bradley interrupted, "Get to it, Doc. What's the bottom line?"

Somewhat taken aback at the gruffness in Bradley's voice and demeanor, the surgeon said, "Very well, Mr. Bradley, we were not able to get all of the affected nodes. The likelihood of complete removal of the cancer is very low. My recommendation is a course of treatment with both radiation and chemotherapy as soon as you are able."

"How long do I have?" Bradley asked.

"Your overall health is strong for your age and condition, which is a benefit in the course of therapy."

Again Bradley interrupted, "Do any of you people ever answer questions directly?"

In an effort to remain calm, the doctor said, "With treatment we have seen patients respond with an additional 12 -18 months."

"What if I decline treatment?" he asked.

The doctor said, "With no treatment, perhaps six months; with radiation alone, perhaps you would have 12-18 months. If you add the chemotherapy on top of that, you could have three years."

The room was very quiet until Bradley finally said, "Thank you." He shut his eyes and continued, "I see I have some decisions to make."

Dylan said, "What decision? We'll fight this like any engagement. We've beat worse odds than this."

Bradley breathed heavily and sighed, "Thanks, old friend, but I've been fighting this war for a long time. It may be time for a strategic retreat."

Dylan stayed as long as Bradley would allow it. After he left, Bradley had some quiet time to think his way through the coming months. The surgery had left him immobilized temporarily. However, that wouldn't raise any particular problem. Nothing could happen until the spring after the bill was passed into law. He was sure the Governor would delay signing it until the end of the legislative session. Even if the state moved immediately to enforce closing the clinics, the process would take months. Houston would be the last to comply. They would fight the law in the courts; there would be restraining orders, appeals.

It looked like summer or even early fall before the plan would need to be implemented. He concluded that he needed to buy an additional six months from the treatment. He had worked too long and too hard not to see the fruit of his labor. Bradley then concluded radiation would be necessary. He'd inform the oncological team the next day.

After Dylan had been dismissed by Bradley, he decided to call John Lucas. While the Senator didn't know Bradley personally, he knew of him through TFI. Perhaps he would have an update that would be an encouragement to him.

It was a surprise for John to answer the phone. Dylan expected it to go to voicemail. "Howdy, General, getting ready for Christmas?" John asked.

Dylan answered, "No. Actually, I'm in Houston with an old friend, Carson Bradley. He was admitted to Houston Methodist and underwent lung surgery yesterday."

John genuinely expressed his concern, "I'm sorry to hear that, Dylan. Is he going to be OK?"

"I'm afraid not," Dylan said. "The doctors have outlined some treatment plans, but none of them give him very long."

John said, "You know I'll be praying for him. Is there anything else I can do?"

Dylan went on, "He's been following your bill's progress closely. He is very supportive. I was wondering if you had any encouraging news I could pass on."

John said, "I wasn't aware our interests intersected, although I am very glad to hear of his support. My staff has informed me the bill will reach the floor immediately upon the opening of the session, and we have enough votes in both the House and Senate to pass it with very little debate."

Dylan said, "That is good news. I will pass that along. Is the Governor still supportive?"

John laughed, "General, I think you know the answer to that better than I do. Perhaps your friend could use his influence on him."

Dylan knew exactly where the Governor stood on the bill. He would delay it until the last moment before signing it. Lucas might be right about Bradley exerting a little subtle pressure on the Governor. It would give him something to do and take his mind off the recuperative process. Dylan said, "That's a great idea, John. Thanks! And, again, thanks for taking my call. Please express my best to your family."

The call from Dylan troubled John. He couldn't help but feel like he ought to do more to help the General's friend. He told Rebecca about the conversation and his concerns. Rebecca always had a solution to his conundrums. She said, "Why don't we fly up to Houston and pick up Jeremiah and Sarah for Christmas? You could run by the hospital and visit with Mr. Bradley in person."

"What are they doing in Houston? He asked.

She said, "Jeremiah is the speaker for Houston Baptist University's fall commencement. They were going to take a commercial flight here anyway."

John agreed quickly. It was a perfect plan. He asked Rebecca, "Will you call them and arrange that? I'll call Dylan and see if he thinks that would be a good idea."

She said, "Of course."

The following day John and Rebecca arrived in Houston early in the afternoon. Sarah met them at the heliport near Hobby International. They planned to split up, with John going to the hospital to make his visit and later meeting them at the University for Jeremiah's address.

John arrived at the hospital and was met by General Walker at the door to Bradley's room. Dylan expressed his gratitude for John coming up to see his friend. He warned him that he was heavily medicated though alert and looking forward to the visit. John did wonder about the preemptory warning about medication. He would find out the reason for that shortly.

As they walked into the room, Dylan made the introduction, and Bradley responded with appreciation for the visit. Bradley said, "I suppose Dylan has warned you sufficiently about my disdain for politicians."

Dylan interrupted, "He's one of the good guys."

Bradley plowed ahead, "He's still breathing. Kinda like snakes; they're no good until you shoot 'em, and they stop wigglin'." Then he looked directly at John and asked, "Why did you come? What is it you want from me?"

John certainly hoped this was the medication doing the talking. He responded, "I don't want anything, Mr. Bradley. I hoped it might be an encouragement to both Dylan and you if I were able to come and visit with you personally."

Bradley softened a bit and said, "I understand you're presenting your bill soon, and it looks like it is going to pass."

"Yes Sir, it does," John answered.

Bradley said, "Good luck getting' that back-room, self-serving Governor to sign it. I wouldn't trust him as far as I could throw him, which I would very much like to do. Those are the kind of men who put me in this bed in the first place. I don't count them worth much more than fodder for the cannons."

John could only say, "I think we can apply enough pressure that it will be signed into law by the end of the session."

Bradley tried to laugh, and it turned into a painful spasm. Dylan started to call the nurse, and Bradley said, "Leave it alone, Dylan. I'm tougher than that. Besides, I do want to hear more from Lucas."

Bradley asked John to tell him why he was so committed to the bill. John told him enough of the story to fill in some of the blanks; and finished the story with, "He'll sign the bill Mr. Bradley. Of that, I can assure you."

Bradley saw something in John's eyes that he had seen many times before on the battlefield. There was a resolve there that made him believe John's commitment. Bradley said, much softer this time, "I believe you Senator. What can I do to help you?"

John was surprised by the sudden turn in Bradley's demeanor and attitude. He said, "I think you could get yourself well, Mr. Bradley. I'm certain we need more men like you. You are a man of considerable bark, though I believe there's also a lot of bite left in you too."

Bradley thought, "If you only knew."

The rest of the visit was pleasant, talking about everything and nothing. They exchanged old stories like fellow warriors returning home scarred but not defeated. John was about to go and asked Bradley if he could pray for him before he left.

Bradley said, "It's been a long while since I've let anyone pray for me. Never thought they were good enough. You may be the exception."

John grabbed his hand and prayed for him. Dylan noticed the watering eyes and saw John to the door. He didn't want Bradley to be embarrassed by the show of emotion.

John left, and Dylan returned to stay with his old friend a little longer. Bradley said, "General, you need to stay close to that one. He may be the real deal, but he's going to need you. Sometimes you have to walk through the rubble of the battle before you can secure the peace."

John met up with Rebecca and Sarah. They made their way to the graduation ceremony in the Dunham Theater within the Joella and Stewart Morris Cultural Arts Center on the HBU campus. On their way, Sarah asked, "Well, how was your visit with Carson Bradley? I hear he's about as crusty an old soldier as there is."

John smiled at the understatement and said, "'Crusty' is a generous description. However, I can say Carson Bradley is not a man I would like to have as an enemy. He did offer his help should I need it with the Governor."

Sarah laughed, "I bet he offered to shoot him in the head and bury his body where no one would find it."

John said, "Well, he didn't use those words exactly, though there was a reference to snakes and shooting them until they stopped wiggling. I have to say that the visit ended much better than it started."

Sarah got very serious then, and said, "John, he is a very dangerous man. He had 70 confirmed sniper kills during his service with Seal Team Seven. He doesn't have much use for the government or the politicians that run it."

John replied, "We may have some agreement on that point."

Chapter 21

The Victory Dawns

January 8, 2019 – May 27, 2019

"We now occupy the proud attitude of a sovereign and independent Republic, which will impose upon us the obligation of evincing to the world that we are worthy to be free. This will only be accomplished by wise legislation, the maintenance of our integrity, and the faithful and just redemption of our plighted faith wherever it has been pledged."

— Sam Houston, addressing his troops before the Battle of San Jacinto

COME AND TAKE IT

The Christmas break was wonderful. John had spent some time with his family and reflected on the coming challenges in the 86th Texas Legislature. Sitting on the swing looking over the longhorn pasture, he began to review some of the changes that had taken place since he began the effort to get Sarah's Law passed.

His staff was one of the bright spots in the evolution of the provisions. The heart of the law had remained the same. However, Patrick had made some very valuable suggestions they were able to incorporate into the bill. These changes made much more sense in light of John's deSire to protect both mother and child. They had combined the ability to protect the unborn child with the personal right of choice for women, who, for dozens of reasons, could not manage to care for a child. With the heartbeat provision in the law, it functionally prohibited all abortions. This fact alone would increase live births in the state by the tens of thousands each year. It was reckless to think this would not result in more neglect and hardship for both mother and child. In the past, this problem was addressed with state or federally funded programs.

His team and some of the brightest minds from Texans for Life and Texas Christians United had spent many late nights developing a fully funded system connecting couples seeking adoption and the additional children born in the state. Funding was allocated for medical, legal, and emotional support throughout the process and beyond to help the women who may have missed education or job opportunities while pregnant to embark on their new life post-delivery. He was pleasantly surprised that the resulting provisions were met with such acceptance from all but the extremes of both parties. There was still strong opposition from Planned Parenthood, but John saw no way to avoid that battle.

John had tried to understand the Governor's deeper entrenchment in delaying or defeating the bill, but he could not see it no matter how he turned it over in his mind. He and David Edwards had many conversations about that point. David's thoughts always came back to the same statement. He had quoted the verse so often that John had it memorized: "They are darkened in their understanding and separated from the life of God because of the ignorance that is in them due to the hardening of their hearts." It was from Paul's letter to the Ephesians.

They had turned that verse over and over in their conversations, and he was still unsure why the Governor was so rooted against the law. He remembered one particular conversation he and David had that dealt with that. The pastor had been in rare form that morning. He brought out the extra napkins and began drawing, which always meant a theological lesson was developing. The bottom line was always the same. He quoted one of his life verses that asserted God was working it all together for good, and that often that good could only be accomplished through challenge and trial. It was not a comforting talk, but it was a very comforting truth. He just wished to avoid conflict and pain.

Looking around at some of the mementos hanging on the walls, he settled on the Davy Crockett rifle, trying to conjure up the thoughts of that great Tennessee hero of the Battle of the Alamo. He wondered if he had the time to think through the events leading to his sacrifice, or if he were just being driven along by the battle. He hoped that he had been wise in his fight. The people in his life who mattered certainly affirmed he had.

However, as was always true in his life, there was that little tug of doubt that never seemed to go away.

As the sun began to set on the sender, January's cooler night air began to settle in. He went to the woodpile next to the outdoor fireplace and built a fire from the mesquite they had cut and stacked there. It wasn't long until the roaring fire reflected a comforting warmth that spread to most of the patio. He was still sitting on the swing when he heard the music begin to play on the outdoor speakers and looked to the doors as Rebecca walked out to join him. She had two glasses of cabernet from the Llano Estacado Winery. The music she had selected was from a playlist she titled *Peaceful Paths*. It was a collection of instrumental music featuring the piano, though she also included some songs featuring Native American flute and water drums.

She sat down closely beside him both because she enjoyed the warmth of being close and the affection they always shared. John said, "Are you too cold?"

Rebecca answered, "Never when I'm sitting beside you."

They sat in silence watching the South Texas sunset until finally, Rebecca broke the silence, "John, are you alright?"

He paused a moment and answered, "I am. In fact, I think I've never been better."

Rebecca said, "I'm glad you feel that way. I've never seen you better. Whatever happens, I know I'll always be on the front row."

They sat in silence until Abby came bounding through the doors and said, "Hey, you two, no PDA on the porch!"

It was an inside joke now since she and Josh Fitzgerald had been caught holding hands in the swing one evening over the Christmas break. John was embarrassed when he walked out on the two of them, clearly displaying *affection publicly*. All he could think to say as he cleared his throat loudly, was, "We have house rules prohibiting Public Display of Affection, you know." Now it had become quite a joke.

Abby wiggled in between her parents and sat on the swing. She said, "What's that awful music you've got playing?" She reached for his iPhone and put on one of her favorite Spotify playlists.

Rebecca said, "You're in a good mood."

Abby said, "This is going to be the best year ever!"

John hoped she was right, though he knew his daughter's reference had much more to do with the growing relationship between her and Josh than the things happening in Austin.

John headed back to Austin on Thursday after the New Year. The session would convene at noon on Tuesday, January 8th. There would be a lot of ceremonial things done that afternoon, including the presentation of the projected annual revenues; a convocation led by a prominent pastor within the state; and, the motion to secede, which was made each year by one of the ten representatives from Bexar County, which is the location of the Alamo. It was never a serious proposal, though it always ended with lifting the "Come and Take It" flag and shouts of "Remember the Alamo!" This year there would be one thing different than in the past. Sarah's Law would have been distributed to every Representative and Senator for review, and it would be formally placed on the agenda presented that day.

John had alerted Mateo that he wanted to have an executive staff meeting Thursday afternoon. He wanted to get ahead of any potential problems well before the weekend. Mateo met him at the helipad with John's driver. They unloaded and made the short drive to the offices.

Mateo said, "I've ordered in some lunch and thought we could get started around one if that works for you, Senator?"

John shook his head, accepting that he was never going to convince Mateo to call him by his first name, and said, "Works perfect. Thanks!"

John was surprised and relieved that the media was not camped out at the door to the office building. He said, "No press today?"

Mateo answered apologetically, "I'm sorry, Sir. Did you want me to call them?"

John laughed so hard he nearly choked. Finally getting control, he said, "No, Mateo. That was sarcasm."

By the time they arrived, the remaining staff had also arrived. They exchanged pleasantries and went to the smaller conference room where lunch had already been set out buffet style at the end of the side table along the wall.

Each, in turn, began their report with the first being Sean O'Sullivan. He started by saying, "As of now we have a very strong majority in both the House and Senate; however, I'll leave the details of that for Patrick's report. We have one additional supporting group that should provide even more solidarity among the Democrats. Catholic Charities USA has fully endorsed the bill and directed all their various district entities within the state to issue formal instructions for a Day of Prayer at the capital early in January. They have applied for permits, and it looks like it will take place on Monday, January 14th, prior to the Inauguration of the Governor and Lieutenant Governor on the 15th. Estimates are an attendance of 10,000. The logistics of the event are problematic because of the BBQ and Inaugural Ball the next day; however, when Texas Christians United joined them in the event, all of the details seemed to be less difficult to handle."

Everyone around the table laughed.

John nearly choked on his BLT. He said, "How did you pull that one off? Catholics and Baptists together on the front lawn of the Capitol without a war? Hope someone told General Walker to have the State Guard ready."

Mateo, missing the sarcasm again, interjected, "He has been alerted, Sir. He will have a contingency of the Guard onsite to complement other law enforcement."

John laughed, "Relax, Mateo, I was just kidding."

"They aren't Sir," Mateo continued.

John said, "Really?" And John made a mental note to call the General and get an update from him as well.

Sean continued to report ending with what he called "the bad news."

"Sir, I'm afraid all our reports indicate that the Governor intends to delay signing the bill until June 16th, which is, of course, the last day available for signing by the Governor."

Patrick added, "I think he is hoping for the maximum time allowable to begin litigation to delay or overturn the law. My sources tell me he has accepted the inevitable passing of the bill. There's just too much support for the bill. He would be committing political suicide to oppose the bill directly."

With that, Sean finished his report with various schedules for press conferences and media appearances throughout the session.

John said, "Thank you Sean. Patrick, can you give us more detail on the vote?"

Patrick called their attention to the report he had prepared and posted to each of their iPads. "As you can see from the report, we have more than the simple majority required to pass the bill through both the House and the Senate with the changes we have made. It is possible that we may need to lobby the group again should the Governor refuse to sign it within ten days of passing. However, I believe it is more likely we will see the Governor reluctantly sign it at the last moment. The fallout from not signing it, or worse, vetoing it, is far too great a risk for him politically."

John asked him if he had sent this information to anyone else.

Patrick said, "No Sir. Though I highly recommend we send it to Texans for Life and schedule a press conference as soon as possible. We need to get ahead of any misinformation campaign by the opposition."

John replied, "Good idea. Mateo, are we on track for that?"

His Chief of Staff said, "Yes Sir. I have a release ready to go out immediately, scheduling a press conference for Monday. Jeremiah and Sarah have already been apprised and agree. I also took the liberty of contacting Michael Brody, from Texas

Christians United, and Maria Ramirez, the Executive Director of Catholic Charities of Central Texas. They all would be happy to attend the press conference that day."

John was impressed. He said, "Great job, y'all. It looks like we're on the downhill side of this journey."

John thought it would be a good idea to call David Edwards and bring him up to speed as well. Perhaps he was in town, and they could have breakfast tomorrow.

As the meeting broke, John's scheduler met him coming out of the conference room, "Sir, the Lieutenant Governor called while you were in staff meeting and requested some time with you as soon as possible."

John asked, "Did he say what it was concerning?"

"No Sir. He just said it was urgent," she answered.

John instructed her to get him on the phone. A few minutes later, she buzzed the call into John's office.

The Lt. Governor was a grave man with a gruff demeanor. He immediately began, "Senator, I am very disappointed that you have scheduled a rally the day before the inauguration, especially with the Catholic Services as one of the sponsors. We have enough problems without involving them."

John was startled by his directness and said, "Good afternoon to you as well."

Interrupting any further conversation from John, the Lt. Governor continued, "We have a crisis brewing here, Senator. I don't have time for pleasantries, and neither should you. Why are they even involved? You know they are the most difficult block of voters to contain in our state. We nearly had a full-scale revolt when the President began to erect the border wall. You need to cancel the protest."

John didn't know where to begin. "First, we have not organized the rally." He was very careful to use the word "rally" instead of the Lt. Governor's choice of "protest." John went on, "They are gathering in a peaceful, permitted rally in expressing their support for the new bill in accordance with their First Amendment Rights. Second, I not only will not cancel the rally,

I will be there in support. I suggest you put on a broad smile and do the same."

It dawned on the Lt. Governor that John Lucas IV had made the transition to becoming an even greater force than his father. Intimidation was not going to work with the new John Lucas.

He softened his tone and said, "John, I'm sure you realize that I cannot hold together all the Republicans if the Catholics are on board. Even with Michael Brody there to soften the visual, we're going to lose some votes."

John said, "Thank you for your concern. I will consult my staff and take it under advisement." With that, he simply disconnected the call.

John did talk with Mateo, Sean, and Patrick. They assured him they had already polled the House and Senate and with only a few exceptions, there was complete support for the rally. The combined political power of Texas Christians United and Catholic Charities Texas was much too strong to oppose and have any hope of reelection in 2020.

Mateo said, "Besides, it's the right thing to do, Sir. This is just the beginning of a new coalition with the potential to bring integrity back to the political process. This is what it looks like when politicians do what the people need and want in government."

Mateo was right, of course. But John couldn't help but feel things were getting bigger than he ever intended.

When John finally got back to his Austin residence, he was exhausted. He called Rebecca from the car, but even her cheerful encouragement didn't dispel the feeling in his gut that a storm was gathering.

John thought he'd better make one more call before trying to get some rest. He reached General Walker on the first ring. "Good evening, General, I hope I'm not calling too late."

The General said, "Of course not, John."

They had gotten to a first-name basis since John's visit with Carson Bradley, though John was still a little uncomfortable with that familiarity. The General went on, "And, John, please call me Dylan. Your kindness to Bradley was an incredible gift to me. I will never forget that. What can I do for you?"

John was humbled. He said, "I hope Bradley is continuing to recuperate well."

The General gave him a short update of the progress of his old friend, and John continued, "I have just returned to Austin, and my staff informed of the details of the rally on Tuesday. Could we get together tomorrow and look at the logistics of that from your perspective?"

The General laughed and said, "Got a call from the Governor already?"

John smiled as he thought how astute Dylan was in political as well as military matters. John said, "Not yet, but the Lt. Governor called asking me to cancel the event."

The General got serious and asked, "Are you thinking of canceling the rally, John?"

"No, of course not. Even if I could, I wouldn't. I just wanted to make sure it goes without incident. I can see how a counter protest could be inflammatory. I'm not looking to initiate another Battle of Concord. The last thing I want is another 'shot heard around the world.'"

The General said, "No shots are going to be fired, John. However, a meeting would be a great idea. In fact, why don't we meet tomorrow?"

John said, "That would be great. Could I have my executive staff there as well? I like as many eyes and ears on the topic as possible."

The General answered, "That would be great. Why don't I get the plans and my Executive Officer and I can come by your office around mid-morning."

"Perfect. I'll put the coffee on." John replied.

As soon as the call ended, John called Mateo and asked him to communicate the meeting to Patrick and Sean. With the call from the General, John felt a bit better, and sleep came much easier.

His driver picked John up early so that he could get a head start on the day before the meeting with the General and his EXO. As they arrived, John saw that his respite from the press had ended. About a dozen media representatives were waiting at the door. He saw Mateo was already wrangling the crowd and instructed his driver to drive to the rear entrance. He knew Mateo would handle the press perfectly. They could wait until Monday for their sound bite.

As John entered the office, the staff was busy getting materials ready for the mid-morning meeting. As He walked toward his office, the scheduler handed him his calls from the morning and a coffee cup. Mateo joined him shortly after he sat down behind the desk already stacked high with files and reports.

John looked up and said, "Just another day in paradise, I see."

Mateo chuckled and replied, "I'm sorry for the crowd at the front so early, Sir. I think I have them satisfied for the moment with the announcement of a press conference Monday."

John replied, "Good job, Mateo. Are we ready for the meeting this morning?"

Before he could answer, both Sean and Patrick walked in. John greeted them. Sean said, "Looks like you had a busy evening, Sir."

Mateo scowled and said, "I'm sure the Senator had a productive evening, Sean."

John just laughed. Mateo had not quite gotten used to Sean's dry humor. John quickly said, "Stand down men. We have enough enemies out there. I don't want any in here."

They all had a good laugh. Finally, Mateo said, "We're ready, Sir. I wasn't sure how much information to prepare, so I had a brief developed for the General to reference."

John said, "I think the General will do most of the talking, though I'm sure we'll have some questions as we go."

They began to talk about a few other matters dealing with the first reading of the bill and legislative procedure when the scheduler buzzed in announcing the General's arrival.

Without waiting to be escorted, General Walker walked into John's office and said, "Good morning, John. Thanks for arranging the meeting. By the way, where's the coffee you promised?"

Mateo was bothered by the familiarity of General Walker using John's first name, but when he asked John for a cup of coffee, he nearly exploded in defense of his boss.

John saw the reaction on his face and said, "Good of you to come over Dylan. Coffee is on in the conference room."

The General introduced his EXO to John with the more formal title of "Senator," and John reciprocated as he introduced his executive staff.

As they walked to the small conference room, the General said, "John, I've asked one other person to join us this morning, Major Robert Hunt, Divisional Commander of the Texas Rangers. I hope that's OK."

John was familiar with Major Hunt. He and John's dad had often spent time together on the ranch when John was a boy. In those days, Major Hunt was the commander of Company D, which stretched across South Texas.

John had learned to respect the Texas Rangers early. The Texas Rangers, now a division of the Department of Public Safety, Texas's state law enforcement department, was also known as "*Los Diablos Tejanos*—the Texas Devils." Some of the mystique of these law enforcement officers came from their history. The Rangers were founded in 1823 when Stephen F. Austin, known as the Father of Texas, employed ten men to act as Rangers to protect the 700 newly settled families who arrived in Texas following the Mexican War of Independence. They were men who gave no quarter in enforcing the law. Today they were responsible for major incident crime investigations, unsolved crime/serial crime investigations, public corruption and public integrity investigations, officer-involved shooting investigations, border security operations, and threats from foreign or domestic sources against the state and its elected officials. They had greater power than the US Homeland Security.

John said, "Sure, glad he could come. I am curious why the Rangers are involved though."

The General's answer was cryptic, "He has some information I think is pertinent at this time."

Major Hunt arrived and was shown to the conference room. He immediately went to John and shook hands, saying, "Good to see you again, John. Did you and JV get a good deer this year?" One of Hunt's favorite excursions each year was riding the ranch with John's dad hunting wild hogs.

John answered with the familiarity of a friend, "He did. A good ten-point with two kickers, it's at the taxidermist now. One of the best ones we've seen in a while. I guess the wet summer helped."

Major Hunt greeted the General, and John made the other introductions. The Major looked toward John's staff and said, "You boys have been busy. Good job. You work for one of the best young men I've ever known. His father and I were old friends."

Mateo, Sean, and Patrick all had to gather themselves, making sure their mouths were not agape in amazement. Patrick once again returned to the thought of the enormous power in John Lucas. He wondered if there was anyone more powerful and still so humble than his new boss.

They gathered around the table as the EXO distributed some materials detailing plans for crowd control and coordination of the various law enforcement agencies for the event. It was a thorough briefing. Every contingency had been anticipated, though John wanted certainty.

He said, "The Lt. Governor called me yesterday with a concern about a counter protest group. He seemed to be anxious about violence erupting between the groups."

Major Hunt fielded that question. "We've anticipated that possibility. We have no requests for a permit for any other groups, and as such, we will be actively denying access through the ingress points already in place for the next day's events. Security will be very tightly supervised. We have also communicated this to both organizations with the proper procedures necessary for entrance into the event."

John was relieved and said, "Looks like all we need to do is show up and enjoy the day. The weather promises to be good, especially for January."

General Walker said, "Well, John, that's not exactly our recommendation as of today."

Major Hunt tried to avoid talking about the next piece of information in front of John's staff, and the General said, "Go ahead, Bob. John is going to inform his staff fully. They might as well hear it from you."

Major Hunt became very serious as he said, "Yesterday, we received a credible threat against the Senator and his family."

John rarely lost control; however, this news hit him harder than anything he had ever experienced. John said with a quiet, menacing tone, "What do you mean 'credible threat'? And what does this have to do with my family?"

The General was completely surprised by this reaction. He had anticipated surprise, perhaps anger, but not this. It seemed as if John had suddenly become a coiled rattlesnake ready to strike. It unnerved him.

The room became very quiet when Major Hunt said, "It is credible because of some of the references made to both the event and your ranch."

John looked at the General and said, "Did you know about this when I called last night?"

The General said, "Not to this extent. Bob called this morning with the update to a credible threat."

Before John could say anything further, Major Hunt said, "We have already mobilized Company D, alerted Homeland Security, and the FBI. We wanted to talk with you before we did anything more overtly than securing your ranch's perimeter and assigning teams of officers to you in cooperation with the State Guard. As you know, they are primarily responsible with the Capital State Police for the Governor's protection detail."

The General did not know about the involvement of the other agencies. As he heard this, he flashed back to Waco and said, "What the hell were you thinking, Bob? Why did you involve the federals? They did that in Waco, and I've got one of the best friends I've ever had dying as a result of that fubar!"

Major Hunt was taken aback at the ferocity of the Generals response. He said, "That's procedure, Dylan. You know that."

The General looked at him as if to bore a hole into his skull and said, "What I know is that's how you get people killed."

John saw the meeting was getting out of hand. He took over the conversation as he issued orders. "Here's what it's going to look like, gentlemen. First, my family comes first. I want them secured and protected 24 hours a day, every day until this threat has been neutralized. That circle will include my wife, children, and my sister and her husband, Sarah and Jeremiah Mann. Second, General, you will coordinate that effort. Work with the Rangers, but get it done. I do not want anything to take priority over that. Is that clear?"

John Lucas had morphed into his father, and no one in that room could do more than acknowledge their ascent. John went on, "Now, Major, you will do whatever is necessary to ensure a plan coordinating through the State Guard under the General's command is executed to apprehend the terrorist or terrorists behind this plot as quickly as possible. The event will go on as scheduled. I will be in attendance as planned. If you cannot with 100% certainty neutralize this threat before the event, use me as bait, and catch these roaches. Is that clear?"

Both Dylan and Bob simply said, "Yes Sir."

John went on, "Who knows about this?"

Major Hunt said, "The circle is contained to executive-level leadership within the FBI, Home Security, the Rangers, and, of course, those of us in this room."

With more control, John said, "Mateo, you and Sean need to manage this immediately. I do not want the press to hear it from a leak." He went on, "Patrick, make sure this does not negatively impact our support."

They all said, "Yes, Sir."

As they were standing to carry out his instructions, John added, "Don't panic, men. God's got this."

John asked General Walker and Major Hunt to remain behind a moment. He said, "I apologize if I seemed to react angrily. However, my family is the center of my world."

They had little doubt of that truth.

He then said, "I will notify Rebecca, along with Jeremiah and Sarah immediately. When can they expect a protection detail?"

Major Hunt looked at the General for his lead and said, "As soon as the General gives the order, we can have them deployed within the hour."

General Walker asked him, "How good are they?"

Major Hunt said, "Excellent."

Walker pressed, "Would you trust your wife and children to them?"

Hunt simply said, "Without hesitation. They are not a parade detail."

The General went on, "John, with your permission, I'd like to put some of my former seals with the details."

John said, "Do it."

Dylan couldn't help but think how this meeting felt like he had been involved in with POTUS and the cabinet many years ago before a major engagement. John Lucas did not sound like a Senator. He sounded like a Commander-in-Chief. Even though a senator had no real authority over him, John Lucas was a man quickly becoming someone well above any mere legislator. Because of his quickly developing friendship and his expanding admiration for John's leadership, he had no problems with John taking charge of the meeting.

The General said, "I think we have our orders, Sir. We will give you real-time updates as we get them." With that, they left.

John immediately went to his office to make the calls to Rebecca, Jeremiah, and Sarah. He found himself thinking that the dawning victory he saw yesterday was being shadowed with the dark thunderclouds that always accompanied an approaching storm.

Chapter 22

The Turn to Secession

January 9, 2019 – January 15, 2019

"To be prepared for war is one of the most effectual means of preserving peace."

—George Washington

COME AND TAKE IT

John made all the calls to his family informing them of the newest development to get the legislation passed. His discussion the day before with General Walker and Major Hunt was terrifying. His thoughts naturally swung toward canceling the rally. He even considered withdrawing the bill. However, he remembered that helpless feeling he had all those years ago while listening to his sister sob with regret after her abortion; and he remembered all those letters David Edwards had delivered to him. This was a small price to pay to end sorrow like that.

John also remembered history. On July 4, 1776, 56 men met in Philadelphia to pass a resolution declaring their independence from England. It was a courageous step in their long march toward the ultimate goal of individual liberty. What they did that day at Independence Hall would cost them greatly in the years to come. Five signers were captured by the British as traitors and tortured before they died. Twelve had their homes ransacked and burned. Two lost their sons serving in the Revolutionary Army; another had two sons captured. Nine of the fifty-six found and died from wounds or hardships during the war. But, it paved the way for a radical new way of thinking about government that would change the course of human history.

John also knew the signers of the Declaration of Independence were not against celebration. In fact, two days earlier, when 12 of the colonies had ratified the document, John

Adams, one of its architects, penned a letter to his wife, predicting that the Second of July would be celebrated every year after that:

The second day of July, 1776, will be memorable epoch in the history of America. I am apt to believe that it will be celebrated by succeeding generations, as the great Anniversary Festival. It ought to be commemorated, as the day of deliverance by solemn acts of devotion to God Almighty. It ought to be solemnized with pomp, shews, games, sports, guns, bells, bonfires and illuminations, from one end of the continent to the other, from this time forward forever.

You will think me transported with enthusiasm; but I am not. I am well aware of the toil, and blood, and treasure, that it will cost us to maintain this declaration, and support and defend these states. Yet, through all the gloom, I can see the rays of light and glory; I can see that the end is more than worth all the means, and that posterity will triumph, although you and I may rue, which I hope we shall not.

Four days later, the Liberty Bell rang out to summon the people to the first public reading of the document. As the words were read, there were great shouts of affirmation, and a great celebration followed. A year later, Congress would authorize fireworks as an appropriate means of celebrating the birth of the new nation.

But amidst his feelings of enthusiasm, John Adams' words above also reflected a somber tone common to all who signed the Declaration of Independence. In doing so, they knew they were inviting a declaration of war by England. They knew that, as traitors, they were legally forfeiting all their possessions to the crown. Essentially, in signing the document, they were putting bounties on their own head. But despite the obvious cost, they considered the impact their actions would have for America's people. They understood from Scripture that government is a sacred trust given by God to protect people's inherent rights created in His image. Their new document stood toe-to-toe against the prevailing governmental idea of the day—the divine right of kings, which held that, when the one on the throne spoke, it was the voice of God. The Founding Fathers believed in the rule of law, not the rule of men.

The Declaration of Independence contended that King George was abusing his God-given power as the leader of England and the American colonies. It was their responsibility as God-fearing men to challenge him on this for the sake of the people. Benjamin Franklin himself recommended a national motto in defense of their actions: "Rebellion to tyrants is obedience to God."

Even though John knew this, he still struggled with the threat against those he loved. It was his doing. He could understand the threat against him. That was a commonly used tactic in intimidation. But, he could not imagine anyone so deranged that they would threaten his family. Again he heard his pastor's words echo in his mind: "How far are you willing to go?" His resolve strengthened. This was not a piece of legislation. This was his obedience to the will of God on behalf of the people of Texas.

Just as he thought he had turned the corner from fear to resolve, John's phone rang. He saw the Caller ID identify it was Dylan. "Good morning, Dylan. What can I do for you?" asked John.

Always direct and to the point, the General said, "I wanted to update you, Sir."

John thought, where did the "Sir" come from? Hadn't they passed that point in their relationship? He said, "Again, Dylan, please call me John."

The General simply answered, "Yes Sir." He informed John that the teams were deployed and on-site at his ranch. He could come over and be more specific about the placement of each of the teams and their schedules if deSired.

John said, "That's not necessary, Dylan. I am confident you have taken every precaution."

The General continued, "Yes Sir. I have also deployed my EXO as liaison. He will be working directly with Mrs.

Lucas and your administrator, Mrs. Lambert. Major Hunt has also assigned individual teams to the children. The agents are young enough that they will not be obtrusive. I have personally screened their protective details. I am very confident their schedules will be minimally disrupted. Your protective detail should have made contact with your Chief of Staff by now and be in place."

John interrupted the General, "They are, Dylan."

Before John could say more, the General continued with his report. "Excellent, Sir. We also assigned protective details to the Manns at their offices and residence. It might be helpful if you talk with them in regard to the necessity of these measures. They seem to be less convinced than we are concerning the validity of the threat."

John told the General he would talk with Sarah again though he doubted he would be any more persuasive than Dylan. General Walker covered a few of the preliminary strategies for the rally and ended the call.

Mateo knocked and entered John's office and said, "Sir, we're ready for the briefing before the Press Conference this afternoon."

John almost forgot about that detail. There was so much swirling in his mind. He needed some time on his swing in the worst way. John acquiesced, "Lead the way, Mateo."

The briefing went well. When they broke for lunch, John asked Mateo, Sean, and Patrick to stay behind for a moment. He said somewhat conspiratorially, "Do you think we could sneak out and get some barbeque?"

Mateo spoke first, "No Sir! There will be no sneaking out!"

John laughed and Mateo realized he had been played again. Then John said, "Ask our jailers if they would like to get some lunch, and let's go to Cooper's."

"Yes Sir."

The protective detail was under orders to be as invisible as possible. However, going to a public restaurant in the middle of a weekday was certainly going to challenge that directive.

They eventually assented to the request though they insisted on riding with the Senator in his car while the others trailed in another vehicle. Mateo secured reservations under the supervision of the protection detail. It seemed they had a protocol for that too.

John needed to call Sarah, though he wasn't looking forward to that conversation. When they entered the cars, John dialed her private cell. She answered immediately, "John, you need to do something about these guards. We can't get anything done with them hovering over us. Our staff is terrified. John, they have full assault gear on with weapons draped on them as if they are expecting an invasion of the building."

Once she took a breath, John said, "Good morning, Sarah."

She shot back, "Don't take that tone with me."

John simply said, "It's just temporary, and it's for your protection."

Sarah calmed a bit and said, "What do you need?"

John said, "I wanted to tell you I spoke with the General this morning and promised I would call and ask you to exercise a little more patience with the protection detail considering the circumstances."

She let out a long, dramatic sigh, and said, "Fine." With that, she hung up. John thought that went about as well as it could have gone.

Arriving at Cooper's, John started to open the door, but he was stopped from getting out by one of the detail, "If you could delay a moment, Sir. We would like to secure the area first."

John thought Sarah might have been more justified than he assumed.

They were all escorted to the back corner where a table was set, giving the detail full control of all the possible weak points. After they ordered, John was relaxing with his Shiner when he noticed the Lieutenant Governor approaching. It was a popular spot for lunch, though he certainly hadn't anticipated seeing anyone he knew. As the Lieutenant Governor got halfway to the table, the detail separated with one shielding John and the other stopping the Lieutenant Governor from coming any closer, "May I see some identification, Sir?"

The Lieutenant Governor was indignant and nearly shouted, "Do you not know who I am? Get out of the way!"

The guard stood ramrod straight and said, "Sir, I am under orders that no one approach Senator Lucas without identification. Shall we do this the easy way?"

The Lieutenant Governor saw this was not a man to be bullied. He showed him his Government ID and was allowed to pass. As the Lieutenant Governor approached John, he said, "You've certainly created a stir, Senator."

John remained seated, "Not my intent at all. What can I do for you?"

The Lieutenant Governor continued, "When I saw you, I thought I'd ask if you have given any more thought to canceling the rally? The Governor and I are concerned with the optics, especially now that you have a small army in tow."

John said, "It's two men, not a small army, and, yes, I've thought about the rally. I wouldn't change it for the world. I thought I made that abundantly clear in our earlier conversation."

With that rebuff, the Lieutenant Governor turned and walked off.

Sean said, "That went well, Sir. I think the 'optics' just got a lot better."

They all laughed. The food came, and they enjoyed a relatively quiet lunch, though John couldn't help but notice the phones all across the room lifted earlier to take pictures of his encounter with the Lieutenant Governor. He was sure some of them would reach the news later today.

He said, "Sean, I'm afraid you may have some damage control to deal with. I may have been a little curt."

Mateo, who was mid-sip of his iced tea, nearly choked with a laugh. He said loud enough for the protection detail to hear him, "Well, Sir, with Los Diablos Tejanos guarding you as if you were Sam Houston himself; it shouldn't be a surprise."

The guards, who were Texas Rangers, knew the reference. They were well acquainted with the story that emerged during the Mexican-American War. General Zachary Taylor, the future President of the United States, gave orders to Jack Hays to raise four regiments of Texas Rangers to go to Mexico. Hays was able to raise three. The Mexicans knew these men as *Los Diablos Tejanos*, and they were greatly feared and hated. As they rode into Mexico City, the locals hurled insults at them. When three men threw rocks, they were immediately shot. Shortly thereafter, another man stole a Ranger's bandanna, and the Ranger answered with one shot from his Colt, killing the man instantly where he stood. When General Taylor questioned Hays about the incident, Hays replied, "no one can impose on my men."

Nothing more was said. Taylor informed Hays that American soldiers were being killed nightly in the red light district by the locals. The Rangers set an ambush for the guilty parties, and when it was finished, eighty-three men died, though not one Ranger was lost. The killing of American soldiers stopped immediately.

This all took place after the Battle of The Alamo - the defeat, capture, and subsequent release of Santa Ana, who returned to Mexico, where he was actively waging war against the U.S. When the Rangers heard that Samuel Walker, a Ranger left in command while Hays was in Mexico, was killed by Mexican troops, it compounded the hate they already felt for Santa Ana. Most of them lost relatives at the fall of The Alamo and Goliad when James W. Fanning and approximately three hundred men surrendered to Santa Ana, yet he had them all killed on the spot. His butchery was infamous throughout Texas and inspired many Texans to take up arms for the cause. The Rangers desperately wanted to catch Santa Ana and missed him five minutes in one small town. Eventually, Santa Ana turned himself in to the U.S. Army because he was so afraid of what the

Rangers might do to him if they captured him. They were forever known as "the devils of Texas" or *Los Diablos Tejanos*.

The two rangers almost smiled despite their strict training to remain focused. The lead guard looked at Sean and gave a quick nod of approval. That one moment gave Sean an idea. He decided to change his introduction at the press conference.

As they arrived at the office, the media was already gathered in the large conference room. All of them were screened closely for security purposes. Cameras were set up around the room, microphones were in place, and reporters scurried about to get settled before the briefing began.

John and his staff entered the room without announcement. The room quickly silenced. Sean was the first to speak. "We are very glad to welcome you to the first press conference of this year. As you may have noticed, security is a bit tighter than normal. We will address that in a bit. However, on behalf of the Senator and all of us, we appreciate your cooperation."

Sean took a breath, and hands shot up all across the room. He continued, "We will have plenty of opportunity for questions in a moment. First, let me express the Senator's appreciation to General Walker and the Texas State Guard as well as Major Hunt and the Texas Rangers, for providing security for the Senator and his family in the face of a credible threat."

That was the first teaser. Sean continued, "You may remember your Texas history and the origin of the Texas Rangers. There is a good reason for them being known as *Los Diablos Tejanos*."

With that, everyone in the room got their headline. Sean continued providing them with a brief history lesson in a way that obliquely but unmistakably compared John to Sam Houston. It was a brilliant move, though embarrassing to John. Sean finished his introduction, "With that, ladies and gentlemen, let me yield the podium to one of the most patriotic men I have ever known, Senator John Lucas."

John stepped to the podium and said, "Thank you, Mr. O'Sullivan. However, I'm not sure I deserve any of those kind words."

John spent a few moments thanking the appropriate personnel and speaking briefly about the security, especially for his family. He used the reference to his family as a segue to the bill. "Our goal in this 86th Legislative Session of the Lone Star State is to provide protection for every individual of every family. Sarah's Law, as it has come to be known, will be presented and considered within the first week of our session. We are confident that it will be passed and signed into law quickly. You all have summaries of the principal points as it has been finalized and worked its way through the Legislative Committee. We are confident it protects both the unborn child and the women who carry them. Now, rather than go item by item, let me simply open the room for questions."

The room erupted as reporters vied to get the first question. Sean did a masterful job of restoring, calling on each reporter in turn.

The day ended with John exhausted and hopeful. He made his way to his Austin residence anticipating a nice long chat with Rebecca sitting in front of the fireplace. When the driver pulled to the curb to let John exit, he was surprised to see a small group of people bundled in their coats and scarves carrying protest signs. He wanted to talk to them. Perhaps if he were able to have a conversation with them, he could change their minds. The ranking guard directed the driver to pull around to the garage entrance, where the evening detail was waiting to relieve them. As they stopped, they instructed John to wait in the car while they checked ID's and made the way clear for him to enter the building.

John reached the penthouse and collapsed on the couch. He was just about to call Rebecca when his phone rang. She anticipated his return to the apartment perfectly. He answered, "Hey! Am I glad you called!"

She smiled with her voice and said, "Do I need to start calling you General Houston?"

He was taken aback, "What?"

She said, "Oh, John, haven't you seen tonight's news? The lead story is titled 'Sam Houston and his Diablos Tejanos.'"

He groaned, "Oh no."

Rebecca said, "It's actually well done, John. Whoever thought of this made a brilliant move."

He said, "This is all Sean. He went off script at the beginning of the press conference. I'm surprised he didn't start waving the 'Come and Take It Flag.'"

She answered, "He didn't have to. FOX News has already inserted some footage with it waving in the breeze over the walls of the Alamo."

John groaned again, "Great."

Rebecca just laughed. "It's going to be fine, John."

He changed the subject, "How are you and the kids? Did they do OK at school today? No one bothered them, did they?"

She answered, "Slow down, John. Everyone is fine. We hardly know they're here, although the armored personnel carriers at the entrance to the ranch might be a little over the top."

He stammered, "The what?"

She said, "I'm just kidding, John."

He finally got control of his thoughts and told her about lunch, the press conference, and the protestors outside the AMLI. They talked for what seemed like hours. The more he heard her voice, the more he was calmed. Finally, he said, "You're being very careful, right?"

She simply said, "Of course I am. All is well."

He closed the call promising he'd call her tomorrow. She said, "I know you will… if I don't call first." She laughed, and they hung up.

John dozed off on the couch. He was startled awake with a banging on the door. He was immediately alert and ran to the door. Opening it, he found the protection detail standing by the elevator and Dylan Walker standing in front of him. He realized it was 10 o'clock.

The General came in, quickly shut the door, and said, "Senator, have you seen the news?"

John was confused, he said, "Excuse me?"

General Walker then realized he had awoken John, and he was not aware of the most recent development. He said, "Senator, I have some news…"

Before he could utter another word, John shouted, "What's going on, Dylan?"

The General calmly said, "Everyone is fine, John. Rebecca and the children are safe and secure, but we did have an attempt to breach the inner perimeter at the ranch."

John nearly collapsed but steadied himself quickly.

The General then detailed the events and the brief skirmish that followed. "At 1900 hours, the south perimeter patrol noted a breach in your fence. They reported it, and we immediately converged on the south inner perimeter nearest the southern facing walls of the main house. Using Blackhawks equipped with infrared technology, we were able to direct a ground assault team to intercept the intruders. There was a brief firefight in which six of the eight intruders were killed or wounded seriously enough that they were transferred to a secure medical facility and are in surgery as we speak. They are not expected to survive. There were no casualties or injuries to our troops. We captured two of the intruders uninjured. They are in custody and being questioned in a secure location off-site."

The General noticed John's features harden as he said, "Where are they? I want to question them."

General Walker said, "Sir, it is in your best interest that neither of those requests be granted. I am going to continue the questioning personally. I promise you we will have answers by morning."

John started to protest, and the General simply raised his hand to stop him, "Trust me, John. This is not Waco."

John said, "I want to talk to Rebecca and the kids immediately. Where are they?"

The General said, "We are having them flown here in a military helicopter with air escort. I feel we can do a better job protecting all of you in one location. I apologize for the interruption of the children's school schedule, but I will keep them safe at all costs, Sir."

John said, "Thank you, Dylan. What can I do?"

The General said, "Sit tight, Sir. I will update you by morning or earlier if I have further news."

The General left, and John immediately called Sarah. She knew something was wrong when John did not exchange any pleasantries, "Do not leave your residence. Under no circumstances are you to go out of sight of your protection detail until I say so. Do you understand?"

Sarah had never heard John talk to her like this. She said, "John, what's going on?"

He said, more calmly, but still in perfect control, "The ranch was attacked tonight. Rebecca and the kids are safe. They are being transported here by military helicopter as we speak. Six of the intruders were killed or mortally wounded. Two are in custody and being questioned by the Texas Guard and the Rangers. Sarah, promise me you will do what I have asked. I cannot risk losing anyone."

She said, "Oh, John, I'm so sorry. Of course, we will wait to hear from you. Jeremiah and I will be praying, as well. Can I call David?"

John said, "Yes, but under no circumstances do I want anyone else to know about this. Tell David the same. I will call Mateo, Sean, and Patrick to coordinate any releases."

Sarah asked one more question, "John, I would like to make one more call. I would like to talk to Peter Bridges. I have a funny feeling about all of this."

John said, "Are you crazy? He's the Governor's Chief of Staff. My God, Sarah, for all we know, the Governor is behind this attack."

Then Sarah said, "I know, John. I think he is. Peter has been my source inside the Governor's office for a long time now. He's on our side." With that news, John put together many puzzles he'd pondered over the last few years.

John said, "A lot of things make better sense now. Yes. Make the call and keep me informed, please."

After he hung up with Sarah, John immediately called Mateo. It was a brief call. When Mateo answered, John said, "Mateo, we have an emergency. Get Sean and Patrick up and get to my penthouse as soon as possible. I'll make sure security knows you are coming and will pass you through."

Mateo had no idea what could have happened, but he knew the tone John used left no room for ambiguity. He made the call to Sean and Patrick. They all arrived within thirty minutes of John's call.

Rebecca and the kids had not yet arrived, though John had been apprised of their ETA. It was a whirlwind of activity. When his staff arrived, he gave them the basics of the General's report. The gravity of the situation was not lost on them. Though none of them had ever been directly involved in an armed conflict, surely this is what it must have felt like. The tension was thick enough to feel. It was palpable.

John drew the meeting to a close with instructions concerning the flow of information, "Make no mistake; we will control the flow of this story. I want nothing, absolutely nothing to delay the presentation and vote on the bill. Am I clear?"

There was a chorus of agreement from the staff.

As they were about to leave, John received a call from Camp Mabry informing him that his family had landed and en route to the AMLI under escort. The General gave specific orders for John to be notified by the Captain of the Watch when his family was safely on the base grounds and about to be transported.

John asked the soldier, "When will they arrive?"

The captain crisply answered, "Unless there are extenuating circumstances, they should arrive within the hour, Sir."

John reacted forcefully, "Captain, it isn't an hour's walk from Camp Mabry to here. I don't want 'should' or 'extenuating circumstances.' I want my family safely transported now. Am I very clear, or do I need to explain myself further?"

The Captain said, "No Sir. You are very clear. I will personally accompany the transport and give you real-time updates."

John said, "Thank you, Captain." And he ended the call.

His staff all looked at one another as Mateo asked, "Will we be reconvening here in the morning, or at the office?"

John said, "You go to the office as usual. I will apprise you in the morning of my arrival. And, Mateo, I don't want to be greeted by the press at the curb when I arrive."

Mateo, nodding, said, "Yes Sir!"

When they got into the elevator for the ride down to the garage, Patrick said, "We just made a hard right turn straight into uncharted territory."

Chapter 23

The Appearance of Benedict Arnold

January 9, 2019 – January 15, 2019

Treason of the blackest dye was yesterday discovered! General Arnold who commanded at West Point, lost to every sentiment of honor, of public and private obligation, was about to deliver up that important Post into the hands of the enemy. Such an event must have given the American cause a deadly wound if not fatal stab. Happily the treason had been timely discovered to prevent the fatal misfortune. The providential train of circumstances which led to it affords the most convincing proof that the Liberties of America are the object of divine Protection.

—George Washington, General Orders,
September 26, 1780

COME AND TAKE IT

Rebecca, JV, and Abby arrived without incident. John insisted he meet them in the garage to the vocal protests of the protection detail, which had now swelled to a dozen Rangers and State Guards who were strategically placed throughout the AMLI Downtown location.

Short of physically restraining John, the commander of the detail accompanied him with two others from the personal detail down through the private elevator to the garage, which was already swept and cleared. John arrived just as the convoy of armored SUVs entered the underground garage area. He ran to the car with Rebecca and the children in it. Before he got to the vehicle, Rebecca opened the door and fell into his arms, followed immediately by JV and Abby.

Always trying to lighten the moment for John, Rebecca said, "I tried to bring the Crockett Rifle, but they wouldn't let me."

He couldn't help but smile as the tension began to fall away in relief that they were safe. They quickly made their way to the penthouse where their security could be more easily managed. They all fell into the familiar comfort of the family room, and John quietly said, "I'm so sorry."

Before he could go any further with self-recrimination, Rebecca said, "Sorry for what, John. This was in no way your fault. This is the work of cowards doing their best to divert your resolve in doing what is right."

Tears came to his eyes.

JV said, "Dad, you should've seen it. It was the coolest thing I've ever seen. The seals came out of nowhere. I was just out there feeding Pancho Villa some apple quarters. I would've seen 'em if I'd just looked, but they were hidden better than a rattlesnake coiled up under a rock. I walked back inside, and when it got dark and all hell broke loose!"

Rebecca broke in, "Watch your language young man."

He went on, "Well, it sounded like hell oughta sound, Mom."

John couldn't help but laugh. His family was alright and safe. "We'll have plenty of time to tell tall tales later. Let's get everybody settled in."

Abby said, "What about school, Dad? I've got tests this week."

John said, "I think I can get your teachers to send it across the school portal for you to take remotely."

JV said, "Don't ask mine to post any. I'd just as soon have a few more days to study."

John thought, "Yep, back to normal." They all finally relaxed, leaving John and Rebecca alone in the family room. Rebecca leaned on John resting her head on his shoulder and softly said, "Tomorrow will be a better day."

They stayed on the sofa for a while longer. Finally, John said, "I don't know what I'd do without you."

She answered, "Let's go to sleep. I have a feeling tomorrow will be a busy day."

Just then, tomorrow began. John's phone rang with the Caller ID announcing it was the General. With the phone on speaker so that Rebecca could hear, John immediately answered. Even if it were another threat, he felt better if she heard the news first-hand. Before John could say anything, the General said, "Senator, please express my apologies to Mrs. Lucas and the children."

Rebecca said, "You're on speaker with John and me, General. There are no apologies necessary. We owe you and Major Hunt a great debt of gratitude for keeping us safe tonight.

Please express our appreciation to all the men and women in your detail."

General Walker thought about how remarkable Rebecca Lucas' strength was. He now saw where John's transformation had come. He said, "It is a privilege to serve you, the Senator, and your family ma'am. And, Senator, I have some news about the attack tonight. The short of it is that we believe it was completely neutralized. I will have more details by morning. Shall I come to your residence for the briefing, or do you want me to come to the office?"

John looked at Rebecca and immediately knew the answer, "I will meet you at the office, General. Our children are here with us, and we prefer to shield them from as much of this experience as possible."

The General said, "Would ten hundred hours be too early for the briefing, Sir?"

John simply said, "Of course not, Dylan. And, please, call me John."

The General said, "Thank you, Sir, for that offer. However, you are my commanding officer now, in principle and soon in position." With that cryptic answer, the General disconnected from the call.

Rebecca said, "Commanding officer? What's he mean, John?"

He answered with a shrug of his shoulders, saying, "I have no clue. I'm just a senator."

Rebecca thought she felt something strange was happening. She said, "Well, it will be a short night. Let's go to bed."

John got up early, though not as early as Rebecca. She was already up and fixed coffee. She also ordered some bagels and muffins to be sent up for everyone. The protection detail nearly frightened the kitchen crew to death with their handguns drawn as the elevator opened. They nearly dropped the trays. Recovering a bit, Rebecca opened the door and explained that she ordered in some light breakfast. Then she said, "I thought y'all might be a bit hungry too. There's plenty for everyone, and I've got some Texas Pecan Coffee brewing inside."

John rounded the corner just in time to see the scene play out and retreated before laughing out loud. He knew Rebecca would not take "no" for an answer. They would be forced to come in and pour themselves a cup of coffee at the very least. He tried to rescue them, saying, "It's OK men, she's very persistent with her hospitality. You might as well come in and get a cup of coffee. It's just one of the ways we can say thank you for your courage and service for our safety."

The commander of the detail said, "Yes Sir." He then issued orders for his men to enter and return two at a time, never leaving the post unmanned. The server followed them in, still shaking from the guns. He hurriedly set everything up on the bar and timidly asked for permission to leave. He was obviously more concerned with leaving than a good tip. John just smiled and got his coffee.

John said his goodbyes to JV and Abby, hugged Rebecca and entered the private elevator to the garage. The driver and another detail were ready to transport John as soon as he arrived. They ushered him into the SUV and sped away.

Good to his word, Mateo made sure no press corps camped out either at the front of the building or at the rear entrance. John had no idea how he accomplished that small miracle, but he was certainly grateful. After entering the building, he couldn't help but notice how quiet the office was. Everyone was there, but it was too quiet. Even Mateo was more reserved than normal. He didn't say more than "good morning" when he met him at the vehicle. Sean and Patrick were at the door to the office suite and also simply said, "Good morning, Sir."

When John entered the offices, he said loudly enough for everyone to hear clearly, "Good morning, y'all. No one but the bad guys died. We're going to be fine. Let's finish what we started."

It was as if someone had let the air out of a balloon as everyone sighed. They all stood, and one by one joined together in applause. John was shocked and embarrassed. He walked toward his office and told Mateo, Sean, and Patrick that the General was due at ten o'clock, and he wanted them to be part of the meeting.

Mateo said, "We have been apprised, Sir. The General asked if we could use the conference room. It seems he's bringing several others with him for the briefing."

Now John's curiosity was piqued even more.

John saw that he had a few minutes to spare and thought he'd better touch base with Jeremiah and Sarah before the meeting. He walked by the scheduler's desk and asked, "Could you get Jeremiah or Sarah on the phone for me, please?"

Mateo said, "Sir, they'll be here any moment. Do you need to talk with them before their arrival?"

John stopped in his tracks and said, "Here? Why are they coming here?"

Mateo thought he had made a mistake and apologized, "I'm sorry Sir. When the General told me to make sure they were expected, I thought he was following your orders, Sir."

John smiled and said, "Relax, Mateo. It's fine. I'm sure the General has good reason to want them here, but we're going to need a bigger pot of coffee." With that, they all finally relaxed. John had a way of doing that innately.

True to Mateo's words, Jeremiah and Sarah arrived, protection detail in tow. Sarah immediately went to John and threw her arms around her brother, nearly in tears, saying, "Oh, John. I'm so grateful you're OK. I talked to Rebecca on the way over, and she told me all about it."

John thought she gave more information to Sarah than she did to him. Once again, Rebecca knew exactly how to handle him. He was more grateful for her than ever.

He said with a deadpan face, "Well, you got more of the story than I did."

Jeremiah laughed and said, "Lucas, women are well known for protecting their men."

John forgot to ask Sarah about her call to Peter Bridges. That was his reason for wanting to talk to her in the first place. All of that took a backseat as the General, and several other officers walked into the office. He was still dressed in black battle fatigues, not having been able to do more than freshen up overnight. He must have come straight from the detention center to Austin. He was an imposing figure in any uniform; however, wearing the clothing of battle armed with his sidearm, he was more than that. He looked almost feral. John couldn't imagine facing him thirty years ago when he was the commanding officer of Seal Team Seven.

John was first to speak, "Good morning, General Walker." He purposefully used Dylan's title to convey the message that he understood both his rank and position. He also wanted to make sure that everyone in the room knew how much respect he had for Dylan Walker. Because of him, his family was safe. That was a debt he would never forget.

The General immediately answered crisply, "Good morning, Senator. With your permission, Sir, may we gather in your conference room and begin the briefing?"

No one missed the deference with which the General now spoke to John. Patrick thought, "I've heard that tone before. That's how DOD personnel speak to the POTUS in the oval office. Something big is happening here."

John said, "Of course. As always, the coffee is hot."

They all walked behind John and the General as they led the way into the conference room. Once they were all seated, the General merely nodded to one of the other officers. That officer began to open and deploy a QtPro Sound Masking device that provided enhanced perimeter protection from any potential electronic eavesdropping.

The General explained the action, "We've brought along some technology making this room secure. While we are in this room, your phones and other electronic devices will become functionally silent."

When the officer finished, he nodded to the General that all was ready.

The General then began, "With your permission, Sir, I'll start with introductions of the officers I have accompanying me today?"

John said, "Please do."

The General went on to introduce each person. "First, I am grateful that we have Major Hunt, Senior Commander of the Texas Rangers, with us. He and his officers were primarily responsible for the takedown of the intruders at the Lucas Ranch last night. Without his first-hand knowledge of both the land and the ranch itself, we may not have been as well prepared as we were. We also have the commander of the protection details assigned to the Lucas' and the Mann's. I also asked the leader of the seal team I assigned to the ranch who captured two of the intruders, to be with us. And, lastly, I asked Admiral Andrew Jackson Crockett, Commander of the Judge Advocate General's office, to join us. Before we get too many questions, Admiral Crockett prefers to be called 'AJ'. He is not related to either of his namesakes, though he's tougher than both Andrew Jackson and Davy Crockett. Glad to have you with us, AJ."

The General took a sip of coffee and continued, "It is also a privilege to have Jeremiah and Sarah Mann, founders and directors of Texans for Life, with us. Additionally, we have Mateo Garcia, the Chief of Staff for the Senator, Sean O'Sullivan, the Media and Press Director for the Senator; and Patrick Beeman, the Senator's Chief Lobbyist and Legislative Director."

John humbly said, "General, let me interject that I, and my family, are grateful for the professionalism and courage displayed last night in the securing of my family's safety. I will never be able to express the depth of that gratitude adequately."

The General continued, "We are each appreciative you would feel that way, Sir. However, it is our privilege to protect a patriot and his family."

The General went on, "The reasons for each of you being in this meeting will become apparent as we continue the briefing."

As he said that, the General turned to the Lt. Commander of the seal team and asked him to begin.

As he directed their attention to the screens set up by John's staff earlier, John noticed they were positioned so that no one in the outer office could see the video. The Lt. Commander began to narrate each frame of the presentation. Some of the video was taken from the Blackhawk and showed the people on the ground as red images. He explained the color was caused by their heat signature being recorded by the infrared cameras. As the video progressed, he explained that the flashes of red light were actually shots being exchanged in the brief, but deadly firefight. For the first time, John realized how bad the battle was. There must have been hundreds of rounds fired from the combatants. As the fight progressed, the enemies' gunshots significantly declined as the seal team was more precise and deadly with their use of weapons. The Lt. Commander ended the presentation with video taken from the ground as the wounded were secured, and the two prisoners were placed in an armored transport vehicle. At the end of the presentation, he turned to the General and said, "Would you like to continue here, Sir?"

The General nodded and began to go further, "We have identified all of the enemy combatants. They are former military and US citizens, who are also known mercenaries. The Texas Rangers were aware of their movement into the state and began tracking them, though two weeks ago, they lost them in Mexico. We did not know they were the ones crossing the border to the ranch until after the skirmish. I can now report four killed, and one more died later at the hospital of wounds received in the skirmish. One other hostile is still in recovery and may survive, though the surgeons are not optimistic. Two were captured unharmed and taken to a secure location for questioning. I personally supervised that interrogation and will report on our findings shortly."

John's anger began to rise when he heard they were US citizens and former military. He knew he needed a break. He said, "Thank you, General. Please continue. I am going to get a cup of coffee while you do so."

Dylan recognized this was John's way of calming his temper, and he respected that greatly. He had already seen that side of John. Now was indeed a time for controlled precision, especially when the rest of the story came out.

The General continued, "When I reached the secure location to begin the interrogation, both enemy combatants declined to speak with anyone without having their lawyer present. However, as fortune would have it, as I explained their situation in more detail, both decided to give a detailed account of their actions, corroborated separately and now verified."

John sat up straight in his chair and said, "General, are you saying you know who hired them?"

The General said, "Yes Sir, beyond a reasonable doubt."

Sarah, who was sitting next to John, recognized the tension building and reached over to place her hand on John's arm. It was a subtle move but very effective. John closed his eyes, took a deep breath, and said, "Please, General, continue. I apologize for the interruption."

The General said, "I understand, Sir. The information is startling. I have not been able to clean up appropriately for this meeting due to the calls I needed to make in preparation for our meeting. And, it is at this point that I would like Admiral Crockett to continue the briefing."

Evidently, AJ Crockett preferred to stand to deliver his report. As he did, John realized how he made him think of "Old Hickory" Jackson. Andrew Jackson was the seventh president of the United States. He is known for founding the Democratic Party and for his support of individual liberty. Jackson's series of military successes, despite the obstacles he faced, stood in sharp contrast to the poor results of other military leaders during the War of 1812. His stunning victory at New Orleans made him a celebrated national hero, revered above all except George Washington. People called him "Old Hickory" because he was a strict and bold military officer. Old Hickory earned his nickname in that war. Not only was Jackson as unbending as a tree, but also as tough as wood.

Admiral Crockett began, "Because the attack came at the hands of former US military, JAG became involved. When I received the initial report from General Walker, I joined him at the interrogation-site to witness and supervise the questioning. Let me alleviate any concerns about the location and methods of interrogation. All were handled according to the law regarding enemy combatants and/or terrorists within our sovereign borders."

John recognized the double-speak immediately. However, he also recognized the results and knew that this information was essential to obtain his family's safety quickly.

Crockett continued, "We have independently verified the veracity of the testimony obtained from the combatants. We have concluded that they were contracted by Governor Perry Thompson through agents he directed. We have followed the financial paper trail that leads at least to the Lieutenant Governor through various offshore bank accounts. There is still an open investigation to close the loop on everyone involved. However, we are very confident that the Governor is at least complicit in the attack."

Sarah, whose hand was still resting on John's arm, immediately bore down with a tighter grip. It took everything within John not to slam his fist on the table and react to this information. But, once again, Sarah was enough.

Calmly, John began to speak. It was not hurried or angry. It was the same tone the General noticed earlier when he and Bob Hunt met with him. It was the tone of a man in control. It was the voice of a man who would not be turned away. John's staff saw this same demeanor before as well. They all held their breath at what might be coming next.

John said, "Let me be crystal clear. First, Admiral, define 'very confident.'"

The Admiral was surprised that was his first statement. He answered, "One hundred percent, Sir. There is no margin of error in this assessment."

John's next question surprised everyone but Jeremiah and Sarah. He looked at the General and said, "What does this mean for the threat level against my family?"

The others in the room were so shocked that they just froze. The General, who was also stunned, stammered, "Sir, we didn't anticipate that question."

John shot back immediately, "Then General, you have badly misunderstood me. I believe I was very unambiguous in our earlier meeting with you and Major Hunt that the first priority for me is my family. Now, once again, what are we going to do to secure their safety from this Benedict Arnold of a Governor going forward?"

The General recovered, "I'm sorry, Senator. I did misjudge you, though, in a very good way. I knew you to be a great patriot; now I know you to be an even greater husband, father, and brother. Nothing about their protection will be changed going forward. In fact, it will be enhanced. Now that we know where the snake lives, we can make sure he doesn't wiggle anymore."

While that reference was lost on some of the others in the room, John's staff and Major Hunt got it immediately.

John said, "Let's me be as direct as I know how. Going forward, I want him and anyone else involved in the attack on my family to be neutralized. I don't want them shot, General. I want them placed under a minimum of house arrest without the ability to make any plans for a second attempt. Second, I do not want this to leak to the press. The time is not right for that kind of diversion. That's probably what the snake was hoping for in the first place."

Using his first name to convey both loyalty and commitment, the General interrupted, "John, I couldn't agree more. May I suggest a plan going forward?"

John, returning the compliment of using the General's first name, simply said, "Dylan, you've been right every time so far. Please do."

The General said, "First, we continue full security detail around the clock for you and your family. They have been and will continue to be our first priority. However, we have another priority in play. The Governor's actions constitute treason against Texas. He cannot be installed next week. I would like your permission to visit with him privately and ask for his immediate resignation. I would also like to have the same talk with the Lieutenant Governor seeking the same result. I believe I can be persuasive enough to secure both of those today. Your staff has the ears of the media. If anyone can steer the news in the right direction, it is them. I want to be informed so as not to step on their efforts, but they should have the lead on this. I also suggest that you continue to lobby for Sarah's Law's passage in the first weeks of the session. With the passage of that into law, the rest will be little more than a mop-up campaign of a defeated enemy."

John said, "I see no problem with any of those steps, Dylan. However, with the resignation of the Governor and the Lieutenant Governor, who will sit in the chair to sign it into law?"

In that moment, Sarah knew why she was invited to the meeting. She said, "You will, John."

Chapter 24

The Die Is Cast

January 9, 2019 – January 15, 2019

Tyranny, like hell, is not easily conquered; yet we have this consolation with us, that the harder the conflict, the more glorious the triumph.

— Thomas Paine, December 19, 1776 in The American Crisis

COME AND TAKE IT

General Walker left the meeting with John Lucas as determined as ever. He called the Governor and the Lieutenant Governor and arranged a joint meeting with them for the following day. He made sure that Bob Hunt and AJ Crockett were able to attend the meeting as well. He knew there would be serious pushback from Governor Thompson. However, the die was already cast.

It is amazing how history finds a way of repeating itself in some of the most unusual ways. The fact that the General was thinking about the phrase "the die is already cast" reminded him of the inevitability of this path, just like the event that inspired that ageless idiom.

This phrase became popular from the Latin, *Alea iacta est*. A Roman historian, Suetonius, attributed the quote to Julius Caesar in the year 49 B.C. According to Suetonius, Caesar said this as he entered Italy with his army. As a result of the invasion, he started a civil war. When Caesar said *the die is cast*, he meant it was too late to stop the war from beginning at that point. He already disobeyed the orders, and now he must win the war if he wanted to keep his life. People still use the phrase millennia later when they realize they are at the point of no return. That was certainly the case now.

Once the Governor received General Walker's call, he knew they traced the attack back to him. He called the Lieutenant Governor into his office. After making sure no recording devices were operating, he said, "We have a problem."

The Lieutenant Governor replied, "We can make another attempt. The Lucas penthouse is not that secure."

The Governor shut him off with a wave of his hand and explained, "It's way too late for that. General Walker demanded a meeting with us tomorrow. He's also bringing Bob Hunt and AJ Crockett with him. Your team must have given us up."

The Lieutenant Governor bore a hole in the Governor and said, "My team? This was all your idea. This is not going to fall at my feet. If I go down, you go down with me."

The Governor was never a man to take responsibility for his failures. As much to the Lieutenant Governor as the air, he said, "Shut up and let me think. No one is going to go down. There's always another solution."

The Lieutenant Governor replied, "Short of our resignation like Nixon and Agnew, we're going to prison for a long time."

The Governor said, "Go put together a contingency plan and get back to me. Maybe they don't know anything, and it's just a fishing expedition."

The Lieutenant Governor said, "You don't believe that any more than I do."

As soon as he left, the Governor called Lydia Smithson. She answered immediately, "Have you heard any news since the attack at the Lucas Ranch?"

He sarcastically said, "Hello, Lydia. I hope you're doing well today."

She was shocked, "What are you talking about? Rebecca Lucas and her children were attacked last night. They could have been killed. When I said I thought something needed to be done to divert the Senator's attention, I didn't know you were going to send people to kill his family!"

The Governor didn't want to admit anything to Lydia Smithson. He became coy in his reply, "How did you hear about the attack? I haven't seen it on the news yet."

She answered, "I have my own sources, Governor." Indeed, she did have her own sources, though she knew little more than that an attack occurred.

The Governor continued, "The Lucases are fine. The terrorist group was neutralized quickly by the Rangers and State Guard. That's part of why I called. Can we meet later?" She agreed, though wondered why he wanted to meet face-to-face. They met for the early dinner meeting at Chez Nous near the Capitol. The old-world charm and quiet of Chez Nous made it the perfect choice for a quiet discussion.

The Lieutenant Governor did a little research to discover that he could not resign without guaranteed immunity from Admiral Crockett. He wrote several contingency plans for presentation to the Governor, though none of them contained even a hint of him seeking immunity in exchange for his testimony.

The Governor received the contingency plans by secure email shortly before he left for Chez Nous. He knew none of these would work without the agreement of Walker and the others. He also concluded that his time as Governor was over. He wanted to salvage what was left of his political future and withdraw quickly and quietly.

The Governor met Lydia at the front door. The hostess escorted them to a quiet corner of the French restaurant. They ordered drinks, and Lydia spoke, "What was so urgent, Perry?"

He was surprised she used his first name, though he thought that was simply her way of exercising superiority over him. He answered, "First, I want to know how much your retainer would be should I retain you as my personal legal counselor?"

Completely surprised by the question, she replied, "Why would you need me as your lawyer?"

The Governor knew better than to take that bait. He repeated, "How much, Lydia?"

She saw that no information was forthcoming without the agreement in place and said, "$5,000 is my standard retainer."

The Governor wrote her a check, immediately handing it to her with a simple contract detailing her as his personal legal counsel.

She quickly scanned it and found no unusual stipulations. Signing it she said, "OK. You've got client privilege in place. What's going on?"

He spent the next few minutes explaining his worries over the upcoming meeting with General Walker, Major Hunt, and Admiral Crockett. He believed they wanted to discuss his involvement in the attack on the Lucas Ranch.

"Do they have any proof?" she asked.

The Governor said, "I don't know. I'm meeting with them tomorrow morning."

She said, "Where?"

He answered, "At my office. They asked for the Lieutenant Governor and me to be present for this meeting."

She said, "Do not say anything to anyone without me being present. This means nothing to your staff or any elected or appointed officials."

She knew he had some culpability, or he would not have asked for her to be his attorney. She pressed further, "How involved is the Lieutenant Governor in this situation."

He tried to dodge the question, "I'm not sure how much he knows."

She looked at the Governor and stated in a very measured tone, "I didn't ask how much they know? I asked how much he is involved."

He quietly surrendered, "He knows more than enough to put us all in prison."

Lydia said, "Great. You managed to throw your presidency away. Let's hope we can keep you out of prison. How could you be so foolish?"

He said with his head lowered, completely defeated, "No one told me they were sending in mercenaries to shoot up the ranch house. The plan was just to scare Lucas into delaying the bill a little longer. Who could predict he would get the kind of support he's gotten?"

Then the Governor became angry and animated. Looking up, nearly shouting, he said, "My God, Lydia, he's got the Catholics and the Baptists rallying together on the steps of the Capitol! Linley-Harris told me to wire the money to an offshore account, and she would take care of the rest. I just told the Lieutenant Governor to send the money from the same fund we used in the past to cover off-the-record operations for Planned Parenthood."

Heads began to turn in the restaurant, and Lydia knew that he was terrified. She tried to quiet him, "Governor, please be calm. You're drawing far too much attention. Let's reconvene this meeting at my office in the morning. I will contact the General and ask him to meet us there."

The Governor took a deep breath and said, "Fine. Just keep me out of jail."

Lydia got up to leave. The server looked surprised and asked if everything was alright. She said, "Everything is fine. I've just gotten an emergency call."

He went to the Governor and asked if he could get him anything. Governor Thompson said, "Bring me a double-bourbon, neat, and the check."

He drained the glass of bourbon and left a hundred dollar bill on top of the check and left. When he got in the car to ride back to his residence, he called the Lieutenant Governor and informed him the meeting was rescheduled for Lydia Smithson's office.

The evening went by as if it were in slow motion. The Governor replayed every decision he made regarding Lucas' bill through in his mind. None of them seemed likely to bring him to this point. He tossed and turned through the night. Thankfully his family was still visiting relatives for the holidays. Mercifully dawn finally came. He got up and dressed to make his way to the Capitol.

When he arrived at the office, he was immediately met by Peter Bridges. His Chief of Staff asked, "Sir, are there new meetings this morning that I am unaware of since yesterday? The Lieutenant Governor insists he has a meeting with you at 10 am this morning."

The Governor didn't want to elaborate to Peter at the moment. He was a bit gruff as he said, "Just do what you're told for once, Peter."

Peter merely answered, "Yes Sir."

The Governor gathered a few things and left as quickly as he arrived. He met the Lieutenant Governor as his car pulled up to meet him.

The Governor said, "Hop in. We can talk on the way to Lydia's office."

The Lieutenant Governor complied, though they said nothing during the short drive to Lydia's office. When they arrived, two armed Rangers met them and informed them that they were both under arrest. After informing them of their Miranda Rights, they were escorted to Lydia Smithson's office. Fortunately, there wasn't any press gathered there that morning.

As he entered the office, the Governor saw General Walker, Major Hunt, and Admiral Crockett along with Lydia Smithson. Perry Thompson was unusually quiet. Normally he would greet them all with some quip or condescending acknowledgment. Knowing that he was facing the literal end of his career, he remained silent.

Lydia was the first to break the silence, "Good morning, Governor. Please do not speak unless I authorize it."

Lydia already informed Walker, Hunt, and Crockett that she was now representing the Governor going forward. She did not know that General Walker spoke to the Lieutenant Governor the previous night, securing his full cooperation in exchange for immunity from prosecution for any and all crimes associated with the attack on the Lucas Ranch.

Since Admiral Crockett represented the military and the state in this matter, he spoke first. Addressing the Governor and the Lieutenant Governor, he said, "Gentlemen, we are here to inform you of the charges against you. There are three counts of attempt to commit capital murder, three counts of aiding and abetting the commission of capital murder by terrorist group or groups, three counts of participation in murder for hire, conspiracy, and high treason against the State of Texas, as well as several other lesser charges. As you know, all of these carry the death penalty in our state. We will be seeking such. Since these crimes involve former military officers of the United States, the Judge Advocates Group will be prosecuting through a military trial's normal mechanism. Do you understand these charges?"

The color drained from Perry Thompson's face. He could only stammer, "Yes."

Lydia jumped in quickly, "Governor, I believe I asked you as your counsel not to say anything. 'Anything' means anything. I don't want to hear so much as a sigh from you. Are we clear? And, Admiral, I would like to know when I might be able to have the prosecutions discovery file?"

The Admiral smiled and said, "When I'm ready to release it."

She fired back, "I demand it by close of business today."

The Admiral looked at her like a cat about to play with its prey and said, "Ma'am, you're in no position to demand anything. We are here as a courtesy to the office. I have every right and intention to immediately have the Governor removed in shackles and remanded to a secure military detention center. There is only one thing that will prevent that from happening. That one thing is his full and open cooperation."

She was about to object when the Admiral cut her off, "Let me also inform you that we already have two of the terrorists who have cooperated fully with us. Their testimony has been cross-verified and validated. Furthermore, with the cooperation of the Lieutenant Governor, we have enough evidence to hang the Governor for treason by the end of the week. Do you still have objections, Ma'am?"

Lydia was horrified. She could only say, "No Sir. However, may I confer with my client in private for a moment?" The Admiral merely nodded his approval.

They retreated to an inner office where they would have some privacy. Lydia said, "As I asked you last night, how much do they have against you?"

He said, "Almost everything."

She saw a glimmer of hope and said, "Almost? What do you know that might keep them from executing you next week?"

The Governor said, "I know who gave the orders."

Lydia said, "Who was it?"

He said, "Ashley Linley-Harris."

Lydia cursed under her breath, "Are you sure? Do you have proof?"

He said, "Absolutely. I recorded her when she told me to transfer the money along with emails detailing the account names and numbers."

Lydia said, "Now, here's the new plan. You will still say nothing. We will go back in there, and I will try to negotiate your immunity just like that snake of a Lieutenant Governor did." Thompson nodded. Even a glimmer of hope was better than nothing.

Lydia Smithson, now with some renewed confidence, walked into the joining room and said, "Admiral, I believe we can reach a deal. My client is willing…"

The Admiral interrupted her with a raised hand as if to say, "Be quiet."

General Walker was about to speak, when the Admiral said, "I got this, Dylan."

The Admiral turned to Lydia and said, "Ms. Smithson, we already know about Ms. Linley-Harris and the involvement of Planned Parenthood."

She interrupted, "But we have emails and recordings clearly showing her involvement."

As though carefully choreographed, the General spoke again, "AJ, let's give them a chance to speak."

While Lydia didn't recognize it, she just got played by the oldest interrogation technique in the book. Many people called it the "good cop, bad cop" routine. The Admiral said, "Very well. Go on, Ms. Smithson."

She said, "We would like some sort of plea bargain. Of course, our first request would be the dropping of all charges and subsequent sentences."

They negotiated for nearly an hour, though the General and the Admiral already discussed where it would end earlier. At the end of it all, the Lieutenant Governor and the Governor would submit written statements. All originals and copies of evidentiary materials would be turned over, and they would resign effective immediately from their positions. Major Hunt also explained they would be placed in WITSEC, the United States Federal Witness Protection Program. They could bring their immediate family with them, though that was not a pre-requisite. This was the only point General Walker was not fully supportive of, but he would consent if they both signed the agreements immediately.

Lydia tried to object to WITSEC, but she had no remaining leverage. There was no turning back from their crimes. Their defeat was final and complete. Not only were the Governor and the Lieutenant Governor finished in politics, so was she. If for no other reason than by association, she hitched her wagon to the wrong horse. The die was cast, and they lost.

Chapter 25

The Crisis Builds

March 1, 2019 – June 5, 2019

There would be no difficulty in securing the rights of the people and the liberties of Texas if men would march to their duty and not fly like recreants from danger. Texas must be defended and liberty maintained.

— Sam Houston

COME AND TAKE IT

A s John sat on his swing, he was finally able to reflect over the last year. The beginning of the year was now little more than a blur. After the meeting between General Walker, Major Hunt, and Admiral Crockett with the Governor and Lieutenant Governor, things changed enormously. The General made a personal visit to John and his family and explained the meeting's events, though he did not share the plea agreement in full detail. The General also assured John that the imminent threat was over. However, he recommended continuing some protection level until he was beyond the first few weeks of the Legislative Session.

The events of the past months felt like a snowball rolling downhill. Not only did the events seem to gather size, but speed as well. The General delivered the letters to the State Attorney General. After he was given some of the details of the attack, he accepted them immediately.

The murky waters of jurisdiction between the Attorney General's Office and the military brought them to a conclusion that rather than make this a federal or state matter, the military was better suited to handle the subsequent legal issues. They all met together and devised a plan for a transition of powers, ultimately leaving John next in line through succession. After all, he had been duly elected as the Senate President Pro Tempore, which made him third in line. That would also give time to set dates for an election."

The cabinet was convened with the heads of both the House and the Senate, and a quick decision was reached to deflect the bad press by redirecting the Inaugural events. The rally to support John's legislation went on as planned, with crowds even larger than anticipated. That day was a turning point for John in many ways. He was the featured speaker at the rally and the only politician given time to speak.

John was on the podium joined by Rebecca, with Jeremiah and Sarah standing with them. He felt that it was an incredible moment bringing him closure to his spirit. It began so many years ago at that horrible meeting with his sister at Coopers BBQ. His failure and regret because of his inability to protect her would finally be redeemed. David Edwards gave the invocation and said a few words of affirmation and faith about the new direction for Texas under John's leadership. Michael Brody shared time at the podium with Bishop Joseph Mecina in a historic gathering of Evangelicals and Roman Catholics. They both spoke in grand gestures of the work begun to unite Christian believers around a central principle of freedom for all people, directly crediting John for this miraculous moment in the history of the Church. General Walker and Major Hunt were also on the dais. He remembered with some humor that the two of them were more a protection detail than participants. Even though security was still very strict, neither the Rangers nor the State Guard was openly visible to the crowd.

He was stirred back to the present when Rebecca joined him on the swing, "Penny for your thoughts?"

John laughed. He knew he could not continue in silence any longer. Rebecca would not tolerate him retreating inwardly for very long. His moment of introspection was over, "I have so many things bouncing around my mind; it may take more than a penny's worth of time."

She smiled and curled up beside him. She gave him that look that always encouraged and stabilized him. John said, "How did we get here?"

Rebecca simply said, "Are you looking for an answer, or is that just preamble?"

John thought, "Yep, I'm not going to wiggle off this hook." He continued, "I was always confident that Sarah's Law would pass and be signed into law. But I never dreamed it would take me becoming Acting Governor to do it."

He was quiet for a moment as Rebecca just waited for the torrent of words to begin. John started, "I should have known at the press conference following the rally. None of them wanted to talk about the bill. Whoever leaked the resignations knew this would force the situation in that direction. I remember the CBS reporter asking if I was ready to take the reins as the new Governor. I wasn't prepared for that question. In fact, I guess I need to talk to Sean about that. I wonder why he didn't prep me for that one? And Mateo looked as surprised as anyone. Nothing surprises him. He knows what time I'll be walking in the door. Heck, he even knows when I need a cup of coffee before I do. Patrick looked like the cat that swallowed the canary. Maybe he was the one who leaked it. After all, he was the one who started the whole Sam Houston thing. I need to talk to him about that. I'm no Sam Houston. That's for sure. And, here I am, sitting on the back porch in a swing, looking at the longhorns, and I ought to be making preparations for the closure of all the noncompliant abortion-sites. I'm not even sure how to do that. Who's going to make those decisions? Somebody's got to make sure we don't inadvertently deny medical treatment to women in the transition. And..."

Rebecca put her finger over his lips and silenced him, saying, "Feel better now?"

John softly replied, "I do."

He knew taking the weekend to come home and relax was just what he needed. She did too.

Rebecca said, "Good. I called down to the barn and had one of the hands saddle up two horses. Let's go for a ride and see if any more new calves have dropped this spring."

They got into the mule and drove to the barn finding the horses saddled and tied to the corral. They rode until the sun was just about to set and ended atop a slight rise and looked to the west. The sunset was brilliant with reds, oranges, and purples streaking across the sky. John said, "God really does know how to paint the sky!"

Rebecca said, "Yes He does. Ready to go home now?"

John nodded and swung his chestnut quarter horse around, saying, "Race you to the barn."

Rebecca was an excellent rider, but John managed to get there a length ahead of her. They dismounted, and she said, "It's not really a fair race when you start first."

They both laughed. One of the hands met them as they rode up to cool the horses and rub them down before putting tack up and turning them loose in their pasture.

John knew all the hands. Some of them started with his Dad on the ranch when John was just a boy. John greeted the hand, "*Buenas Noches*, Tomas. How's your wife?"

It reminded Rebecca why she loved him so much. Even in the midst of so much responsibility, John remembered the needs of the people around him first.

Tomas' wife was frail. Diagnosed with COPD some years ago, she was especially struggling these past few months. Tomas said, "Very well, Senor John. She is getting the best of care. Dr. Fitz says she will be stronger on the new medicine. *Gracias* for helping us find him."

In the middle of everything else, John made the call to Fitz to explain the situation with Tomas and Juanita. They came into the United States illegally decades ago, but now lived and worked at the ranch under a permanent visa. John did not want to put Fitz in a potentially compromising circumstance. Fitz assured him nothing would please him more than to take them on as patients personally. Even though his specialty was pediatrics, he could still treat them.

They got into the mule for the short ride back to the main house, and Rebecca said, "Thank you."

John said, "For what?"

She said, "Thank you for letting me win your heart all those years ago at A&M."

John looked at her and smiled. He knew that wasn't what happened. He was so fortunate she chose him, not the opposite.

The weekend went by so quickly. John found himself boarding the helicopter for the trip back to Austin much too soon. Touching down at the helipad, his driver met him along with the now ever-present protection detail of Rangers. To John's surprise, Mateo was also at the helipad.

John greeted him, "Good morning, Mateo. How are things at the office?"

Mateo was even more animated than usual. The attack at the ranch severely unnerved him. He said to John, "Not good, Sir. Things have taken a turn for the worse, Sir."

John was still in a great mood from the weekend at home and said, "I'm sure the world is not coming to an end in the next thirty minutes. Let's talk on the ride over to the office."

His driver unloaded and stowed John's things into the black armored SUV, and they began the short trip to the office. John said, "So, tell me what's happened."

Mateo said, "Sir, the press is becoming more and more problematic. They camp out at every entrance around the clock. They are now hoping to get a sound bite from anyone, including the interns."

John was quite accustomed to Mateo's panic, as well as his coping mechanism. He asked Mateo, "What time is the press conference?"

Mateo nervously responded, "Well, Sir, I didn't want to bother you with the details while you were at home. I know it has been a very difficult transition since the attack."

John interrupted, "Mateo, I'm not mad. You have the authority to act in my best interest, and I trust you to do so."

Mateo said, "Thank you Sir, but the press conference is scheduled for this afternoon. The complicating factor is the other appointments prior to meeting with the press."

John said, "And, what might those be?"

"Mateo said, "I've also put time on your schedule for a meeting with General Walker."

John said, "No problem."

Mateo went on, "Yes Sir. However, Ms. Linley-Harris wants time with you today as well."

John's curiosity piqued, and he asked, "About what?"

Mateo said, "That's just it, Sir; she wouldn't say."

John thought for a moment and finally said, "Don't schedule her until after I speak with the General."

Mateo sighed with relief and said, "Thank you, Sir."

As the car arrived, John saw Mateo was right. The press was everywhere. The Ranger in charge of the protection detail said, "Don't worry Sir, we will clear the way."

John said, "That's OK, Captain. I can hop out and handle this quickly."

Mateo was alarmed, "No hopping out, Sir. These people haven't been cleared. What if they start shooting!"

John said, "We'll hope they're bad shots. Go ahead, Captain, run a little interference for me, but I do want to talk to them."

The Captain thought this man was indeed like Sam Houston. He said, "Yes Sir."

Even though they cleared the crowd, when John emerged from the SUV, it was a melee with reporters all jockeying for the closest position. John simply lifted a hand and said, in his best Texas drawl, "Mornin' y'all. How's everyone enjoying our spring weather?"

All the reporters began shouting at once. John was still uncomfortable being addressed as Governor, though that would be made permanent with the final vote in the joint session as approved earlier by the State Supreme Court. That legislation had sailed through even faster than the approval of Sarah's Law.

Finally, he shouted above the din and said, "I promise I will have a full statement for you along with ample time for questions this afternoon. Until then, I must attend to my other duties."

As he started to press forward with the Rangers clearing the way, he once again heard someone say, "There goes Sam Houston and his *Los Diablos Tejanos.*"

The Rangers smiled to themselves. Mateo just shook his head in disbelief, thinking, "I just hope there aren't any Alamos in our future."

Things were nearly back to normal in the office, though it was busier now due to his appointment to the Governor's chair. John entered and said, "Good morning, y'all. Hope everyone had a great weekend."

Sean and Patrick fell into step with Mateo trailing John to his office. Sean whispered, "Looks like the boss is chipper this morning." Patrick said a little too loudly,

"I hope so. It looks like today is going to be a crazy day." John picked that up and said, "I heard that, Patrick." They all had a good laugh.

The scheduler handed him his messages and said, "The General is on his way over, Sir."

John thought, "Yep. Patrick's right, today's going to be a crazy day."

He was still feeling the good effects of the great weekend at home with Rebecca and the kids. Hopefully, it would be enough to get him through the day.

Once they were all inside the office, Mateo said, "Sir, we believe it would be good to cover some preliminary questions in a one-pager. Hopefully, we can limit the conference to an hour."

John said, "What preliminary questions do you think we need to cover?"

Mateo nodded to Sean to take over the briefing. Sean said, "Sir, we believe there are three primary questions that will be asked. First, what are the locations of the former Governor and the former Lieutenant Governor? No one has said a word about their whereabouts. Second, who was responsible for the attack on your family and when will they be brought to trial? And, last, when will the Planned Parenthood in Houston close its abortion procedures. It is common knowledge that they are currently in violation of the new law without any consequences. A possible follow-up to that last question is what we are prepared to do if they refuse to comply?"

John said, "I think there are more than three questions in your list, Sean."

Sean fumbled with his words thinking he had been reprimanded, but John quickly added, "Sean, I'm kidding. Everything is OK. You guys need a drink. Relax. It's not the Alamo. Santa Anna is not encamped around us. Besides, we've got the *Los Diablos Tejanos* on our side."

They couldn't quite muster a laugh, though John smiled and said, "I can see Cooper's and a bucket of Shiner in our near future, men."

Then John got a bit more serious, "Mateo, are Jeremiah and Sarah going to be at the press conference?"

He answered, "I don't know, Sir. Do you want them here?"

John said, "Yes. I'll make that call. I also want the General to be there. I'll take care of that when he arrives."

As if on cue, John's scheduler buzzed in announcing the General's arrival. The General needed no one to let him in, though John waved him through the closed door.

John said, "Howdy, Dylan. How are you and how's Bradley doing?"

General Walker was always disarmed by John's knack for putting him at ease. He answered John's question, "Fine in answer to both your questions."

John interrupted the General before he could continue and said, "See, the General can count the number of questions in a conversation as well as I can."

The General had no idea what John meant and looked around puzzled. Then John said, "It's an inside joke, Dylan. My staff and I were just discussing the details of a one-pager that answers some questions before we open the floor to the press.

They said there were three principal questions to be covered, but there were actually five."

The General laughed and said, "I see. You boys having a little PTSD?"

Finally, some air returned to the room as they all laughed.

John said, "General, what brings you to the poor side of town?"

The General answered, "I heard the natives were restless, so I thought it would be helpful to give you a full report. Much of it is classified. Have all your men been cleared?"

Mateo spoke up, "Yes Sir. We received our clearance last Friday."

The General continued, "Good. I'm glad they expedited the process. Perhaps you should recite those questions to begin the briefing."

Sean said, "Sir, where are the former Governor and Lieutenant Governor? No one seems to know their whereabouts."

The General answered, "Their exact locations are unknown, even to me. They agreed, along with their immediate families, to be placed under the protection of WITSEC. I don't even know what office is supervising them. Because of this, I suggest you simply defer to the Governor or myself to answer that question if it is raised. What's the next question?"

Sean referred to his iPad and repeated the next question, "Sir, who was responsible for the attack on the Governor's family, and when will they be brought to trial?"

The General said, "I see the reference to multiple questions now. That's four so far, Sean."

Sean said quietly and somewhat embarrassed, "Yes Sir."

The General said, "They're still a little tightly wound, Governor."

John laughed and nodded, "I think Cooper's and a bucket of Shiner later will help."

The General smiled and continued, "All the identities of the attackers, those killed in the firefight and those captured, are currently being withheld because it is still an ongoing investigation. That information will be forthcoming in the weeks ahead. The Judge Advocate Group's office made it clear that a trial will be held under the authority of the military as soon as the investigation is complete. I took the liberty of inviting him to the press conference today. He may have more to say at that time. What I can tell you is that the threat was completely neutralized. And, while we do not expect any further threats from this source, we are fully prepared for any future possibility."

The General turned directly to John and asked, "I do have the identity of another one of the conspirators, Sir. Do you want that information now or later?"

John said, "Now is fine, General. They are cleared through Top Secret."

The General continued, "Governor, as you already surmised, Ms. Ashton Linley-Harris, the Director and CEO of Planned Parenthood, was one of the principal directors of the attack. We now know she made the initial contact with the former Governor, who then enlisted and instructed the former Lieutenant Governor to divert state funds from a black ops account to the mercenaries. We have enough evidence to arrest her and convict her."

Mateo said, "Why haven't you done so?" That comment drew a look from John that silenced Mateo from making any further comments.

John then said, "I'm sure Admiral Crockett and General Walker have their reasons, Mateo. I'm also sure that your question is simply a reflection of your surprise at the depth of the conspiracy. Please continue, General."

The General continued, "We still have a few unanswered questions as to motive. Therefore, I would insist that none of this information I have given you be communicated beyond this group. Governor, according to my information, it is my understanding that you have been contacted by Ms. Linley-Harris requesting some time with you."

How the General found out about that was unimportant to John. He said, "Yes, I have not returned her call or made the time available to her."

The General replied, "Good. Let's see if she shows up at the press conference. I think she may be turned into an asset. She could be invaluable in determining how far up the chain of command the orders for the attack goes."

John agreed with the General. He then turned back to Sean and said, "There was one more question, Sean. Would you like to continue?"

John was angry that his suspicions were now confirmed. However, he was still completely in control of his emotions.

Sean continued, "General, there will be numerous questions concerning the continuing of abortions at the Planned Parenthood facility in Houston. Do we have any plans in place for this contingency that we can relay to the press?"

The General answered, "Yes, we have several potential recommendations for the Governor. However, I would stress that none of these will be made public until the Governor agrees we should proceed. Therefore, I recommend that the Governor address this question personally if it arises."

John said, "I agree."

Mateo said in summation, "I think we have our marching orders, Governor. May we be excused, or is there anything else we need to be informed about?"

Having calmed himself, John said, "The bigger question may be whether any of you have questions?"

They expressed appreciation for being asked but were satisfied they had enough information to finish preparing for the press conference. Once again, the General was pleased. John Lucas' leadership skills were exceptional.

As they left, John noticed Admiral Crockett waiting to see him. He walked out and extended his hand, "Forgive me, AJ, I didn't know you were waiting. Please come in."

The Admiral responded, "Thank you for your kindness, Governor. However, a moment of downtime was most welcome." He greeted the General, and John shut the door.

John said, "The General gave me the full report, Admiral, and we do have a request of you. The General suggested, and I concur that you should field any questions at the press conference concerning the disposition and ultimate trial of the attackers. Does that meet with your approval?"

Immediately the Admiral said, "Of course, Sir. To what level of detail do you want me to speak?"

John answered before the General had a chance, "As little as possible." Realizing he may have overstepped, John apologized, "I'm sorry, Dylan. I hope that you agree?"

The General said, "John, you're officially my commanding officer now. I do agree, but regardless I will follow your orders. I will do so because that is the chain of command and, even more so, because I trust you completely."

John said, "Yep, I am certain of it. Cooper's Barbeque and a bucket of cold Shiners are definitely on the list of imperatives for this evening." They all laughed.

John needed to make one more call before the press conference. As he dialed Sarah's cell number, the General and Admiral rose to excuse themselves. John motioned for them to remain seated.

Sarah answered quickly, "John is everything alright?"

He quickly said, "Everything is fine, Sarah. Are you going to panic every time I call?" She laughed.

John continued, "Can you and Jeremiah be at the office for the press conference this afternoon?"

She said, "Jeremiah is still in DC, but I can be there. Will that work?"

John said, "Of course. And thanks!"

As predicted, Ms. Linley-Harris did show up for the meeting. The Rangers stopped her at the door since she had no credentials. She began to shout insults at them. As she tried to push her way past them, the General and the Admiral walked out of

John's office. General Walker saw her and ordered, "Detain that woman immediately by any force necessary!"

The Rangers were forceful, but not nearly as physical as possible considering the circumstances. She shouted at the General, "You have no right to keep me out of this meeting. This is a public meeting."

The General was about to speak when John stepped forward and softly said, "Ms. Linley-Harris, first I would remind you that you are not a credentialed member of the press; second, this is neither a public place nor a public meeting."

She took a breath to shout at John, but before she could utter a syllable, he said, "Please, calm yourself and come into my office. Perhaps we can have a chat before the press conference begins."

He then turned to Mateo and said, "Mateo, will you please get a visitor's badge for Ms. Linley-Harris."

Ms. Linley-Harris almost stomped into John's office. Dylan, AJ, and John nonchalantly entered once Mateo handed her the ID. Before Mateo gave it to her, he said, "Ma'am, do you need help putting the badge on or are you calm enough to do so without injury?" John almost laughed out loud.

The three men all took seats in the chairs surrounding the hide-covered sofa while Ms. Linley-Harris stood defiantly. As he gestured at the sofa, John said, "I'm sure we'll all be more comfortable if you take a seat."

She said, "I'm sure you would. However, I prefer to stand."

Like a mongoose stalking a cobra, the General said, "Sit down, ma'am. I insist." His tone shook her so badly that she sat without a word.

The Admiral began, "I'm not sure we've formally met."

Some of her composure returned, and she sarcastically said, "I don't believe I've had the dubious pleasure, though I'm sure you will attempt to impress me with your high position."

John broke in, "Admiral, let me do the honors. Ms. Linley-Harris is the Director and CEO of Planned Parenthood, headquartered in Houston. Ma'am, this is Admiral Crockett, the commanding officer of the United States Judge Advocate Group of Texas, headquartered here in Austin."

The Admiral liked the way John subtly used the familiar title of "ma'am." The Admiral said, "Thank you, Governor. I appreciate you taking the time to meet with us earlier for a complete briefing of the facts surrounding the attack at your ranch. And, ma'am, I believe it is in your best interest to communicate with us in a much less combative demeanor. Don't you?"

Linley-Harris' mind began to race. The pieces of the puzzle were falling into place very quickly. She said, "Am I being detained?"

The Admiral immediately became the "good cop" leaving the "bad cop" to the General. This placed John in the position of an interested observer. The Admiral said, "Do we need to detain you?"

Immediately the General said, "Cut to the chase AJ. Let me get the Rangers in here and take her into custody. I'm sure she would look good on the news tonight handcuffed and escorted out of the office."

She thought one more attempt at bravado might work, and she said, "Shall I call my attorney now or later for this harassment?"

Admiral Crockett looked her in the eye and said, "If you call your attorney now, long before they can arrive, you will be in custody and charged with three counts of attempted capital murder, terrorism, and plotting to assassinate an elected official and/or his family. There are also about a dozen other lesser charges we are prepared to bring, though you will get the death penalty before those cases are brought to court." The Admiral paused for effect. Then he said, "Perhaps you have something you would like to say now?"

She replied, "I want my attorney present before I say anything." The General got up to go to the door, and she nearly shouted, "Where are you going?"

The General smiled and said, "To ask the Rangers to come in. I detest shouting through a closed door."

Ashton Linley-Harris was undone. She could barely whisper, "What do you want?"

The Admiral said, "We want all the names, written documents, and communications between you and your coconspirators regarding this act of terrorism."

She said softly, "What will I get if I give you everything?"

The General, still in "bad cop" mode, said, "That depends on what 'everything' looks like."

Linley-Harris hesitated, and then said, "I'm dead either way. They will make sure there's a bullet in my head before I get out of this building. They have ears everywhere."

The Admiral said, "Ma'am, if that is true, I'm sure you recognize the wisdom of placing yourself in our protective custody while we depose you."

She was caught in a trap with no good way out. She never felt more helpless. She said, "What comes next?"

Before anyone could say another word, one of the Rangers burst into the office and nearly threw John to the floor, covering him with his body. The General was first to grab Linley-Harris and pull her to the floor behind the sofa. Suddenly a loud pop came from the window to the office, and immediately two shots rang out. There was some chaos though the office was now flooded with State Guards ordering them to shelter in place. Within moments, Major Hunt came into the office. Going to General Walker, he said, "The sniper has been neutralized, Sir. I'm afraid we were not able to take him alive."

He turned to the Governor and said, "Sir, are you alright?" John said, "Looks like it's two buckets of Shiner tonight, General." The General merely smiled.

Later, after everything was sorted out, the press was briefed with some of the story. After Ms. Linley-Harris was safely secured, Bob Hunt approached John and said, "I'm sorry we didn't tell you the whole story, John. I knew you'd be safe in your office. I helped your Dad install the bullet-proof glass years ago during the Lone Star Steel strike in '68. We needed the shooter to reveal himself so we could get him."

John looked at Dylan and said, "Well, I did tell you to use me as bait."

The General said, "Sir, we do not think you were the target. Our preliminary information was that Ms. Linley-Harris was targeted the moment the attempt on your family was neutralized. While we were prepared for it here, that was as much a result of our continued surveillance and protection of you as it was a trap. We will never use you as bait, Governor."

John continued, "Thank you, Dylan. However, I have a very serious question, to which I want nothing – I repeat, nothing – left out. Is my family safe?"

Dylan looked at John for a long moment, knowing this was the completion of a deep bond between them, and said, "I gave you my word they would be. I can assure you they have never been safer."

John was relieved. He then said, "Do they know anything about any of this?"

The General said, "As she has requested, I have kept her in the loop for the duration of your stay in Austin. She ordered me not to bother you with her safety. In fact, her exact words were: 'General, make sure my husband comes home.'"

John could hear her saying just that. The General went on, "I have her on a live satellite communication if you'd care to speak to her."

The General gave the order for the communications officer to bring the Sat Phone in. Handing it to John, he said, "Rebecca?"

She answered, "Yes, John?"

He quickly recovered, "How's the weather there?"

She said, "It was a little hotter than usual for this time of the year, but I think we got a cooler breeze blowing now."

John said, "You know I love you?"

She said, "Always."

John looked at the General and said, "Thank you, Dylan. I am forever in your debt."

The General said, "No Sir. It is I who am in your debt."

John wasn't up for barbeque, but he knew it might be a good way for everyone to unwind. As Sean had earlier predicted, it was a crazy day! He asked his staff, Bob, Dylan, and AJ, if they would like to go to Cooper's. They all agreed it would be a great way to end the day. Later, after way too many ribs and a few Shiners, John thought about how fortunate he was to have so many good people around him. There was still a crisis building, but he felt like they could handle it when it came. He knew they still had to deal with Houston.

Chapter 26

The First Shot

June 1, 2019 – October 2, 2019

War is declared... public opinion has proclaimed it.

*— **Stephen F. Austin, written two days after the***
Battle of Gonzales

COME AND TAKE IT

The end of the 86th Texas Legislative Session found John as the newly appointed Governor of Texas, with a special election to confirm that soon. Sarah's Law was quickly put into effect with every abortion clinic closed except the Houston facility of Planned Parenthood. Even that location was nearly closed. It was just a matter of time before he could begin to see real fruit from his labors.

As he sat in his favored spot, swinging on the porch of his ranch, he thought about the whirlwind of activity this summer was going to be. JV graduated high school with honors, even with all the interruptions of his schedule. He and Rebecca were already helping him make plans for his first semester at Texas A&M. Fish Camp, an Aggie tradition that began at the end of July.

John couldn't believe how quickly the time passed between his Fish Camp and now his son's. It would be different in many ways. JV was not planning on joining the Corps of Cadets, as John did. Much of that decision was in the fact that JV and Katy Fitzgerald were now nearly inseparable. That certainly was the primary reason Katy decided to follow JV to A&M.

She was the eldest child of Dr. Gregory and Barbara Fitzgerald. The Fitzgerald's and Lucas' were good friends, made even closer by the relationship developing between their oldest children. Fitz, as Dr. Fitzgerald preferred to be called, always chided John about the power of a Tennessean and a Texan working together. He would say, "You know, John, the Alamo would have fallen the first day except for Davy Crockett."

John could not deny that Katy was a brilliant young lady. However, her greatest attribute was how she seemed always to know what to say to keep JV focused in the right direction. She reminded John so much of Rebecca.

All the principal players in the attack on him and his family were either in WITSEC or incarcerated, awaiting their sentencing hearing's final disposition. The biggest surprise was how far up in the private and public sectors the conspiracy went. Planned Parenthood involved itself throughout its administrative directory. Ms. Linley-Harris took the brunt of the responsibility and, as a result, would not be seeing a day of freedom for the rest of her life. She did manage to escape the death penalty in exchange for her cooperation detailing the involvement of several other directors of the national Planned Parenthood organization. They were still awaiting trial, but the cases against them were strong.

John was still lost in thought when Rebecca walked around the swing and sat down beside him. He didn't hear her and was a bit startled.

She smiled and said, "Did I startle you?"

It was the way she said it more than the words, so all he could do was laugh. "I guess I'm still a little gun-shy."

Rebecca encouraged him, "Oh, John. Everything's going to be just fine. Besides, Sam Houston's 'Texas Devils' are still on guard."

They both laughed.

When Rebecca saw she succeeded in breaking into his train of thoughts, which would likely end in self-recrimination or remorse, she said, "Let's do something fun tomorrow."

John said, "Well, I thought we'd all go to church as usual. What do you have in mind?"

She said, "Oh, I didn't want to change that. I was thinking about tomorrow evening. Since it's Sunday, most folks are available. Let's have a cookout. The weather should be perfect."

John said, "Who do you want to invite?" He knew she was probably a step ahead of him as usual and might have already invited the folks she wanted to be there.

He chuckled, and she said, "What's so funny?"

John answered, "I'm getting better at this than you think. What time are we eating and who's coming?"

She was coy as she answered him, "Just a small group. I thought if folks wanted to come over after church, say two or three, we could visit and eat around six o'clock."

John said, "How many is 'a small group'?"

She said, "Just our close friends and family… Jeremiah and Sarah, the Lamberts, the Edwards, the Fitzgeralds, your staff, Dylan Walker, Bob Hunt, and AJ Crockett… about twenty altogether."

John said, "I see it's going to be a 'small' group!"

She laughed. "Well, John, they're all going to be here anyway."

John had no clue what that last statement meant. He did not know that there was a new conspiracy working in the background. David Edwards called her weeks ago and told her he wanted to surprise John with the news that John was the recipient of The Distinguished Alumnus Award from Texas A&M University. It is the highest honor bestowed upon a former student of the university. The award is jointly sponsored by The Association of Former Students and Texas A&M. It recognizes those former students who have made significant contributions to society and whose accomplishments and careers have brought honor and distinction to Texas A&M and The Association of Former Students. In over fifty years, only 291 former students received this award. David submitted John for consideration last year, and he was unanimously approved. The actual awards ceremony wouldn't be held until October. David was given the honor of breaking the news.

Everyone was sworn to secrecy. Even Abby promised not to say a word about the plan. John woke up as usual and took his coffee to the back porch. It seemed to be the perfect day. It wasn't nearly as hot as it could be in South Texas. There was a little breeze blowing in from the south, across the *sendero*. Even Pancho Villa looked happy now that Bevo had been moved to another corral to prepare him for the University of Texas' football season. Those two didn't get along at all.

Rebecca joined John on the porch, but only to remind him they needed to leave earlier than usual.

John questioned her, "What's the hurry? I sure don't want to be there too early. The last thing I want is to have David ambush me with another impromptu press conference."

Rebecca knew better than anyone how to sidestep John, "Oh, did I forget to mention Jeremiah and Sarah are meeting us there. I wanted to be sure and get there early enough for us to all sit together. You know how crowded it is at church since you became Governor."

He still wasn't used to that. He apologized to David every time he saw him. It was definitely an imposition with the additional security and crowds that gathered to see him.

David simply laughed him off, saying, "Well, at least we get all these folks at church once, don't we?" David Edwards never chased a crowd, but he never wasted an opportunity to tell them the Gospel either.

They all got ready and hopped in the SUV, with the protection detail leading the way in another SUV. He no longer drove anywhere alone other than along the roads and trails of the ranch. John quit complaining about their constant supervision months ago. His family was more important than any embarrassment he felt from the entourage.

They arrived at the main campus of Grace Restoration Church, and John saw a much larger group of reporters and cameras than usual. He also saw some of the church's security personnel herding them inside. They remained in the SUV until the last of them walked away. The Rangers opened doors and escorted them inside. Jeremiah and Sarah were there, waiting inside the doors. After the hugs and greetings, John saw General Walker, Major Hunt, and Admiral Crockett standing near the Coffee Corner, talking with some of the press. They all wore their dress uniforms. He thought perhaps that was because it was a Sunday. They did strike an imposing threesome. By now, everyone knew of the part each of them played in the attacks and the days that followed. Before John could walk into the auditorium, Mateo appeared with Sean and Patrick.

Now John was concerned. He said, "Howdy, men. What's going on?"

Thankfully, David was nearby and rescued them, "Good morning, Governor. Rebecca, how are y'all?"

David shook hands with John. Then David turned to Jeremiah and Sarah saying, "It's always great to see y'all. He shook Jeremiah's hand, but as was his custom, he hugged Sarah. He was as much a grandfather to her as a pastor.

He continued, "It is always such a pleasure to see two of my favorite people in the world. Glad y'all could come by today. I'm looking forward to catching up this afternoon."

John realized he was probably getting suspicious for no reason. Maybe nothing was going on after all. They all just decided to get an early start to the day and drove in earlier than he expected.

David turned them over to some of the greeters, and they were all ushered to some seats nearer the front than usual. John thought it strange that the Fitzgerald's and Lambert's were all seated in what he now saw was reserved seating. He pushed the thought aside as the worship team began to sing. John didn't know some of the songs. They were always introducing new choruses based on the theme of David's current sermon series. When the Scripture passage was read, John's interest was particularly piqued. David was in the middle of a new series from the Book of Genesis and the life of Joseph. Today's reading was from the last chapter. The last verse of the reading caught John's attention. The context was Joseph speaking to his brothers, who came to beg for his forgiveness: "You intended to harm me, but God intended it for good to accomplish what is now being done, the saving of many lives" (Genesis 50:20 NIV).

David used this verse with John many times to encourage and comfort him.

When David stepped to the center-stage, he began by reading the twentieth verse again. Then he uncharacteristically stopped with a lengthy pause. It looked as though he was trying to find the right words to push through a very emotional moment.

Finally, David said, "I know I often use stories in my teaching to illustrate a principle of Scripture. In fact, I often get criticized for telling too many stories. However, today's truth cannot be better illustrated without such a story. It took place last year on a typical October morning in South Texas as I met a dear friend for breakfast at our own Downtown Café. As my friend sank into our normal booth, he was particularly troubled. His exact words were, 'I'm done.' My friend continued by releasing a torrent of words about his deep feeling that something drastic needed to be done in Texas to protect the lives of the tens of thousands of unborn children in our state. He recounted his own personal story and the effect his inaction might have played in the life of someone very close to his heart, his sister. He told me he was committed to doing something so that no one would ever be forced to endure those same feelings ever again in Texas. It wasn't a terribly long dialogue. However, at the end of it, I asked one question: 'What are you prepared to do?'"

John knew early on that the pastor was talking about his meeting with him. He also knew that when David Edwards spoke, no one dared retreat. John was stuck. The pastor continued, "My friend did not waiver or hesitate. With the same resolute determination of the likes of John Adams, Benjamin Franklin, Thomas Jefferson, Roger Sherman, and Robert Livingston, who he quoted, he answered my query with a simple truth, 'It's the right thing to do.' We have another Founding Father in our reading today who came to the same conclusion. His name was Joseph. We know him as a Patriarch of Israel."

David Edwards went on to tell the story of Joseph. Rejected and sold into slavery by his brothers, he came to the foreign land of Egypt. While there, he was falsely accused of attempted adultery with his master's wife and endured years of imprisonment. One day Joseph was called out of his prison cell into Pharaoh's presence. He had the reputation of being able to interpret dreams. After explaining the dream to Pharaoh, the mightiest ruler in the known world, he was appointed to Egypt's second most powerful position. He was the providentially appointed to be a savior to an entire nation by storing away food for the coming famine. The abuse and hardship he endured was not easy. His brothers put him through immense pain and suffering. However, when he could have retaliated in a way that many of us would have justified, he told his brothers, 'You intended to harm me, but God intended it for good to accomplish what is now being done, the saving of many lives.'

David continued, "As you probably have surmised, my friend is now the Governor of our great state, John Lucas. He endured a different kind of betrayal, not from his family, but from those who took an oath to do the very thing he has done – protect the lives of the citizens they serve. His family was attacked in a cowardly act of terrorism. He patiently endured the attacks of those who would rather hurl insults at him than engage in a mutually profitable discussion. He never sought to promote himself. He merely wanted to defend those who could not do protect themselves. I am proud to know him. I am privileged to call him my friend. He made good on his commitment. Sarah's Law is nearly fully implemented in our state."

The entire congregation began to applaud, and David raised his hand to silence them, "Though I would join you in honoring this good man, please hold your applause for a moment."

David went further, "We are honored today to have many of the key figures who brought us to this incredible moment in our state's history. Let me introduce each one of them to you."

David instructed the audience to hold their applause until he finished. He also asked each of them to join him on stage. He wanted to make sure everyone watching the simulcast could see them as well. He called each of their names beginning with Rebecca and included everyone sitting with John. For those unfamiliar with their titles and positions, he included that information along with their introductions. The press pushed their way forward to capture all of it for their evening news. It was an impressive line of men and women.

Finally, David said, "All of these men and women played a pivotal role in the process. What started out nine months ago as a conversation with John at a little café in South Texas resulted in Texas being the first state to protect human life from conception since Roe v Wade. This all began with our own John Lucas, now the Governor of our great Lone Star State!"

He called John to the stage, and the congregation could not be contained any longer. Some burst into shouts while others applauded loudly.

As John made his way to the stage, he could hardly contain his emotions. They were mixed with gratitude, humility, and genuine love for this great man of God who meant so much to him.

John was about to speak when David said, "Before Governor Lucas speaks, I want to be the first one to announce the well-deserved award of The Distinguished Alumnus Award from Texas A&M University, which will be formally presented to the Governor in October."

John could not contain his emotions any longer. Fortunately, Rebecca was standing beside him, and she slipped her hand into his to steady him. Nearly in tears, John looked at her, turned to David and said, "You know better than anyone, Pastor, I deserve no credit. It is only by the grace of God through Christ that I stand here today. He deserves all the glory."

The press tried to ask questions, though security quickly ushered them away from the stage. So many people wanted a moment with John that David finally said, "There will be another time to say a personal word to the Governor. However, for now, we have some special cards placed in the seatbacks for you to convey your prayers and thoughts. Our worship team is going to come and sing for a bit while you do that. There will be boxes at the exits for you to place the cards. They will be delivered to the Governor this afternoon."

As the worship team came, David led the congregation in prayer. His protection detail ushered John and his family out to the SUV as quietly as possible. General Walker, Major Hunt, Admiral Crockett, and the staff went to their prearranged spots for people to speak with them on John's behalf. David remained with the press to take the brunt of the questions.

When they were in the SUV, Rebecca, still holding John's hand, said, "I hope you're not mad, John. You are truly a great man."

John, having regained his composure, smiled and said, "Of course I'm not mad. Besides, who has ever been able to tell David Edwards 'no' to any of his schemes!"

They all laughed and JV said, "Does this mean I should start calling you a Founding Father?"

Even the Rangers in the front seats laughed at that. It was a very pleasant ride back to the ranch. No one knew how quickly that feeling would evaporate.

Everyone arrived at the ranch by mid-afternoon. They all gathered on the porch to enjoy the sights and smells of the ranch hands cooking over the open pit. Cabrito was a favorite and always on the menu at the Lucas' cookouts. David and Meg were the last to arrive. John was glad to see he changed into a more comfortable choice of jeans and boots.

The conversation was light and personal. No one wanted to talk "shop." They would be returning to Austin soon enough, and that could wait. John did ask Dylan about Carson Bradley. He knew he didn't have long to live. Dylan simply said, "He's a fighter, though I think this fight is almost over."

John said, "I wonder if he's up for a visit next week?"

The General said, "I think he would like that. I'd be happy to accompany you if you'd like?"

John laughed as he pointed to the ever-present Rangers, "You think they're not enough, General?"

Dylan laughed. JV and Katy went off riding horses. Abby and Josh got the Mule and took off on their own. Rebecca reminded them that dinner was at six.

After dinner, the "boys" gathered on the porch, and the ladies made their way inside. It was now a little rowdy with so many war stories being told. No one knew whether there was any truth to the tales though John suspected much more that could have been told. The General and Admiral, both former seals, had seen combat in several theaters. Major Hunt witnessed as much or more in his tenure fighting the drug cartels along the border. However, they rarely talked about those details. Their stories were more humorous, detailing some of the mess-ups they were a part of.

Sean remembered his history doing some quick calculations concerning the General's service record, and asked, "General, did you know any of the seals who were involved in the Waco Siege?"

It was entirely innocent. Sean didn't have any idea of General Walker's involvement in that operation. John knew and came to the rescue, "Well, that's enough war stories for one night. Let's go see if Pancho Villa is hungry."

John got up and walked to the corral, where they pastured the longhorns. Bevo was just across the fence engaged in an epic stare-down with Pancho Villa.

John said, "That steer doesn't understand just how badly he is outmatched."

Jeremiah said, "I don't know, John. Sometimes youth and persistence win over age and strength."

It was a perfect ending to a great day.

The next morning at breakfast, Rebecca asked John, "When do you plan to fly down to see Carson Bradley?"

John didn't know she was aware of that and said, "I know better than to ask how you know I was planning to do that; and, I know you were not eavesdropping. So, who's the tattler?"

She laughed, "Jeremiah mentioned it this morning before they left for Austin."

John said, "Oh, I didn't want to miss saying goodbye. I hope they don't think I was lazy for not getting up earlier."

Rebecca said, "You know they would never think that. They have some meetings later today that they needed to get ready for. They wanted to get an early start on their drive. Now, back to my original question…"

John interrupted her, "Oh yeah, I chased a rabbit, didn't I?"

She said, "John?"

He laughed. He was particularly good at this kind of gentle torment. Finally, he surrendered the information, "I was thinking about flying to Houston tomorrow."

Rebecca reminded him with a question, "Have you let the General know?"

He answered with as much contrition as he could muster, "Yes ma'am."

The General was at the Texas Air National Guard base in Austin, waiting for John's helicopter to touch down. They transferred to a military jet for the flight to Houston. John told the General that the jet was not necessary since his helicopter could complete the trip. The General told him he preferred to land at Hobby International in Houston and transfer to a motorcade to the Hermann Hospice Facility, where Bradley now resided.

John asked Dylan, "Why do we need a motorcade for a personal visit?"

The General said, "Until we get Houston Planned Parenthood facility closed, Sir, I would err on the side of caution."

They settled in the Gulfstream G650, and John continued the conversation. "How are things on the ground there, Dylan?"

The General explained they were still unable to gather any actionable proof. Planned Parenthood was locked down with very tight security under the auspices of a private group. The General went further, "We do have strong indicators; the group is an illegally operating adjunct of the CIA."

John said, "What do they have to do with us?"

The General explained, "Nothing at all, Sir. But they have several black ops groups on their payroll. They are primarily used in South America against the drug cartels, but we used face recognition protocols to identify two individuals who have a history with the CIA."

John said, "More mercenaries, Dylan?"

Recognizing the source of John's concern, the General said, "Yes Sir. However, I'm only acting out of an abundance of caution. There is no reason to suspect any threat to Rebecca or the children."

That was troubling news to John, but they had other things to deal with today.

They did talk about some of the engagement plans the General developed earlier in the summer. There were a few modifications, though nothing of substance changed. The last thing either of them wanted was a standoff between the State Guard and the US Army in downtown Houston. They soon landed and made the trip to the hospice center uneventfully. The route chosen did take them by the Planned Parenthood facility. John was surprised at the numbers of protestors in front of the entrance. It seemed to be peaceful but surprising to see people from both sides of the issue in a stare down of sorts.

John laughed and said, "Looks like Bevo and Pancho Villa to me. Maybe we ought to put up some fencing and corral them in separate pens, so they don't hurt one another."

The General thought that was more correct than he knew.

Bradley, expecting his visitors, was sitting up in bed when they walked into the room. It was spacious and well-appointed, though it was still a hospital setting.

John was first to speak, "Mr. Bradley, how are you? I hope you are comfortable?"

Bradley answered, "I'd be fine if it weren't for these infernal nurses constantly fussin' over me. They're about as cuddly as a ground hornet."

John laughed, and he was glad he was in good spirits and full Texas drawl.

The General said, "Good to see you, Bradley. John and I wanted to drop by before things get crazy in Austin."

Bradley knew things were going to get a lot crazier in Houston before they knew it. He smiled and said, "The way I hear it, they're a couple of sandwiches shy of a picnic over there at Planned Parenthood."

Bradley changed the subject and asked John, "How's your family Governor? I heard it got a little exciting at the ranch last spring. I heard the Rangers did a damned fine job. They sure ain't all hat and no cattle."

Dylan jumped in, "It wasn't much more than a skirmish, Bradley."

Bradley tried to laugh but started coughing deeply. The charge nurse rushed in and made some adjustments to his IV. It wasn't long before Bradley started to drift off to sleep. The morphine drip started to take effect.

Before he closed his eyes, he reached out a hand to John and said, "Thanks for coming, Governor. Would you pray for me one more time? I think the Man Upstairs will hear it a lot better comin' from you than me."

John was deeply touched and prayed for a moment before they left Bradley in a deep sleep.

They left the facility in silence. Once they were in the SUV, the General said, "Thank you, John. It means the world to me that you would take time to come. It should've been me in that bed instead of him. I can never make up for that mistake."

John knew that wasn't true. And he also knew the torture of feeling responsible for the past.

June passed entirely too quickly for John. His office scheduled him to be back in Austin for the July 4th activities and in his
office Monday, July 8th. Rebecca planned to stay at the ranch to
help JV finalize his preparation to move to College Station. Of
course, Abby also wanted her help in making her fall wardrobe
choices. Abby was quite capable of selecting her clothes for the
year though Rebecca knew she was beginning to feel the absence of her older brother and needed a little extra attention.
Rebecca thought they could fly to Austin and do some shopping together. It would also give her a good excuse to see John
after settling into the routine and demands being placed on him
as Governor. Before any of them knew it, the summer was gone.

September 3rd began as typical as any workday following a holiday. His staff greeted John as he entered, Mateo was
waiting with a cup of coffee, and his scheduler had a handful of
messages. Now, no one was particularly fazed by the Rangers
who accompanied him. The General was insistent that Rangers
make up the protection detail rather than the Capital Police. He
could ensure John's safety much better working in conjunction
with Bob Hunt than the local law enforcement.

The General called early in the afternoon, and when John
took the call, he knew something was wrong. Dylan said, "John,
I just received word that Bradley died this morning."

John could only say, "I'm so sorry, Dylan. What can I do
for you?"

The General, composing himself, said, "Yes Sir, there is
one thing I'd like to ask."

John said, "Whatever you need, Dylan. I am at your
service."

Dylan said, "Bradley didn't want a lot of ceremony for
his burial. However, since I am the executor of his affairs and
he has no family, I believe he should be buried at Arlington.
I've made all the arrangements. Since he was a Medal of Honor
recipient, he was given a space years ago. All that's left now is
to finalize the plans."

Dylan realized he was rambling on and said, "I'm sorry, Sir. I know I'm rambling."

John said, "No problem Dylan, would you like me to speak at the ceremony?"

Dylan once again was amazed at John's perception. He said, "Yes, Sir. I think it would be perfect."

John said, "It would be a privilege." Then he added, "Would you like me to invite Pastor David to say a few things as well."

The General was relieved, "Thank you, Sir. That would be perfect."

And, he went on to say, "There's one other thing, Sir. Since Bradley was a Medal of Honor recipient, the president will be in attendance. He will not be speaking, but I have been informed by his Chief of Staff that he would like to attend."

John said, "I'm sure we can put enough fence between us not to disrupt the services."

"Thank you so much for understanding, Sir."

The General gave him the date and time of the service and assured him that he would make all the travel arrangements. John reiterated his encouragement as they disconnected.

Two days later, they boarded the state jet, flew into Reagan Airport, and went by motorcade to Arlington Cemetery. The interment went without incident. The President did not insert himself into the ceremony at all. Even the press was respectful for the solemnity of the time. They did photograph and video the entire ceremony, though no one anticipated the headline that would accompany the story: "Hero of the Waco Siege Laid to Rest."

The President did spend a bit of time with General Walker and Governor Lucas following the service. He offered his condolences ending his conversation with a request for John to call him soon.

His invitation was cryptic, "Governor, I hope we can get together soon. I would hate to see the Houston situation blow up in our faces."

Before Dylan could say anything, John snapped back, "I'm sure this is not the time or the place to talk about a situation we have well in hand. None of us wants another Waco, do we, Mr. President?"

POTUS had no ready return for the force of John's words, though he understood the reference precisely. He was a member of the Subcommittee on Crime of the House Committee on the Judiciary that jointly investigated the Waco Siege along with the Subcommittee on National Security, International Affairs, and Criminal Justice of the House.

He stumbled a moment, then recovering, the President said, "When you're ready to negotiate, give me a call."

The General saw John's fuse get shorter and said, "Mr. President, thank you for your presence here today. You must excuse us. We need to get to the airport. Our flight window is very narrow."

With that, John's protection detail stepped in to lead John to the SUV, and the Secret Service detail moved into position between the Rangers and the President.

The cameras caught the move in its entirety, and the press made the most of it. It became "Breaking News" on every network. CNN led the story with, "Sam Houston and his *Los Diablos Tejanos* face-off with the President."

John was barely on board when he received a call from Mateo, who said, "Sir, we're on speaker with Sean and Patrick. I suggest you turn on the Sat Feed to CNN."

John was too tired to deal with that and said, "Just give me the one-pager, Mateo."

Mateo said, "They're talking as if your protection service assaulted the President, insinuating you are contemplating a move to lead Texas to secede."

John said, "Maybe we should."

Mateo nearly shouted, "Sir! What happened? What do we need to do?"

John said, "Mateo, just take a breath. Everything is going to be fine. What time is the press conference tomorrow?"

Mateo said, "Sir, I haven't done that this time. I didn't know what to do. This looks bad, Sir."

John said, "For whom? Them or us? The General and I will confer in a moment. Schedule a staff briefing for first thing in the morning; then call a press conference for tomorrow afternoon."

It was about a three-hour flight from Reagan International in DC to Austin-Bergstrom International Airport. While John and the General reviewed the situation plans, John was informed the White House was on the Sat Phone. John told the co-pilot unless it's the President tell them we'll get back to them."

The co-pilot said, "It is the President, Sir."

John thought this couldn't end well. John said, "Put him through." John flipped the speaker switch so the General could hear the conversation and said, "Good evening, Mr. President, how may I help you?"

The President was nearly shouting, "You can secure a full and complete apology from those goons of yours along with their resignation, effective immediately. Then I want you to immediately repeal that ridiculous unconstitutional law you people put into effect down there."

The General thought this might be the defining moment in the Independence of Texas.

John remained calm and measured as he said, "Mr. President, so far, I have been patient and tolerant of the federal intrusion into our state. However, I can assure you that my patience is not without end. I suggest that you employ whatever coping mechanisms you may have to calm yourself. While we are not at war, you are acting like an enemy of our state. We both know you do not want to be our enemy any more than we want to be yours. When you are able to speak in a more controlled manner, please call back. Thank you for your call. Good night."

And with that, John disconnected the call.

The co-pilot looked at the pilot, since they were able to hear the whole conversation, and said, "The Governor just hung up on the President. I've never seen that before. Gutsiest move I've ever seen."

The entire plane looked at the Governor, while David Edwards said, "Well said, John."

The General sprung into action. "Sir, with your permission, I'd like to scramble a couple of F16's from Ft. Worth to meet us as soon as possible to fly our wing home."

John knew better than to question the wisdom of Dylan when it came to military matters. He said, "Make the call, Dylan. That man may be crazy enough to do something really stupid. While you're at it, do you think it's also time to mobilize the Guard to keep the peace in Houston?"

The General was impressed that John was already thinking a step ahead. He said, "Yes Sir."

It was now very quiet in the plane. That gave John time to think. His mind wandered to his love for Texas and the first lessons he learned about the Texas War for Independence. The first shot was fired at what came to be known as the Battle of Gonzales. In reality, it was nothing more than a minor skirmish. It was the political consequences that were so impactful. As the Battle of Lexington, which initiated the American Revolution, Gonzales served as Texas' version of the "shot heard around the world." He remembered the story well. The Texans, at last, took up arms to defend their rights against Santa Anna's despotism. On the surface, it appeared to be a disagreement over a small cannon. However, to the Texans, it was about their right to freedom. Two days after the short battle, Stephen F. Austin, who staunchly counseled peaceful negotiations, wrote, "War is declared... public opinion has proclaimed it."

Chapter 27

History Repeats Itself

October 28, 2019 – December 11, 2019

"Keep under cover boys and reserve your fire; we haven't a man to spare."

— *James Bowie, spoken to his men at the Battle of Concepcìon, October 28, 1835*

COME AND TAKE IT

The aftermath of the confrontation between John Lucas and the President at Arlington Cemetery was not a trifling matter. Perhaps nothing would have come of it had the situation not escalated so quickly. While he and the General flew home from Washington DC, the General ordered an escort of four F-16 Falcons from the Texas Naval Air Station in Ft. Worth, which were scrambled to meet their plane along the flight path. John remembered that sight very well. It seemed as if they appeared out of nowhere. While looking through the window of the Gulfstream G650 at a clear sky, they suddenly just appeared. The four distinctively marked fighters from the Texas Air Guard took up defensive escort positions forward and aft and port and starboard of their aircraft. They bristled with armament making a very imposing show of force.

This didn't surprise John. He knew this fighter jet intimately. He was part of the committee that authorized the first purchase of the newer models in 1995 from Lockheed Martin after merging with General Dynamics. The General Dynamics F-16 Fighting Falcon was considered the most versatile single-engine supersonic multirole fighters developed by the aviation unit of General Dynamics. While it was originally designed as an air superiority day fighter, it evolved into a successful all-weather multirole aircraft. Over 4,600 aircraft had been built since production was approved in 1976. The F-16 has an internal M61 Vulcan cannon and 11 locations for mounting weapons and other mission equipment. The F-16's official name is

"Fighting Falcon," but "Viper" is commonly used by its pilots and crews due to its resemblance to a viper snake.

John was glad they reached their plane so quickly, though that shouldn't have been a surprise. They travel at Mach 2 and were able to join them before they crossed the Kentucky-Tennessee line. About an hour later, they landed in Austin.

The next two weeks passed quickly. Monday, October 28th, John arrived at the office with a full schedule of briefings ahead. When John walked into the office, Sean said, "Happy Independence Day, Sir."

John was startled, "Good morning Sean. Independence Day?"

Sean was a little confused and answered, "Yes Sir. Today is the 184th anniversary of the beginning of the Texas War of Independence. Jim Bowie won the Battle of Concepcìon 184 years ago today."

The Texas Revolution began on October 2, 1835, with the Battle of Gonzales. Stephen F. Austin formed an army of 500 men to march on the Mexican forces in San Antonio with the cannon that precipitated the fight. The name *Texian Army* was the name applied to this militia. On October 22, Austin asked Bowie, now a colonel in the volunteer militia, and James W. Fannin to scout the area around the missions of *San Francisco de la Espada* and *San Josè y San Miguel de Aguayo* to find supplies for the volunteer forces. The scouting party left with 92 men, many of them members of the New Orleans Grays who just arrived in Texas.

After discovering a good defensive position near Mission Concepcìon, the group requested that Austin's army join them. On the foggy morning of October 28th, Mexican General Domingo Ugatechea led a force of 300 infantry and cavalry soldiers and two small cannons against the Texian forces. Although the Mexican army was able to get within 200 yards, the Texian defensive position protected them from fire. As the Mexicans stopped to reload their cannon, the Texians climbed a bluff and picked off some soldiers. The stalemate ended shortly after

Bowie led a charge to seize one of the Mexican cannons, only 80 yards away. Ugartechea retreated with his troops, ending the Battle of concepcìon. One Texian and ten Mexican troops died in the skirmish. One of the men under Bowie's command during the battle later praised him "as a born leader, never needlessly spending a bullet or imperiling a life, who repeatedly admonished... Keep under cover boys, and reserve your fire; we haven't a man to spare."

Sean said, "You remind me of Bowie, Sir. You have no problem charging the enemy, but you always count the cost before doing so. Authorizing the State Guard to go into Houston was a brilliant move. It completely shut down their illegal procedures."

John said, "Thank you, Sean."

Then Mateo added, "The General is waiting in your office, Sir."

John walked into his office and greeted Dylan, "Good morning, Dylan. Any good news from Houston?"

The General replied, "Good and bad, Sir. Which would you like to hear first?" John said, "I'd like there to be nothing but good news for a change, but let's have the good first. Then we can figure out how to deal with the bad news."

The General briefed John concerning the successful deployment of the State Guard. Functionally, the Houston complex of Planned Parenthood was completely shut down.

John inquired, "Have they closed their medical services?"

The General replied, "No Sir. But folks figured out that it's just not worth the hassle going through the crowds of protestors and security checkpoints to get any of the services offered. We also noticed more women seeking medical services from other sources, along with an increase in adoption support. Sarah's Law is working, Sir."

John said, "That is good news, Dylan. What's the bad news?"

The General began to detail the latest intelligence showing a ramp-up of US Army forces at Folk Polk, Louisiana. John remembered from an earlier briefing that Fort Polk is located in Vernon Parish in Louisiana seven miles from Leesville, Louisiana. It is strictly a US Army post 63 miles from Lake Charles, Louisiana and 50 miles to Alexandria where the nearest municipal airport is located. The General reminded John that there were only two units stationed there, the 3rd Brigade Combat Team, 10th Mountain Division and the First Battalion of the 509th Airborne Infantry.

John asked, "Why does that concern us, General?"

The General became very serious, "Sir, we believe they are mobilizing two of the units into Houston as a show of force."

John said, "What do your sources inside the Pentagon say? Surely, they wouldn't involve the military to keep Planned Parenthood open, blatantly violating Texas's state rights. We have a binding law in place that the US Supreme Court already ruled as constitutional."

The General said, "Yes Sir, that is correct. However, not being a political man, I can only guess the motivations of the POTUS in giving the directive."

"Go on," John said.

The General explained, "One of the Joint Chiefs unofficially reported to me that they strongly advised the President against moving troops into Houston, but his response was one of 'open disdain,' to use their words. My guess is that he feels a lot of pressure to flex some muscle, hoping we will withdraw and ignore the operations of the Houston Planned Parenthood facility."

John thought for a moment and asked the General, "Dylan, do you know the story of James Bowie and his death at the Alamo?"

Dylan didn't recall the details and confessed he was a little rusty on the battle's last days. John went on to detail the report from Alamo survivor Juana Navarro Alsbury, who stated in 1898 that she witnessed soldiers enter Bowie's room upstairs in "the old church," bayonet him and carry him out into the plaza below while he still lived. They tossed him up and caught him on their bayonets until a cavalry officer dashed in and lashed the soldiers with his sword until they stopped. Enrique Esparza, a child survivor of the battle, gave his version of the story in 1907. He stated that Bowie, though sick with fever, fought on until he was wounded and had to be carried to a cot in one of the rooms on the north side of the church. He fired his rifle and pistol at the enemy from his cot until they closed in on him. As they made their final rush, he rose up in his bed, burying his knife in the breast of one as another fired a shot, killing him. His body was then riddled with bullets.

John said, "As you can see, no one really knows how he died. And, as with most aspects of the Alamo battle, the exact details of Bowie's death may never be known. However, his mother, Elve Jones Bowie, gave us one of the best insights into this great Texian. Walter Worthington Bowie quoted her in his book written in the 1899's, The Bowies and Their Kindred. I'll never forget memorizing that quote years ago. He wrote, '…it is said when told her gallant son James had been killed by the Mexicans at the Alamo, she received the news calmly, remarking that she would 'wager no wounds were found in his back.' General, I do not want another Alamo. However, we will not be found with any wounds in our back. Am I clear?"

The General understood perfectly as he replied, "Crystal clear, Governor."

He finished his briefing and said, "I will keep you informed, Sir. I am flying down to Houston today."

John thanked the General, and the meeting adjourned.

The General arrived on-site in Houston and met the commanding officer. He was briefed with the latest intelligence, especially as it concerned the mobilization of the units from Fort Polk. They moved the troops and some mechanized units into a staging area near Lake Charles, Louisiana. From there it was no more than three hours to their position in Houston. The General relayed the information immediately to John.

John said, "Thank you, Dylan. I'll initiate the first contact with the Chairman of the Joint Chiefs per our engagement plan."

The General replied, "I'll hold our forces here rather than meeting them at Beaumont. Surely, they will listen to reason, Sir."

John said, "I hope so, Dylan. However, make sure all the men, down to the last man there, know we will not fire unless fired upon should it come to a face-off."

"Yes, Sir." Then the General closed the communication.

John called Mateo and asked him to get the Chairman of the Joint Chiefs on a secure line. General Crawford, confirmed just six weeks ago by the Senate, was a strong supporter for the president. That was the primary reason for his appointment. The president's staff constantly changed since the beginning of his term of office. Regardless of his political affiliation, he was a military man. Surely some plain talk would go a long way toward avoiding a confrontation.

It didn't take as long as John anticipated for the call to go through. When Mateo connected the two men, John spoke first, "Thank you, General, for taking my call."

Crawford answered, "It is my pleasure, Governor Lucas. What can I do for you, Sir?"

John went directly to the point, "General Walker informed me this afternoon that the US Army is moving forces to our border between Louisiana and Texas at Beaumont. Is that true, General?"

The question did not surprise General Crawford. He knew how well informed General Walker was. He merely replied, "Yes Sir, that is correct."

John went on, "May I ask what your orders are, General?"

Crawford couldn't see any advantage in withholding information. He knew about the competence of John Lucas and his staff. In fact, he heard it said they would have been a better team than the one presently in the White House. These men would not be trifled with, nor bullied with a mere show of force.

He answered John, "The POTUS signed an executive order requiring us to move into a position guaranteeing the continued operation of a nationally based organization, legally operating under national law in Houston."

John's staff were all together with him in his office and listened to General Crawford's call on speakerphone. After the last response from Crawford, John couldn't help but laugh, "You do recognize the tenuous platform you just described, don't you General?"

Crawford regretted trying even that small deflection and said, "Sir, I am simply following orders."

John flatly replied, "General, I suggest you order your troops to stand down. Neither of us wants another Alamo. We know how that ended for the Mexicans at San Jacinto."

Pulled into a confrontation he did not want, Crawford said, "No Sir, but I am bound by my orders."

John saw that he was talking to someone without any overriding authority. John ended the call by asking the General, "General, I hope you are familiar with what today's date means to us here in Texas. It is the anniversary of the Battle of Concepcìon. The Texians drove the Mexican army back to San Antonio, inflicting significant casualties on them all over a little six-pound cannon. As a result of that battle, they created a new flag. You know it as the 'Come and Take It' Flag. We still fly that flag here in Austin. We do it every year on this day as a reminder of our disdain for anyone violating our constitutionally adopted rights and freedoms. And, by the way, as you come into Houston on I-45, you will notice the world's tallest statue of any war hero. It is a memorial to Sam Houston. He's watching over what happens in Houston, General."

Crawford caught the double entendre and simply replied, "Yes Sir."

John disconnected the call, and Sean said, "Well, that went well."

They all laughed. Mateo asked, "What's next, Sir?"

John said, "Give General Crawford a chance to run my conversation up the line. His next call will be to the President. Hopefully, the president won't be as reckless as he appears to be."

John's instincts proved to be correct. Crawford did call the President. However, John did not expect a call from the President. Barely an hour passed before Mateo came into John's office and said, "Sir, the White House is holding for you. Shall I put them through?"

John expected a call from General Crawford and was surprised it was the White House. He said, "Put them through, Mateo."

Mateo answered with a smirk, "Oh, by the way, Sir, it is the President."

John couldn't help but laugh.

The call came through, and again John assembled his staff in his office and put the phone on speaker. The President started the call with an effort at intimidation, "What are you doing down there, Lucas?"

John said, "I might ask the same question of you, Mr. President."

Astonished by the direct assault from John, he said, "Well, I don't know what you're talking about."

John came back quickly, "Is your age starting to affect your memory, Mr. President?"

Patrick saw this headed the wrong way. He negotiated with the President once before. He interrupted, "Mr. President, this is Patrick Beeman, the Governor's Senior Advisor, and Policy Director. You may remember me from our meetings dealing with the border wall."

The President fired back, "I remember you very well, Beeman. Governor, what am I doing on speaker with your staff?"

John explained, "Unlike some leaders of state, I highly value the opinions of my staff. They have kept me from making rash decisions on many occasions. Who's listening on your end, Mr. President?"

The President could not get the upper hand. During his time as President, his favorite tactic when negotiating with heads of state was bullying. He'd never encountered such strong opposition and didn't expect that to start with a Governor, especially a Governor from Texas.

After taking a moment to gain his composure, the President said, "Mr. Governor, perhaps we should start over? Can we schedule a meeting to negotiate the reopening of the Planned Parenthood in Houston?"

Patrick looked at John as John gave him the thumbs' up. John said, "Mr. President, their office is not closed. In fact, General Walker has the State Guard on-site to ensure the peaceful protests do not interfere with any of their legal activities."

The President said, "Perhaps we can allow them to offer all their services while we await the result of the appeal filed this week by the Attorney General with the Supreme Court?"

John countered, "Mr. President, you know that is not only illegal but also unwarranted. The bill was signed into law in June. We have exercised great restraint by not sending the Rangers in to make arrests, though warrants have been issued for all the staff in violation of the present laws in Texas regarding abortion."

The President saw the conversation was not going anywhere and said, "Governor, what is it you want? We're already pouring millions of dollars into your economy by building the wall. I'd hate to see that stop because of some misunderstanding. Perhaps you could do me a favor and give me a little more time to reestablish the main offices of Planned Parenthood to another state?"

John easily read between the lines. For the past few months, the President tried moving the Planned Parenthood office to another state but could not find a home for them. None of the southern states wanted them, especially now that Texas provided them with the blueprint for successfully stopping abortions. The President stood to lose millions of dollars from his Super PAC if he appeared to be so weak that he could not control the Texas Governor. He could care less about the issue of abortion; he needed to get re-elected to his second term. This meant he needed to keep this Planned Parenthood office fully functioning.

He also knew his efforts to delay the closure by filing the appeal of the recent ruling from the Supreme Court would not prove productive. He wished he could go back in time and make some different appointments to the SCOTUS seats that vacated recently. John finished the conversation with one more attempt at clarification, "Mr. President, perhaps I haven't been clear. I do not need to negotiate a quid pro quo between the Federal Government and the State of Texas. Sir, you have nothing we need or deSire."

Evidently, the last mention of "quid pro quo" was more that the President could deal with as he nearly shouted, "There is no quid pro quo!"

John calmly answered, "I'm glad to hear that, Mr. President. I believe we understand one another perfectly. Thank you for your call." Then John disconnected the call.

The day ended with no movement from either side. John returned to his Austin residence and called Rebecca. There were only two things that could ease his troubled mind. The first was Rebecca's voice. That was a sure remedy to all of the torn emotions that he seemed to experience when circumstances pulled at him. He tried the remedies David Edwards continuously preached to him. They worked too, but nothing did the trick like Rebecca's voice. The second thing he always counted on was currently unavailable to him – sitting on his swing overlooking the sendero at the ranch and getting lost in the vast horizon.

She answered immediately, "Hi, how's Sam Houston today?"

He answered in his best Eeyore voice, "OK, I guess."

Rebecca caught on immediately, "Tough day at the office?"

John didn't want to burden her with any of the mess, though David was right about one thing – "unloading your train" was the only way to feel free from the burden. He said, "Tough day is one description that I could use."

Rebecca said, "You aren't worried about Houston, are you?" She could always get to the heart of his burden.

"I am. The President threatened to send in troops today. He has already moved two units from Fort Polk into position by the Texas line."

Rebecca knew she could not solve this problem for him, but she knew who could. She simply said, "John, you have great people around you. What are they telling you?"

He suddenly realized the problem. He hadn't asked for their opinion. John unknowingly drifted into his father's heavy-handed style of positional communication. They must have felt like he didn't need them. He confessed, "I haven't been asking."

Rebecca said, "Well, that's easily fixed. Why don't you invite them to breakfast on the balcony tomorrow morning? Get them some time away from the office and just let them talk." John knew that was the answer. Everyone but Dylan could be there.

John and Rebecca talked for a while longer about everything and nothing. JV loved it at A&M, and Abby seemed to be adjusting to life without her big brother well. Rebecca offered to come to Austin for the weekend. John jumped at the chance to have her and Abby come up. As soon as he finished his call to Rebecca, he called the staff, and they heartily agreed an off-site working breakfast would be great. He also called Dylan and arranged to video conference him into the meeting. John determined to be more intentional in engaging others with a greater sense of relationship. He was the Governor, but he was a brother-in-arms first.

The next morning when everyone assembled, John felt refreshed. He had enjoyed the best night's sleep in months. The meeting went extremely well. Dylan's report was somewhat encouraging. The regular Army troops were on their way to Houston; however, it would not be a full show of force, according to his sources. The President suddenly changed his mind about the optics of two full units of regular troops suddenly pushing their way into Houston.

Mateo gave some suggestions about handling the press when that took place. All of them agreed it needed to involve as many House and Senate members from the Houston area as possible. Mateo was responsible for contacting the appropriate members of the legislature while Sean handled the press itself. Patrick offered the consideration of opening up a backchannel to negotiate with the President. John thought that was a great idea, though it felt a little strange since "foreign state" typically used back channels. Dylan was the last to speak. He suggested he make another contact with General Crawford. John agreed that the more conversation they generated the better the odds were it would not escalate into an unmanageable situation where their choices were severely limited.

Over the next few days, the team returned to their typical personal, cooperative unit. John felt very good about the strategies they had developed. As predicted, the US Army units sent a minimum of personnel and supporting units. Since there was not a good place for them to bivouac, General Walker suggested through a backchannel Mateo developed that they use the Sam Houston National Forest in New Waverly. It was national park land and could be legitimately used for their base of operations. It was only about 50 miles from the Planned Parenthood office. They could rotate a contingency of men and equipment out of Houston relatively easily. It would not go unnoticed, but the impact would be minimal.

Mateo enlisted several legislators from all three parties for the press conference. The Democrats and Republicans were now minority parties in Texas due to the rise of the Independence

Party, who now was in full control of both the House and the Senate. Sean managed to be very selective in choosing the press in attendance. John handled the release of information to everyone outside of their group. In their preparation for the press conference, they knew the most important question would be about states' rights. The elephant in the room would be, "Did Texas have the legal right to do this?" Sean saw this issue come up in so many other things that the state regulated. For him, it was no different than speed limits on the Interstate Highways throughout Texas. The state regulated and enforced them, not the Federal government.

It was late November before the troops finally moved everything into place in the command center at New Waverly. The troops were in Houston for a couple of weeks before the press conference was to be held. Though tensions ran high, there was not any incident of more than passing notice. People working in the building grew accustomed to the constant military presence. Most of them could not tell the difference between US troops and the State Guard. No one seemed to care.

John, the state legislators, General Walker, and John's staff all agreed that it would be a good idea to hold the press conference in Houston the first week in December. The weather pattern continued to be unpredictable, and they decided to hold the conference in the WesternGeco Building across the street from Planned Parenthood. WesternGeco was a subsidiary of Schlumberger dealing with Seismic and Geophysical Services for Maximum Hydrocarbon Recovery. They had a conference room big enough to house the press conference and close enough to give the press ample opportunity for video recording of the military on-site. The company directors were happy to assist John. They did a lot of work on his ranch and knew his family well.

So many people knew about the press conference it was impossible to keep it from becoming as much of the news as the actual conference. The groups protesting were larger than ever. People milled around the street and parking lots of both buildings nearly at will. General Walker coordinated with General Crawford to ramp up security. They both agreed the worst case scenario was if the crowd got out of control and someone got hurt.

The President wanted to be in attendance, but the Presidential Security Detail of the Secret Service strongly advised that they could not adequately secure the area. It was simply too hot.

In fact, the Director of the Secret Service said, "Sir, I am surprised the Rangers are allowing the Governor to be in attendance."

The President scoffed, "What do they know? They're just a bunch of cowboys down there."

The Director realized how little the President knew about the Texas Rangers. The Governor of Texas was safe in their presence.

The press conference began, and the major news channels carried it live. Sean spoke first, introducing the principals who would speak. Some of John's interns distributed a one-pager explaining the history of the events leading up to the present situation.

Everything seemed to be progressing perfectly until a deafening roar split the air, blowing the windows in and sending glass shards flying through the building. The impact was so great it shook the ground causing everyone standing to grab whatever was nearby to keep from being thrown to the floor. Smoke from the explosion seeped in from the broken windows as the Rangers moved the Governor to a secure place within the interior of the building. It was complete chaos. It felt like they were in a live battle zone.

No one inside the WesternGeco Building was seriously injured. John was thankful for that miracle. After they secured the area, General Walker came to John with an initial report. It was bad, in fact, it was very bad. All the major hospitals and first responders responded along with the medical corps from both the US Army and State Guard. They triaged the injured and began identifying the dead. By the time John's security detail verified it was safe for him to go outside, most of the dead and wounded were no longer outside the Planned Parenthood facility.

John was completely overwhelmed. He hadn't felt this way since the time he met with Sarah as she described her abortion. Even then, this was worse, much worse. He saw the front of the building was simply gone. It looked like someone ripped it away, leaving just the shells of rooms visible from the street.

As he walked through the rubble, he asked General Walker, "What happened, Dylan?"

He softly answered, "I don't know John. It wasn't us. And, General Crawford is as stunned as we are. He swears it wasn't any of his men. This is worse than Waco."

Chapter 28

The Chaos Deepens

December 25, 2019 – March 6, 2020

"I prefer dangerous freedom over peaceful slavery."

— Thomas Jefferson, written in a letter to
James Madison (1787)

COME AND TAKE IT

Dawn was just beginning to show its winter colors on the horizon as John sat in his swing at the ranch. It was cold in the early morning before the sun warmed the *sendero*. He was thinking so intently about the days that followed the explosion destroying Planned Parenthood in Houston; he didn't notice it. The blast killed 268 people, and there were still hundreds more recovering from injuries sustained in the blast.

It was now the second-worst attack on American soil; even the bombing in Oklahoma City was less devastating. Some of the more rabid federalists remarked that one would need to go back to the American Civil War and the Lawrence Massacre to make a comparison. That tragedy, also known as Quantrill's raid, was an attack by Quantrill's Raiders, a Confederate guerilla group led by William Quantrill, on the Union town of Lawrence, Kansas. It happened on the morning of Friday, August 21, 1863. They targeted the town because it supported abolition and reputation of being Jayhawkers, free-state militia and vigilante groups known for attacking plantations in pro-slavery Missouri's western counties.

Only the coordinated terrorist attacks of September 11, 2001, were more destructive. Most of the victims this time were people who had been standing outside the building, though the number of missing and presumed dead was still very high. The effort was now a recovery instead of a rescue. The final death toll could easily climb over 300. John felt personally responsible for every one of those.

General Walker and Major Hunt insisted they move John to the ranch until they could be sure he and his family were not in danger, and luckily JV was home on winter break, so he would be home already. No one knew who or why the explosion happened. No group stepped forward, claiming responsibility. General Walker strongly felt that it was not a terrorist group. He believed it was an attempt by some group to stop the new law from going before the Supreme Court for its final appeal. John reluctantly agreed with them and went to the ranch. He also insisted that Jeremiah and Sarah, as well as his office staff, be relocated to the ranch for the time being.

In the two weeks since the bombing, the chaos only continued to grow. The FBI and ATF were on-site, though John knew that was more an effort to deflect any responsibility from the Federal government than to find the perpetrators. It was strange to John how easily the President and his cabinet managed to point fingers at everyone but themselves. He couldn't help but wonder if the US Army weren't present, things might have gone very differently. He certainly would not have called for a press conference at that location. There would not have been any need for the press to be there. The crowds of protesters would have been much smaller. It may not have even been a target for the bombing. All of those people, mothers and fathers, children, old and young, now dead. He would never be able to shake the feelings of guilt. Maybe it was time to rethink his position.

Just then, Rebecca joined him on the swing. She was wrapped in a soft afghan throw.

John, nudged back to the present, said, "Good morning. I've gotten us in a mess. I never should have attempted to change the law."

Rebecca watched John spiral like this many times over the years. He always seemed to take personal responsibility for everything bad and no credit for the good.

She answered, "It's a little cold out here this morning. Maybe it will warm up a bit as the sun rises more."

John couldn't believe she ignored him, "Huh? How can you think about the temperature at a time like this?"

She looked at him for a long moment and said, "Maybe I wasn't talking about the temperature out here. You know John, the sun will shine again. God knows what he's doing. You haven't failed. We just need to build a different bridge to cross this new river in our path."

That broke the spiral. She always had a way of doing that so perfectly.

John put his arm around her and said, "I could never make it without you. You know that, right?"

She smiled, "Yes I do. Now come on in or get the hands to build a fire for you out here." He laughed and followed her inside.

He was greeted by Abby first, "Dad, did you see the presents under the tree? I think you must have been a very good boy this year. You got a big one."

He laughed as he remembered it was Christmas Day. He said, "Well, let's get a bite to eat, and when everyone is up, we'll open presents."

Jeremiah and Sarah were scheduled to come to the main house by mid-morning. Since coming to the ranch, they stayed in the guest house. It was a more permanent solution to their "temporary relocation." Mateo, Sean, and Patrick would be joining them for dinner along with the Fitzgerald's. He wished Dylan could be here though he was still in Houston.

The General didn't trust either the FBI or ATF to get to the bottom of the bombing. He had specialists from the Rangers and the Guard doing their own investigation. It didn't help that Diane Hernandez, the SAC present at the Waco Siege, was onsite. She rose to the position of Deputy Director as the years passed. Dylan trusted her even less now than he did then. John had come to trust the General's instincts more than his own in these things. He saw they were rarely very far off the mark.

Abby insisted that her Dad open the "big" present first. "Come on Dad, it's huge. Open it!"

John put her off, "We'll wait for Jeremiah and Sarah. I'm sure they'll enjoy seeing what it is too."

He was curious about who gave him the gift. He went into the family room and asked, "Where is this big gift?"

Abby said, "Oh, it's outside on the front porch. It was too big to get into the house. But here's the card that came with it." She plucked it off the tree where Rebecca put it and gave it to him.

About that time, JV came into the family room and said, "Morning, Dad. Getting an early start?" Rebecca laughed.

John said, "Well, it's just the card."

John pulled out his pocket knife and slit the envelope open. It was plain white stationery. Glancing quickly at the signature at the bottom, he saw it was from Dylan. He said, "It's from Dylan."

Rebecca said, "Well, you've opened it. Don't keep us in suspense. Read the note."

John said, "It just says, 'Here's a little something the boys in the armory and I cooked up for you. We hope you will display it with pride. It is a working replica, though we certainly hope you will never need to use it. Merry Christmas, my friend.' And, then he signed it with just his first name, 'Dylan.'"

Now John was curious. Before he could walk out to the front porch, Jeremiah and Sarah came in from the back. They hugged one another, and Abby said, "Daddy's opening his big present first."

Jeremiah said, "We saw some of the Guardsmen unload it yesterday. They needed a forklift to get it out of the truck. It must be on skids."

Now, John had to open it. They all walked out to the front of the house and saw a gift-wrapped crate. It was about four feet high and wide on all sides.

John said, "Well, it's too small to be a tank." He jokingly went on, "Maybe it's a cannon." He carefully tore off the paper and saw it was an enclosed crate.

Jeremiah said, "You're going to need some pry bars to open that."

John said, "I've got one in the shop. JV, will you get it and the impact drill with a star driver for the screws?"

JV was as excited as his Dad, "Sure."

He ran off to the shop and came back quickly with the tools. They opened the crate and saw it was packed with straw. Digging down, John was amazed. He exclaimed, "You'll never believe it. It's a replica of the six-pound cannon from the Battle of Gonzales!"

They all finished unpacking it and saw it was a perfect replica down to the finest detail.

Jeremiah said, "It's got a note attached."

He picked it up and gave it to John. It was signed by the Texas State Guard Armory of New Braunfels and read, "Merry Christmas, Governor. 'Don't fire until you see the whites of their eyes.'"

John was hoping it would never come to that, though he often fought off the temptation to go down that road. He already went there today, and it didn't go well. It never did. He said, "Well, I guess I need to get some black powder and cannonballs to shoot this thing. I bet we could do some serious damage to the feral hog population with it."

They all laughed, and Rebecca said, "All right, enough toys for now, let's go inside to the other gifts and a warmer place."

Later, when there was a lull in the activities, John called Dylan, "Merry Christmas, Dylan. I was completely surprised by the gift you sent. 'Thanks' is way too small an expression. It was perfect."

The General said, "You are very welcome, John. It wasn't my idea, though. The men came to me with the suggestion, and I thought it was an apt expression of our confidence in your leadership."

John, flattered by the compliment, simply said, "It means more to me than you will ever know."

They talked briefly, and Dylan said he would be on his way to the ranch in a day or so to brief him more fully concerning the progress of the investigation. What neither of them knew was that the next wave of the crisis was about to erupt in Houston.

The recovery operation and investigation into the Houston bombing seemed to be slowing to most people who still had an interest in the outcome. This was especially true for Planned Parenthood. The resulting frustrations led to larger and larger crowds at the Houston-site. Even the colder than normal temperatures of late December did not deter the crowds from swelling.

Pro-choice demonstrators teamed up with more militant groups protesting other issues, while large crowds from the pro-life groups joined with militant secessionists. Both groups reached a point of frustration the Friday following Christmas. General Walker moved the Texas Guard back from the site out to a three-block radius. This did not compromise the security of the immediate area. However, the US Army did not follow suit. Major Crawford ordered them to maintain a security perimeter of no further than 100 feet from the blast site. This put the crowd within arm's reach of the soldiers.

Early Friday morning, as the crowds began to build, some of the people began chanting their slogans, and from somewhere in the crowd, a brick fragment was thrown at the Army guards. One brick turned to dozens more as people turned to violence in their frustration. The soldiers answered by standing their ground and launching tear gas canisters to disperse the crowd. It was bedlam. The soldiers were outnumbered but better equipped. Their ballistic shields protected them from anything less than a cannon round. However, the young second lieutenant in charge of the detail panicked and ordered several soldiers equipped with shotguns and bean bag rounds to fire into the crowd. Instead of falling back, the crowd rushed faster into the small numbers of soldiers. They were overrun within seconds. Wisely, the young officer ordered a full retreat.

When the melee subsided, one of the protestors lay lifeless in the parking lot between the barricades previously set by the military for the protestors. She was a young woman protesting the presence of the US military. She was inadvertently killed as the intended non-lethal round of bean bags struck her chest, fracturing her rib cage and piercing her heart, killing her instantly.

The news of her death went viral. General Crawford called General Walker, who was now at the ranch informing him of the disaster. General Walker, justifiably outraged, knew this was not a time for him to lose control. He said, "General Crawford, I am with the Governor. I am putting you on speaker. Please repeat your report."

Crawford did not want to engage Governor Lucas but was trapped. He repeated to the Governor the details of the confrontation and the mistake of firing on the crowd. General Walker asked, "General, for clarification, were these the orders of engagement you posted?"

Crawford was really in a tough spot now. He could only say, "These are the rules of engagement I was under orders to follow."

John broke in, "Who ordered those rules of engagement, General Crawford?"

He answered, "I was not in that planning session, Sir."

John went one step further, "General Crawford, I am not a man who likes to repeat himself. However, given the obvious confusion on your end, I will ask you again, who is responsible for the death of one of our citizens?"

Crawford answered, "I can only say it came from the highest level of command, Sir."

General Walker then asked, "Where are your troops now, General?"

Crawford said, "We have fallen back to a three-block radius north of the site."

General Walker requested that they vacate the city and return to the temporary base in New Waverly. General Crawford told him that it was impossible without disobeying direct orders from the Commander in Chief. He also said that he expected to have updated orders within the hour. He added that the Secret Service took a request for orders to the golf course where the President was with some of his cabinet members. General Walker looked at John to check if he needed any further information.

John said, "Thank you, General Crawford. We'll take it from here."

With that they disconnected the call abruptly.

John turned to Dylan and asked, "Dylan, can you get in touch with your contact from the Joint Chiefs and find out what those bureaucrats in Washington are trying to do. They must be crazy if they think we will sit idly by while they trample on our freedom."

The General said, "I can reach him now if you like, Sir?"

John was much calmer than Dylan anticipated, and that might not be a good sign. This was the John Lucas he had seen only once before. This was the John Lucas who was willing to do whatever it took to protect his family, which now included every man, woman, and child in their state. John said, "Get him on speaker, Dylan."

The General simply dialed the number as he said, "Yes, Sir."

What John didn't know was that the General's contact from the Joint Chiefs was actually the Chairman, Admiral Samuel Burroughs. He and General Walker were both members of Seal Team 7 and at Waco during the Branch Davidian Siege's debacle. Even though he was second in command of Seal Team 7, Burroughs was left out of the penetration of the compound due to food poisoning he contracted the day before they were deployed. He felt he owed Dylan his life for allowing him to stand down that day.

Burroughs answered the call, "Merry Christmas, you old dog. How are things in Texas?"

Obviously, he wasn't up to speed on the most current developments.

Dylan said, "I'm fine, Sam. And, who are you calling old? You're just as old as I am." After the laughter subsided, Dylan got serious, "Admiral Burroughs, I am with Governor Lucas. I have us on speaker. Have you heard the report from Houston?"

The tone of the call changed immediately. Burroughs said, "No, General, I am unaware of anything beyond the tragedy of the explosion before Christmas."

Then Dylan recounted the report from General Crawford about the confrontation between protestors and the US Army on-site that resulted in one civilian casualty.

Burroughs let out a deep breath and said, "I tried to warn the President not to provoke the situation. Hell, he practically laughed me out of the Cabinet meeting. Where is the detachment now?"

General Walker said, "Our understanding is they have withdrawn to a three block radius and are holding for further orders from the President."

The Admiral said, "Let me get involved immediately and see if we can de-escalate this mess. The last thing anybody needs right now is Waco. I'll get back to you within the hour."

John called his staff to join him in the office they were now working from at the ranch. His home office was simply too small, so they converted one of the other buildings typically used by administrative and clerical employees for the oil and gas side of the ranch. After they assembled, the General brought them up to speed. John instructed Mateo and Sean to work on the media side of the event, and Patrick to contact the leaders of the State Legislature to inform them personally.

Mateo was first to ask, "What do we say when we're asked who was at fault, Sir? I don't think we can stall this one by saying it is 'an ongoing investigation.'"

John agreed and said, "Tell them the basics. We know the details. Make sure they understand these were not our men. We were three blocks away, purposefully avoiding such a confrontation. Also, tell them that we are in direct contact with Washington going forward at this time, but avoid making any direct references to the President."

Sean, trying to lighten the atmosphere yet still convey a truth, used a new idiom he recently picked up, "Yep, there's a light or two burned out on his string. No telling what this President might do if we accuse him in the press."

John said, "Any other time that would make me laugh, and maybe I need to be laughing, but you are right that the inmates are running the asylum."

The General said with uncharacteristic humor, "There or here, Sir?" And, thankfully, they all laughed, easing the tension that had built so quickly.

Their relief was short lived, however. Admiral Burroughs called back and informed them that the President just issued an order to place Houston under martial law while also imposing sundown to sunrise curfew. General Walker explained that though the POTUS technically has the authority to do so, rarely has such a measure been taken without the cooperation and consent of the state's Governor.

Burroughs said, "I know, Dylan. I wish I could do something, but my hands are tied."

General Walker simply replied, "Ours aren't. I strongly suggest that you countermand that order and withdraw beyond the state line. I do not want us being on opposite sides in this one."

The General disconnected the call before Admiral Burroughs could say anything in response.

John looked at the General and said, "Dylan, do I need to get you some gunpowder and cannonballs for the Christmas gift?"

Even though it was an attempt at humor, no one was laughing.

Chapter 29

The Flag of Freedom

March 6, 2020 – April 21, 2020

"I have said that Texas is a state of mind, but I think it is more than that. It is a mystique closely approximating a religion. And this is true to the extent that people either passionately love Texas or passionately hate it and, as in other religions, few people dare to inspect it for fear of losing their bearings in mystery or paradox. But I think there will be little quarrel with my feeling that Texas is one thing. For all its enormous range of space, climate, and physical appearance, and for all the internal squabbles, contentions, and strivings, Texas has a tight cohesiveness perhaps stronger than any other section of America. Rich, poor, Panhandle, Gulf, city, country, Texas is the obsession, the proper study and the passionate possession of all Texans."

— John Steinbeck, 1962.

COME AND TAKE IT

Admiral Burroughs' faced one of the most difficult decisions in his life. He, along with all the Joint Chiefs, sat in a conference room filled with cabinet members, the Speaker of the House, the Senate Majority Leader, the Vice President, and various aides and interns, listening to the President describe the need for Martial Law in Texas. There was little doubt that Martial Law would be imposed. It was well within the President's authority.

Historically, martial law in the United States was used during several periods throughout the history of the United States, wherein a region or the nation as a whole was placed under the control of the military. Only the president has the power to impose such a drastic measure. In each state, the Governor has the right to impose martial law within the borders of their state. In the United States, martial law was implemented on only a few occasions, such as directly after a foreign attack. It happened after the Japanese attack on Pearl Harbor and in the War of 1812 during the Battle of New Orleans. It was also used after major disasters, such as the Great Chicago Fire of 1871 and the San Francisco earthquake of 1906. Most notably, martial law was the conduit for the United States to restore order to the Southern States after the Confederate Surrender. That included Texas and continues to chafe some of its citizens to this day.

The waters were murky at this point. In United States law, martial law is limited by several court decisions handed down between the American Civil War and World War II. In

1878, Congress passed the Posse Comitatus Act, which forbids military involvement in domestic law enforcement without congressional approval. Ironically, a Texan, George W. Bush, signed the John Warner Defense Authorization Act for Fiscal Year 2007. In addition to allocating funding for the armed forces, it also gave the president the power to declare martial law and to take command of the National Guard units of each state without the consent of state Governors. However, it expired in that fiscal year.

Burroughs was torn thinking about the legality of martial law in Houston. As he listened to the Attorney General, he realized he was not alone in this quandary. That being the case, he was not wavering in his moral conclusion about it. It was simply wrong. And, it was wrong on many levels. This could very likely be the spark to ignite the people of Texas to unify, driving them to become one voice and one people separate from the rest of the nation.

Admiral Burroughs was jolted from his thoughts as the President said, "Burroughs, are your men in place to enforce the declaration of martial law?"

He almost stumbled but responded smoothly, "Sir, that depends. What is the scope of the declaration?"

The President jabbed his finger in his direction and said, "As large as you need it to be to get Houston under our control again."

Burroughs then said, "Sir, The Houston Metropolitan area covers 10,000 square miles. It is bigger than the individual states of Rhode Island, Delaware, Connecticut, New Jersey, New Hampshire, or Vermont. With the entire complement of forces in place from Fort Polk, we could not contain nearly a tenth of that area. So, no Sir, we do not have enough men in place to enforce martial law in Houston, much less the surrounding area of Harris and Galveston Counties."

The President now red-faced nearly shouted, "If you can't get the job done Burroughs, I'm sure there are others who would jump at the chance."

That threat was enough to push Admiral Burroughs to his decision. He said, "I am aware of the conundrum this places on you, Sir. Therefore, as indicated in the letter I am bringing to your attention now, I formally resign my position and announce my immediate retirement from further military service."

With that, he slid his letter of resignation across to the President, stood and walked out of the room.

Admiral Burroughs was not a rash man – not many career military men are. He planned his exit from the White House as thoroughly as any battle plan in his past. As soon as he reached his office in the Pentagon, he called his old friend from Seal Team 7, General Walker.

Dylan saw the Caller ID and answered immediately, "Well, Sam, are you calling with more bad news?"

Burroughs laughed and replied, "I suppose that depends on your perspective. I just resigned from my position as Chairman of the Joint Chiefs and slid my retirement letter across the conference table to the President."

Dylan laughed, "Well, hell, Shark! What happened? Did you leave him in one piece?"

That last reference was one few others knew about. Then Lt. Commander Walker and Lt. Burroughs were on assignment off the coast of Viet Nam. Their team, Seal Team 7, was tasked with a night water intrusion from a submarine holding three miles off the coast. Their specific engagement rules were to enter just east of Da Nang, reconnoiter the area in sector 19 to determine if the reports of surviving POW's were true. If so, they were to determine the viability of extraction. They made their way to the sector from the shoreline by way of several deep canals. Upon arriving, they immediately confirmed eight American soldiers being held in an old POW camp. Freeing the prisoners was short work, even though the casualty list of the enemy topped out at eighteen confirmed dead and more wounded. The prisoners were weak, but they made their way back to the South China Sea without delay. Six of the team inflated a raft for the rendezvous with the submarine. Dylan Walker, Sam

Burroughs, and Carson Bradley remained in the water as cover for the extraction. They were the three cowboys on the team, perhaps as much because they were Texans as they were deadly in or out of the water. The team with the prisoners was almost to the submarine when another inflatable patrol skiff was spotted racing toward them. The water was relatively shallow, at 15 feet, as they made their way across a long sandbar.

The three "cowboys" slowed their swim to engage the enemy and allow the others to reach the submarine safely. There were six "targets" on the pursuing boat. It was dark enough that they never knew the three seals were there. Reaching the sandbar, the enemy combatants slowed enough for the seals to engage them in close quarter combat. Dylan reached for the rope running across one side of the pontoon boat and swung up enough to use his pistol to take two out with quick succession. Bradley shot the engine, stopping the progress of the boat and then immediately shooting one of the enemies in the head, killing him instantly. The other three decided they were better off in the water than in the boat but realized too late the foolishness of that decision.

One nearly landed on top of Burroughs, who used his knife to cut through both carotid arteries before he was fully wet. The other two didn't know that Burroughs was under the surface below them. He pulled each one under and used his knife to eliminate them quickly. It was not pretty, but it was deadly. The three cowboys made their way to the submarine with a crew standing by to help them boarding and stowing their gear.

The Captain watched from the conning tower and could only say, "My God, they killed six men as quickly as a shark!"

The story circulated through the submarine's crew, and the moniker stuck with Burroughs.

The Admiral said to his old friend, "He's still in one piece. You're never going to let me escape those old days, are you?"

Dylan answered with just one word, "Nope."

Burroughs went on, "I'm thinking of coming home. I was wondering if you needed an old frogman."

Dylan said, "It would be our privilege to have you on the team again. When do you arrive? I'll make sure I personally pick you up."

The Admiral said, "It will take a few days to wind everything up. I can get everything packed and put into storage until I find a place to settle in. Do you have any room for me to bunk in?"

Both of them were single. Dylan never married. Sam's wife divorced him years ago when he was on a mission in the Mediterranean Sea. Neither had any children; their love was always the Navy.

Before he disconnected the call, Admiral Burroughs said, "Dylan, you should prepare the Governor for martial law. The President has all but signed the order. He's just trying to figure out how big an area to commandeer."

The General said, "Can you fly into Laredo? I'd like you to meet John in person. We transferred his office to the ranch for security reasons. I think he will surprise you."

Burroughs said, "If he's half the man everyone in DC is complaining about, I can't wait to meet him. I'll send you the flight info when I get it."

Dylan said, "Great. Good to have you onboard old friend."

Houston was relatively quiet. The Army was all but absent, with the State Guard the primary force tasked with security. Even the protestors were gone. The former headquarters of Planned Parenthood was still a danger and required a military presence to keep people from climbing through the rubble looking for *souvenirs*. The recovery effort was now completed with everyone accounted for and the building itself was scheduled for complete demolition later that summer.

The media shifted its attention to the rumors coming out of Austin from some of the Independence Party members. More than one *reliable source* reported a strong contingent of legislators moving toward some legal remedies in view of the deepening federal intrusion. It was difficult to find anyone sympathetic to the presence of the Army in New Waverly. Patrick was spending a great deal of time lobbying US Representatives and Senators for a movement of censure, if not outright impeachment of the President. While that was gaining some traction, no one in Washington was interested in such an assault on a man known to retaliate with such force that their careers would be in jeopardy.

Sean had his hands full with the press camped out on the road leading up to the main entrance of the ranch. They could not get on to the property itself as the State Guard was posted at every possible entrance. John personally paid to have a wide area paved at the main entrance. This prevented them from blocking the road in or out, as well as giving room off the road to install electrical lines and necessary facilities for them. It became a virtual camping area much the same as Highway 6 did during the Waco Siege.

Abby continued to attend high school in Laredo though she was accompanied at all times by her assigned team of Rangers. The same was true for JV. While he was at Texas A&M, his protection detail was never far away. John didn't like the intrusion into his family but knew it was the only way to manage their safety with some semblance of normalcy. He liked being home. Rebecca and his swing were his anchors in life. He even managed to go to the Downtown Café a few times to have breakfast with his old friend David Edwards.

Recently on one such breakfast he told David some of the source of his anxiety. It seemed he was being driven inextricably down a path he didn't choose or deSire. The pastor's response was classically *David-esque*.

He would say, "So? What did you expect? The journey was determined long before you took the first step. God has got it, John."

John would always answer that he was not fond of the path. Then David would say, "I know. Read the Book of Jonah again. Remember, it didn't end well for him when he tried to run from his path."

At the end of each breakfast, David would remind him, "John, you're not an American. You're a Texian. Don't forget that."

The pastor was right about that.

A week passed, and Dylan was waiting at Laredo International Airport for Sam Burroughs, now officially "Retired Admiral Burroughs."

Burroughs greeted the General, "Great to see you, Dylan."

Dylan introduced him to the two aides accompanying him, and they were taken to the waiting SUV.

Dylan said, "I really wished you would have let me send our plane for you. I hope the flight wasn't too bad."

Burroughs laughed, "You know we've flown on much worse in our day."

The General said, "I've arranged a meeting with the Governor for us later this afternoon. He has insisted that you stay for dinner and meet the rest of the staff. I hope that's all right?"

Burroughs laughed, "I'm at your service General."

Dylan seriously replied, "Please, Sam, call me Dylan. It is great to have you home. I just wish Bradley could be here to see it."

Sam became more serious and said, "He was a good friend and great man. I wish that I could have seen him before he died."

Dylan changed the subject, "I've arranged for your housing in Austin, but the Governor would like to know if you could join us at the ranch. We've managed to remodel some of the existing buildings into very comfortable quarters."

Burroughs wasn't quite sure what to read into that request, though he quickly agreed.

John and Rebecca greeted everyone as they came into the main house for dinner. Dylan introduced Sam Burroughs to everyone, and John simply said, "It's good to have you home Admiral; and, it's even better to have you on the team."

Burroughs said, "Please, Governor, call me, Sam."

John was quick to respond, "I will do so if you will call me John." Like Dylan, he would not do that except in the most unusual of circumstances.

Burroughs said, "Yes Sir."

John laughed, "I thought it would be that way. By the way, I understand you no longer go by the name 'Shark.' So, I promise not to call you by that name as long as you avoid referring to me as 'Sam Houston.'" He immediately looked over at Sean with a sly grin.

Burroughs said, "I've heard some make that reference before. I've also heard it is a well-deserved description, Sir. However, I will not repeat their error, Governor."

Rebecca then took up the conversation, "John, take the men outside for a Shiner while the staff and I finish up preparing the dinner."

The days were getting longer and there was still enough light to look across to the pasture with the longhorns lazily grazing before they bedded down.

Burroughs asked, "Which one is Bevo? I've heard the stories of how an Aggie owns him. That's got to be difficult for the teasips to swallow."

John laughed and said, "He's the one on the south side of the fence. We have to keep him and Pancho Villa separated. He hasn't figured out that youth only goes so far."

Burroughs was a graduate of the Naval Academy but very familiar with the old rivalry between Texas A&M and the University of Texas. They all grabbed a beer and sat down in the comfortable outdoor furniture. Burroughs couldn't help but gawk at some of the things on the wall of the porch. His attention centered on the small cannon. He asked, "Is that the Gonzales Cannon?"

John answered, "No. That's a recent addition to my collection. It was a Christmas gift from the State Guard and General

Walker. The men at the New Braunfels Armory made it for me. It's an exact working replica."

Burroughs continued looking at some of the collection displayed and settled on the long rifle and powder horns. He asked, "I'm not familiar with this weapon. Where is it from?"

John said, "That's the only authenticated Crockett rifle known to exist. Some have told me that I may need it if I ever face the President again." They all laughed.

Burroughs said, "Well Sir, I'd suggest the six-pound cannon just to make sure."

John trusted Dylan when he told him what kind of man Sam Burroughs was, but now he knew for himself. This was a man he wanted on his team. He said, "We don't usually talk business in the evening, Sam. However, I want to give you something to chew on overnight. I am certain that we need you on our team. The General and I talked about it and conclude that we'd like to offer you a commission in the State Guard. My hope is that you will accept the rank of Admiral and work in conjunction with General Walker to oversee the build-up and training of our Texas Guard. Right now, the Texas Coast Guard is under the Department of Homeland Security. However, I think in view of the vulnerability of both the Gulf Coast and the Rio Grande, we're going to need someone of your ability to get us where we need to be. Give it some thought, please."

Before he could say anything, Patrick said, "Admiral, he never goes slowly. I suggest you think it through, of course. However, when it comes to the final decision, I can speak from personal experience: you will never regret coming on board."

Rebecca interrupted the conversation with the announcement that dinner was ready.

Patrick couldn't help himself, he asked the Admiral, "Sam, what happened when you resigned? I'd love to have been a fly on the wall at that meeting!"

John said, "I'm sure the Admiral would like to talk about other things, Patrick." It was a gentle rebuke that fell on deaf ears around the table.

Dylan jumped in, "I know my old friend well enough to know it didn't go well for the President."

At that tantalizing comment, Sam thought he better explain. "Honestly, even though I was prepared to retire, I hoped that sound judgment and wise counsel would prevail. However, after thirty minutes of the President's diatribe, I was nearly comatose when he called on me to give a status report of how big an area the troops already camped nearby could contain under martial law."

Dylan interrupted, "You don't need to clean up the story, Shark. These boys have seen plenty in their young lives. In fact, they would have been great seals on our team back in the day."

John rolled his eyes. He knew all the stories, but no one else on the staff did. They weren't his stories to tell, and he didn't feel comfortable gossiping even with the truth.

Sean chimed in, "Why did the General call you 'Shark,' Sir?"

Sam said, "I guess I assumed you knew that old story." He looked at John and said, "I'm sure the Governor read the files and knows the root of that old nickname."

Rebecca knew John would be uncomfortable with this conversation because of her presence. He was always overly protective of her. She said to the group, "Why don't y'all retire to the porch? Sarah and I will help the staff put everything away. I'm sure John has an extra Cuban for those of you who would care to have one. I'll have one of the kitchen staff bring around that new bottle of Ranger Creek .36 Bourbon."

John knew that was his cue to move the group to the back porch.

There was a fire in the pit to drive away the cooler air of the evening, and they all naturally gathered near. John offered cigars though not everyone took one. As expected, both Dylan and Sam joined John in a cigar. As promised, the bourbon arrived with glasses for everyone.

Settling into their chairs, John said, "Well Admiral, I guess it's your show."

Sam said, "I'm sure the story would be much more entertaining if Dylan were to tell it, Sir."

The General said, "It is a great story. Let me summarize it by saying that Sam Burroughs is one of the most courageous men I have ever known. His bravery in the extraction of eight imprisoned American POW's who were being held after we withdrew from Viet Nam continues to be the standard for every frogman today."

Sean pressed for more, "But Sir, how did you get the nickname?"

Sam said, "Honestly, I think it came from a lot of bubble-heads who added more to the story than was really there."

Dylan laughed, "They don't know what a 'bubblehead' is, Sam."

Mateo jumped in and said, "Sure we do, Sir. They are the men and women who serve aboard a submarine."

Sam was impressed. Mateo went on, "But Sir, we also know you don't get the Medal of Honor for rumors started by a bunch of 'bubbleheads.'"

Dylan said, "I told you they were smart, no-nonsense, men."

John smiled at that. Dylan continued, "Let's just say that while Bradley and I were engaged with three enemy combatants, he took out the other three in hand-to-hand combat while still in 15 feet of water. The story goes there wasn't much left of them after the 'shark' attack."

There was a long moment of silence finally broken by Sam. "Governor, you may not want me on your team after that story, but I would be honored to serve. There is one question I have, Sir."

John said, "What's that?"

Sam asked, "Are you an American or a Texian, Sir?"

John said, "Strange that you would ask that. That's the second time I've been reminded of that recently. My answer is the same now as it has always been. I am a Texian."

They enjoyed the rest of the evening together breaking up only after the mesquite in the pit was reduced to a pile of glowing embers and ash. They knew the next few weeks would bring incredible challenges to all of them.

After the meeting in the President's office, he issued an executive order placing Houston under martial law, effective immediately. All the troops were readying for deployment to Houston as General Walker contacted General Crawford. Dylan said, "General, we understand that martial law has been declared with a sunset to sunrise curfew for Houston and Galveston County. Is that correct?"

Crawford said, "Yes Sir, it is."

Dylan said, "General, are you aware of the untenable position this places you and your men in?"

Crawford answered, "General, I am very busy. Is there any specific communication you wish to convey, or is this another lecture about the states' rights that you feel are being violated?"

Dylan knew he was aware of all the numbers just as he was. The State Guard outnumbered his men in every category. They simply could not carry out their orders should there be any resistance.

He was very direct when he said, "General, should you or any of your troops move from the temporary bivouac in New Waverly, we will stop and detain you for transport outside the state line. Please do not test our resolve."

General Walker was good to his word. Before any troops or vehicles could be moved from the park, every exit was blocked by Texas State Guard troops. Without starting a shooting war, they were paralyzed in the park. Crawford tried to communicate with Washington, but with the resignation of Admiral Burroughs, there was confusion as to who exactly was in charge. The situation was also rapidly deteriorating. Numerous other resignations came in from across the military chain of command. In fact, most of the National Guard based in Texas was now a de facto part of the Texas State Guard. Those resignations came all along the chain of command. The men, equipment, and munitions *appropriated* made the Texas State Guard more than able to secure the state.

Admiral Crockett was one of those resignations submitted to the President. When he joined the State Guard, he became the chief advocate responsible for filing litigation to prevent the President from abusing the power of his office, evidenced by the declaration of martial law. Things were moving slowly through the bureaucratic red tape of the federal courts. However, if the Democratic majority in the House was an indicator, the President had much bigger problems than martial law in Texas. An impeachment inquiry began as a result of other accusations. All of that would take time, but time was now on Texas' side.

Crawford was now wavering in his command commitment. His call from the President didn't help. The news reports did not help the situation either. Every station carried video of the tanks, and men from the State Guard moved into position at the park exits. Even Fox News was asking whether the President was attempting to start a war with Texas.

The President was incensed, "Crawford, are you going to move those troops to Houston, or do I need to get somebody who will?"

Crawford simply answered, "Sir, I can move them. However, unless you want another Alamo, I suggest you try more diplomatic solutions. We might win the battle, but we will surely lose the war."

The President was not one to back down. He said, "General Crawford, consider yourself relieved of duty. I will communicate with your next in command to immediately move the troops with any force necessary to Houston." The President then disconnected the call.

In their staff meeting, Sean brought up the media attention being focused on the New Waverly standoff. He said, "Governor, I think we need to get way ahead of this."

John said, "I agree. However, press conferences have not been very effective recently. I have been thinking about another approach. What if we use the season of the year to remind everyone in our state of history indirectly? That may buy us some time to negotiate further."

Sean remembered his Texas history well. "That's brilliant, Sir."

He agreed that the timing was perfect. From March to May in 1836, Mexican forces once again occupied the Alamo. For the Texans, the Alamo's Battle became a symbol of heroic resistance and a rallying cry in their struggle for independence. On April 21, 1836, Sam Houston and some 800 Texans defeated Santa Anna's Mexican force of approximately 1,500 men at the Battle of San Jacinto, shouting "Remember the Alamo!" as they attacked. The victory ensured the success of Texan independence. In mid-May, Santa Anna, who had been taken prisoner during the battle, signed a peace treaty at Velasco, Texas, in which he recognized Texas' independence in exchange for his freedom. The citizens of the so-called Lone Star Republic then elected Sam Houston as their president.

Many of the leaders of the Independence Party were urging John to develop a contingency plan of secession should diplomatic negotiations fail. The breakdown of peaceful talks seemed more likely with every move the POTUS made. John saw the wisdom of the contingency plan. He put together a group of men and women from all the parties represented in the State Legislature. Their task was singular. They were to draft a new Declaration of Independence, pronouncing Texas as its own nation once again.

With all the activity, the fateful choice for Texans came to be summarized throughout the state by the question: "Are you a Texian or an American?" The "Come and Take It" flag began to fly again over the Capitol in Austin.

The second-in-command of General Crawford's detachment in Texas was a young major who had no battle experience. He served most of his time in the Army as an engineer. He transferred into Fort Polk to lead the training program for the Army's Joint Readiness Training Center based there. His primary responsibility was the maintenance of the combat vehicles used in training. His order to "saddle up" struck the other officers as a line from one of the John Wayne movies he was so fond of watching. However, an order was an order. The men loaded into the armored personnel carriers and began the drive out of the park toward Houston.

They were stopped from exiting by two M1 Abrams tanks blocking the road; turrets turned toward the approaching column. The M1 has undergone a steady stream of upgrades, from the introduction of the German-designed 120-millimeter gun to the addition of depleted uranium armor and networking capabilities such as Blue Force Tracker. It was known as the deadliest tank in the world for a good reason. The commanding officer of the State Guard detail radioed a warning to the approaching column. General Walker issued very specific orders that they were not to fire unless fired upon. He also commanded them to stand their ground. No one was allowed to leave that park.

The major did not consider that the news media was on-site. By now, they were broadcasting a live feed of every detail of the confrontation. They were broadcasting when the captain of the Guard's detachment dismounted his tank and walked to the gate. He was hoisting a white flag in an effort to engage the commander of the column. Fortunately one of the officers from the lead vehicles stepped out to approach the captain.

The captain looked at the young second lieutenant and said, "Son, you're outmanned and outgunned. Turn your vehicles around and head back to your base while the politician's sort this out. No one needs to die today."

The young lieutenant was brash, "Do you really think those two Abrams are enough to stop our entire column?"

With that, the Captain keyed his communicator as a pre-arranged signal for six AH-64 Apache attack helicopters to make their presence known. They seemed to materialize out of the thick pines on either side of the road almost magically. The Captain then said, "Son, we've got a lot more than that. You are surrounded. I've already got more than 200 troops placed on your flanks. No one needs to die today. Turn around and get some coffee. Live to tell the story to your grandchildren."

The lieutenant was wearing a sidearm strapped to his waist. When he made a move just to put his hands on his hips, it looked like he was moving for his weapon. The Captain recognized it was not a threat and made no move in response. However, one of the young soldiers in the lead vehicle was standing outside the vehicle with his rifle at the ready. He saw the move and fired, striking the Captain in the chest. While his vest would prevent the wound from being fatal, no one else knew that. Both Abrams fired at the lead vehicles, immediately sending them skyward in an explosion that shook the ground. Before the cease-fire could be issued, the US forces were taking fire from both flanks and the air. The Apaches were deadly in their instant counter-attack. The vehicles that were not destroyed were abandoned. Many of those men fell under withering fire from their flank.

The Army was forced to surrender to the State Guard. The wounded were triaged while those unhurt were disarmed and marched back to the camp under heavy guard. It was not a fair fight. Many newscasters remarked that this must have been what Santa Anna faced when his retreat was cut off at the Buffalo Bayou.

John was again cast into the spotlight. He was repeatedly asked to explain what happened. He reiterated over and over the steps that were taken to prevent such a tragedy. He also became the hero of the latest battle in Texas history. It became known as "the Battle of New Waverly." And it was the last step in the march to Independence for the Lone Star. The people of Texas rallied behind John and their shared obsession for their freedom.

Chapter 30

The Declaration

April 21, 2020

"Is life so dear, or peace so sweet, as to be purchased at the price of chains and slavery? Forbid it, Almighty God! I know not what course others may take; but as for me, give me liberty or give me death!"

— Patrick Henry

COME AND TAKE IT

This day had been coming for some time for John Lucas IV, even though he had done his best to avoid it. He panned the crowded courtyard in front of the George H. W. Bush Library. It overflowed with media from every Texas outlet, as well as all the national organizations. The area could not contain all of the reporters. The large number of interested parties and onlookers spilled over to the parking lots surrounding the library. The cameras were placed on scaffolding allowing a better vantage point for the event. Microphones covered the podium while reporters jockeyed for the preferred positions.

John's eyes were drawn to Jeremiah and Sarah. It was amazing to realize that all of this began with a lunch in Austin with his sister, Sarah. He never dreamed that her confession of brokenness all those years ago would lead him to this moment. He stood before her, knowing that she was proud of him. He saw General Walker seated with Sam Burroughs, now the commanding officer of the Texas Navy. He recalled the wisdom of both of these powerful, single-minded men. He looked, and he saw A. J. Crockett, once the commanding officer for the Judge Advocates Group of the US Armed Services, now the Attorney General of Texas. He now served as the counselor to every agency and legislature on behalf of the people of Texas. His counsel proved invaluable in writing the declaration. It was hard for John to imagine them writing it without him.

His eyes continued to pan the crowd as he recalled the deep friendship of his mentor and pastor, David Edwards.

His encouragement in the faithfulness of God was a mainstay during the many days of doubt and uncertainty. Even now, his words that "God's got this" steeled his resolve. His eyes fell next on his staff, Mateo Garcia, Sean O'Sullivan, and Patrick Beeman. Providentially he had been given these faithful men. They reminded him of the Gibborim, David's Mighty Men. The nation of Israel would have a much different story if not for them. So it was with the new nation of Texas. He knew history would reflect their actions as that of true patriots and heroes. Finally, John's eyes were drawn to the front row. As always, Rebecca was seated there along with JV and Abby. How could he have ever survived without her? She never left his side. She never wavered even when her life was in jeopardy. Seeing her today on the front row gave him all the strength he needed to make this bold declaration to the world.

John felt absolutely sure about the direction they all committed themselves to follow. He was a keen student of the constitution and the Founding Father's sacrificial intent in the establishment of the union. He was a patriot but deeply committed first to his beloved state of Texas. After all, his lineage pointed directly to some of the brave men who fought beside Sam Houston, securing the independence of the Lone Star State. He was well aware of the stories passed down through the generations of his family by Juana Navarro Alsbury, the adopted sister of James Bowie's wife and the niece of Texian leader José Antonio Navarro. She survived the Battle of the Alamo with her young son and her sister, Gertrudis. Those stories only steeled his resolve for the day he now faced.

This April day dawned promising a perfect Texas spring day. The weather forecast was accurate, with temperatures in the mid-seventies with just a hint of a mild Central Texas wind blowing. It was entirely appropriate that John chose the front entrance of the George H. W. Bush Library on the campus of Texas A&M University. It is located just 170 miles northeast of the Alamo and a mere 30 miles from the place where Texas first declared their independence from Mexico, 200 years earlier on March 1, 1836, at Washington on the Brazos.

Founded largely by immigrants from the southern United States, Washington-on-the-Brazos is known as the *birthplace of Texas* because here, on March 1, 1836, Texas delegates met to formally announce Texas' intention to separate from Mexico and to draft the constitution for the new Republic of Texas. They organized an interim government to serve until a permanent one could be elected and inaugurated. The delegates formally declared independence on March 2, 1836. They adopted their constitution on March 16. The delegates worked only until March 17, when they had to flee with the residents of Washington-on-the-Brazos, to escape the advancing Mexican Army. The townspeople returned after the Mexican Army's defeat at San Jacinto on April 21. Town leaders lobbied for Washington-on-the-Brazos' designation as the permanent capital of the Republic of Texas, but leaders of the Republic favored Waterloo, which later became Austin.

However, John intentionally chose a different location for today's event. This declaration would be made public in College Station on the campus of Texas A&M University. This was the location of the presidential library of Bush 41 (George H. W. Bush). After all, he was the one who said, "We know what works. Freedom works. We know what's right. Freedom is right." It was here that a monumental bronze sculpture named *The Day the Wall Came Down* was erected. It was in honor of the fall of the Berlin Wall.

Texas A&M University was perfect for another reason, though. Being a land-grant university made it the perfect location. He understood this place personally and corporately. First, as a former student, and then by supporting numerous student scholarships from the fund started by his great-grandfather long ago.

A&M began with monies granted through the Morrill Acts of 1862 and 1890. These acts funded educational institutions by granting federally controlled land to the states for them to sell, to raise funds, to establish and endow *land-grant* colleges. The mission of these institutions, as outlined in the 1862 Act, is to focus on the teaching of practical agriculture, science, military science, and engineering. This mission was in contrast to the historic practice of higher education to focus on a liberal arts curriculum. Even though these universities were begun with federal monies, each of them was known for their strong sense of State's Rights. A&M was perhaps even more so inclined than the others because of the Corps of Cadets' strong military presence. They were Texans, first and foremost. John knew, if his effort were to be successful, all of these things would be vital to Texas's ultimate independence.

Further, he saw the symbolism of the 1-1/4 life-size bronze monumental sculpture, *The Day the Wall Came Down*, as an unmistakable message. There were two of these commissioned and completed. Each is a composition of five horses, one stallion and four mares, running through the rubble of the collapsed Berlin Wall. One casting was placed in a reunited and free Berlin on July 2, 1998. It was delivered by the U. S. Air Force on the 50th anniversary of the Berlin Airlift, installed by the German Army, and unveiled by former President George H. W. Bush. The sculpture was a gift of friendship from the American people to the people of Germany.

He also saw the symbolism in *The Day the Wall Came Down*. It was never about horses. It was about freedom. In this monument, the horses symbolize the personal drive for freedom shared by people of all nations. The Berlin Wall was a visual reminder of the oppression in many parts of the world. This sculptural wall also represents all walls or obstacles to personal freedom, both past and present. The collapse of the Berlin Wall on November 9, 1989, was a moment of joy shared around the world, captured by the artist in this sculpture. Now John Lucas IV was about to declare new independence for the Lone Star of Texas.

It was now time. Speaking softly with the passion of conviction, he stood ramrod straight at the podium, with little preamble or introduction, and said:

"When the president and Congress took office they took one oath - that oath was not to devalue our currency by printing money and taking us off of the gold standard. It was not to invade our privacy by having the NSA reading our emails and hacking into our computers. It was not to invade countries that were not a threat to us or send our troops into over 100 different countries each year. It was not to set up the CIA, FBI, Homeland Security, or the Federal Reserve to deepen our oppression. It was not to seek power as individuals. It was not to use their office to promote themselves or their personal agenda. That oath was that they would, to the best of their ability, preserve, protect and defend the Constitution of the United States. They have broken that oath. Therefore today, we, the sovereign people of the state of Texas, declare ourselves a free and independent nation. To that end, we pledge our lives, our fortunes, and our sacred honor. Come and take it!"

The silence was stunning. Even though he spoke many times about the importance of states' rights, especially as it was so clearly revealed in the federal overstep recently in Texas. Yet, here it was, for the world to see and hear. The silence lasted but a few moments until the symphony of voices erupted with a barrage of questions. As stunning as the silence, the confusion of the shouting voices of reporters and media representatives was unsettling, even for a man like John Lucas.

The FOX News reporter was either the quickest or the loudest, but she was recognized first. In an effort to gain the upper hand in the verbal sparring, she asked, "Mr. Lucas, are you declaring war against the United States?"

His answer was measured and temperate. He said, in his best Texas drawl, "No ma'am. I am declaring the independence of this great Lone Star of Texas. As we once stood independently, it is time for us to return to such a position in the world."

Quickly, the reporter retorted, "You can't do that! It's against the law!"

John smiled as the Officers of the Day from the Corps of Cadets, stationed at the flagpole in the backdrop, lowered the American flag, and removed it. They attached the Texas flag with the Come and Take It flag beneath it and raised it as the Aggie Band began to play "Texas Our Texas."

All the reporters stood in stunned silence while all of the Texians sang the words, adopted in 1929, composed by William J. Marsh of Fort Worth, with lyrics by Marsh and Gladys Yoakum Wright. There are only three verses and a chorus, though it was the chorus and last verse that said it all:

God bless you Texas! And keep you brave and strong, That you may grow in power and worth, Thro'out the ages long.

Texas, dear Texas! From tyrant grip now free,
Shines forth in splendor your star of destiny!
Mother of heroes! We come your children true,
Proclaiming our allegiance, our faith, our love for you.

And, so it began.

Coming Soon....

You've been on an adventure with John Lucas and all the other great characters of *The Lone Star: Independence*. It's merely an indroduction as the adventure continues.

The Lone Star of Texas – Fight for Freedom (Vol. 2)

John Lucas finds himself in a maelstrom of activity as a result of the reading of the Declaration of Independence. A flashback of the events that led to the drafting and reading of the declaration takes place. Included in this is the committee organized to develop the first draft of the document, called the "Gonzales Draft." The committee includes John Lucas, David Edwards, Dylan Walker, A. J. Crockett, and Sarah Lucas-Mann, among others who have been in a supporting role. Sarah has begun to transition from her position with Texans for Life to Secretary of State for the new Lone Star.

In the ensuing weeks and months, these new *Founders* of the nation find themselves facing the world's greatest military power of the modern era. In addition to the brewing war, they are forced to forge a new government. Other states and nations become surprising new allies coming to the aid of this new nation. The intrigue and suspense is reminiscent of the early months of America's War for Independence. An Olive Branch Treaty is drafted and delivered to the White House and summarily dismissed. War begins with a battle off the coast of Galveston. John Lucas struggles with the cost of what he put into motion as he finds himself faced with losses greater than he imagined possible.

Finally, after months of intense struggle, peace and independence are secured. The treaties are signed at the newly developed capitol in College Station. The work of governing now begins.

The Lone Star of Texas – A New Government Rises (Vol. 3)

With peace, the real work of government begins. John has become part of something much bigger than could have ever been imagined. With the aid of his faithful friend, David Edwards, the new government begins to emerge. The process is not without challenge and dissent; however, a greater nation rises from the ashes of war destined to become a model for the world. Modeled after the design of government in the Bible, freedom and equality become more than just words. All Founding citizens receive permanent land grants in the new country. There are no direct taxes on the people. All debts, public and private, are cancelled every seven years. The new currency is based on a gold and silver standard. With the new nation and its identity established, the question is will they be able to keep it?

Don Emmitte is the Founder and Executive Director of *Grace Restoration Ministries*. He is now semi-retired though he has been involved in Christian ministry for over fifty years with college students, prisons, and at-risk children. Don has also served as a Senior/Lead Pastor of multiple churches in Texas and Tennessee. His focus has always emphasized ministry to families through counseling and life-coaching by way of GRM. Don continues to write *Morning Devotionals*, a daily inspirational thought distributed through the GRM website (www.grace-restoration.org), and various other social media sites. He and his friend, Alex Pazdan, have also written numerous articles and position papers in conjunction with their first of three volumes, *The Lone Star: Independence*. These, along with podcasts from the perspective of two of the main characters in the fictional story of Texas Independence, can be found on their website - www.lonestarindependence.com.

Alex Pazdan lives in Franklin, TN, with his son Jonathan and daughter Ashley. He owns an investment company and has worked in finance for the past 25 years. He has always had a deep interest in the historic battles for liberty–from the Reformation and the American Revolution to the ongoing struggles that continue today. This interest only grew after he became a Christian 23 years ago. He was born and raised in the suburbs of Chicago, IL, and graduated from Vanderbilt University in Nashville, TN. He is still amazed that his friend, Don Emmitte, was crazy enough to take an idea he had for a story and write a book together with him!